I0589479

THE CITY OF QUARTZ

THE CITY OF QUARTZ

IAN IRVINE

(HOBSON)

THE CITY OF QUARTZ
is copyright © 2016 IAN IRVINE
Bendigo VIC 3551
Telephone: +61 3 5439 3662
Author's website: http://www.authorsden.com/ianirvine
Band site for *Interstitium*: https://www.reverbnation.com/Interstitium

This is a work of fiction. Names, characters, businesses, places, events and incidents are either the products of the author's imagination or used in a fictitious manner. Any resemblance to actual persons, living or dead, or actual events is purely coincidental.

Copyright is retained by the author.
The moral rights of the author have been asserted.
All rights reserved. Without limiting the rights under copyright reserved above, no part of this publication may be reproduced, stored in or introduced into a retrieval system, or transmitted, in any form or by any means (electronic, mechanical, photocopying, recording or otherwise), without the prior permission of both the copyright owner and the above publisher of this book.

The Australian Copyright Act 1968 (the Act) allows a maximum of one chapter or ten per cent of this book, whichever is greater, to be photocopied by any educational institution for its educational purposes provided that the educational institution (or body that administers it) has given a remuneration notice to Copyright Agency Limited (CAL) under the Act.

First published in Australia in 2016
By Zoetics Institute

ISBN: 978-0-646-95632-9

Book design and cover illustration
Peter Wiseman *Anomalies and Glitches* digital collage, 2016.

CONTENTS

BOOK ONE
PART ONE: ARRIVAL AND DEVELOPING THE CURRICULUM

BOOK ONE
PART TWO: THE TEACHINGS OF ABRAHAM ISLES

BOOK TWO
PART ONE: DINAS YARKUK
(THE CITY OF QUARTZ)

BOOK TWO
PART TWO: THE SONGS OF ABRAHAM ISLES

Dedication and acknowledgements:

Special thanks to Sue King-Smith, John and
Ev Charalambous, Peter Wiseman, Win King-Smith,
John McNab and the members of *Scribblers Writing Group*.

To the Indigenous peoples of Australia.

PREFACE

The manuscript which here bears the title of *The City of Quartz* (or *Dinas Yarkuk*), was discovered in an ornate wooden box on a 100 acre property about 30 kilometres south-east of Bendigo. It was accompanied by some trinkets, a USB stick containing media content belonging to "Dinas Yarkuk Transmedia Cooperative" and four other manuscripts that we intend to publish in the near future. It was discovered on February 12th 2007 by the current owners of the property. It had been left at the rear of the property in a small cave complex created by a boulder formation. The complex is near a large dam and about seventy metres from the property's boundary with the state forest. At the same location there was a sign nailed to an ancient redgum that stated: 'University This Way' —though puzzlingly no university exists immediately south-east of Bendigo.

Dr Douglas Green, one of the previous owners of the property, who died in January 1998, figures prominently in the purportedly factual narrative. The property passed into the hands of Douglas Green's step-daughter, 'Rhiannon', later in

1998. Acting on requests made by Green in his will, it appears as though the property was used without rent and with all rates paid by one 'Rowan Sweeney' (fictional name) from Green's death until the trouble-free hand-over to Rhiannon.

At the request of Sweeney, who is curiously silent on the matter of this book, the real names of many of the characters, including 'Anika Miraj' and Rhiannon have been changed for the purposes of publication. Rowan, Anika and Rhiannon all deny that they are the authors of this manuscript.

Who then is the author of the book? Some have pointed to Douglas, who owned the property during 'Rowan's' time there. Unfortunately, the paper upon which the manuscript is handwritten clearly dates to 1999 at earliest, and is not recognizable as belonging to Green, or for that matter Rowan, Anika or Rhiannon[1]. The other logical possibility is that it was written by the person who professes authorship on the title page of the manuscript, that is, Philip Ungaru. On that page Ungaru professes to be a Maori Scot (or Scottish Maori?) aged thirty who is studying toward an MA at MUCT (Marin University of Creative Thinking). He also states that he is on an Aotearoan government scholarship and is a trainee 'tohunga' skilled in 'karakia,' or spell-making.

Ungaru also tells us that he has assembled his story about Rowan and Anika from various sources and he hopes that by writing his manuscript he will help solve a particular mystery. Sadly, given the character of Ungaru is, so far as we can ascertain, entirely fictional—being confined to the alternate present that is Marin-e-bek (which roughly translates as 'the

---

[1]We note that although all three are internationally respected in their given art forms none of them, to our knowledge, possess skills in fiction writing or even creative non-fiction writing (though Rowan and Anika possess PhDs that demanded academic non-fiction skills).

splendid land'), it doesn't progress us far to make Ungaru the author of the MS. 'Ungaru' itself is a kind of cipher word, rather than a real Maori name. It is composed of the words 'Unga' ('seek' or 'expel/cause to come forth') and 'Ru' ('shake/ agitate/ scatter/ upheaval') and if we put the two meaning constellations together we perhaps have a metaphor for spiritual exorcism—a concept paralleled in the text.

So much for the puzzle of authorship!

We are left with an authorless book written about a fantastic alternative present in which much Australian history is unrecognisable to the average modern reader. The book thus contains some factual and some fictional characters. Given these facts we've decided that we can only really present the story to the reading public for the purposes of entertainment.

In relation to Douglas Green, his sister Irene—a Melbourne beauty consultant— says simply, 'Douglas was certainly a very odd fellow—something like a modern day alchemist … and he did publish odd books now and then.'

Olwen Ghent
Commissioning Editor
Ghwilian Books
South Wales
United Kingdom

BOOK ONE

PART ONE: ARRIVAL AND DEVELOPING THE CURRICULUM

CHAPTER ONE

THE COSMOS OPENS UP
(Thursday August 15th 1996)

It was an unseasonably hot day in August as Rowan Sweeney left the outskirts of Melbourne driving north. The blue EA Falcon station-wagon he'd inherited after separating from his wife was loaded down with the miscellaneous debris of his life. The car was unserviced due to lack of money and Rowan kept a close eye on the temperature gauge, aware that the radiator was dodgy on longer trips. Likewise, the air-conditioner wasn't working properly—it needed re-gassing. As a result, Rowan was soon sweating profusely.

The vehicle struggled in the hillier country around Mount Macedon, forcing Rowan to pull off the highway to give the radiator a break. At the same time, he took the opportunity to peel off his cumbersome black suit jacket—the only one he owned. He could always put it back on again for the meeting with Douglas Green, his future employer. After Melbourne's long, cold winter, he enjoyed the sensation of wearing only a short-sleeved but collared black shirt. Part of him also wanted to exchange his long pants for a pair of shorts and his shiny black shoes for sneakers or sandals. *Not the ideal way to present to your future employer*, he thought. Besides, given the chaos behind the driver's seat, it might take a while to locate some clean casual clothes.

As he leant against the car bonnet sipping water, he noticed dozens of large wattles lining the road-side. Many were laden with thousands of tiny yellow flowers. Despite feeling emotionally heavy, he thrilled at these early signs of spring. As he slipped back into the driver's seat and headed for Harcourt—where Douglas's rough map said he should make a right turn out past Mount Alexander—he began obsessing about the state of his life.

He was leaving behind his wife, Kerryn, who had agreed to a trial separation a month earlier. They'd been together for over a decade and though they'd grown apart in recent years she'd seen him through some difficult times. He felt slightly giddy, unstable at the thought of her no longer being a part of his life. He'd lost five kilograms as a result and looked sickly, even to himself.

His mother, on her last visit from Geelong, had said 'Rowan, you look too pale and thin for your own good—what's up?' Being 'too pale and thin' made him feel tall for some reason—even though he was just above average height. She'd also said 'Why not take a holiday—go get some sunshine,' as well as 'And stop wearing black all the time! Why can't you buy some colourful clothes?' *Fair enough advice to a thirty-three year old*, he thought, as he overtook a red tractor, *but holidays cost money and I can't even afford to fix the bloody radiator. And as for my clothing, well black is the Melbourne colour.*

As the engine temperature started to climb alarmingly north of Kyneton—forcing him to estimate the distance to the small town of Malmsbury—his thoughts turned to the woeful state of his career. His dreams of a tenured academic position, after many years of study toward a PhD, had failed to materialise. There were no tenured positions on offer in History or Cultural Studies in Victoria, despite the fact he'd been published in a dozen suitably stuffy journals and had attended a dozen recent conferences.

After eight months of only occasional academic job interviews he'd been forced to think about returning to the community services work that had been the cause of a near breakdown some years earlier. The very thought of it made his stomach muscles tense up.

He left the Calder Highway again at Malmsbury, near a small but picturesque lake. While the radiator and engine cooled down, he wandered off in search of coffee at a nearby milk-bar. As he ordered the flat white, he felt some trepidation at what lay ahead east of Castlemaine. The position he'd accepted was unlikely to solve his career problems. He'd taken it in desperation, with his debts mounting and his self-esteem plummeting. It was the only position he'd seen in weeks even remotely connected to the kind of work he'd been trained for during his PhD studies. One section of the brief job description requested a person qualified to 'undertake research toward the eventual publication of a book dealing with a prominent 19th century Australian politician.' Another section stated that the person would also be required to teach at an 'innovative university'. There was only one university in Bendigo so Rowan assumed that his job would be based there. However, friends in the loop knew staff at Bendigo and no one seemed to have heard about the position. *Perhaps it's a privately funded position,* he mused, as he paid for the coffee and headed back to the car.

Rowan left the Calder just north of the Castlemaine turn off and headed into boulder country. The road soon became narrower and he had to slow down and concentrate more. His thoughts turned to the oddness of the recruiting process. He'd mailed the company named at the bottom of the ad, 'Douglas Green Publications'. A week later he'd received a brief job description attached to a personal note by Green stating:

> Rowan,
>
> Please mail me your resume plus a photograph (I can tell a great deal from a photograph) plus a recording of you lecturing (everything of any importance about personality can be discerned from a person's voice).'
>
> Sincerely
>
> Douglas Green

Despite seeing the process as unprofessional, Rowan had done as requested. Within a week he'd received confirmation of employment—'for the fixed term of at least one year'—and a start date—'Be here August 15th, no later.' The hand-drawn map he was now using to locate the property had been stapled to the offer letter.

He'd mailed an acceptance letter with a request for the company's phone number and more details regarding the teaching and research duties. The reply letter was equally brief:

> Rowan,
>
> I'll reveal most of the details of the position upon your arrival. In the meantime don't bother contacting me over the next four weeks—I'll be in Europe. I'll see you on August 15th. In the meantime, I suppose you need to know that you'll be researching for two units in the first year, the first is "An Introduction

to Global Spiritual and Philosophical Traditions"
(combined second/third year unit), and the second
is "An Introduction to Cultural Studies" (a first year
unit). You'll prepare classes appropriate to a 15
week semester unit (roughly three one hour classes
per subject per week). Please note: eventually a
significant part of your working week will be taken
up researching and writing a biography on one
Abraham Isles.

PS: Attached to this letter is a postal order for one
thousand dollars—it's to assist you with your
relocation costs.

Regards

Douglas Green
(Alternative Psychologist and Publisher of Curios)

Although Rowan felt he'd easily be able to handle teaching the
Cultural Studies unit, he felt more apprehensive about the other
unit—though the vagueness of Green's curriculum description
hadn't helped. Rowan had only ever tackled religion from
the perspectives of Sociology and Cultural Studies, and his
philosophical knowledge was limited to a handful of the post-
Enlightenment giants—he'd passed three undergraduate units
in the discipline, not even enough for a sub-major.

Nevertheless, the money was a life saver—though he'd made
no immediate attempt to relocate. Instead, he'd spent it on his
share of the mortgage, as well as the bond for a rental unit in
Melbourne—just in case he needed to return to the city quickly.
Though Kerryn suggested that the job was a scam, Rowan had
ignored her advice to turn it down.

As the lush late winter slopes of Mount Alexander flashed by on his right, he dared to dream. Maybe he really had landed a position with a cutting-edge independent publishing company to write a biographical history and teach. He'd been given real money after all and the job represented a better option than returning to the hard slog of community services work.

Just for a moment he allowed himself to feel excited about the position. Though the teaching brief was just that, brief, Rowan was experiencing something he hadn't felt for many years—a sense of the cosmos opening up to him. Such feelings, however, were balanced by heart-ache. His chest had been tight for weeks and he often felt uncried tears behind his eyes.

A few minutes later, he found the dirt road depicted on Douglas's map and decided to drive more cautiously on its loose, gravelly surface.

CHAPTER TWO

DOUGLAS GREEN AND THE RED-BELLY BLACKSNAKES

Rowan rolled up at the front gate of Douglas's hundred acre block with the temperature nudging 30 degrees Celsius. He peered upwards through a forest of mature gums as he entered. Further up the hillside he saw fruit trees and other non-natives. The gravel roadway wound upwards on a steep gradient toward a distant home site.

The site was composed of a series of old train and tram carriages and a number of sheds surrounding a two storey wooden barn. Rowan wondered where Green's house was. *Surely he has a civilised place to welcome his clients.* Down the escarpment, less than a hundred metres from the barn, Rowan spotted the compacted red-clay wall of a large dam. Further above the home site the hillside culminated in a bouldered crest.

Rowan pushed the blue Ford into second and entered the property's driveway. He was surprised at the unkempt nature of the property's dirt road. Jagged rocks leered up at him from a baked clay road surface and here and there exposed tree roots made the track bumpy and uneven—several times he had to get out of the vehicle to clear away fallen branches. To make matters more difficult, deep welts of erosion scored the road—obviously drainage run-off from the hillside ended up on the road.

It was shady under the mottled canopy of yellow gums, iron-barks and, further up, peppercorns, jacarandas, and smaller desert ash trees. Besides the larger trees all manner of native bushes, smaller trees and wildflowers huddled together on either side of the road. The place had the feel of a permaculture farm—Garden of Eden fertility mixed with chaotic native grandeur. The relative dryness of neighbouring farms was all but forgotten as the car wound its way up the hillside.

The car's axle buckled and bobbed over all manner of rocks and organic protrusions until Rowan arrived at a small clearing perhaps half way up the hill. A large sun-faded sign said: VISITORS' CARPARK. Directly beneath the sign stood a gigantic stone boulder hewn into the form of a couch. Various native trees shaded most of the area. Rowan decided to park the car then walk up to the barn to inquire about Green's whereabouts.

Before he'd even turned off the ignition, however, he observed two large, dark shapes slither into the clearing in front of him. His heart missed a beat when he realised they were abnormally large blacksnakes—their bodies as thick as men's wrists. Each snake looked to be over seven feet long as they wriggled in the gravel before proceeding to wrestle with each other aggressively. Rowan sat in the car petrified, surely they were unusually large for the region—perhaps the fertility of Green's property was the reason.

The battle continued and Rowan wondered whether he was witnessing mating, play or a territorial stand-off. He stared past the wrestling serpents to a wooden archway threaded with a lush purple coral pea vine. He figured that Green's house lay somewhere beyond the archway. Grabbing his mobile phone, he found Douglas's number and rang it.

'Hi, Douglas, Rowan Sweeney here.'

'Rowan, good to hear from you. I've been expecting you all morning.'

'I'm in your visitors' car-park,' Rowan stammered as the serpents stopped their wrestling and raised their heads in unison.

'Must have a bad line, I can barely hear you. Look, better late than dead, as they say. If you follow the path up to the barn-house I'll make you a cuppa.'

'There's a problem here, Douglas, I'm staring at two of the largest red-belly blacksnakes I've ever seen. They're directly in front of my car.'

'Ah, my dear guardians of the primordial enigma! They're familiar with humans those two—I have a licence to handle and keep reptiles, you know.'

'To what?' Rowan spoke louder than he wanted to.

'I'll explain it later. Look, I'll get my snake-catching gear. I don't have any sacks at the moment, so we'll have to carry them. They're usually fairly slow at this time of year—just out of hibernation I'd say. I'll be down in five, in the meantime, no unexpected movements and don't even think about starting the car engine—you don't want to scare them off.'

Rowan began to sweat profusely. He was frightened to move an inch in case the monsters somehow noticed his presence. At some level, he imagined them as dream-serpents, to which the mere shell of a car held no particular challenge. He'd heard stories of snakes holing out under the seats of cars (or even curled around accelerators, clutches and brakes), where they'd bite ankles, shins or calves when the unsuspecting owner entered the vehicle.

For ten minutes, though it seemed like an eternity, he sat

and watched the snakes whip about—a tangled clump of muscular darkness—on the road beside him. As they wrestled they flicked loose gravel across the road.

Finally, Douglas appeared wearing a straw hat, brown cord shorts that had been hacked off at the knees and a blue t-shirt that had to stretch over a small pot-belly. He stood in the archway surrounded by green from the Happy Wanderer. For a moment Rowan imagined a leafy halo around his future boss. He carried two large metal poles each with some kind of metal attachment at the end lined with felt. Spying the writhing serpents, Douglas smiled a broad, mostly toothless smile and approached them at a crouch. The creatures soon ended their hostilities and turned, almost in unison, to face him. Douglas bounded forward another three or four steps then abruptly froze, one pole poised high above his right shoulder. The creatures seemed confused and one, the smaller of the two, took the opportunity to retreat closer to Rowan's car. The other confronted Douglas.

Rowan noticed dark sweat patches under both of Douglas's armpits and smiled. Already Rowan realised that the old man was far removed from others of his ilk in the worlds of academia and publishing. It was also difficult to imagine him as an alternative psychologist. He looked nothing like the slick New Age gurus, healers, yoga experts and celebrity channelers headlining at alternative spirituality festivals up and down the country.

Douglas had closed to within six or seven feet of the more aggressive monster. It was coiled in a thick black-red spiral out of which poked a thin, explorative head.

'Get out of the car slowly, I need a favour from you,' said Douglas, eyeing the giant reptile.

'A favour?'

There was a long pause as man and reptile dared each other to blink.

'Yup, I want that other red-belly—you'll need to follow my instructions.'

It felt like some sort of test, and Rowan, who'd been fifteen years in the city, felt doomed to fail it.

'You really want me to catch this red-belly blacksnake?'

'Yup, I'm studying their behaviour via tracking devices. It looks like we have a male and female pair here—very useful.'

'Mr Green, I … I'm just as likely to get bitten.'

Douglas gave Rowan a look that said cut the crap and get out of the car.

Not wanting to fail the job interview on the spot, he found the courage to leave the car. As he did the other serpent slithered defensively then stopped.

'Great! Now stand stock still a minute and I'll throw you one of these metal poles. What are you like at catching?'

'Pretty good—I used to play cricket,' replied Rowan, feeling his blood freeze.

'Here we go then.' Douglas threw him the pole, but with the shadows of the car-park and his own jitteriness, Rowan failed to secure it. It dropped noisily to the gravel alarming both snakes. The one closest to Rowan fled into the bush. The other swivelled, then slithered in Rowan's direction.

He froze, rooted to the spot in case the creature decided to strike at movement. He felt his heart thumping in his throat.

Douglas, meanwhile, took the opportunity to move closer to the creature before wielding the metal pole and pinning it, behind the head, to the ground.

'You can do better than that, old uncle,' he said, applying pressure via the pole. 'We aren't going to hurt you.'

'You sure you know what you're doing?' asked Rowan, picking up the other pole.

'Does granny ever swallow the egg upon which she sucks?' asked Douglas. But the creature was stronger than anticipated. In a flash, it had wriggled a metre free of the pressure point, its head facing Douglas.

'Grab that other pole, Rowan—I need a little help here. They're damn quick in this heat.'

Rowan slowly moved to a position behind the snake's head.

'I'm going to edge closer and put a bit more downward pressure on him for a moment. It should push his head down into the gravel—you can pin him then.'

As he spoke the creature tried to strike—its small fanged head seemed bound for the leathery throat of a crouching Douglas. But the old man moved deftly back whilst simultaneously applying more pressure to the steel pole. The manoeuvres stifled the creature's strike, sending it backwards like a jack-in the box. Enraged, the snake started to thrash around at Douglas's feet.

'Don't just stand there you lazy bugger, now's your chance! Look he's a bit dazed, poor old thing.'

Rowan aimed the steel pole at the neck of the snake, but was terrified of the consequences should he miss. He connected, putting probably too much pressure on the creature's neck. It was now pinned to the gravel in two places.

'Now hold on tight—he's a big bugger. It's going to take both of us to hold him. Jesus, they'd revoke my license for this mess. He's as strong as an ox.'

Rowan held on for dear life. He was well aware that the stressed creature would strike at one of its captors the moment the metal rod slipped even an inch.

'Its body is getting traction off the roadway. I can't hold him much longer,' said Rowan, perspiring and full of adrenaline.

'Keep the pressure on as we *slowly* swap metal poles. Then I'll nab him behind the head so we can lift him off the road together.' As they did this the snake curled aggressively around their knees and ankles.

'As I grab the neck with my hands, you'll need to get a solid grip of the rear end—maybe four foot of it anyway—then quickly lift it off the road surface. Be warned, he'll keep thrashing about. He's scared and angry.'

Again Rowan did as asked, despite having to leave behind the safety of the steel pole. The thrashing reptilian body reminded Rowan of times he'd handled carp as a kid, up on the Murray River. For a moment he felt unable to contain the monster's muscular palpitations. The back part of its body and tail wrapped around his wrists and waist as for a moment the snake resembled some kind of gigantic tropical python. He had to fight a strong urge to drop the angry beast and run.

'There, I have him,' said Douglas, 'now it's up the path we go!'

The two men trotted the angry reptile up to Douglas's camp. Douglas tripped several times—almost dropping the huge creature. At the house-site they climbed a small embankment before releasing the snake into a large, battered rainwater tank set up as a guesthouse for captured reptiles. A tall peppercorn shaded the area and the creature quickly disappeared among logs, boulders, straw and other reptile amusements, including a pool of water.

'He'll be right in there for a while,' said Douglas, panting, 'he needs to rest a while. He's exhausted himself chomping on the pole.'

CHAPTER THREE

DOUGLAS GREEN

Rowan's first meeting with Douglas Green was hardly auspicious. He felt amazed that the old man had expected him to partake in such a crazy, probably illegal, activity. However, he also felt vaguely guilty that he'd let Douglas down by dropping the steel pole and letting the second snake escape.

Apparently Douglas harboured no ill-will and after leading Rowan back to the double storey shed-cum-barn, promptly sat him down on an old couch in his 'lounge-room'. Though hardly a real house, it seemed well-insulated—quite cool inside despite the inferno outside—and was decorated in a haphazard, cluttered sort of way, with remarkable sculptures and paintings. Books, magazines and CDs covering all sorts of topics were strewn everywhere, and Rowan noted a computer connected to a large home theatre system. Douglas would later tell Rowan: 'I can't stand commercial TV. I read—and increasingly listen to—everything that matters via the internet.' There were pot-plants everywhere as well as tanks and cages harbouring native snakes, reptiles and fish. Rowan stared for a long time at a large tank containing a four foot brown snake draped over a log.

'Do you want tea or coffee—or a cold drink perhaps?' shouted Douglas, from another room.

'I'll have mineral water if you have it, thanks.'

Douglas reappeared soon after with two grubby looking glasses of water, one of which he handed to Rowan. He then slumped tiredly into a nearby chair before putting his feet up on the room's only coffee table. 'I don't handle the strenuous stuff like I used to. The way it's going, I'll have to employ Rhiannon to help out two or three months a year.'

'Rhiannon?' Rowan asked, trying to find a polite way to ask some of the questions on his mind.

'Yes, my 27 year old step-daughter—from my second marriage. A very creative young woman—she's studying acting and dancing in Melbourne. We get on well, but she hates me smoking—probably for good reason.' He took a gulp of water.

'What's with the brown snake? Do you collect them too, like the blacksnakes?' Rowan pointed at the tank containing the snake.

'I don't really "collect" any animals. I retrieve them injured from the roads—echidnas, wallabies, snakes, blue-tongue lizards, magpies, kookaburras, even the occasional wombat. Some are no good for the wild after I've nursed them back to health—they tend to hang about.' Douglas took another gulp from his cup.

'Including that brown snake?' Rowan eyed it warily.

'She'll go home in a week or two—once the weather heats up and she can move a bit faster.'

Both men paused for a moment.

'I suppose you have some questions …'

'Yes, I do—about the employment offer. There's some teaching and a research project—is that correct?'

'The research project will be on Abraham Isles—a biography,

one year to complete. This publishing house', he gestured around the room with a sweep of his arm, 'will publish it, if it's half decent.'

'This publishing house—do you run it directly from here?'

'An eye so easily deceived,' said Douglas cheerily, 'Yes, I run an independent publishing house from this very location, well one of the sheds here about. Everything is outsourced these days—I have excellent copy editors in India of all places, and designers and illustrators in Europe. My favourite printer operates out of Hong Kong—very unpatriotic, I know. A lot of stuff can be done online these days—I have no idea what half the people I work with even look like. Unfortunately, however, your biography may well be our last book,' he glanced around the room thoughtfully, before drinking slowly from his glass of water.

'Financial problems?'

'No, not at all. A problem, that's all.'

Rowan decided not to probe further, the old man obviously didn't want to discuss the 'problem'.

'And the university teaching—you mentioned that in your ad?'

'Not exactly teaching; well not immediately at any rate. Though a big part of your contract will be to write lecture content and assemble learning resource packages for two university level units.'

'Are the units being delivered at the Bendigo campus of La Trobe?'

'They'll be delivered here and there as of early next year, but not specifically at Bendigo. My company is contracted as a publisher of off-campus academic content to an overseas university. The conditions of the contract, however, preclude me from giving you more details at present—suffice to say it's in *Europe somewhere*,' he chortled, before leaping up excitedly. 'I'll be damned, two wedge-tailed eagles and a rabbit.'

Rowan followed him to the north facing bay windows beside

the front door. He spotted movement further up the hillside—toward the back of Douglas's block. Two huge wedge-tailed eagles were hunting a large rabbit in a clearing.

'You see that?' asked Douglas, thoughtfully, 'that's two visits in under an hour, we have our man. The Government of Souls has well and truly spoken.'

He and Rowan watched quietly as the eagles tore the frightened rabbit to pieces by way of tandem dives. Their huge brown-black wings flapped like sinister kites on an irregular breeze as they worked hard to block the nimble creature's escape routes. Whilst one terrified the rabbit from the front, the other attacked from behind—talons and beak quick to rip at the small creature's fur and flesh.

Douglas returned to the couch and took another gulp of his drink at the conclusion of the display.

'You might imagine the university as up there, at the back of the block for the present. When the time is right I'll show you the exact location.'

'When the time is right?' repeated Rowan, trying to hide his agitation.

'There's a four month probation period.'

Rowan pondered Douglas's offer, he felt a little cheated since Green had withheld important details about the position from him.

'Look, Mr Green ...'

'*Doctor* Green,' said Douglas, pointedly.

'Doctor Green, maybe there's been a slight misunderstanding. I thought I'd be lecturing at a genuine university.'

'And you will be ... next year. But first you have to write some content. I'm sure you're aware that many junior academics are given up to a year to prepare content before delivering lectures,' said Douglas impatiently.

'I do thank you for the money, of course, and I'm happy to

work it off here on your farm, but I was expecting a position in a genuine academic institution.' Though feeling a little guilty, Rowan's years as a social worker had taught him to be up front with people.

Douglas wore a mischievous grin as he gestured to a computer humming away beside a large fish tank, 'Of course a young man like you, fresh out of a major university, would understand that the University is everywhere these days.'

'How so?' asked Rowan, puzzled.

'The web of course! Many academics prepare classes entirely for online delivery. They sit in the backblocks of North Vietnam, or Mongolia, or Nepal up-loading classes to "cyber universities". Soon they'll be creating audio and video files as well for students to download at their leisure. The very idea of the teacher is changing. I'm sure you're well aware of all this given your time at a prestigious university,' said Douglas, sounding smug.

Though Rowan hadn't looked at online education for a while, it was unlikely that the download speeds were fast enough—and the connections reliable enough—to run online classes just yet. Maybe by the new millennium. Despite these doubts, he felt ashamed of his earlier pushiness, 'I suppose a lot is starting to happen online. Is that what I'm being employed to do?'

'There are new worlds out there to discover for the adventurous.'

'What about the biography of Abraham Isles? I couldn't find any record of him anywhere, and I checked the databases of all the major Melbourne universities.' Rowan tried not to sound accusative.

'All in good time! Look, if you want the job, your probation period begins today. During that time you'll be paid your full salary. With luck you'll enjoy what you're doing and we'll proceed to bigger and better things by February next year.'

Douglas rummaged about under the coffee table for a moment before producing a crumpled and grubby employment contract for Rowan to read through.

Rowan's mouth felt dry as he scanned the pages of legal jargon. The contract looked legitimate enough, though in many ways it seemed more like a publishing contract than an academic position. In truth, Rowan was desperate for any paid work that made use of his academic skills. Family poverty during his teens had made him value a regular wage as an adult—many couples, he recalled reading somewhere, fought over financial matters. It was central to many divorces, and of course he reminded himself daily that Kerryn had supported him for years during his PhD studies. The reality was that his work at Melbourne universities had dried up. After graduating, postgraduate students were expected to find contract positions elsewhere in the state—even interstate or overseas. Unfortunately for Rowan, he'd graduated at a time of large cuts to humanities and creative arts budgets across the country.

As he signed the employment agreement, tax declaration form etc. a little voice in his head said: *Why are you risking your future as an academic to this madness?*

Douglas looked pleased, 'Excellent! But why so bloody grim?—it's not the end of the world. If after a few days you change your mind you're free to terminate the contract with only a day's notice. No hard feelings—easy as you like.'

'I noticed that,' said Rowan, reminding himself that he was now earning the salary of a junior academic. Kerryn would have to eat a little humble pie.

'Now, part of our time together will involve me updating you on important Quant developments in your primary discipline area, i.e. Cultural Studies. We'll need to do some *reframing* before you begin teaching next year.' Douglas's face gave nothing away, but Rowan thought he caught the slightest hint of friendly mischief.

'I'm fairly up on the main international developments for my discipline,' said Rowan, 'I've just finished five years of intense study in the area.'

'Oh, I do not doubt it. But they think differently overseas. No problem for someone as learned as yourself of course—you'll just need to adapt what you think you know. Look, we'll talk specifics in coming months,' said Douglas.

Though frustrated, Rowan decided not to push Douglas further. The bottom line was that he'd be paid good money for four months at least, and whatever activities that entailed— apart from grappling with poisonous snakes—had to be better than returning penniless to Melbourne with egg on his face. He resolved to check the Melbourne newspapers and phone his contacts at various universities the following morning—best to keep his hat in the academic ring. The two sat in silence as Rowan contemplated scanning more job descriptions (thick with Key Selection Criteria) and writing more application letters. As he slumped further into the couch Douglas lifted his cup of water close to Rowan's face.

'Here's to a fruitful partnership!'

As the two cups went *chinka*, Rowan felt himself relax. If nothing else he'd have an income for a few months.

CHAPTER FOUR

THE INTERROGATION

Immediately after they toasted Rowan's acceptance of the position, Douglas put down his drink and said; 'Now, I have a few questions for you.'

Rowan flinched. After the incident with the snakes and the perplexing way Douglas had described the position, he'd forgotten that Douglas might want to question him.

'Ask away, Dr Green.'

'But you'll be calling me Douglas—that'll be fine.'

'Okay, Douglas.'

'I checked out your old rock band on the web by the way— just put your name into a search engine and *voila!*' He reached over to a stack of CDs and tapes on the table in front of him and to Rowan's amazement picked up a battered looking tape-case containing the mid-eighties first album by *Interstitium.*

Rowan felt embarrassed, 'Jeez, that's from a long time back. I never thought anyone would still have a playable recording. We were never all that successful—I mean I was pretty young then. Punk was all the go.' He knew he sounded flustered.

'It's not clear from the cover who wrote the songs. Did you write the songs?'

Rowan frantically tried to recall some of the lyrics. What the hell had he said back then that might incriminate him? He'd underestimated Douglas—obviously he did his homework.

'I wrote most of the lyrics for the band—though we shared some of it. Look, that was a very long time ago. I think my PhD research is probably much more relevant to your position—and my years as a social worker.'

'I read your exegesis, *Alfred Deakin, Federation and Cultural Modernity*. A bit long winded, but that's modern academia for you. Alfred Deakin was a very interesting fellow—consulted fortune tellers, channelled great poets, supported poets and writers. It's a wonder he had any time left to be, well, the Prime Minister.' Douglas laughed at his own wit before continuing, 'I'm not sure he had much to do with the arrival of modernism in Australia, but your argument is interesting and the work proves to me that you can write—that's useful. Have you tried to get sections published?'

'I was going to, but a couple of months back I delivered a chapter at a conference in Western Australia. I felt I was doing okay—people looked interested—but an Aboriginal guy, I never caught his name, stood up during the question time and started to rant about Deakin, White Australia, the Doomed Race theory and so on. He said "All very well, Doc, telling us how bloody *progressive* ..." he hissed the word *progressive* at me, "and *cultural* Mr Deakin was, but he did bugger all for Aboriginal people, for Aboriginal *culture*." He kept going for about five minutes—wouldn't let me get a word in. I wanted to say "Mate, I've worked with Koori kids and young people, I know how tough it is," but I never got a chance. He said his piece, turned his back on me and then casually left the auditorium.'

'Why should that be a reason not to try and get sections published?' asked Douglas.

'Though I was shitted with him at the time—I felt humiliated actually—I thought later: *In a way the guy was right.* I realised that writing the thesis wasn't about Deakin or the founding of Australia—it was about *me* hunting pathetically for something creative to research in the world of post-Federation Australian politics. During the PhD, I think I became a bit fake, at least in comparison to what I was like as a social worker.' Rowan went quiet, worried he might be confessing too much too early to his new employer.

'The PhD is essential, as is your experience in social work. You probably did a lot of advocacy as a social worker—a very useful skill—it'll make you more grounded as a lecturer. Not many are. To be honest, I'm just as interested in the therapy you underwent.' Douglas seemed to be enjoying himself—the tables had certainly turned.

'Where did you get the information about my therapy sessions? That should have been kept confidential.'

Douglas smiled and tapped his head, 'I'm not trying to cross-examine you here. Your moral failings or otherwise according to the "conventional wisdom" don't interest me at all. Besides, you have the job already, so no need to be defensive. Now tell me, what happened to your band?'

'We parted company in the mid-eighties—after a friend committed suicide. Around the same time, I also split up with my then girlfriend. After a very tough period, I cleaned myself up and met my wife, Kerryn. Around the same time, I became a social worker.'

'The therapy helped clean you up, yes?'

'That, quitting the band and finding Kerryn.'

'What kind of therapy?'

Rowan took a deep breath, 'We talked about my childhood—I

had a lot of feelings about my parents' divorce, including my father's mind-games. There was also an emphasis on *will* and *choice* and *authenticity of response*.' Douglas appeared sympathetic, though Rowan deliberately avoided stating that the therapy was part of a drug and alcohol detox program.

'There you have it, all my deepest secrets, though obviously you've got hold of them already from somewhere else.'

'Web postings by your former bandmates, as it happens—apparently they went on playing together for some years after you left.'

Rowan felt vaguely bitter.

'They did, but they weren't the reason I gave up music. Jesus, it's been almost a decade!'

'Nevertheless we have a son of the Muses, a composer, among us.' Douglas sounded delighted.

'If you call writing catchy alternative rock songs "composing"', Rowan joked uneasily.

'Well, I happen to be a connoisseur of both 20ᵗʰ century popular *and* experimental music. Do you know how many alternative rockers incorporated techniques developed by avant-garde poets, artists etc. into their songs and stage performances? The list is huge.'

Rowan felt relieved, Douglas was far from stuffy. Besides, deep down he was still proud of some of the songs he'd written as a nineteen year old.

Douglas pulled him out of his reminiscing, 'Your musical knowledge will come in very useful since Abraham Isles composed songs—excellent songs. When you begin writing the biography you'll need to brush up on everything you've ever learnt about music. Have you brought a musical instrument with you?'

'With all due respect, Douglas, I thought I was being employed to teach and write a book. I haven't played music professionally for almost a decade.' Rowan knew he sounded touchy.

'I'll take that as a *no*. There's an old classical guitar upstairs, you can play it whilst you're here. Playing music again will help get you in the right frame of mind to write the Isles biography. You'll also need to retrieve your knowledge of the French language, and you'll learn other languages besides.'

'I only really have high school French. These days, it amounts to what I'd call "reading French". Useful, I guess, when I had to deal with French theorists in the original for my PhD, but I'm hardly proficient. I'd struggle to understand anything among native speakers.' Rowan was starting to feel anxious about the long list of conditions attached to his employment contract.

'Nevertheless, that's very useful—the Government of Souls chose well.' Out of the blue, Douglas began humming one of Rowan's more poetic and eerie songs before signalling toward the car-park, 'If you want to go and grab your luggage I'll show you the way to your "hut", it's up the hill a bit, a mud-brick place. By the way, what sports do you play?'

'I've played indoor soccer on and off for the last couple of years.'

'I know nothing about soccer. Any other sports?'

'Cricket, I guess. There was no way of avoiding it in high school. I was a wannabe pace bowler. But after my parents split up, mum didn't have much money, so I missed out on specialised training. I failed to "reach my full potential". I did, however, play a season or two in A grade after the band folded, but I haven't picked up a bat for at least three years. Why do you ask?'

'It's very easy for intellectuals to become *disembodied*. And if they neglect their bodies and become physically unfit they're in danger of becoming *intellectually* unfit. In the Early Modern period people believed that the melancholy humour accumulated in particular body organs, the spleen for example. Scholars, due to the long periods they spent sitting on their arses reading and writing, were prone to such toxic accumulations. If you work for me you'll need to keep mind and body in balance. I like watching test cricket now and then in the summer. Let's make it your extra-curricular activity. And what if we set you some goals—to keep you motivated. How about you work primarily on your pace bowling, but secondarily you work to improve your batting?' Douglas sounded definitive about the goals—there was no sign of humour.

'Sport isn't in the employment contract,' Rowan joked.

'You can sign a revised one if you like.'

That afternoon Rowan settled into his hut. It was made out of thick mud-bricks with two large verandahs on the southern and northern sides. The main windows of the lounge and study faced north, thus with the help of a couple of fans (run on solar power) and the afternoon shade of several large desert ash trees, the place would probably stay remarkably cool even when the temperature pushed into the high thirties during the summer. There was also an en suite, a visitor's bedroom and a study complete with a computer and a large bookshelf, currently empty except for some dictionaries, a thesaurus and a couple of other reference books.

Seeing Rowan's interest in the study, Douglas said, 'That's your office and library whenever you're here. The computer is state of the art with dial-up internet access and it's your job to fill that book shelf.'

'That's great—I have a boot full of books I'd like to bring in later.'

'And I'll loan you many more in coming days and weeks, including …'

'Books on Isles? If you have any material on him, I'd be

keen to start reading it as soon as possible. As I said, I haven't been able to locate any information on him at all.'

Douglas chortled, then said, 'I'm very sorry Rowan, but it will be a while yet before I can allow you to look at the Isles material. There's a fair bit of class prep and PD to get through first.' Douglas was fiddling with some blinds over by the northern window of his small lounge area.

Rowan looked at the back of the old man a long time before responding, 'The sooner I get to look at the books, the sooner I'll get some sort of grounding in ...'

'The overseas university we'll be working with needs the material for the two units by December. It's a tight deadline.' He sounded emphatic as he turned to look at Rowan.

Rowan looked puzzled, causing Douglas to add, 'Look there are also confidentiality issues with some of the Isles material. The owners of his diaries, for example, want to be absolutely sure they can trust the person doing the research—it's a family thing. They're responsible for the clause about the four month probationary period. I hope you're okay with that.'

In that moment, Rowan realised that despite the odd circumstances of his employment, Douglas was quite definitive about timelines.

'Now, some nights I put on a feed up at the house. Otherwise you're welcome to buy food in Bendigo or Castlemaine and bring it back here. You have a kitchen including a fridge and a cooker—there's no television, however, but there's a stereo and of course the internet—feel free to use both. Also, if you need anything I'll be up at the house.'

'How long can I stay here? My plan is either to commute back and forth to Melbourne or to find cheap accommodation in Castlemaine or Bendigo as soon as possible.'

'Most days you'll be working 9am to 4pm here with me on this block. Also, the hut is yours for the duration of your employment—though you may prefer finding accommodation somewhere in the region. If so, I'd suggest Bendigo, since you'll also be working quite a bit at the university library there—I have a library card for you up at the house. We're only forty minutes or so from Bendigo by road, where I've also snared some academic office space for you through Dr Ian Campbell, a friend and lecturer in Celtic and Norse studies up there. You'll be sharing an office with a PhD student.'

'I'd like to keep my flat in Melbourne for the moment, it's a bit of a financial drain, I know, but it's close to my, er, wife. So I may take you up on the offer of staying here during the working week—at least for the next month or so. Is that okay?'

'No problem—as I said this is your hut. Also, when you do begin serious research on the Isles material, you won't be permitted to take any of it off the property. It'll need to be stored here somewhere.'

With those words, Douglas scratched his broad old man's chest and loped out of the room.

CHAPTER FIVE

ASTRAL TRAVEL IN AN OTHERWISE NEWTONIAN UNIVERSE

Later that night, Rowan lay in bed thinking about his first day. Douglas seemed friendly enough and was genuinely seeking an employee. Although Rowan wouldn't immediately be lecturing, he would be *writing* lectures and developing learning resources. As for the biography, for all he knew, Isles might well be a neglected figure in colonial Victorian history. Perhaps Douglas was a descendent of Isles, which may have led him to overestimate the man's historical importance—a common phenomenon these days with people desperate to mine the colonial past for identity.

Also, given all the state of the art technology around the place—dial-up internet, high quality copiers, expensive phones, etc.—it seemed likely that Douglas was indeed a publisher of some sort. There were books everywhere, and Rowan hadn't seen even half of the rooms in Douglas's barn-house. Perhaps he worked in a large room upstairs or maybe even in a shed.

So far so good, but as Rowan listened to frogs croaking in the reeds and shallows of a nearby dam, he felt more and more uneasy. Unable to pin down the cause, his thoughts drifted to Kerryn. Perhaps she'd met someone at the radio station. Why else had she been so acquiescent about the separation? Perhaps she was tired of supporting him financially. After all, he hadn't earned a decent wage since leaving his job as a social worker years ago. But that was only part of the story—and he knew it. *More likely*, he thought, *she's sick of me avoiding the "let's have children" issue.*

Unable to sleep, he switched on the bed-side lamp. He'd been finding it difficult to sleep alone at night since moving into his flat after the separation. Propped up beside the bed-head with a pillow supporting his back, he stared across the room at the pile of boxes he'd brought with him from Melbourne. The cheap classical guitar Douglas had lent him that afternoon was resting against the pile. At the top sat a cardboard box full of photograph albums—they'd been carefully vetted by Kerryn. Beneath the box sat a battered, blue case plastered with stickers from various late 80s music festivals.

Despite being drawn to it now and then over the past month, he'd been unable to open it to inspect its contents. Of course he knew exactly what was inside—folders containing band posters, newspaper clippings, magazine articles, song lyrics and music sheets, as well as band photo-albums. It also contained a print summary of his four years with *Interstitium*, and old recordings of the band's music—four-track tapes, some live recordings, rough recordings of jam sessions and radio interviews, some reel to reel studio recordings and copies of the two albums the band had released in 1985 and 1987.

On a whim, he decided to pull it out of the pile and place it on the bed. He circled it a while, but lacked the courage to open it. His cowardice brought him to an uncomfortable question: *Why don't I want to become a father?* Some days he saw himself as a selfish bastard intent on keeping his options open. This led to another question: *Open for what?* The answer was usually: *For Anika,* though that relationship too had ended in disaster.

Some days the first question took him back to his own father, Dylan, who lived in a mansion overlooking an estuary near Mooloolaba, north of Brisbane. Dylan had recently married his third wife, Carmel, a thirty-three year old tour guide on the Great Barrier Reef. Their life together, so far as Rowan could make out, consisted of fitness and dieting regimes, playing the stock market and endless overseas trips. During a phone conversation the previous year, Dylan had asked 'How is the old slag?'—meaning how was Rowan's mother. Rowan had told him to fuck himself before slamming the phone down. They hadn't talked since.

The memory of slamming down the phone jolted Rowan back into the present. The battered, blue suitcase seemed to leer up at him. Avoiding looking at it directly, he grabbed Douglas's guitar and tried to play the chords to one of his old band songs. Though he couldn't remember much—he wasn't a guitarist after all, and his singing was rusty—he found it comforting to play for a while, even though his fingers soon felt sore from holding down the strings.

As he sang, he thought about Anika—which led to darker memories about the death of Eric, his best friend. Meeting Kerryn and finding employment as a social worker had saved him from what he called 'all the young adult shit'—the subject matter of much of his early music. *Good riddance!* he mumbled, as he put the guitar down and returned the case to the pile of boxes. *Good bloody riddance!*

After putting out the lights and returning to bed, he was still unable to sleep. Memories of life with Kerryn haunted him. Their last year together in the big, new house in Dandenong—suburbia all around—had been a year of silences. While she worked long hours at the radio station, he'd wasted whole weeks at home surrounded by gloomy, minimalist furniture and sterile, white walls. The current year had started with him anxiously editing the final draft of his PhD. By May, he'd found himself writing applications for endless positions he was overqualified for.

After being awarded the PhD, it gradually dawned on him that he and Kerryn had been growing apart for years. Drunk one night after attending a friend's wedding alone, he'd said, 'This isn't working is it?' Within a fortnight he'd moved into his own flat. Even now, however, he was still telling himself that their relationship wasn't completely over—perhaps because divorce represented the kind of instability locked up in the battered, blue suitcase. He drifted into sleep with the word DIVORCE repeating in his head.

For many years Rowan had not been altogether honest with himself about certain Anomalies in his worldview. On the one hand, he was as atheistic and scientific as the most hardnosed sceptic. Nevertheless, things occasionally happened to him that defied his scepticism. He'd often noted a strong emotional element to the 'happenings'. He sometimes knew things about people he loved that no one had ever divulged to him. He didn't like to talk about these 'space-time ruptures' because they undermined his largely realist approach to life. Besides, it wasn't a perfect gift by any means—information often arrived in garbled or impossibly symbolic form. He hadn't abandoned his atheism, because he didn't yet understand the underlying system behind the happenings. As a songwriter he'd been uncomfortable with the 'happenings' for other reasons—he knew that they heightened his creativity.

On the whole, he associated the 'happenings' with the lifestyle of his younger, darker self. Avoiding such a lifestyle didn't stop them occurring, but it did allow him to mentally distance himself from them. He'd indulged in one particular 'happening' routinely over the years. He liked to visit Anika occasionally in his sleep. He saw such visits as examples of lucid dreaming. Some of the meetings were clear and vivid, others were indistinct and blurry.

After drifting into sleep, Rowan found himself standing at a hotel door. He knocked tentatively, then waited. She only rarely came to the door to greet him—their sleep relationship was as ambivalent as their relationship had been in real life. After a moment or two, however, the door slowly opened.

She was in some sort of up-market hotel since the carpet beneath his feet was plush and the numerals on the polished wood of the door were in gold. He sensed that she was somewhere overseas, perhaps touring. Her life for some years had revolved around folk-music performances at prestigious venues, as well as lectures and workshops at major universities. Of late, her career had blossomed further, and her recordings as a soloist were starting to sell internationally.

Despite all the success, he sensed that she was spending a lot of time alone.

He paused before entering, suddenly aware that it was daytime in her part of the globe. Although he hadn't seen her in person for many years, he knew what she looked like from pictures in newspapers, magazines and on the web. She was thirty-two years old, with long, brown hair and green eyes. She was also a little above medium height, and though her face had developed small lines in recent years, her eyes remained vivid and alive.

As he entered the room's main living area, he noticed travel luggage sitting on a single bed. Anika herself was seated at a small table. She didn't acknowledge him immediately—conversations were rare—but she did glance over at him as he entered the room. She was reading a letter that seemed to be both annoying and confusing her.

When she'd finished reading, she looked at Rowan and said, 'I'm coming back to Australia. There's something I have to deal with.'

She refused, however, to share the contents of the letter with Rowan.

'How are you and Ishmael getting along?' he asked, after a period of silence.

She glanced at him with something approaching bitterness, before turning away.

'Kerryn and I have separated,' he said quietly, to her back. The words provoked a wave of sadness that almost woke him up.

'You'll get through it, Rowan—you're a survivor … and a bastard! A good combination for dealing with life's major challenges.'

The words jarred him out of the dream.

CHAPTER SIX

THE SERAPEUM

(Friday, August 16th 1996)

Since Douglas was nowhere to be seen come 9am the following morning, Rowan spent the morning relaxing and surfing the web. Eventually Douglas strolled out of a stand of gum trees at the back of the block around midday. He wore knee-hacked jean shorts, impractical thongs, a black shirt with a collar and the outlandish straw hat. He seemed agitated and deep in thought.

Rowan offered to prepare him a drink and some lunch since he looked exhausted and dehydrated. Douglas accepted, but insisted they eat up at the barn where he had aspirin and re-hydration tablets.

'I'm not made for this climate, you know—especially now that my thermostat is faulty. I'll be okay in twenty if this stuff works,' Douglas said, lying on his couch—fingers massaging temples and scalp.

When Rowan returned with sandwiches and cut-fruit from

the kitchen, the older man was sitting up.

'You look as though you've been pondering something,' said Rowan, handing Douglas the plate of food.

Douglas took a bite of a sandwich, swallowed then brushed crumbs from his unshaven chin before answering, 'Yes, I am—I may have miscalculated.'

'Miscalculated?'

'Yes, I thought you and I had a couple of years, to prepare. Not so, apparently! So much to learn—so little time.'

'Meaning?'

'Meaning we will have to cram.'

There was an uncomfortable silence as Rowan waited for Douglas to elaborate. He didn't.

'Where did you go to learn this? I didn't hear a vehicle approach and your own car has been in the garage all morning.'

'Quite the detective, aren't we? Never-mind, that trait will be useful when it comes to tracking down information on Abraham Isles.'

Rowan pushed on, despite the parry, 'I've seen the maps, there's only state forest up behind your hill—unless you've been down the dirt road along the northern boundary. There are no roads to the east or south for ten kilometres.'

Douglas seemed amused as he chomped heartily on his salad sandwich.

After swallowing again, he said, 'Tenacious lad, aren't we? Won't take fob for an answer.' He took a gulp of apple juice.

Rowan sat opposite, waiting patiently for more information.

'How's your eyesight after all that PhD study?' asked Douglas.

'Twenty-twenty blinkers on.'

'Good, we're going for a walk after lunch. There are some books you need to read.'

Rowan finished his sandwich and drink in silence. Douglas,

unperturbed by the quiet, stared out the window as he ate. Outside, the sky turned an hallucinogenic blue as the heat intensified. When he'd finished eating, Douglas rose, burped loudly and brushed crumbs off his stomach and jeans.

'Okay, we're nourished. I'll meet you in ten minutes—over by that shed you passed coming up from the car-park. It's shaded by peppercorns and ash trees—camouflage!'

Douglas struggled with a large padlock as Rowan arrived at the shed. It struck him, as he watched the old man puff and wheeze due to the exertion, that he had to abandon the idea that he was being employed as an academic. He almost laughed at the ridiculousness of the situation.

The lock finally clicked open and Douglas pushed hard with his shoulder against the door. It didn't budge the first few attempts, so he moved back a metre and kicked it solidly with the heel of his right foot—a deft karate kick. The door swung open.

'I haven't had the need to come in here for a while—pardon all the books; it contains the overflow from my house library. I gather a 'crop' and take them up to the house. I try to bring back an equal number of books from the house.'

He searched for a switch. It was dark and cool inside the shed, due to a lack of windows in three of the walls, as well as shade from the peppercorns and ash trees outside. As Rowan entered, he was hit by the unmistakeable odour of books—lots of books. He knew the smell well from time spent in second-hand bookshops and libraries in his youth: a certain papery dankness, old knowledge mouldering, or maturing. The odour receded only slightly after Douglas flicked the light switch and began opening windows.

Glancing downwards, Rowan noticed that the floor was made of glazed mud-brick slabs, whereas around him three of the room's walls were covered, almost to the ceiling, with large, dark-grained wooden bookshelves. Each shelf was crammed with an inordinate number of books and trinkets. Smaller shelves also jutted out at right angles into the room's interior. Only the northern wall—where Douglas was struggling to open a large wooden shutter—was free of books. There were four shutters and therefore four windows in all. Sections of each window featured coloured glass—green, red and yellow were the dominant colours—and each window developed a narrative by way of four images. The windows were arched, and framed by thickset wooden ledges at the bottom and stone-work up either side. Unlike the other walls, the northern wall was made of mud-brick. As Douglas pulled open each shutter more light poured into the room.

Rowan quickly realised that the room contained much more than books. There were paintings—framed and unframed—above every bookshelf, and he couldn't walk two paces without stumbling over a clay pot or modernist statue. He also noticed a comfortable couch—a little dusty perhaps—two armchairs and a desk piled high with books and magazines. Deities and other fabulous creatures peered from every nook and cranny. Some were wooden; others were metallic or made of stone. Some were large and imposing, others could be held in the palm of one's hand. From numerous nations, they'd been positioned so that they all gazed at a two foot high, six foot square box at the centre of the room.

'What's that—some sort of stage?'

'In the sense that stages transport us to other realities, yes, I guess so,' answered Douglas, before guiding Rowan gently by the elbow. 'Today we're here for the books.'

Struggling to stay focused, Rowan began scanning the shelves. He noticed that Douglas possessed a first rate classical and world religions library.

'This is like the library of Alexandria—gods and books (scrolls) everywhere,' said Rowan, still looking for books by authors he'd heard of.

'Some of the material goes back a long way in the history of the species—it's the Serapeum *plus*,' said Douglas, surveying the dusty vastness of his collection for a moment with pride.

'It's quite a collection, you must have taken decades to assemble it,' said Rowan, still awed.

'Very true, but we have to focus. You need to be up-to-date with a number of important spiritual traditions.'

'I'm a little perplexed—I don't see many Cultural Studies books. Am I missing a shelf?'

'There's more to academic life than glib new theories.'

Over the next two hours, Douglas presented Rowan with the details of his gruelling work-study timetable for the next four months. Much of it seemed unrelated to the original job description.

He was given a detailed reading list for only one of the courses he was supposed to be researching—the "Introduction to Global Spiritual and Philosophical Traditions" unit. Neither Rowan's professed lack of interest in the subject, nor even his lack of a basic grounding seemed to bother Douglas in the slightest. After unveiling the timetable, he brought a shonky red wheelbarrow into the shed before roaming the book-shelves like some kind of wild animal—crouching or standing on tip-toes to snare books on Hinduism, Buddhism, Alchemy, Gnostic Christianity, and other topics. Douglas was quite aggressive with the books. He flipped their pages over in a kind of frenzy—trying to locate specific sections or chapters. Sometimes he threw them from a distance into the wheelbarrow. Rowan winced repeatedly as crisp white pages were stained by Douglas's grubby fingers. Perhaps he'd been working all morning in the veggie garden or among the grape vines.

After twenty minutes or so, the wheelbarrow was overflowing. Douglas seemed determined to wheel the barrow up the hill to the hut himself, despite the flat tyre. He looked comic to Rowan as he puffed and panted up the path with the red barrow, spilling books every ten paces or so.

Half way up, he stopped and rested on a jagged piece of quartz jutting out of the clay. 'Sit down a moment,' he said.

'I'm fine. Do you want me to help with the wheelbarrow?'

'Please sit down. I want to show you something.'

Intrigued, Rowan did as he was asked.

'Do you see anything remarkable about what we're sitting on?'

'We're sitting on a large rock—so what?'

'Look up and down the hillside carefully—try to follow the path.'

Again Rowan followed Douglas's instructions.

'I see large slabs and boulders of quartz four or five metres apart either side of where we stand. Some look partially buried and together they form a kind of line—perhaps they've been placed like that deliberately.'

'Correct. They form a line that emerges from the Serapeum following this path up past your hut to the crest of the hill. The line continues for 300 metres downhill to the back dam. Strange don't you think?'

'Did you place the rocks in that formation?'

'No, they were here when I bought the block—I even dreamed about them on my first night in the house. I was outside in the dark—standing under a full moon—when the rocks lit up, one by one, like a line of street lights. They'd become transparent, like huge crystals—and clusters of many-coloured lights, *scintillae,* swirled inside each rock. Quite beautiful! I followed the rocks up to the hill's crest and then things got really weird. I heard a grinding and crushing sound. The very earth seemed unstable—like what happens in an earthquake. The cause? Well the line of quartz appeared to be moving slowly through the soil, up and over the hill. And the rocks had changed into spikes that marked the spine of some kind of gigantic prehistoric reptile. At the crest of the hill I froze with terror. Off in the distance, further down the hillside, I spotted a bulbous reptilian head. It was drinking water from the small spring just above the back dam. Strange dream, eh?' said Douglas, struggling to stand up.

'Like you'd eaten the wrong type of mushrooms,' Rowan joked.

'Well, we do find mushrooms on the south side of this hill in the winter, but mushrooms were not the cause my dream.'

Rowan helped Douglas to his feet and they continued up the hillside. When they reached the door of the hut, Douglas said, 'I'll let you unload this lot. Once done, bring the barrow back to the library. There'll be another pile waiting. Who would have thought the gods could be so heavy!'

'These alone will keep me busy for weeks. Are you sure I'll need more right now?'

'The next pile is different. If you look closely at your timetable you'll see that you'll be studying some of the Aboriginal languages of South-Eastern Australia, likewise French. Part of your learning each day will involve *speaking* the languages. Here's your work timetable.' He handed Rowan a crumpled piece of A4 paper.

'Why these languages? I mean, I won't be preparing resources for language subjects will I? I'm useless at languages. I gave up on French in senior high school—I barely remember any of it. And I don't know the first things about the Aboriginal languages.'

'The French will come back and there are certain techniques for learning unfamiliar languages in accelerated fashion.'

Rowan felt perplexed.

'I also want you to be able to read Scottish Gaelic and Welsh.'

'Why, for heaven's sake?'

'Isles occasionally wrote in Welsh and Gaelic,' Douglas said casually, whilst picking up a book on the devil that had fallen out of the wheelbarrow. He handed it to Rowan.

Rowan located a language session on the timetable—it was on a Tuesday 1pm-4pm in 'The Clochan'. In fact most of the language sessions were in The Clochan.

'What is *The Clochan*?' he asked, as he placed the devil book gently in the wheelbarrow.

'It's a triangular stone building at the back of my block of land. It doesn't have any windows, making it perfect for learning languages.' Douglas was thumbing through a book on Egyptian religion as he spoke.

'Why is that?'

'There are no distractions down there, and it's totally dark inside—which aids memory.' He threw the Egyptian book back in the wheelbarrow.

Perusing the timetable, Rowan noticed an error—there appeared to be 10 sessions a week of 'Cricket Tuition' i.e. two sessions per work day. The morning sessions focussed on batting, whereas the evening sessions were about bowling.

'There's a muck-up here, Douglas. It says I'm to have *two sessions per day* of cricket tuition. Is that a misprint?'

'No, that's deliberate.' Douglas was already strolling back down the hillside. 'The goal is for you to be able to bowl close to 125 km per hour by the end of the year.' He wore a mischievous grin as he looked over his shoulder at Rowan.

'You're joking—I told you a while back that I haven't played cricket for ages. Even at my best as a bowler, I was little more than medium pace cannon fodder. Do you realise that 125km per hour is close to the pace of first grade bowlers down in Melbourne?'

'Yes, and if you can achieve that speed—and can maintain control of the ball—maybe you can push on to 130km per hour. You also need to be able to face the same pace with the bat.'

Rowan looked incredulous, 'And you're paying me to learn this stuff?'

'It will help keep your humours balanced. By the way, I have access to a bowling machine. It goes to 145km per hour—I just turn the dial clockwise. Also, it swings the ball both ways. You'll love it. And I know a savvy coach—he's agreed to help me set up some nets in the tractor shed over there between the hut and the barn.' He waved a hand in the general direction. 'He's also agreed to coach you in pace bowling. His name is Ramsay Philips, though I call him Rammer—he used to play high level cricket and has connections to a local club.'

Rowan sighed, 'What's the point of all the training? I mean it seems a bit over the top—there are other ways for me to keep fit.'

'Well, by September the plan is to have you playing games every Saturday. We have lots of work ahead. I've organised for you to attend a four day clinic in Queensland in a month. It teaches batsmen how to face high quality spinners—that's an area in which Rammer and I are, let us say, *lacking expertise,*' he chuckled. 'The machine doesn't do spin, and I'm no Shane Warne. And coaching tapes only give us the theory—you need to actually bat against good spin bowlers. Right after the batting clinic, I've also booked you into a three day clinic for fast bowlers in Adelaide. That'll be a busy week for you since you'll need to keep up with your readings whilst away.'

That night, Rowan had a quick look at Anika's website. He found an announcement to do with her forthcoming 'Antipodean Tour'.

The text read as follows:

Acclaimed folk soloist, Anika Miraj, will return to Australia later this year to perform her award winning music, deliver lectures and conduct workshops. She will remain in Australia for most of 1997 and thus will not tour internationally until 1998.

CHAPTER SEVEN

HERMES AT THE POINT OF DELIVERY
(Monday, August 19th 1996)

Ramsay Philips, forty something local cricket coach and part-time illustrator, listened patiently as Douglas described the capitalistic ethic behind cricket. 'The game of cricket is the capitalist game *par excellence*. And in that sense there is something austere and Protestant about it.' Apparently Philips occasionally attended therapy sessions with Douglas in the clochan, which made him more tolerant than Rowan of the old man's eccentricities.

'Scorers have a lot in common with accountants—they have to be precise. Indeed, the record of a completed game of cricket looks very much like a balance sheet. Everything is accounted for—wides, no balls, etc.—and each participating player product possesses a numerical value (a bowling or batting average) that we could loosely associate with capitalist sales figures. If a bowler gives away too many runs, we call him "expensive" and the batsman is said to have "profited" from the crap bowling. The individual's accumulation of runs over a season (or a career) makes the sport all about numbers—one's contribution to a team is essentially statistical. A regular sporting stock market: "Given performance indicators so far [i.e. the player's batting *average*] Slamuel Quickbatter promises a high *investment yield* in the coming season."'

Ramsay, or Rammer as he was nicknamed, started to look agitated.

Rowan smiled to himself as he surveyed the make-shift sports arena. Half of the large shed in which they stood had been cleared of building materials, tools and old machinery—including vehicles—to make way for an indoor cricket pitch complete with carpet, nets, wickets, a video camera either end of the pitch and, worryingly for Rowan, a bowling machine. The other half of the shed was packed almost to the rafters with piles of junk, and the whole place smelled of oil, fertiliser, mice and rat droppings, sawdust and other unmentionables. Douglas had rigged up a series of theatre lights that dangled precariously from the rafters above the pitch. Rowan had been told that the large tractor doors at one end of the building would be opened, permitting him a good sized run up. He'd been assured that the run up would also be 'mostly flat'. 'Not ideal, I know,' Douglas had said, 'but it'll mean you can practice bowling here whenever you like.'

'I think we should get young Rowan in front of the wicket—so I can have a look at his batting technique,' Rammer said, turning to Rowan who was outfitted in batsmen's pads, a thigh pad and gloves that Douglas had borrowed from the local cricket club.

'I want Rowan to approach cricket with an awareness of the deeper meaning behind the sport. We Australians, as far as I'm concerned, rarely play sport with the right attitude.'

'What are you saying we're bad sports or perhaps that we

aren't dedicated enough?' Rammer asked, 'those are very big generalisations.' He handed Rowan a Gray-Nicolls bat that felt heavy to hold given he hadn't wielded a bat for years.

'No, I'm saying we aren't *reverential* enough.'

'Reverential? Christ, I love cricket, but all that crap about the "baggy green" —I mean spare me! Cricket is not war. We're not fighting at bloody Gallipoli—we have too much artificial *reverence* as far as I'm concerned.' He leant over as he spoke to pick up a battered looking helmet. After dusting it off, he handed it to Rowan.

Douglas lost his train of thought for a moment.

'Are you ready for a bit of middle aged pace, Rowan? I'll bowl you a few for starters, though I'm coming back from a shoulder injury,' said Rammer.

Rowan looked to Douglas for permission, but Douglas was not finished, 'Okay, Rammer, I agree there's too much *false* reverence, but I'm talking about something different—sacred reverence.'

'Meaning?' asked Ramsay, as he began a series of warm-up exercises and stretches.

'Behind the exploitative capitalism of the 19th century was the ancient love of trade—a tribe exchanges objects with another tribe for primitive currency or for other things it needs. A social relationship is established. Now, which classical God presided over such exchanges?'

Ramsay was doing an exercise that involved him bending over from a standing position and lightly swinging his arms back and forth between his two feet. It allowed him to break eye contact with Douglas.

Not missing a beat, Douglas turned to Rowan instead, 'Which God, Rowan?'

'I don't know,' Rowan said, as he struggled to adjust the strap on his helmet.

'Hermes to the Greeks, Mercury to the Romans and Odin-Wodan to the Northern pagans. God of magic and healing—though Hermes was also God of athletes.'

'Well, Rowan here had better pray to this God of Cricketers right now, 'cos I'm feeling pretty nimble today for an old bugger!' joked Ramsay.

Douglas ignored him and instead produced an old photo of the great Australian fast bowler Dennis Lillee in full flight. The image had been taken some time in the early 1970s and it featured Lillee at the point of delivery. He was mid-leap—so high above the wicket that he appeared to be flying. Douglas pointed a grubby forefinger at the image saying, 'That's what you're going to look like.'

Rowan chuckled, 'Then Hermes-Mercury will also need to be a god of miracles.'

'In a way Lillee *is* Hermes in this moment. The photo captures him in an eminently Hermesian posture.' Douglas flicked the page to a picture of a famous statue of Hermes about to take off for Mount Olympus. Only the tip of a single toe was earthbound—everything else belonged to the element of air (his winged sandals, his winged helmet). His chest was also thrust forward, reminding Rowan of the posture of sprinters as they hit the line, or long-jumpers at the point of maximum acceleration just prior to jumping. Everything about the statue strained for the heavens, for Olympus— realm of the Gods.

'Apart from being god of athletes, Hermes is also God of writing and communication—of thought moving swiftly, swift as the wind, swift as air. That's Hermes,' said Douglas, to a loud crack from one of Ramsay's old bones.

'So what's the deeper lesson, Doug—I don't get it?' said Ramsay shaking himself off after the stretches and exercises.

'If we apply Early Modern capitalist thinking to cricket—and I could say a lot more about *class conflict* in cricket—batsmen are the Knights, bats are even called *blades*, batsmen *flash the blade* and bowlers are exploited proletarian workhorses.'

'Really, Douglas?'

'But underneath the economic Darwinism we still sense the survival of ancient notions of trade and sport—trade as social exchange between tribes to maintain civil communications, and sport as inter-tribal ritual, display, the mutual honing of skills. And over such exchanges presides, even now, Hermes—god of cross-roads, travellers, thieves and fast talking entertainers. God of interstitial *zones*—places where *my* reality meets *your* reality.' Douglas paused, apparently out of breath, before summing up.

'The photo of Dennis Lillee captures a transcendent moment. There is a *joy* in becoming Hermes, but it isn't primarily an aggressive experience. Lillee looks aggressive, sure, but he's really in a kind of ecstatic trance—love of flight, love of the dance. All athletes are really dancers—never forget that, it's the real secret of sport.'

'I get what you're saying, Doug,' said Ramsay, struggling to stay respectful, 'but we're playing cricket here, not admiring ballet. Rowan, let's get to work, shall we?'

Douglas looked directly at Rowan—determined to have the last word, 'Always remember, cricket, indeed any sport, is about dance, it's about theatre—it should enact archetypal dramas, it should be a cathartic Group Ritual. In the background is Luna, the Great Moon Mother, and King Sol, the resplendent Sun! Sport should be about extremes—extremes of fate, birth and death, morality and immorality, good and evil, etc. Show us ecstatic triumph and heart-breaking defeat! Anything less results in boredom.' Having said his piece, Douglas put down his photographs and trotted over to a ladder behind the batting wicket. His intention was to film Rowan batting and bowling via a camera in the shed's hay-loft.

The first session of batting went well. When Rowan got to bowl, however, he found the going tougher. The run up jarred his ankles, knees and back and given he hadn't done much physical exercise for a while, he tired quickly. Douglas took the video-footage and after an hour Ramsay ended the session saying, 'Let's call it quits for the day—before Rowan collapses.' The process of analysing the strengths and weaknesses of Rowan's batting and bowling began after dinner that night. Identified faults were noted down to be addressed in the following day's sessions.

So began the cricket component of a gruelling weekly work regime composed of research, learning various languages and endless cricket training sessions. These activities were supplemented occasionally by labouring and handyman duties around the farm—cutting firewood, mending fences, pruning fruit trees, etc. The activities provided relief from the isolation associated with constant study and writing—though they'd been absent from the original job description. Rowan's language lessons were conducted in the strange windowless triangular building made of bluestone situated at the back of the property called 'the Clochan'. Apparently it also doubled as a therapeutic centre—in it Douglas conducted psychotherapy sessions with clients. Rowan was fascinated by the building's strange interior. Bizarre mythological images from numerous traditions were painted on its interior walls as well as on the floor. The room was also stocked with piles of foam mattresses and other padding (which had been stacked around the walls), a powerful (and expensive, Rowan thought) sound system with large speakers as well as dozens of large, though dusty, statues and figurines—a veritable menagerie of forgotten gods, goddesses, ancestor beings and fabulous creatures from numerous mythological traditions.

The speech development component of the language lessons took place in this building, often in near total darkness, with Rowan answering Douglas in the particular language being learnt. Douglas had advanced skills in French—though the lessons were often punctuated by outbursts of exotic swear words. When Rowan asked Douglas why he had to learn French, he was told, 'Isles wrote in French now and then … and he approved of the French Revolution.'

Rowan also had to spend time every day learning some of the aboriginal languages of Victoria, South Australia and New South Wales. Again, Douglas seemed proficient, though Rowan noted a tendency to randomly merge bits and pieces from various languages. It was as though he was teaching Rowan a hybrid inter-regional language composed of words, phrases etc. drawn from multiple tribes. Inevitably this involved grossly 'unscholastic', not to mention politically incorrect, leaps of faith. The strange thing, however, was that many of his intuitive leaps seemed quite logical after Rowan learnt more about the languages in question. He began to suspect that Douglas had Koori heritage, though Douglas invariably parried the question. The fluency of his pronunciation, made Rowan suspect that he was using some of the languages in conversation with native speakers.

When Douglas wasn't conducting the sessions himself, he provided Rowan with tapes featuring native speakers—'Just to be on the safe side.' Usually he'd play the tapes over the clochan's stereo system, with Rowan, sitting or even lying in darkness, struggling to absorb phrases, grammar etc. by rote. 'High decibel language immersion,' was how Douglas described the technique. After switching on the tape, he would typically leave the building to attend to business tasks, or perhaps to his fruit trees and animals.

The first few weeks were also eventful with regard to the

two units Rowan was being employed to research—there was an early snag. The promised office space at the university in Bendigo didn't eventuate. According to Douglas, space and computers were at a premium, and the Head of School had overruled his academic friend's earlier offer. At least Rowan's lending rights at the library were confirmed, though he only ever visited the campus to pick up or return books. He was disappointed since it diminished his chances of finding work there as a tutor or lecturer. It also meant that instead of making friends in Bendigo, he found himself gravitating to the region's arts capital, Castlemaine, to socialise.

Interestingly, Douglas's library seemed at least as extensive as the university library—especially when it came to material on the Axial Age Religions unit. Douglas's encyclopaedic knowledge of the world's spiritual and philosophic traditions meant Rowan spent long hours on the barn's second storey balcony watching his boss thumb through then quote from dozen of books on shamanism, Christianity, Buddhism, Islam, mysticism and so on. Occasionally, Rowan would take notes, ask questions, debate a point or wander off to make tea or fetch a plate of the jaffa flavoured chocolate biscuits that Douglas loved. Occasionally, when Douglas was absorbed in a book or a thought, Rowan would gaze out across the orchard or marvel at the way the landscape was drying beyond its green rectangular boundaries. Despite the pleasant setting, he had little interest in religion, mysticism, theology, metaphysics or general philosophy, and thus struggled to retain much that they discussed. Such topics, however, were Douglas's favourites— he rarely talked about the contents of the Cultural Studies unit.

Douglas was less able as a cricket coach. The task of teaching Rowan how to bowl fast and bat competently was mostly given to Ramsay. Apparently, Douglas had bartered therapy sessions for Rowan's coaching sessions. To Rowan, however, the sessions where Ramsay wasn't around were the most fun, largely because Douglas seemed to struggle with his failings as a coach. Often, the expert training videos Ramsay had passed on proved impenetrable and Douglas would become theatrical. 'What on earth did he say there? Can you work out what he's saying, Rowan—what does he mean by *reverse swing*?' Such sessions tended to deteriorate into good-humoured farce. He'd chat with the bowling machine, 'Hey, Robot—let's bowl him a toe-cruncher!' or he'd address the Gods of Cricket requesting guidance—'Sir Donald, I ask you, how can we keep Rowan in-line with the ball when the speed hits 130km per hour? He seems to want to shit himself.' Just as often he'd make obscene comments mimicking the voices of famous cricketers from various countries.

CHAPTER EIGHT

THE HARCOURT TURN-OFF
(Friday, Sept. 6th 1996)

Rowan sat outside his hut picking at a breakfast of cut mango, kiwi-fruit and muesli with honey. The food was being washed down by freshly ground coffee. The sun had risen by the time he'd finished eating, and he sat drinking the last dregs of coffee under the verandah surrounded by the morning sounds of numerous insects and birds. He felt agitated—evidence that he was in two minds about the decision he was about to make.

The urge to pack his bags and leave the block had grown over the past week. He would have to return all Douglas's money and then write a sincere resignation letter.

In truth, he was missing Kerryn and had many misgivings about Douglas. Given Rowan did not see himself as a spiritual person, he was finding it very difficult to stay interested in the subject matter. The plethora of languages he'd been asked to learn also brought special challenges—again Rowan lacked motivation, which made the learning slow and tedious. The interior of the Clochan and its remote location on the block didn't help—likewise, the fact that Douglas also used the building for therapy sessions with clients. When asked what type of therapy he practised, Douglas had replied, 'Oh, people scream and cry and hit pillows. If they stick at it, they get to travel to other dimensions of being—transpersonal dimensions.' Rowan's social work training had made him suspicious of most New Age therapists.

Finally, Rowan's body was aching from the constant cricket training. Although he was getting to live out a childhood dream—i.e. being paid to play the sport—he knew it was too late for him to become a professional cricketer, and thus he saw little point to the physical suffering. For example, he was nursing a severely bruised left thumb due to an accident the previous night. A ball delivered by the bowling machine had reared sharply to jam Rowan's thumb against the bat handle—the pain had been excruciating.

Douglas wasn't about—so the timing seemed perfect. He'd announced the night before that he needed to visit a neighbour for a day or two, 'I'll leave the front door to the house open in case you need anything. There's plenty of music up there and instructions to feed some of the animals and reptiles. Anything that could cause harm is under lock and key, so make yourself at home. And of course, read 'til your eyes are sore.'

By 1pm he'd reached a decision. Soon after, he began lugging his belongings down the hillside to the car. He then wrote a 'thank-you, but no thank-you' note to Douglas and placed it in an envelope on the hut's dining table.

He felt strange as he drove toward the Melbourne turn-off at Harcourt. Suppressing for the moment an impulse to turn left there, he crossed the road and headed for Castlemaine. He decided it was only fair to restock the hut with fruit, cereal, milk, coffee etc.. This meant returning to the property, of course, to place the food in the hut—an act Rowan couldn't immediately countenance.

He ended up sitting in a coffee shop for two hours—all the time pondering what to do. The first thing he noticed was that people seemed strange to him—the changed perceptions were so dramatic that he seriously wondered whether Douglas had brain-washed him. He noticed the soul ugliness of people, for example, and here and there suppressed anger. Most difficult to deal with was the sadness and despair. He felt as though the people who passed his table were figures in a Bosch painting, like the people depicted in the Garden of Earthly Delights. It was as if their core personalities and life-long anxieties, desires and fears were on display to him. This changed perception of people surprised Rowan—something about life on the block had made him excessively sensitive.

Just after 4pm, he decided to visit the auto-teller and withdraw some money. He'd return it to Douglas along with the food.

He entered his pin into the machine, pressed the savings account option, then the withdraw cash option followed by the amount. In that moment, as the machine processed the withdrawal request, he felt his decision was final.

The hundred dollar notes, all new and shiny, felt good in his hands. He recovered the card and the transaction receipt, and on a whim glanced anxiously at the account balance.

To his surprise, it was up over seventeen hundred dollars—his first full pay from Douglas's company had been deposited in the account. The money represented a triumph of sorts—hadn't Kerryn been dismissive of the job from the start? She'd have to admit now that however dodgy it appeared, it paid real money.

He walked back to car deep in thought. If he resigned, he'd have to give back almost three thousand dollars. The thought of it stressed him—the rent on the unit was due, not to mention his share of the house mortage. Regardless, he resolved to take a right turn back to Melbourne at the Calder intersection near Harcourt—after all, he didn't need to post all the money back immediately.

Fifteen minutes of driving later, he found himself leaving the Melbourne turn-off to its busy meditations. Once again, he was driving through the apple and pear orchards in the foothills of Mount Alexander. Before he knew it, he was dragging his possessions back up the hill to the hut. *I have to give it a few more weeks*, he told himself.

CHAPTER NINE

SPRING GIVES WAY TO SUMMER

By the end of September, Rowan's cricket skills had improved enough to allow him to practice with local players. 'Rammer says he can get you a game in the seconds the Saturday after next,' said Douglas one day, 'I think it would be useful for you to apply what you've learnt to a game situation.'

After all the coaching and fitness work, Rowan had discovered that he could bowl at a remarkable 125km per hour. He was also much fitter and marvelled at the improvements he'd made to his run up and delivery action (particularly the more effective use of his front arm). Clearly, Ramsay's introduction of strength work was paying off. His batting too had improved markedly.

One evening in September—during a video analysis session—Douglas unveiled new goals for Rowan, who was lying on the couch nursing a bruised thigh. The old man had cranked the bowling machine up to around 130km per hour that day, and his employee had been too slow to react to the first delivery.

'125km is good as a bowling speed — about as fast as anyone around these parts ever bowls. But we need to push you to 130km, then if possible, to 135km per hour,' said Douglas, sitting on his grubby couch thumbing through a training manual. 'Also, you need to be able to handle 135-to-140km with the bat.'

'I didn't even *see* that first ball today — how am I supposed to handle stuff travelling at the speed of light?'

Douglas simply smiled his gapped smile.

'That's why coaches Ramsay and Green are researching *reflex improvement* exercises. Apparently, it all comes down to pre-delivery footwork, maintaining verticals and horizontals (horizons), not moving the head too much, watching the ball out of the bowler's hand (the robot's maw), and er … someone bouncing cricket balls at your head, chest or thigh full tilt from 15 metres. Practice makes perfect!'

'Sounds like tomorrow's sessions will be great fun.'

By the time he fronted for the second grade match in mid-October, he was quicker than the other local pace bowlers and could competently keep out spinners and medium pace bowlers when batting. Though he only took one wicket and was wayward at times, he more than held his own as a bowler. Ramsay was delighted, 'We'll have you in the first grade within a month if you can tighten up your line a bit.'

Rowan, however, was exhausted. Though away at the training clinics, Douglas had demanded that he maintain his reading in religious studies topics (including summarising whole books into 2,000 word lectures), Aboriginal languages as well as French and Gaelic.

Whilst away, he was afflicted with a number of nightmares. One involved soldiers in full battle-dress — including infra-red goggles and machine guns — chasing him through a forest of ironbarks and grey-box gums. The dream always ended with him facing a gun and he'd wake to his heart racing and the bed-clothes saturated with sweat. In another dream, equally menacing, he'd find himself running through the streets of an unknown city—but always the same city. Usually he'd be running hand in hand with Anika as air-raid sirens sounded and fighter-jets, helicopters and bombers circled overhead like gigantic mechanical birds of prey. Terrified locals would shout at him as he ran, 'Hurry to the shelter! The Northerners are coming!' Perhaps due to the languages Douglas had been teaching him, the people in the dreams usually spoke French or a hybrid Koori language, instead of English.

As the weeks passed, Rowan had to revise his earlier assessment of Douglas's academic status. Apart from his vast knowledge of history, literature, philosophy, art history and languages—all of the traditional humanities subjects—he had an uncanny ability to draw together complex theoretical insights into simple, evocative language that provided a key to understanding any given topic. He rarely presented his own personal perspective on the material under discussion, preferring to methodically present an important perspective before critiquing it via an important opposing perspective. The result was a sense of being involved in the debate.

Then there was his ability to create vivid narrative out of reams of boring factual detail, not to mention his abundant theatrical skills—he had superb voice modulation and possessed a remarkable ability to become the person he was talking about. Sometimes he'd play two characters at once, switching seamlessly between personalities as they dialogued on some obscure historical disagreement. These talents were even on display during cricket training sessions—which led to much hilarity. He often pretended to be famous cricketers—

Rod Marsh, Ian Botham or Viv Richards.

He was also an excellent editor, fast and efficient at rearranging the confused material Rowan typically presented to him.

Although Douglas didn't discuss his private life with Rowan, he did talk openly about his many publishing and editing ventures. His aesthetic in this area seemed to be experimentalist—though never simply for the sake of it. He believed in the social responsibility of the writer/artist, and distrusted those who submitted to 'the regime of self-inflicted censorship'; a 'disease', according to Douglas, afflicting many Australian writers and poets. 'I publish work that makes people feel uncomfortable,' he said one day. Similarly, although the internet was new, Douglas believed it would revolutionise reading, writing and publishing, and would birth entirely new literary forms. He was fond of declaring the reign of the "publisher tyrants" all but over.

During these first months, Rowan often wondered how anything he was learning related to the Abraham Isles biography he was being employed to research and write. Likewise, though the job was doing little for his academic career, he did nothing to change the situation. Indeed, he took pleasure in refusing to recommit immediately to suburbia and a conventional existence. Life on the block was peaceful, and the bits of farm work and the training sessions had made him feel fitter and healthier than he'd felt in years. As the weeks wore on he found himself fantasising about a future that he knew, deep down, to be an impossibility. He imagined that he and Kerryn might reconcile, leave Melbourne and settle as postmodern bohemians somewhere in the hills around Castlemaine—Victoria's unofficial arts capital.

BOOK ONE

PART TWO: THE TEACHINGS OF ABRAHAM ISLES

CHAPTER TEN

THE FINALITY OF DIVORCE
(Boxing Day, 1996)

During their Boxing Day meeting to discuss mortgage payments and other financial issues, Kerryn announced that she was filing for divorce. 'The papers are in the mail' she stated gently. The announcement panicked Rowan, and for the rest of the meeting he all but begged her for more time.

'More time for what, Rowan?' she asked in a level voice. Her stylish dark gray suit jacket, cream silk shirt and gray skirt made her words seem formal and definitive.

'For me to work out who I am … to work through stuff.'

'What *stuff* … exactly what *stuff* do you mean? You've had four months to work through your *stuff*.' They were sitting at the dining-room table of their large Dandenong home. Everything around them looked clean and contemporary—even if the furnishings were a little sparser than normal due to the absence of some of Rowan's possessions. The late afternoon sun slanting its way through the kitchen blinds produced a warm but melancholy mood in the room. The same lighting on Kerryn's shoulder-length, light brown hair with blonde highlights made Rowan pause before answering.

'Stuff to do with my father—to do with fatherhood. To do with what the hell I'm supposed to do with the rest of my life that doesn't make me feel like I'm well ... already dead ... in here,' he pointed to his heart, 'and here' he tapped his forehead a couple of times.

After sighing and looking away, Kerryn said, 'You know, even if you worked through those issues—and we both know that's been a long-term project—I doubt that would change anything important between us.' She was fighting back tears as she spoke.

'You don't know that—we've had some good years together.'

Again she sighed—though a little more definitively this time, 'I know *that* because I've read some of your diaries over the past month or so. And they say pretty categorically, actually, that you need, quote: "someone like Anika" in order to feel "completely alive", unquote.'

Rowan didn't know whether to feel angry that she'd read his private diaries or guilty about what he'd written. He felt numb and defeated as she quietly listed her reasons for divorcing him.

'I'm not angry or even jealous, Rowan. In a way reading the diaries was a kind of liberation, you need to understand that, but I can never be Anika, or even "someone like Anika". My happiness in life isn't dependent on some pie in the sky commitment to "creative living" as you like to call it. I guess I've tried to hide that fact from you—perhaps from the very beginning. But I'm through pretending—to myself and to you—that I'm "creative" in any meaningful way. I pretended, you know ...' her voice was cracking slightly, 'so that you would continue to want to be with me. A pointless exercise, as it turned out—as the diaries confirm.'

The rest of the meeting passed in a blur: 'Fifty-fifty division of assets? Do you intend to challenge that?' 'No—let's keep the solicitors out of it.' 'Fifty-fifty on house-related maintenance bills and on the mortgage until it's sold?' 'No problem.' 'What about the furniture?' 'You paid for and chose most of it—I only want a few things. I live like a monk these days.' 'Okay, make a list—and the diaries are in that box over there. Please take them with you today.' 'Of course', etc.

As they sorted through the debris of their time together, he tried to think of something to say that might change her mind about the divorce. Her having read the diaries, however, made the task pointless.

As the meeting drew to a close they walked, without speaking, to the front gate of their home. After passing the empty bedrooms she'd hoped would one day echo with the voices of children, the loneliness he'd always felt there became unbearable. They halted at the gate—right next to the FOR SALE sign. After the briefest of hugs, she said, 'If I set my own situation aside for a moment—and under the circumstances that's pretty hard—I really do feel for your dilemma. You messed up with her when you were young and we both know she'll never take you back.'

'Kerryn … I know I have some growing up to do.'

'Just hear me out, please. There's "growing up" and "growing up". I know now that the "growing up" I offer you isn't what you want or even need. You don't want all of this, do you?' She waved at the house as she asked the question.

'No … not really.' He stared down at the pavement, his side of the confession complete.

Kerryn paused, shocked by his candour. 'Okay, a day for home truths! Well, maybe she can make you feel "completely alive", but I really hope for your sake, that she isn't just a mirage. And I really hope that the image—the fantasy of her— isn't just a defence against really embracing adulthood.'

The meeting had left Rowan despondant, not least because it meant a definitive end to their relationship—a moment he'd avoided confronting during their separation. A precipice had appeared in front of him and, like it or not, he was being forced to jump.

He'd replayed the meeting a hundred times since Boxing Day, and was doing it again now as stark treeless paddocks gave way to a stretch of native forest east of Mount Alexander. *Welcome to the New Year*, he kept saying to himself as he drove the now familiar road. His mind also drifted to developments with his job. He'd done everything required of him over the first four months of his employment. He'd prepared the resources for the two units—even the unit on global religious and spiritual systems that he had no real interest in. Likewise, he'd started to get a genuine grasp of the various languages Douglas had asked him to learn; though he was still quite confused about the Koori languages he was being taught. This was partly to do with Douglas's tendency to jump between languages, and partly to do with the fragmented state that many of them were in due to the ruthless efficiency of the colonisation process in the 19th century. Strangely enough he'd begun speaking bits of Scottish Gaelic, even though Douglas had only requested that he be able to read it. He felt an instinctive attraction to the language.

Douglas had sent the edited unit resource material overseas before Christmas. Consequently, Rowan was looking forward to some New Year revelations to do with the Abraham Isles biography. Likewise, he intended to raise with Douglas the possibility of teaching—whether face to face or off-campus. Though most of the staff at his old university were on leave over the January period, there was a rumour afoot among the post-grads that the PhD student they'd employed to lecture on contemporary literary theory in 1996 had experienced an emotional melt-down over the Christmas period. Given the course was due to begin in late February, Rowan was the logical replacement. He'd been told by a PhD student in the know, however, that the head of department would employ him only reluctantly. When his name had come up at a meeting as the obvious replacement, Professor Styles had said, 'Dr Sweeney? A little rough around the edges don't you think? And exuberantly political as well as being prone to creative flourishes ... Well, I suppose he might do for a semester—until we can find a proper replacement.' The comments had stung Rowan since Professor Styles was listed on his resume as a referee.

Besides, Rowan had bigger problems. He'd developed a nervous tremble after Kerryn's divorce announcement. Perhaps it was due to all the physical activity related to moving his possessions into storage after giving notice on his Melbourne flat. The decision had reduced his financial stress, but it also meant a definitive break with the secure, stable world he'd enjoyed with Kerryn for over a decade. Even his former friendship group seemed to have splintered, with many mutual friends already taking sides or retreating after the split. In a way, he was glad to be away from it all.

When Rowan arrived at the property, Douglas was nowhere to be seen, so he dropped his bags at the hut, as well as a pile of household debris from his Melbourne flat, and prepared himself some lunch. He opened a can of mineral water and made a turkey sandwich. Douglas, as usual, had stocked the gas fridge-freezer full of lean-meat, fruit, vegetables and drinks. Rowan then wandered down the back of the property to look for Douglas. Perhaps he was pumping water up to the house or working on something at the clochan.

The temperature had soared by the time Rowan reached the back paddock, but still Douglas was nowhere to be seen.

Swatting summer bushflies, Rowan decided to walk in the direction of the clochan—which stood beside Forest Track Road at the northern boundary of the property. The building had its own entrance and carpark.

Rowan heard loud music—heavy bass, thundering toms—punctuated by blood curdling screams and wailings as he approached the wooded ridge that led down to the clochan. At the top of the ridge, he was greeted by an unusual scene—about a dozen cars, bright and reflective in the sweltering heat, were parked under the large white cedar trees of the clochan's makeshift gravel car-park. Outside the clochan stood an open tent and a dozen white plastic seats sat higgledy-piggledy under some mature ash trees.

Rowan wandered nervously down the familiar dirt path leading to the clochan. He knew that Douglas would not approve of him walking in on a therapy session, so he decided to hang around outside instead.

As he approached the large, blue-stone triangular structure, the cries of cathartic despair seemed to grow louder and more intense, until he began to feel his stomach churn and his pulse quicken. He found a concealed spot amongst a stand of late black wattles and settled down to listen. For a time, he was transported back to the rehab therapy he'd undergone after quitting the band, but before meeting Kerryn. As he listened, he recalled again the experiences that had surfaced as the drugs began to leave his system—anger and sadness related to his parents' divorce, and memories of his mother's tiredness and anxiety as a single parent. The intense, sometimes cathartic, sessions with drug and alcohol counsellors had been life changing—assisted cold turkey after years of substance abuse and denial exacerbated by life on the road with the band.

His therapy had ended after he'd gained control over his drug habit. By then Kerryn was on the scene. Not for the first time, he asked himself where their relationship had gone wrong. His usual answer was that after meeting Kerryn he'd stopped seeing life as an adventure. The years prior to their meeting had been so intense, so tumultuous, that he'd been blind to the possibility that the security she offered might one day amount to another kind of imprisonment. Slowly but surely they'd become victims of the 'great sleep'—otherwise known as 'the middle class professional thing'—a large mortgage, late model cars, secure but unimaginative work routines, private health cover, plans for a comfortable retirement and— he felt nauseous just thinking about it—hypocritical new left 'activism'. The only thing he hadn't agreed to was parenthood.

This had been his narrative—Kerryn as a contributor to his inner deadness, Anika as the cure. Of late, however, with Kerryn gone, the narrative had collapsed—leaving only failure and loneliness.

He was so absorbed in his thoughts, that he didn't see Douglas leave the clochan mid-session for a breather and to visit the outside toilet.

'What the hell are you doing standing over there?' shouted Douglas, obviously angry at Rowan's presence.

'I-I didn't find you up at the house so I decided to search for you near the dam, then down here,' he said sheepishly, stepping out from behind a large late black wattle.

'Get back behind those trees—you mustn't be seen. I have clients in there and some of them are paranoid about being seen here. I need you to make your way back up to the house right away.'

In that moment, Douglas noticed that Rowan wasn't his normal self—something in the disconsolate way Rowan stood there—because he immediately softened, 'Look, I guess it's a while since I told you about not coming down here during therapy sessions, but you do need to make yourself scarce.'

'Sorry, Douglas—hearing all that took me back to my detox treatments.'

Douglas drew nearer, 'She wants a divorce doesn't she?'

Rowan nodded and looked down.

Douglas put a hand round his shoulder before turning him gently in the direction of the main house.

'We'll talk later, okay? I'll be back up at the house at 8pm—this is an intensive, people will be around all afternoon and into the evening.'

Rowan was relieved to see Douglas return to the barn a little after 8pm. He looked exhausted, however—the therapy sessions had obviously knocked the stuffing out of him. Nevertheless, Douglas listened to Rowan recount the details of his Melbourne trip.

Finally, around 9pm, with Rowan trailing off into repetitive reminiscences, Douglas stood up, saying, 'Tomorrow might be a good time to introduce the main principles of Isles's spiritual system. I'll prepare a new work-plan for you in the morning—we're done with developing unit resources, but I still want you to work on your languages, likewise the cricket sessions will continue as per normal.'

'Douglas, I really don't see the point. The last match I had before Christmas—the A Grade match …'

'Yep, you took 4-25 and bowled with real pace,' said Douglas.

'But it was 40 degrees Celsius by the afternoon—I had dehydration after bowling just ten overs. I was sick as a dog. My body doesn't cope with extreme heat.'

'Stop catastrophising—we can get around dehydration. You drank water when you should have been drinking rehydration fluids. It's that simple. The cricket sessions will continue as before. However, from now on you'll devote some time each week to academic *and* experiential research into Abraham Isles. It's time to start writing that biography we talked about last August.'

Later that night, as Rowan trudged up the hill to the hut, he felt profoundly alone. The stars—usually so clear and bright in the heavens—seemed cold, and indifferent to his struggles. Likewise, the moon—in all its white luminescent glory— appeared stark and inhuman.

CHAPTER ELEVEN

THE UNDERGROUND NEMETON
(Tuesday, January 7th 1997)

Douglas was standing beside the small square stage at the centre of the library. It was late in the afternoon on a forty degree Celsius day and thus the interior of the library-shed, despite being reasonably well insulated, felt like a sauna. Rowan had never paid any attention to it before, but today he knew that this square stage was the gateway to his first lesson on Abraham Isles.

'If we lift off this wooden sheet we'll find two clamps on each side of the square. That's right ... pull each clamp lever up gently—they're spring loaded. Now give us a hand lifting this sheet off.'

Rowan did as he was asked and together they uncovered a large hole—the entrance to a mine-shaft. Rowan leant nervously over the wooden rail-track sleepers that framed the entrance—they were stacked three deep—trying to peer into the hole. He immediately made out a rusty metal ladder descending, rung by rung, into the cool, dank smelling mine shaft.

'Don't jump in there yet,' joked Douglas, 'I need to switch the air pump on for ten or fifteen minutes, otherwise unhealthy gases that sometimes accumulate in mines and leach from the rock, might turn us into sensitive new age canaries as we descend.'

'As we descend?' muttered Rowan.

'Welcome to my classroom!' said Douglas, flicking a light on before switching off his torch.

Rowan halted four or five steps above the cavern floor. It felt damp and cool in the mine. As he surveyed the dimly lit scene, he saw a small number of plastic seats facing a flat wall-space about five metres wide. At the centre of the wall, he noticed an alcove hollowed out of the rock. It was just over two metres high and under a metre wide. It appeared to house a statue of an Egyptian god or royal—Rowan searched back through his memories to work out who the figure represented. It was male and its limbs were in perfect proportion and it was dressed, as per ancient style, in an elaborate, though scanty costume embroidered with various types of painted jewels. Despite this, the main colour emanating from the alcove was gold. The god—Rowan was now certain it was a figure representing a god—was seated on some sort of rock throne and held an ornate golden bowl in its left hand. Rowan also noted that the cave was thick with the smell of incense.

'What the hell is this, Douglas?' said Rowan, his voice slightly higher than normal.

'Like I said, a classroom—but far from prying eyes and the heat.' Douglas seemed to be looking for something on a desk to the left of the statue at the far end of the cave theatre's projection screen. He wasn't looking at Rowan as he spoke, but the words carried easily. *The acoustics are amazing,* Rowan thought.

'Looks more like a pagan shrine,' said Rowan nervously,

'what exactly do you do down here?'

Douglas looked up at Rowan and said, 'Come on, get down here! Thoth doesn't bite, he prefers to write.' The old man chuckled at his own joke.

But Rowan wouldn't budge—he wanted to have a good look around before descending any further. As his eyes adjusted, he spied other, smaller deities, on pedestals, or in the shadows of chairs. The lighting in the cave was pointed at the lectern at the front. Some of the deities he recognised, for example, there was a statue of Hermes-Mercury—god of thieves and intellectuals. He was poised at the point of take-off and seemed so graceful with his right arm—and attached caduceus—outstretched and pointing to the heavens. Rowan observed that only the toe of the lead foot was attached to the pedestal/ground. The heel was just off the ground, and the other leg—raised horizontal from the waist backwards—was already airborne. *Douglas is right, he looks like a dancer or an athlete*, thought Rowan.

Directly beside Hermes-Mercury stood a statue composed of three female figures. *Graces*, thought Rowan, but he wasn't certain. They wore loose peasant dresses and were bare-foot. They danced together joyously in a circle but the centrifugal thrust of the dance made the piece seem unstable—only each woman's physical connection to the other two 'Graces' kept the dance circle intact.

There were other deities too, but most were too much in shadow for Rowan to be certain of their identities. He thought he made out a many-armed, dancing Shiva on the far side of the cavern, but couldn't be sure since a chair impeded his view. Likewise, there was a Celtic theme to some of the statues. Rowan knew practically nothing about the Celtic pantheons except that they were complex and speculative given the lack of written sources. One figure looked particularly striking— seated in a Buddha-like posture; it displayed large antler horns attached to an otherwise human head and body.

In the same area, behind the chairs, a projector began to fire up. It lessened his anxiety, since it suggested an educational purpose for the cave. The extra light of the projector also illuminated two tunnel entrances, one either side of the central projection screen. *Probably they lead into the mine proper*, thought Rowan, which immediately made him feel nervous about dark stretches of tunnel harbouring any number of unpleasant surprises.

Rowan decided it was all too weird. He'd tolerated the poisonous snakes, the wacky lectures, the bizarre obsession with cricket, the unfulfilled promises of a teaching position, the expectation that he write a biography about an unknown politician, and so on, but he was not about to step into a mine featuring all the paraphernalia of a pagan shrine.

'Douglas, I'd like you to tell me exactly what all this is about—if you don't I'm climbing back up this mine-shaft and when I reach the top I'm going to walk to my unit, pack up all my things and leave the property for good.'

There was a long tense pause, at least on Rowan's part. Douglas, however, was absorbed in starting up what looked like a small computer on the desk in front of him.

'Don't be so … *earnest*, Rowan. Here's a guy tells me he's a teacher, but how does he intend to teach? Surely not in a *mon-o-tone* to the *ass-em-bled stu-dents*! Mr *Listen-to-me* as I bore the pants off you, you poor bastards. Surely not!' said Douglas, still struggling with his computer console.

Rowan took a step back up the ladder, but not out of fear—more out of wounded pride. He paused for a while with one foot on a rung, and the other dangling comically from the ceiling of the cavern.

'Come on! Get down here—I put a lot of effort into this. We

need to discuss some of the concepts at the heart of Isles's 19th century intellectual system. You need to understand this stuff if you're going to write a book on the fellow. Besides, his ideas lend themselves to spatial elaborations. Haven't you ever heard of experiential learning?'

Rowan was descending again. His head soon appeared below the level of the ceiling and his feet were only a metre above the rock floor. Once again, he surveyed the scene. The projector cast a bright blue light against a screen behind Douglas.

'I didn't realise how utterly devoid of theatrics most universities are these days. Besides, I thought you'd studied history—how can you study history without being exposed to the weird and the wonderful, the sheer *otherness* of the past?'

'I studied, uh, mostly contemporary history—Australian history from Federation to the 1920s. I also taught some post-settlement— or post invasion, depending on your perspective—stuff.'

'Oh, it was an invasion all right; let's not mince words— murderous, greed-fuelled, self-righteous and above all ruthlessly effective. But even the study of Australian history should have made you aware of the uncanny beauty of the past?'

'I did mostly economic history and the history of ideas— also a little social history and some Medieval and Early Modern history. That was before they, uh, shut that stream down as irrelevant to modern Australian students.'

Douglas looked stunned—like a military leader handed bad news about the loss of a critical battle. 'There appear to have been many casualties at the hands of the prevailing paradigm.'

'The prevailing paradigm?'

'Yes, neo-liberalism in alignment with postmodern secularism.'

Rowan stepped off the ladder onto the cave floor.

Douglas was struggling to make his computer connect to the projector.

'Do you need a hand there?'

'The damn thing is just out of the packet—I've only used it a couple of times. I'm trying to remember what I did. Ah, that's right … the hand-held console—where is it now?' As he spoke, he opened a small drawer in the desk under the computer.

'Of course,' ventured Rowan, 'some argue that humanities disciplines like history articulate a distinctly colonialist European view of the world. So what if no one studies ancient history, let the flawed past die! Three cheers!'

Douglas clicked a button on the hand-held console and the image on the computer screen was instantly replicated on the wall behind him.

'Yes,' he said ironically, 'three cheers indeed.'

'You sound dubious?'

'Because I am dubious! Anyway, we have another topic entirely today—if I can find the bloody files! It may take me a few more minutes.'

Rowan was also content to change the subject.

'For a moment there, I thought I was entering a pagan shrine. You'll agree that an abandoned mine is a strange place to hold a class?'

'Who says it's abandoned—this mine is still producing gold.'

'Surely the old miners would have exhausted this area very early in the piece … sometime in the 1850s?'

Douglas was fumbling with a stack of computer discs. 'This area was part of the so-called Mount Alexander diggings, on the edge of it actually. Look, it will take me a while to transfer some of the material on these discs to the computer and I've forgotten which folder I put the lecture in.' He sounded flustered.

'Have you found the odd small nugget then or just flecks of gold?'

'Can'a trust you, Rowan, me laddie?' Douglas mimicked the accent of an old Scottish miner.

'Aye, that you can,' answered Rowan, playing along.

'We-eell, if you be a trusty sort, capable o' keeping mum—e'en with the rum in ye—and not afflicted with the gold fever that turns a man into the divil his good sel I'll let ye peruse my patch, while I proceed with this gadgetry. Here take this torch. The tunnel behind us will answer all your questions.'

Rowan hesitated, 'How far does it go? Is the air clean?'

'Sure. Do you hear that soft hum off in the distance? Also, can you feel the cool draft right where we're standing? That's the air pump in operation. It brings surface air down here into the tunnel, forcing the musty stuff up top. When you go through that doorway you'll see what looks like a large wind sock worming its way along the tunnel's roof.'

'Then what?'

'Find the gold, young digger, find the gold.'

'Are there other levels?'

'I've never needed them.'

Rowan didn't know much about gold-mining, or any kind of mining, but there was something odd about the place. He remembered hearing that many of the gold mines around Bendigo went down 1500 metres or more—the upper level quartz reefs having long since been exhausted. There was no evidence here of machinery capable of transporting uncrushed gold quartz out of the mine, unless of course there was another exit. No doubt the puzzles would be solved simply by having a quick look down the tunnel. Rowan imagined that Douglas was probably something of an amateur miner, perhaps more interested in the romance of gold than the hard work of mining it. He'd be very surprised if the old man had fished out anything but trophy nuggets (nuggets costing more in diesel, oil, man-hours and worn out machinery than they were worth to uncover).

Rowan shone the torch at the roof of the tunnel before

directing it down the walls on either side. The light faded out twenty or so metres down the tunnel, which was straight, with just enough headroom for walking. Here and there bits of timber helped reinforce a roof or a wall and in other places the roof seemed reinforced by concrete occasionally speared with thick metal supports threaded into the concrete by way of triangular metal slabs. About ten metres along, Rowan also noticed the large white air sock. It threaded its way through a series of metal hoops at head height as far as the torch illuminated. A vent directly above his head announced the birth place of the giant worm, and its link to the upper world of fresh air and light.

'Go on,' shouted Douglas, 'have a gander—it will prepare you for the lecture. Assuming I can find the file containing the bloody material. What better a place to discuss Isles and alchemy than in a gold mine located in diggings that were, in the 19th century, the wonder of the world.'

CHAPTER TWELVE

OF SULPHUR AND SALT

Rowan wandered cautiously down the tunnel. For the first thirty metres or so he saw nothing but grey rock on all sides. Further along, however, he noticed little alcoves to the right and left—though there was no machinery around capable of transporting rock debris and gold-bearing quartz to the surface. Of course, if the mine was inactive then all of that dirty work would have been done many decades ago. These facts suggested to Rowan that Douglas was probably playing some sort of game with him.

However, perhaps ten metres from the end of the tunnel, his torch caught the glint of a shiny material embedded in the quartz reef running through the end-wall. Rowan assumed it was fool's gold—or perhaps fake gold placed there by Douglas for fun. *They do that in the tourist mines*, Rowan thought, *tourists like to think they're seeing gold in its natural state.*

Rowan moved closer. The wall's dull glint betrayed the presence of large quantities of some sort of metal.

Close up, Rowan noticed the first signs of industry—a sledge-hammer and a very large chisel. He almost laughed out loud; this was pure theatre. And to him the fake gold nuggets looked genuine—not that he could really tell the difference. The larger nuggets looked particularly pure. Rowan wondered about how many ounces of fake gold he was looking at.

As Rowan wandered back along the tunnel, he pondered how Douglas had managed to make the scene look so real.

'How did you do that? How did you set the wall up to look so … so genuine?' he said as he returned to the main cavern.

'It is genuine,' answered Douglas, not looking up from his computer. 'I have had most astonishing luck. How else do you think I acquire capital for my publishing business? The Quartz Dragon provides—and Hermes, god of gold mining and cultural endeavours.'

Rowan stared at Douglas in amazement, 'It is either fake gold down there, or placed gold—I'd bet my life on it. There's nothing but a sledge-hammer and a chisel in the tunnel, and no evidence of any means to transport quartz rock to the surface for crushing.'

Douglas looked up, 'You saw the lead, there's no need at this time to crush too much rock—though I'll grant you at times I've had to haul buckets to the surface.'

There was no trace of humour in Douglas's voice. Likewise, his facial expression remained deadpan. Rowan stared at him for a while, hoping to catch the hint of a smile. Douglas, however, simply returned to his job of setting up the projection facilities.

'This place does look like a pagan shrine,' Rowan said again, as he sat on an old wooden seat close to the front. He was drowned out by Greek folk music playing through the room's main speakers. At the same time the rock face projection screen lit up with a photograph of the Greek god, Hermes.

'Isles adapted certain pagan elements inherent to Early Modern Alchemy to his system, merging them with beliefs drawn from other sources.' Douglas spoke in fits and starts, still concentrating intently on the computer. When he eventually looked up, he said, 'Don't sit at the front. I need you to sit back-row centre.'

As Rowan stood up, he heard footsteps coming from the other tunnel followed by voices in the main mineshaft.

'You have an audience?' he said to Douglas, uncertainly.

Douglas ignored him, but went a few paces toward the other tunnel entrance before disappearing out of view. Rowan soon heard him conversing quietly with someone who did not enter the cave until Rowan was re-seated at the back. Meanwhile a pair of black shoes appeared on the highest rung of the ladder near the cavern's ceiling.

'Are you decent, Douglas?' It was a man's voice.

'As decent as I'll ever be. Did you bring wine?'

'Our poet carries the wine. This humble novelist carries only grass, but 'tis divine grass—grass that would sate the heavenly cow herself!'

'Did you pick up Isobel?'

'Isobel the artist? Yes, in a manner of speaking.'

A loud female *harrumph* came from further up the mineshaft. Moments later a stocky middle aged man was visible at the foot of the ladder about two metres away from Rowan. He was dressed in black jeans and a black t-shirt. The next person to come down the mineshaft ladder was also dressed in black. He was taller and thinner and had bushy, silvery hair and stylish glasses. He seemed quieter than his blustery friend. Both men said a cursory hello to Rowan before hailing Douglas, who embraced each in turn.

Moments later a third person appeared on the ladder, Isobel he presumed. She was a tall attractive woman of fifty or so dressed in an ornate gypsy dress—greens, purples and blacks swirled as she negotiated the last three rungs of the ladder. Her arms were bare to the shoulders and she wore innumerable bangles and bracelets. She seemed hot and bothered as she adjusted her eyes to the dimness of the cavern.

'You must be the young academic?' she said, after spotting Rowan. 'I bet he's leading you a merry dance.'

Rowan wanted to ask her what she meant, but she'd already turned to the others, apparently after hearing Douglas's voice. 'There he is—my dear old beast of the woodlands.'

'Your "beast"? Last we met I was your "antipodean Merlin". What next?' He said with obvious delight, 'I prefer the title Merlin, since that would make *you* the youthful Viviane. According to some traditions the two sorcerers were married— until she stole his knowledge and imprisoned him!'

They hugged with affection, 'I am neither your Vivian, nor your Lady of the Lake. In truth, I am but a mortal fish returned, all-be-it exhausted, from the oceans of the world. Who have you bedded since my departure? Are you still on with that composer wench? What's her name?'

Douglas looked a little sheepish as the burly fellow clapped him over the back whilst announcing, 'Do not jest with the gypsy, Isobel—painter of marvellous panoramas. Behind her brush lurks the bite of a cobra!'

Isobel immediately mimicked a cobra striking at Douglas's pot-belly, but it came across to Rowan as a kind of foreplay. He now recognised the two men. The silver haired man was John Shelman, one of Australia's leading poets. Rowan recalled that he lived near Castlemaine, but also spent a lot of time overseas—he had academic posts in the US and the UK. The stocky man was George Millicent, an award winning novelist. Rowan had read a couple of his books.

'I've been told you have a performance for us today,

Doug,' said George, 'something about alchemy and Hermes Trismegistus. I don't mind listening to your Medieval guff so long as you continue to publish my fiction.'

'Likewise, my poems,' joked John.

'You don't need me to publish your bloody poems,' said Douglas, 'they just about publish themselves these days. Likewise your fiction, George.'

The two men looked coy.

'I need an informed audience for my friend, Rowan, over there. And for our young *world soul* over here.' Douglas pointed to a figure emerging from the right-hand tunnel. Smaller than the others, he or she was dressed in a hooded monk outfit. Due to the cavern's gloom and the cloak, it was difficult for Rowan to discern anything else about the figure as it took a seat in the front row.

'Why have you put such a gaudy image of the Egyptian god Thoth in the central alcove, Douglas? From an aesthetic perspective, he dominates everything,' said Isobel, as she took her seat in the front row to the left of where Douglas now stood fiddling with something under the desk.

'This performance is not about aesthetics, Isobel. It's about Thoth and Hermes, or rather Thoth-Hermes—for the two gods all but merged after Alexander the Great kicked the Persians out of Egypt.'

George began lighting up a joint as John found himself a seat near the front.

When everyone was seated, Douglas brought out three identical boxes and placed them in a line on the desk in front of him. The figure of Thoth seemed to tower studiously over Douglas's left shoulder. Also on the desk was the computer, which was now hooked up to the projector and the cave's stereo system.

'Okay, we're almost ready,' said Douglas, in a deep, booming voice. 'Thank you everyone for coming. This isn't exactly the largest audience I've ever addressed, and I'm probably a bit rusty, but let's proceed regardless. Let me introduce Sol and Luna—two of the three fundamental substances, or should we call them characters—associated with alchemy.'

Douglas paused to clear his throat. On cue, John Shelman leant down between his legs to begin fumbling in a bag of some description. He eventually surfaced with a large gold-painted crown, which he placed on his head. When he was finished, Isobel followed suit—though she wore a silver crown featuring three small moons: one waxing, one full and one waning.

'Thank you, King John and Queen Isobel! Now, in the three boxes in front of me are three virtually identical "stones". They are each made out of mineral salts extracted from the same species of plant. All the plants used were harvested from the same field at the same time of the day. Indeed the only difference between these three "vegetable stones" is that an alchemist poured positive emotions into one of them whilst it was being created. The other two stones did not enjoy the affections of the alchemist. The alchemist's stone exhibits his initials on its base.' To Rowan, Douglas seemed more like a stage magician than a lecturer.

'Rowan,' Douglas said, 'please choose a box ... any box, but try to pick the box that speaks most emphatically to you. You may need to meditate on your choice for a moment or two.'

Rowan wanted to poke fun at the entire procedure, but the seriousness of the others restrained him.

'I gave up on New Age festivals a while back—besides you've employed me as an academic and a history researcher. But okay, to keep with the spirit of the occasion I'll do my best.' He stared at the three identical boxes for about thirty seconds each.

'Has the young scholar reached a decision?' asked George,

projecting his voice like a Shakespearian actor.

'Stupid as it sounds ... I guess the middle box sort of speaks to me most.'

'Thank you, Rowan. You've just chosen the vegetable stone created by my alchemist friend from Zurich.' Douglas took the lid off the box and held it up at an angle. Inside was a multi-coloured stone. George immediately leapt up and examined both the stone (about the size of an emu egg) and its base, 'Engraved it is—with the letters R I,' he declared, before returning to his seat.

'Let's try it again, shall we? Rowan, if you will be so kind as to turn away for a moment whilst I rearrange the stones and the boxes that contain them.'

Rowan did as he was asked.

'Okay, this time, Rowan, please choose the box that you feel best represents physical and emotional well-being.'

Rowan felt ridiculous. In all probability this was some kind of elaborate trick, like the fool's gold down the passageway, like everything about Douglas—but to what purpose? Of course, Rowan would select the alchemist's stone again—third rate stage magicians knew how to engineer such outcomes.

'Try to hold your scepticism in abeyance for a moment, Rowan—I need you to concentrate on the stones.'

'Oh, I'm trying, Douglas, but I don't see the point of all this.'

'For Christ's sake, give your brain a rest, mate!' snorted George. The novelist's impatience made Rowan feel flustered. Once again, he tried to concentrate.

'Okay, okay—the one to your left, our right,' he said.

Douglas was delighted, 'It normally takes quite a few selections to illustrate the point. Yes, once again you've chosen the box containing the vegetable stone prepared in the presence of my alchemist friend. Congratulations!'

'Harrumph,' snorted George, 'Let me have a look at that.' He seemed to pounce on the box Rowan had chosen, 'Okay, yes, we have the initials again, but show me the other two "stones".'

Douglas made a move toward the middle box, but George grabbed his wrist lightly, 'I'll do the physical labour, thank you.' He then opened the middle box and examined the stone therein. 'No engraving,' he declared, perplexed. He did the same with the next box. Again, no engraving. He looked at Douglas for a long time, then said 'You old bugger, you're up to something? What is it? Obviously Isobel and John here are in on it, not to mention Rhiannon over there. Come on, out with it Doug.'

'I needed an impartial observer for the performance. I knew you'd be just the man—George the eternal realist.' Rowan noted a hint of mockery in Douglas's tone.

'Now, as for what I'm up to, let's proceed to the actual lecture shall we. Oh, and Rowan, you can come down here and examine the "stones" and their boxes too if you like.' Douglas was obviously un-phased by George's outburst.

Rowan declined the offer saying, 'I'll take your word for it.'

Douglas then clicked on the first of a series of thumbnail photographs running as a strip across the bottom of the projection screen. The image of a large lump of gold flashed up on the wall behind him.

'This is a photograph of the Hand of Faith nugget found near Rheola some years back. It's one of the largest nuggets ever found in alluvial soils—a real *monster* nugget worth a great deal of money. The transformation of this entire region, including the Castlemaine and Chewton fields, also the Bendigo field— *Big Gold Mountain* as the Chinese called it—not to mention numerous other diggings at Maldon, Rheola, Inglewood and Wedderburn, began with the discovery of large nuggets close to the surface. Many were literally sitting in the walls of creeks and waterholes when Europeans arrived in the late 1840s.'

Douglas paused for a moment as the cloaked figure rose then gracefully walked to a position beside Douglas—directly in front of the Thoth statute. The figure then turned to face the audience—though with head lowered, making it difficult for Rowan to see its face, though he did make out long brown hair.

George had given the person's gender away—Rhiannon was a female name. The pseudo monk was probably a woman with straight brown hair. She stood very still as Douglas spoke. Her arms were at her sides and the palms of her hands faced the audience.

'The theme of today's talk concerns Abraham Isles's relationship to gold and, perhaps more importantly, to Mercury.'

Douglas allowed his words to settle for a moment. George was squirming in his seat—perhaps because this next phase of the performance had the aura of an occult ritual. Moments later, John/Sol and Isobel/Luna rose from their seats. With their crowns almost touching the cave ceiling, they walked slowly but gracefully to positions at the front, either side of Douglas and the hooded figure.

Douglas waited for them to join him before continuing.

'Abraham Isles did not perceive minerals the way we in the modern world perceive them, which is to say as inanimate matter. By the mid-1820s Isles had renounced much of his Enlightenment derived scientism and had become, let us say "pre-scientific." He refused, as a result of his readings in alchemy, astrology and Mesmerism, and as a result of his acquaintance with William Blake's later poetry, to completely detach soul and spirit from matter. To put it simply: Isles, prior to his shipment to the colony of New South Wales around 1833, had developed a working knowledge of Hermeticism and, by extension, the key principles of late Medieval alchemy. The difference between Abraham's relationship to gold and that of the diggers, jolly puddlers and Quartz Kings who flocked to these parts during the gold rush was marked and was related to his interest in alchemy. We note that Great Britain adopted the International Gold Standard in 1821. In that moment gold (and silver, to some extent) became canonised as the life blood of Empire, colonisation and industrialisation, things Isles despised.' Again, Douglas paused before signalling to the hooded figure.

Taking Douglas's cue the figure pulled back its hood, exposing a narrow female face decorated with numerous bizarre patterns. Her cloak was soon pulled apart at the neck, allowing the entire garment to slip down over bare shoulders and breasts on the way to the cave floor.

Rowan had to catch his breath. Strange circular tattoos covered the girl's chin, cheeks and forehead. They also covered her neck, upper chest and breasts. The tattoos seemed to combine a Pictish blue wash (featuring ogham notches) with green and black coloured Maori spirals. In places Aboriginal dot art coloured white or ochre was also in evidence. Rowan was particularly interested in a large sun and a crescent moon that faced each other either side of her neck. Each radiated small spiral tattoos that Rowan took to be symbols of Isles's planetary orbits. Rowan noted that the girl's entire body was covered in a mass of astrological, alchemical and ogham designs and symbols. The girl—or rather the young woman, for her maturity was now clear to Rowan—was staring at him without intimacy. Indeed, he had the sense that she was in some kind of trance.

'To put it simply,' Douglas continued, 'Isles held to a very ancient view that the etheric soul energies of the "adept"— who could be a physician, alchemist, poet, musician, or white or black magician—could be purified by way of various alchemical transmutations. This *work* determined the efficacy of any healing objects, art-works, etcetera that the adept created.'

Douglas paused in order to reach beneath the table to retrieve what looked like a caduceus. Douglas placed it in front of the young woman. She grasped it slowly with both hands, before directing it at an imaginary point just above Rowan's head.

'To spiritual alchemists our human emotions, desires, thoughts, etc. subtly permeate the matter we come into contact with. *The quality of consciousness influences the shapes matter takes.* The job of the spiritual alchemist is to concentrate positive, life nurturing energies in matter. Such energies are innate to those who have purified themselves through devotion to the *work*, the *opus*. The primary job of the adept is spiritual—to be courageous and patient enough to work through the various alchemical transformations. The initiate seeks to resolve important dualities—feeling/intellect, body/spirit, and, most importantly, divine/mortal.

'So Isles's alchemy—really a kind of protoscience—allowed him to regress to an essentially spiritual view of life. I sense a god behind the scenes somewhere!' said George, snorting.

'True ... in a way. Isles did not believe that human beings could transcend the dualities, or the suffering implicit to the cosmos, on our own. We need the help of the Hermesian Principle—an aspect of consciousness outside time and space. Only this principle, activated through creative *work*, could temporarily neutralise what he called *the flaw in the fabric of the cosmos*.

'Which is?' asked Rowan, convinced now that both Abraham and Douglas were neo-Romantics.

'The flaw is the fact that suffering has apparently been built into our universe,' said George impatiently

'To Isles these epiphanies, originating beyond time and space, can feel like bolts of energy emanating from the very wand of Hermes—though the *anima mundi*, or world soul, was usually implicated.' Douglas gestured in the direction of the young woman. 'Historically the *anima mundi* often took the form of a beautiful, though strangely distant, woman.' Douglas paused for a moment to look directly at Rowan.

'For a young man, the bolt that initiates the initial *nigredo* phase—the dark, chaotic, harrowing first phase—is often delivered by the beloved. Of the three graces—the lover he is with, the lover who desires him (but cannot possess him), and the lover he longs for but cannot possess—it is the third that will usually motivate his commitment to the work of genuine self-transformation.' Douglas paused again to bend down and retrieve the young woman's discarded cloak.

'Thank you, Rhiannon—exactly the right tone for the occasion!' Douglas turned to Isobel as Rhiannon recovered her cloak. 'My step-daughter makes a wonderful World Soul—she assures me that the trance is genuine. She's taught herself how to enter into it at will. And you, Isobel, did a wonderful job with the body painting—so striking, and historically accurate, I might add.'

Rhiannon, now fully clothed, smiled gracefully and bowed to applause from John, Isobel, George and Douglas. Only Rowan didn't clap—he was too stunned to speak. When Rhiannon had pointed the caduceus in his direction he'd recalled with uncanny vividness an event from his past—the moment Anika had announced her intention to split with him after his friend, Eric's, suicide.

'Our performers now have to leave us. However, Rowan, I have more to discuss with you. George, you're welcome to stay if you wish.' Douglas then halted the presentation for five minutes as Isobel, John and Rhiannon left the mine.

As they were leaving George began teasing John, 'PoMo Shelman discovers his inner occultist—would you believe it.'

'Or his inner *performer*,' said Douglas.

'True, occultism is all about *performance*,' said George, 'or maybe the right word is *ritual*—think W.B. Yeats and the Golden Dawn. However you look at it, we're a long way from an anti-oppressive poetics.'

John took the bait, 'Who says everything I write has to be political in the narrow sense? I happen to believe that experiencing a transpersonal expansion of consciousness is to have a political experience of sorts.'

'I'm not telling you how to write or think, *Clarke*. It's just that, well—it's *such* a change of spots.'

'I've been interested in alchemy for decades, so when Douglas asked me to participate, I thought it might be interesting.'

'Come on, John,' shouted Isobel from above, 'never explain or justify—let your actions do the talking. Besides its time for a glass of red, some delicious sea-food and the smelliest cheese we can procure from the beast-man's fridge.'

'Sorry, George—Luna has spoken' said John, before making a *zip-it* gesture with finger and thumb. He then removed his crown and clambered up the mine-shaft ladder behind Rhiannon and Isobel. Douglas returned to his computer as the echoes of their voices died away. Rowan noted that George intended to stay for the next phase of the performance.

Douglas began flicking through dozens of late-Medieval and Early-Modern alchemical illustrations. The screen lit up with colourful images of fabulous dragons, green lions, numerous personified suns and moons, a multitude of snakes and other reptiles, a procession of birds, various archetypal royals (to Rowan they looked like they came from very old card decks).

The hermaphrodite also featured often, as did strange trees—some of which sported suns or moons in the place of leaves. Occasionally, images of humans mating in bathtubs or in the woods appeared.

Eventually, Douglas ran out of images and the screen went blank. He turned slowly to the much diminished audience and said quietly: 'Isles asked us to ponder something fundamental, gentleman: Is our consciousness bound only by the rules of the universe as constructed around us—with its implicit brutality, suffering, unfairness, etcetera—or do aspects of consciousness originate elsewhere i.e. in worlds that do not affirm the necessity of suffering? If you are to be Isles's biographer, Rowan, honest reflection on what he meant by the *flaw in the fabric of the cosmos* is required. The science of his day, not to mention the atheism of ours, answers "yes" to the first part of this question, and "no" to the second part, but where do you stand?' Douglas fell silent, as if to emphasise the challenge in his words.

Rowan felt irritated. Despite the multimedia bells and whistles, the presentation was enough to convince him that putting his name to a biography on Isles represented career suicide. Specialising in an unknown white, male, British colonialist (no matter how economically oppressed he may have been) professing bizarre spiritual beliefs was no way to get a job in the humanities in contemporary Australia.

'Actually, I have a question—but it's not really to do with your presentation.'

'Fire away, Rowan.'

'Well, it was all very interesting, Douglas and I do not doubt that there will be a skilled historian of the ... er ... occult, somewhere, interested in writing about such matters.'

'Get to the point!' bellowed George scrunching up his face and scratching behind his ear as if irritated that Rowan was beating around the bush, 'We're not at a bloody academic conference now, you know. Doug here has a very thick skin—you can tell him outright if you think he's talking crap.'

Rowan flinched, 'I guess what I'm trying to say is: What does alchemy have to do with me? I know nothing about such stuff and I have no interest in religion—except perhaps to critique it. In fact, I'm an atheist—so, yes, I guess I do answer the question Isles sets us with that in mind. Why on earth would you employ someone specialising in Materialist philosophies to write a book on an unknown 19th century mystic?'

Douglas and George exchanged odd looks for a moment before the novelist chuckled, 'Jesus, a young Doctor Faustus if ever I saw one. Quite a *tool* ...' he swung around to look at Rowan with a grin on his face '... *kit* you have there, Doctor. I'm sure you'll make merry with Promethean monsters the very moment you gain a tenured position.' He swung back to Douglas, 'If you want my opinion, Doug, you'd best leave him to his feverish utopias.'

Douglas, however, decided to answer Rowan's question, 'There are three obvious reasons why I need you to write this biography. Firstly, you're an historian who wrote a book about Alfred Deakin—a mystic of sorts. Secondly, you're a musician and song-writer and Abraham Isles was a wonderful song-writer. Thirdly, what he drew from alchemy is but a small part of his overall system. There's much more.'

'Such as?' asked Rowan, a little too aggressively.

'Mesmerism, Rousseau's ideas about childhood and certain motifs drawn from Celtic mythology are also relevant. During the 1820s Isles was sampling dozens of spiritual systems and philosophies. He was looking for something to address what he later termed his personal *nigredo*—he felt he went through a kind of "dark night of the soul" in the mid-1820s. He was eventually treated by a London mesmerist who encouraged him to engage in cathartic purges whilst under hypnosis. Though the treatment worked, Isles didn't understand why it had worked. Spiritual alchemy provided part of the answer. Isles viewed the body as a kind of *alembic* and the central alchemical act—i.e. the adept meditating on the contents of the alembic whilst facilitating physical "circulations" (and tending to the transformative fire)—was really a kind of metaphor.'

'A metaphor for what?' asked Rowan, struggling to keep up.

'For the real secret underpinning spiritual alchemy—the existence of certain archetypal postures and breathing exercises designed to transform the soul's noxious energies, i.e. 'vices', or 'spiritual parasites' into positive energies, i.e. virtues.'

'But such occult systems are notorious for bizarre forms of ritualism.' Rowan didn't even try to sound objective.

'True—but this is where Isles became truly original. His political activism and interest in a number of Enlightenment philosophers made him reject the more bizarre, i.e. ritualistic, aspects of spiritual alchemy. As far as he was concerned, his system was primarily a *psychological* system.' Douglas let the last sentence hang in the air a moment before beginning the shut-down process on the computer.

George began clapping loudly, 'Nice wrap-up there, Douglas.'

Rowan started to ask another question, but George was laughing as he rose from his seat, 'I'm thirsty and hungry, my friends—and I've had quite enough of Magic 101 with Professor Green and his undergraduate. Doug, we need to talk about my short story collection. I need another month or two to complete it.'

Douglas was also keen to pack up. 'Save any questions for tomorrow morning, Rowan. For now I'd like you to return to your hut since I need to catch up with Rhiannon and my friends over the next few hours. I'll bring you down some food in a little while.' He paused a moment before adding, 'By the way, think about going to bed early tonight. We'll be observing the sunrise tomorrow morning. You need to understand Isles's thinking about "the Orbits".'

CHAPTER THIRTEEN

THE ANCIENT STAMPEDE OF DIONYSUS

Lying in bed in the early hours of the morning Rowan listened to the party in the main house boom experimental music out across the hillside. He was struggling to sleep—the lesson in the mine had left him reflective and on edge. Besides, he was beginning to lose track of time; was it a Friday or a Saturday? He also had to deal with Anika's failure to respond to his recent emails—admittedly the first had contained a long and garbled summary of his life since the late 1980s. It hadn't bounced, but maybe she'd accidently overlooked it. But how was he to account for her not responding to the second message. It had been a week now.

Smarting at being excluded from the party, he decided to have a party of his own. He'd been given a couple of bottles of honey-mead for Christmas—a sick joke from Jed, one of his old band mates, 'To get the creative juices flowing, mate.' Jed had given Rowan alcohol every Christmas for years, and each time Kerryn had quietly whisked it away—never to be seen again.

This year, of course, there'd been no Kerryn around to do that.

Rowan grabbed a wine glass from the kitchen before filling it with the sticky liquid. *Why not get rotten pissed?* he thought. *No one around to give a fuck.* Nevertheless, he hesitated and on a whim, before taking a sip, he wandered back into the bedroom to retrieve the battered blue case containing all his old band paraphernalia. He carried the case into the lounge and placed it on the coffee-table unopened. He circled the case for a while—glass of honey-mead in hand—before mustering the courage to open it. Although he couldn't face looking through the photograph albums, he found it easy enough to approach the band's last recording. The tape cover featured stylised images from the work of Hieronymus Bosch and, once open, unrolled to half a dozen miniature pages featuring pictures of the band members as well as copies of Rowan's lyrics.

Five minutes later he was lying on the couch listening to the thundering drums and soaring effects-laden guitar riffs of 'Triptych'. The song had been inspired by some of the imagery in Bosch's work *The Garden of Earthly Delights*.

As the alcohol kicked in Rowan felt lost for a while in the gloom-laden chord progressions, melodic lead-breaks and haunting vocal harmonies. Now and then, however, he flinched at subtle recording errors. Other times, he recalled incidents at gigs or in the recording studio. The memories were bitter-sweet since Anika featured often.

In the middle of Rowan's reverie, he heard several loud knocks on the hut's front door. He struggled out of the couch to switch the stereo off before opening the door. It was George Millicent.

'Hi,' said Rowan noticing a slight slur to his voice. What was the guy up to visiting in the early hours of the morning? George also seemed a little drunk.

'Looks like the sorcerer's apprentice is on the grog. Having a little party of your own, I see?'

'I was just listening to some music,' said Rowan, wandering over to the coffee-table to quickly repack the blue case, 'What do you want at this hour?'

'I thought I'd pop down to apologise for my display this afternoon,' said George, watching Rowan gather together the tapes and folders before placing them back in the case. 'Douglas said I'd misread you. Apparently you were the lead singer of that 80s alternative rock band *Interstitium*.' He paused a moment as though waiting for Rowan to say something. 'He seems to believe you're more than some puffed up culture theorist. I've had a bad run with them lately—the idiots are always firing oh so abstract pot-shots at creative types from their financially secure positions in the towers of academia.' He stopped again to observe Rowan closely, before holding out his right hand. Rowan turned to face him.

'No hard feelings, eh?' continued George, 'God I might have achieved a lot of things in my creative life, but I've never in all my days been cheered by thousands of screaming fans—even if they'd struggle to assemble a single brain between them. What is that like?'

Rowan noted the double edge to George's apology—what was he up to?

'I barely remember—I was stoned most nights'.

'Sex and drugs and rock-n-roll, eh? Oh to re-enact for each new generation the ancient, sacred stampede of Dionysus! Death to reason! Back to the senses! You know I've long worried about the fascist subtext to many of those huge musical events. The prevalent ideology is always capitalism—clothed, I've noticed, in narcissistic individualism. Maybe that's just professional jealousy. The girls rarely rip off their clothes for novelists.' As he spoke, he strode past Rowan into the lounge.

'It's all a little more civilised is it, in the literary world?'

Rowan turned to catch George smiling mischievously—perhaps he approved of Rowan giving a bit back.

'Do you want something to drink?'

'I could do with a good strong coffee. I'm getting older you know—I'm 46. I can't hack the party pace these days without the caffeine—the alcohol sends me to sleep.' He laughed at himself.

'But the naked maenads—if they were so disposed?'

'But one doesn't want to end up like poor Pentheus, does one?' said George, wearing a sardonic little smile.

Rowan wandered over to the kitchenette and lit up a gas burner. Behind him George continued talking—though his tone had changed. He'd settled into the only couch in the room and now had his feet up on the coffee table, with his arms folded across his stomach in a relaxed way.

'So what are you here for?' George asked, 'There are only three possibilities with Douglas: you're his literary or intellectual prodigy, you're his apprentice magician/shaman or you're in therapy with him.'

Rowan turned to face George, after placing the kettle over the lit-up burner.

'I've signed a confidentially clause. I can't divulge the details of my terms of employment.'

'Must be serious if he's paying you. But I can tell you're all at sea with the old bastard—you have no idea what he's up to, do you?'

Rowan let the comment pass. He was standing with his back to the sink. George looked at him in silence for an uncomfortably long time.

'Okay, let me tell you something—it might help. Douglas collects people. He collected me. I'm in the "literary prodigy" category. He mentored me, still does, though these days he frequently says: "I have nothing to teach you about writing, my friend." Later, as life got difficult—fame, you know, leaves you with nowhere to hide—I entered therapy with him. He reckons he adopts no one method or approach, but he's always on about Abraham Isles. I sometimes think *Isles* is my therapist— even though I've found no bloody trace of the guy in the history books.'

Rowan bit his tongue. George made him feel uneasy, but the guy obviously knew a lot about Douglas.

'I was in a bad way about three years back—depression with mild mania—I won't go into the details, suffice to say classic high achiever issues. I'd masked it since my 20s. And depression fucks with your ability to write. I couldn't keep anything in my head, least of all a novel. Douglas's therapy was the only thing that helped. Though I'm still not really sure what he actually did that produced the breakthrough. Regardless, it got me off the drugs—and I was on bloody heavy doses, I can tell you, zonked out most of the time.' He paused for a long time as though deliberately giving Rowan the chance to divulge something personal in exchange.

Rowan took the moment to check on the kettle instead.

George tried another tack. 'Look, I know there's other stuff going down here. Dozens of musos, poets, artists, playwrights, novelists, thinkers, etc. visit Douglas—have slept in this very hut. I've met many of them. I've also met some of the people who visit Douglas for therapy—most of them, it must be said, are also creatives. But there's another, smaller group—the *apprentice magicians* I referred to, though that is probably a bit of a simplistic term.'

There was another period of silence, which Rowan refused to break. George continued when it got uncomfortable, though he seemed a little more tight-lipped.

'As an academic, Douglas was very dodgy you know—took

seven years to get his BA. He studied in Melbourne, I forget the university—but he indulged in activism, mind-expanding drugs and God knows what else. He immediately left for Europe after graduating. Wait for it—he got his PhD in Eastern Europe—a philosophy PhD. Something to do with Goethe's attitude to science—no extant copies, hmm.'

Rowan finally responded, 'Did he ever teach?'

'A bit—in the late 60s and into the 70s—but he never seemed to seek or be offered tenure. That happens when you specialise in Early Modern occultism. Guaranteed to give any modern Humanities academic the willies, eh?' He made the sign of the cross at Rowan. 'Obviously the old fellow has been somewhat silent on his own biographical details, hmm. Look, don't worry, someone obviously believed his PhD qualification was legitimate—though they'd have needed the CIA to do the resume and references check, eh?' He laughed sardonically. 'Hey, in those days you didn't actually need a PhD anyway, academia wasn't so bureaucratic. You just had to, well, *know* something.' He chuckled again.

'Anyway, about fifteen years ago he retired to set-up his publishing house and alternative therapy practice. That was just after he bought this block of land.'

The kettle began to whistle, 'How do you have your coffee?' asked Rowan.

'White, two sugars and a heaped spoon of coffee.'

George regrouped as the coffee was prepared. Rowan imagined George for a moment as a journalist, struggling to find the magic question that would lead to a story angle.

'Look, I think we have a lot in common. I'm no mystic/occultist. In fact—putting aside for one moment what I think about literary critics and French post-structuralist philosophers—I consider myself a postmodernist. Probably a postmodern socialist actually.' He let the statement hang in the air.

The social worker in Rowan held back from admitting the obvious common ground—*always resist the urge to jump in … let the client do the talking.*

'I think my "perverse realism", as Douglas puts it—or my "postmodern, dirty realism", as the university critics label my writing style—doesn't appeal much to Douglas—at least in terms of letting me learn more about what he calls "The Greater Mysteries." That particular *experience* is reserved for his "apprentice magicians", as far as I can tell.' George sounded bitter.

Rowan cleared his throat, 'I'm probably in Douglas's first category—though I'm certainly no literary prodigy, little more than an apprentice scholar, really. And to tell you the truth, I'm not sure what it is he really wants from me. However, I'm not in therapy with him and I'm certainly not an apprentice magician.'

'But you're getting vintage Douglas—a show like that today, all that alchemical and Hermetic crap—hell, I couldn't walk two feet down there without tripping over some bug-infested wooden deity from this or that tribe of animists. He has something special planned for you.'

'Why don't you ask him what that might be exactly? I get precious little sense out of the old bugger.'

George sipped on his coffee. 'You know—and I'd only confess this to a fellow artist ...' he said, with a sly glance at Rowan.

'I'm not an artist—these days I'm a social worker and historian. I haven't performed music in over a decade, though I still write songs now and then.'

'Once an artist, always an artist! When an artist takes a break for such a long time, he or she is usually pondering the big question.'

'Which is?'

'What kind of artist *am I?* Find the answer to that and you'll be back performing in no time—the ancient stampede of Dionysus will resume.' Again the trademark smile.

Now it was Rowan's turn to smile, 'You really can't see past the image of intoxicated maenads can you?'

'Look, to level with you, my problem is that I think my creativity is linked to Douglas in some strange way. I don't just come here for therapy; I come here for creative ideas. I think I need to explore the "Greater Mysteries" Douglas sometimes talks about—even if there's not a spiritual bone in my body. That's where the creative charge is right now—the *gleam*, as Tennyson put it ... the haunting melody that seduces us into the land of the faeries.'

'Sounds more like you want to use him,' said Rowan.

'The creativity of postmodernist writers is fundamentally amoral—though it all works out *in the end*. Problem is, the wily old bugger won't let me in. It's like he's placed a thick stone wall between me and whatever convoluted secrets he's hiding.'

'Perhaps you need to transcend that scepticism of yours—or at least pretend to, if you really want to pursue the "gleam".' Rowan realised with irony that he was counselling a much published novelist on matters of creativity.

'Easier said than done, mate. Easier said than done.' He stared glumly into his coffee.

Rowan noticed that the music had stopped up at the house. George also heard the change.

'Shit, I'd better get back up there. We were told not to disturb you tonight—you're supposed to be deep in meditation, or some such shit. I'd better get back up to the house before Douglas notices I've been grilling his apprentice.'

'I'm no apprentice,' said Rowan emphatically as George emptied the rest of his coffee down the sink, 'and I'm not a literary or intellectual or even musical prodigy for Douglas to mentor.'

The older man laughed, 'Neither was I, or so I thought. There's nothing formal about how it happens you know, you wake up one morning and it suddenly seems like a fact of existence. That's how he operates.'

Rowan ignored the comment.

'Anyway, life after receiving the Douglas Epiphany isn't so bad, look at me—I've come a long way thanks to Douglas. The problem is, once you're hooked, once you cross the line, there's no going back. Hang on to your sun-hat and buckle up your seat-belt! With Douglas you never know what's around the next corner—mystery upon mystery. He'll have you cavorting around in druid robes before you know it.'

George looked up at the sky, 'The wind's getting up and no stars in the heavens. Looks like we're in for one hell of a storm later tonight.' He flicked on the torch he'd been carrying as he spoke and took an exaggerated sniff of the night air before wandering off into the darkness.

George's visit set Rowan thinking. The fact that a famous literary figure should have such respect for Douglas—not to mention all the others who apparently sought the old man's counsel—forced Rowan to rethink his shaky resolve to leave first thing in the morning. He decided tentatively that he wouldn't act on the decision until Douglas had given him the promised biographical information on Isles. Secretly Rowan hoped there would be political dimensions to Isles's work—something to satisfy the social worker/cultural theorist in him.

Eventually, after finishing the entire bottle of honey-mead, he turned the stereo on again and began listening to the *Interstitium* tape he'd been playing earlier. The quieter ballads at the end of the first side invited reflection and he found himself pondering the long-term absence of creativity in his life. He'd long believed that the alternative rock muso life had contributed to the near breakdown of his early twenties. It had bloated his ego, making him dependent upon the fickle judgements of total strangers (*The Audience*). He didn't want to return to that space—and yet he realised, perhaps for the first time, just how much he'd missed writing, recording and performing music. In truth music made him feel alive—even if it also had a destructive side for him. These epiphanies lulled him into sleep.

CHAPTER FOURTEEN

WALKING THE LAND OF THE SELF IN ORBIT
(Wednesday, January 8th 1997)

Around 3am the clouds amassed in the west put on a fireworks display worthy of the tropics. As the wind grew in intensity, so did the volume of the approaching thunder. At the same time the temperature dropped perhaps ten degrees in a matter of ten minutes—the night had been in the high twenties due to the way the clouds had trapped in the previous day's heat. Unable to sleep due to the noise, Rowan decided to sit under the front verandah and watch the fireworks. The scene unnerved him—flashes of lightning illuminated the entire hillside as violent thunderclaps vented electrical charge into the arid earth.

When the rain started, it fell so heavily that for perhaps half an hour it became difficult for Rowan to see anything beyond twenty metres from the hut—even with a torch. At the height of the downpour, it was hard to make out the hillside at all since it resembled a vast shallow waterfall wherever Rowan shone his torch. Though the drainage around the hut seemed to work alright, he still felt he was sitting on a small fragile island. After perhaps thirty minutes the rainwater tank beside the hut overflowed and a little later he heard a loud crack as the branch of a gigantic yellow-box further up the hill was sundered from its main trunk. It fell silently before crushing wattles and other understorey culminating in a loud thump.

The rain continued to fall steadily until perhaps 4am, by which time Rowan decided to return to the hut to get some sleep. With the windows open, he fell asleep to the strong, refreshing scent of eucalyptus released by the downpour.

A short time later, however, he heard indistinct voices on the barn side of the hill followed by the sounds of cars starting. Before long they were slowly winding their way down the block's probably muddy, perhaps unstable, driveway. At one point Rowan heard the wheels of one of the vehicles spin for thirty seconds or so. It recovered, however, and the vehicle sounds gradually faded. He drifted back into sleep soon after.

'PD time!' shouted Douglas, waking Rowan out of a vivid dream of being stranded as a child in an outback motel. In the dream his mother, working at the petrol station across town, had not come home in the early hours as per usual, leaving Rowan to feed his little sister a make-shift breakfast of salted peanuts, a chocolate bar and a can of coke. In the nightmare the hours ticked by and Rowan woke to the terrifying possibility that his mother had been killed or had abandoned them. At the climax he heard someone banging at the motel door. 'Open the door, Rowan—I know you're in there. Officer, I hope you're taking notes here—she's left two children on their own in this motel room all night while she gallivants around the town.' It was the voice of Rowan's father—smooth and inauthentic as ever.

But it was not the voice of Rowan's father that woke him,

rather it was that of an eccentric old man banging on the front door of the hut, 'You awake, Rowan? It's PD time.'

Rowan glanced wearily at the electric clock next to the bed. It said 5.15 a.m.

'There's cereal on the shelf above the cooker, milk in the fridge and wholemeal bread in the bread bin. No need to thank me—you can visit the supermarket later this morning if you don't fancy the food I've bought for you.'

Rowan could barely believe his ears, 'Where in the employment contract does it say anything about me having to turn up for work before sunrise—and why are you awake at all, you were partying half the night?' Rowan grumbled. His words sounded lumpy in his throat.

'Good to hear you're alive, young fellow. We'll walk the land at 6a.m. sharp—it's important to watch the sun come up over the back hill. You're welcome to join me for a cuppa in the house at five-thirty if you like. Oh, and you'll need hiking boots—there are two or three in different sizes on the shoe rack in the cupboard.'

Rowan heard Douglas trudge off back down the gravely path to the barn. He didn't want to walk the land, he wanted to sleep. Unlike his mother, he wasn't a morning person.

It was almost six by the time Rowan fronted at the barn. He wore old black jeans, a green t-shirt and a pair of brown safety boots one size too big. He felt somewhat grubby since he'd neither shaved nor combed his hair.

Douglas was seated on his front step enjoying a hot drink as Rowan approached. He stood up slowly and Rowan observed that he was dressed in blue fishing pants, Wellington boots with waterproofing attached up to the groin, a stained t-shirt with the arms cut off and his beloved battered straw hat. His small old-man's pot belly hung out over the belt of the pants. He seemed amused at Rowan's tiredness and generally dishevelled appearance.

'Right on time. Very important for trainee biographers, but where is your sun-hat?'

'I figured I wouldn't need it, given the sun is struggling to rise over South America right now,' mumbled Rowan sleepily.

Douglas chuckled, 'Given it's only your second day as a biographer I'll go easy on you. Follow me.'

Everything smelt fresh and alive after the rain. Rowan followed the old man as he wandered out into the front yard before hanging a left up a path behind the barn. Douglas then produced a large key, which he used to unlock a metal gate that opened into a walled garden area behind the barn. Rowan had never entered this area before. In the dimness the two men splashed through puddles from the night before as they passed strange monoliths that looked to Rowan like abstract sculptures. Douglas halted in front of a large bronze monstrosity about three metres tall.

Douglas sounded pleased with himself, 'Duchamp would have appreciated a splendid object like this. Hundreds of years from now historians will confuse it with art. What is it, Rowan?'

Rowan struggled to adjust his eyes to the dimness on this southern side of the barn. The building's shadow, combined with a large peppercorn tree in the centre of the courtyard, effectively blotted out the first glimmers of dawn to the east.

'Can't make head nor tail of it in this light,' said Rowan.

'Wait for it,' said Douglas, leaning toward the barn wall and pressing a light switch.

Now there was too much light and Rowan had difficulty seeing anything due to the glare. Gradually, however, the large metallic contraption became clearer to look at—it seemed to feature a complex array of metal balls, cogs, pulleys, levers and rubber belts.

'It looks like some kind of model of the solar system …'

'It is indeed—so they didn't just give you a PhD out of pity.'

'It looks out of place—too ornate, perhaps, for our much more utilitarian age.'

'Spot on again. It's from the early nineteenth century and it's linked to a vision of the universe Abraham Isles was familiar with. Of course we know much more now.'

Rowan marvelled at it. It really was a well-constructed piece of machinery, the cogs and pulleys that connected to the various planets were beautifully constructed. He half imagined that if he pulled one of the levers, Jupiter or Mars or Earth would commence a slow but measured orbit around the large and beautifully polished gold coloured sun at the centre.

'Remember how I ended yesterday, with some comments on the importance of orbits to Isles's thinking? Well, I wanted to show you this because this morning will be all about orbits.'

'Orbits? Was Isles an astronomer … or perhaps an astrologer?' Rowan was wide awake now.

'Neither, we're going to talk about different kinds of orbits— the orbits of the soul. They're at the heart of Isles's mystical system. Come on, I fancy we need to meet a certain lady friend down by the dam.'

Rowan followed tentatively. It was still quite dark and the last thing he wanted to do was to tread on some relative of those red-belly blacksnakes he'd encountered in late winter.

'You know, I've been thinking a lot about where we encountered those snakes. Do you remember—it was when you first came here? And what about the place those eagles chose to hunt that rabbit? Interestingly, I found a seven foot snake skin—you guessed it, a red-belly black—wrapped around a fencepost near the car-park the other day. Anyway, while I was walking down to the unit this morning to wake you up, it finally clicked. I thought, yes, precisely what I'd expect from the Government of Souls.'

'The Government of Souls? I'm not familiar with the term—

it sounds religious.' Rowan kept close to Douglas.

'We'll talk about the Government of Souls soon enough. You have some homework to complete first—and there are other things we need to discuss.'

He was wheezing slightly, even though they were walking down-hill.

'What sort of homework?'

Douglas turned with his right forefinger touching his upper lip, 'You'll need to speak a little quieter—otherwise you'll scare her ladyship off.'

'What sort of homework?' whispered Rowan, unconsciously refusing to move any further. They weren't far from the car-park now and the grass beside the path was quite tall. He had to take a deep breath to pluck up enough courage to follow Douglas further down the path and into the woodland—close to the large dam—at the front of the property.

Douglas saw Rowan's hesitation and mocked him gently by nonchalantly walking backwards along the path as he spoke, 'There's experiential homework and there's factual homework. The first involves elements of self-disclosure.'

Rowan flinched. He didn't feel like self-disclosing anything this early in the morning, 'Look, Douglas, I know you're a therapist, but frankly my idea of writing a biography does not involve …'

'Have you ever known things you shouldn't know? There are technical terms for it, but I've forgotten them. You possess a recent PhD—you should know what I'm talking about.'

Rowan was tired of the mind games, 'What could pre-cognition and the like possibly have to do with my work as a biographer?'

'Quite a lot actually, Isles was a nineteenth century mystic after all. Look, I know you're a reasonable writer and researcher, but I also need to know whether you're capable of understanding the types of experiences Isles wrote about. Think of the question as a part of your post-probation performance review.' Douglas's voice was direct but gentle, which disarmed Rowan. In fact the entire exchange seemed strangely unreal since it was at precisely this moment that the sun poked over the hillside behind the barn—the first beams striking the sunglasses perched on top of Douglas's straw hat. The moment seemed to demand a kind of honesty from Rowan.

'I haven't talked about the uh … *happenings* … to anyone—not for years anyway. They're infrequent and I can't control them. I don't consider myself a psychic or anything. In fact, I despise most psychics—ripping off damaged, vulnerable people all the time.'

Douglas said nothing, simply wheeled about as he walked and whistled, then coughed a little before pausing again to announce, 'Your first assignment as a trainee biographer will be to describe on paper all of the *happenings* that you've experienced in your life. I want you to list the minor *happenings* as well as the major *happenings*. Oh, and remember to include the musical *happenings*. I'll give you a few days to complete this homework—it's important that you do a good job.'

Rowan replied, 'I wrote songs, what's so mystical about that?'

'I want to know what state you were in when you wrote *particular* songs, for example "Golem", "Soul in Motion", "Bunjil's Cave", "Lovers in the Nigredo" and a couple of others. I've written them down somewhere. I'll give you the list when we get back to the house.'

They walked in silence for a minute or two until Rowan, after falling behind, found himself alone on the path and panicked. Douglas had disappeared round a bend. As he trotted to catch-up, he was hit by a series of vivid memories. He'd been under Anika's influence for many of the songs Douglas was interested in. They'd often discussed the topic of inspiration and the

Muses. He remembered snatches of drunken conversations—her quoting extracts from some of the bizarre books she threw his way. One night, standing naked above him as he lay on the bed—his back against the pillows, her long brown hair flowing forward over her breasts and ribs—she'd adopted a kind of biblical voice, 'Thou must invite Her into your soul, Mr. Songwriter!' The conjuring had been a bit of a joke at first, but under Anika's influence—she spoke of the Muse as if she were a real woman present in the room during jam sessions—there were times he almost believed she existed. These days, however, the Muse seemed to blur with Anika—though, in truth, she was different to any women he'd been with: serious, like Kerryn, but otherworldly and fun like Anika. After that night, the songs began arriving at regular intervals—'Muse FM', he'd joked, 'playing in the back of my mind'. And he was in love. He'd forgotten all that stuff—Douglas had exposed a raw nerve.

After another couple of minutes of brisk walking through box-ironbark woodland, Douglas halted near a pump-house on the shore of the large dam close to the front of the property—about seventy metres down-hill from the car-park. It would be half an hour or more before the morning sun reached this spot, though a thin moon shone some light from directly above. Rowan stayed close to the old man. He knew snakes liked to drink and swim—and the dam was very close.

'Can you hear that?' whispered Douglas.

'Hear what? I'm still trying to work out what you mean by *happenings*,' replied Rowan, pondering whether to tell Douglas all about the Muse games of his young adulthood. Douglas however cut him off by stopping dead still and pretending to listen to something over by the dam. From Rowan's perspective, Douglas seemed to be taking undue pleasure in making him feel ill-at-ease.

Though concentrating on bush sounds, Douglas had

another question for Rowan, 'Did your therapist talk about the importance of individualism?' His voice was very low; inviting Rowan to answer in like manner.

'I guess you could say that …'

'Of being an *authentic* individual?'

'Yes, the whole idea, though it wasn't put in as many words, was that I had to um … *free myself from the expectations of others.* I had to become who I really was.' Rowan thought he heard movement on the water behind them.

'You had to *self-actualise*—had to leave behind all the limitations and constraints of those who wanted to keep you in your place.' Again Rowan noted unexpected gentleness.

'Yes, I guess so. I mean, plenty of people never have to think about who they really are. The approach worked okay for me.'

'Really? So just how well have you been doing "transcending" all those relationships that kept you inauthentic all those years?'

'As a therapist, surely you know that people can easily be imprisoned by other people's neurosis. I don't imagine that you'd send an abused kid back to an abusive parent?'

'Of course not, and keep your voice down, her ladyship is about. All I'm saying is that there might be another way to look at it. There is, after all, no getting away from our need for people—we're all in orbit, or to put it slightly differently, we all orbit "others". And just as in the solar system there are many unique planets, likewise, in the realm of soul orbits, there are many kinds of relationships. The delusion of individuality—as defined by inane consumer capitalism—veils a terrifying fact: our daily dependence on myriad others.'

'So why exactly are we down here in the near darkness, so far from the house?' Rowan asked.

'We're at an outer orbit. Can you hear her splashing about in the water?'

Rowan listened carefully—there was indeed something moving in the dam. 'What is it?' he asked, fearing the worst.

'Probably that female red-belly blacksnake that got away back in August.'

'You're joking?'

'Not at all. It's not a duck or water-bird and it's not a kangaroo or wallaby—they make different sounds. There are three Eastern Greys over to our right actually, behind that late black wattle. They've been watching us since we arrived.'

Rowan glanced to the right and after a moment or two spotted the shadowy outlines of three large kangaroos.

'If you think I'm going to try and catch that bloody blacksnake in this light you can think again.'

'That's not why I brought you down here. I just wanted to confirm something—the two snakes live near the dam?'

'Maybe ...'

'But they came up as far as the car-park to greet you last spring.'

'If *greet* is the word. Look, shall we head back up to the house, the, uh, splashing has stopped.'

'Over the years, Rowan, I've learnt to think about space and time the way Abraham Isles did. I'll give you an example; this block of land is the cosmos as perceived by the soul of Douglas Green. There is a pile of stones to the left of this pump-house— not far from the water's edge that I call my "outer orbit".' He pointed at the pile—it stood about a metre tall, and looked to be constructed out of medium sized quartz rocks. It seemed dwarfed, however, by the large late-black wattle that towered above it.

'There's another personal "totemic site" just like this up the back of the block, near the other dam—the strange dam. Just behind your unit actually, close to a sign that reads "University This Way". It's near where those wedge-tailed eagles did their thing a while back.'

Rowan was even more confused.

'When they speak through animals—specific animals, beautiful dark creatures with red markings and fangs full of venom—you listen long and hard. She's listening now, our representative from the Government of Souls. Whatever is about to unfold here-abouts is of importance not only to us humans, but to the animal and plant worlds as well. This is a difficult orbit to work with—it's where we humans morph into animals and plants—the interspecies issues are huge and complex. Did your therapist ever talk about this orbit?'

'Of course not—they only deal with human problems.'

Douglas chuckled before summarising, 'We modern *individuals* are quite comfortable blaming everything that causes psychic distress on other humans, but if you sit here by this dam long enough you'll begin to sense the non-human energy exchanges taking place all around us. Even the most urbane city person is *dependent upon* the world's non-human bio-mass.'

'What about the car-park' asked Rowan, worried he might be feeding the old man's madness, 'which orbit is that?'

'My clients—people who don't know me well—park there before they enter my more intimate circles. I tend to visualise it as the orbit of acquaintances—bank managers, employers, doctors and the like. You're an acquaintance. And the clochan you've been doing your language sessions in is roughly the same distance from the main house as this car-park—that's because I also use it for therapy sessions. The point is: what did I find when I came down to meet you? You and two extraordinarily large blacksnakes out of their orbits—what does that tell me Rowan?'

Rowan saw the method in the madness, 'And where you've put me—the hut—is about the same distance from the barn, though at the back of the block, as the car-park is from the barn at the front.' He almost felt pleased with himself, though he was aware that he'd dodged the question Douglas was asking.

'Yes, you're getting it—and there are imaginary buildings here as well, in among the real ones. My first wife lives in an imaginary house just up from the car-park—about forty metres from the house. We parted in our forties—life got very tough for a while. It was in the late sixties—the Vietnam War was in full swing.' Douglas fell silent a moment, 'We remained friends—there are some experiences that weld couples for life, even after they stop being lovers. Short of it, she isn't in the orbit of acquaintances because I don't want her ghost swanning about the house uninvited. Only Gillian, my second wife (Rhiannon's mother), also dead now, gets to mingle with me there. That's because I need to talk with her daily.' There was sadness in Douglas's voice.

In truth, the day's lesson was sounding very nutty indeed to Rowan. Only the fact that he imagined astral travel at night to meet with Anika, made him withhold judgement.

'For a long time Rhiannon lived in the house with me. As with all young people however, she eventually moved out to become what Isles would call a "living ghost". She now lives in an imaginary house not far from the orchard—about twenty metres from my house—when she's not visiting, that is. Anything unusual happens in that orbit and I worry about her.'

They'd returned to the front of the barn, so Douglas pointed out the vacant spot where he said his step-daughter lived in his imagination.

'Perhaps if you let me read some of Isles's works, I could understand what you're getting at more clearly.'

'Some of this stuff has to be experienced—book learning only takes you so far. I often know what's happening to family and friends according to what I call "spatial dreams"—dreams, day-dreams or what I call "cross-times" or "possessions"—that involve events at a certain radius from the house. The spatial unconscious is very precise you know—distance indicates specific people in specific "orbits". The two events last spring we've been talking about were "cross-times", and outer orbit ones at that. In "cross-times" or "possessions" there is a disruption to the space-time continuum. High valence emotional happenings collapse for a time conventional space-time laws by amplifying quantum indeterminacy. Those snakes were unnatural large don't you agree?'

Rowan nodded in the affirmative—he was thinking about a few 'happenings' in his own life over the years. 'How did Isles come up with ideas like this?'

'Isles's spirituality encompassed respect for energy exchanges between all the important 'orbits' of being. To Isles, we are nothing but our orbits and the self doesn't exist except in orbit, i.e. what we'd now call "in relation". To him, the decision to submit to an alchemical purification of our personal orbits needs to be an act of free will. To heal damaged orbits, is to challenge what he called "the flaw in the fabric of the cosmos"— it means to both address the facts of suffering and evil, and to work to balance in our daily living the energies we absorb from others with the demands of our best possible selves. The ancients saw our best possible selves as "gods", but to Isles the term was far too epic—he called them the "Domestic Deities" or, more simply, "the Principles".

He came to his theory of the orbits via Rousseau's work on childhood, but also out of the years he'd spent as a political prisoner far from his wife, family and friends. He experienced painful bouts of longing and depression, but believed that his wife, Miriam, spoke to him in dreams about the health of his parents, village gossip and the like—domestic things, mostly. Eventually, of course, she joined him here on the other side of the world.'

'He knew what his wife and kin were going through back in where, Britain?' Rowan noticed the sky brighten considerably to the north-east.

'England and Wales—though he was born in Scotland.'

'Just by walking around his home here in Australia?'

'The diaries say as much. Look, all you need to remember is that Isles didn't accept the "flaw" passively. If the self is at the centre of a metaphoric "solar system" of relationships—some negative, some positive—then our life task is to transform negative orbital energies into positive, healed ones. The system of "postures" that he and Miriam developed was a medicinal system. To "dance the orbits" was to heal the orbits—a necessary element of genuine happiness. Now, any more questions before we head up to the house for some tea?' asked Douglas

'Not right now. I'd like to reflect upon what you've told me for a while.' To Rowan the system sounded like a kind of proto-psychology.

'Okay, tea it is then! However, when you write his biography you'll need to remember how important soul orbits were to him.'

CHAPTER FIFTEEN

THE ORBITS IN COLLISION

In the afternoon Rowan began working on the 'experiential research' he'd been set by Douglas—despite feeling morose and tired. He'd been asked to create complex orbital charts related to his own life. To help, Douglas had given Rowan a workbook. Each page featured a diagram of circles within circles. 'A page for each year of your life', Douglas had explained. He'd also asked Rowan to list all the 'transpersonal events' he'd ever experienced—synchronicities, telepathic communications, prophetic dreams etc.Douglas had ended the morning on orbits by saying, 'Though things have moved on since Abraham's day the orbits exercise is still worthwhile—especially if you take your time and try to describe significant memories in detail. I want you to assess the state of each orbit for each year of your life—you may have to reconstruct some childhood memories a bit. You are at the centre of each diagram—the surrounding circles represent "significant others". As an example, in your current diagram the first circle would represent your relationship with Kerryn.'

'Not any longer,' Rowan had interrupted.

'The next circle would represent your *current* relationship with your parents and sister and so on out to your relationship with your vocation. The second to last circle on each page is transhuman—there you will assess your relationship with the plants and animals of the natural world. Finally, the broken outermost circle—the one featuring short, outward pointing lines— represents your relationship to time and space—to the cosmos itself and perhaps to other dimensions of being.'

Douglas had given Rowan five days to complete the workbook—he'd hinted that some of the orbital material might be tough going. Rowan, however, wanted to get both the orbital charts and the transpersonal events list back to Douglas by the following morning.

After making a fruit smoothie and switching on the fan in the hut's lounge, Rowan set the orbits workbook on the coffee-table and set to work. Though skeptical, he decided to work on the 'transpersonal events' list first (though he preferred the term 'happenings'). After staring at the blank page for ten minutes or so, however, he began to feel agitated. It was as though seeing such weird 'happenings' listed on a page threatened some fundamental aspect of his world-view. Surprised at his resistance to the exercise, he put the task aside and turned instead to the orbital charts. The problem there was different—he had trouble remembering specifics about his life. Luckily there was a solution close at hand. He'd brought with him from Melbourne a box full of photograph albums. Whilst retrieving it from the bedroom, he noticed he was sweating a lot—clearly the hut was warming up due to the inferno outside. He decided to swap the black jeans he was wearing for a pair of khaki shorts.

Rowan was soon sketching in bits and pieces related to a number of the charts. In the current chart labelled '1996' he wrote KERRYN between the second and third circles. He pondered this placement a long time and found that it made him feel anxious. He scrawled the word 'VERTIGO' next to her name, which he then crossed out symbolising her decision to delete herself from his life. This act brought him close to tears. To steady himself, he lay back on the couch and closed his eyes. The sensation of the cool fan air on his face felt calming, but he was soon thinking about the contrast between his life with Kerryn and his earlier life as a teenager. When he thought about Kerryn, the phrase *She gave me a centre*, ran through his head. When he tried to summarise his adolescence and childhood, a kind of formula came to mind: *Rowan the teenager = four states, six schools. Rowan the child = five countries, nine schools. Conclusion: Too much change. Rowan is a tree unable to take root anywhere.*

After a while, he sat up, drank some of the fruit smoothie and scribbled down the insights on a couple of the orbital charts.

Next, he plotted his current relationship to his parents. He hadn't seen his mother much over the past few years due to his PhD and teaching work, but the relationship was warm whenever they met. She lived in the suburbs of Geelong these days with her second husband, Linus, a Greek truck driver with a big heart. Linus was despised by Dylan, Rowan's father, due to his lack of education and money, but Rowan got on with him well.

Rowan then wrote the word 'DAD' in the same circle before lifting the pen for long moments. The word sat there on the page like some kind of curse. As a consequence, he underlined it a couple of times, but struggled to write anything else. *Maybe come back to him later*, he thought. As he and Kerryn had become increasingly middle class and conventional over the years, Rowan had felt himself move closer and closer to the world of Dylan Sweeney, "successful businessman". These thoughts made him write: *Rowan doesn't want to become a father*, beside the word 'DAD' on the chart. This done, he went looking for photographs taken before his parents had split up. There were lots of them—often taken in exotic locations—The Franz Joseph Glacier, New Zealand; Edinburgh Castle, Scotland; the big old house with servants in Jakarta, and so on. After thumbing through these images for a while, he added: *Rowan doesn't want to become his father* to the Dad circle on several later charts. Though Rowan rarely saw his father these days, he hadn't forgiven him for the way he'd treated his mother after the divorce. In Dylan's jealousy, he'd used legal connections to try to ruin her financially. She'd been left with nothing but her children and her pride. After writing some of this down, Rowan sat back on the couch and thumbed through a photo album containing more images from his childhood. He smiled at two pictures of himself cradling his baby sister—he was two and half years old.

The orbit of his sister, Cheryl, was without conflict. Her husband's job with an NGO had taken her to New Zealand five years ago. They phoned each other every month or so and caught up in person a couple of times a year. *No problems there*, he thought. He leant over the coffee-table and wrote 'CHERYL = LITTLE SISTER' in his third circle followed by the word 'Protective'.

Next he spied photographs of his mother's parents, John and Margaret. They'd been taken on the Isle of Anglesey in North Wales beside a large green hump—a prehistoric burial mound. Rowan's parents and Cheryl were also in these pictures. The sky above all of them was black with distant rain clouds and as a consequence both John and Margaret seemed paler than Rowan remembered them. His grandparents were clearly enjoying spending time with their daughter's young family. Dylan, on the other hand, tanned and clean-cut as ever, looked distinctly uncomfortable.

Rowan wrote on his chart that the family links on his mother's side were infrequent but warm—he still visited the UK every five years or so to catch up with his ageing grandparents, as well as numerous uncles, aunts and cousins strewn all over England and Scotland.

The situation on his father's side was not so positive. He found it difficult to even write the names of some of these extended family members on the charts. Most of them, including both of his father's parents, had sided with Dylan during the divorce, and he still resented them for it. Still, he had fond memories of two of his aunts, largely because they'd stood up for his mother on a number of occasions. After writing down their names and adding comments, he felt emotionally exhausted and decided to brew a pot of tea. As he lit the gas burners and pondered the task Douglas had set him, he noticed the afternoon sun setting behind the barn and surrounding gum trees.

He had to admit that his 'orbits', as Douglas would put it, were in a state of disrepair. He'd never thought about his life in quite this way before and the social worker in him was interested in how the idea might be useful to clients. The contrast between his childhood (which involved periods in numerous countries due to his father's business commitments) and his adolescence (which involved his mother moving from town to town around Australia trying to make ends meet for her children) struck him as immense. It was during this period he'd taken to learning guitar—he recalled the cheap acoustic guitar his mother had bought him for his fourteenth birthday. Its dark red-wood colouring had seemed magical at the time.

These thoughts naturally led to memories of band life and, after brewing the tea, he returned to the coffee-table and randomly began filling in some of the orbital charts related to his youth. He first plotted the year of the detox therapy (1988)— which also encompassed nine months in Britain, where he'd lived with his grandparents on a farm near Liverpool. He'd left the band by that stage and had also split up with Anika. He wrote the words MY INFIDELITY and ERIC'S SUICIDE in the appropriate circles, but did not elaborate.

In 1989 he'd returned to Melbourne, determined to move away from the band scene for good. He'd met Kerryn during a summer holiday camping trip to Apollo Bay. Soon after, and with her encouragement, he'd decided to train as a social worker. Rowan paused after writing all this down. It was getting dim in the hut, so he decided to stand up and switch on some lights. Out the kitchen window the skyline to the north was a patchwork of colours—purple, light blue, orange and pink. *Just the kind of scene*, he thought, *that made me want to write songs*. He wandered back to the coffee-table deep in thought.

After writing the word MUSIC across the two outer-most circles of one of his young adult charts, he crossed it out. It was the only thing he could think of to put there. Douglas's association of those orbits with 'nature' and 'cosmos' seemed irrelevant to Rowan, after all he'd been living in the city for almost fifteen years. His father had always said 'You can't *eat* a panorama of gum-trees or ocean.' Even in his current orbital chart Rowan had nothing to write there but 'Indifferent' (Music having left his life). He instinctively knew what Douglas's response to such a statement might be, '*Indifference* equals spiritual deadness?'

After these additions to the orbits booklet, he decided to quit for the day. Writing about band life had triggered an impulse to contact Anika by phone. Over tea with Douglas, he pondered the ethics of making a phone call—hadn't Kerryn relinquished any claims over his fidelity? Later that evening, he found Anika's business phone number at her web-site and decided to make a call using Douglas's house phone—his own mobile phone wasn't working so far out of town.

Douglas was eating a salad—washed down by light beer—and watching a European comedy with English sub-titles on VHS, as Rowan mustered the courage to dial the Sydney number. The phone rang seven or eight times without response—each ring brought back something of the angst, guilt and euphoria of his youth. He knew that she'd been overseas on and off for some years, but her website said that she returned to Australia regularly to perform and present master classes at various Australian Universities.

Though he'd planned what he wanted to say in some detail, his mind went blank as the ring-tone changed into an automated answering machine message. 'This is the business number of Dr Anika Miraj, folk musician and music educator. Anika is not here at present, but if you leave your number, she or her admin staff will respond to your inquiry as soon as possible. Please note that Anika is not accepting international engagements throughout 1997, but is happy to discuss domestic engagements, as well as teaching appointments. Please leave your number or contact details after the beep.'

Rowan introduced himself quickly and left Douglas's phone number before the machine cut him off.

CHAPTER SIXTEEN

CERRIDWEN OF THE CAULDRONS
(Thursday, January 16th 1997)

The teachings about Isles's spiritual system paused for over a week—apparently Douglas needed the assistance of both Rhiannon and Isobel for the next 'lesson' and both were away at that time. Rowan busied himself with language studies, gruelling cricket training sessions and menial farm-work in the interim. Given his melancholy over the final split with Kerryn, rote learning and physical exercise were just about all he could manage anyway. Even a trip to the university library in Bendigo to search one last time for genuine historical material on Abraham Isles hadn't dispelled his gloom—though he had met, of all people, the former lead singer of *Goya's Child*—a band he'd enjoyed listening to for years. Over a coffee they'd discovered they had a lot in common—both had survived the music industry to become arts academics. By the end they'd exchanged contact details and had agreed to swap recent original material. Overall, however, Rowan knew his time with

Douglas was coming to an end—despite the irrational paralysis he'd been experiencing lately.

It was a Thursday in the middle of January before Douglas was ready to share the next Islesian revelation. After returning from an afternoon cricket session with Rammer in Castlemaine, Douglas told Rowan that come sunset they'd be heading down to the clochan. He was to wear track-suit pants and a t-shirt. He also had to bring two towels, a change of clothes, a pillow and some insect repellent. 'After you sleep down there alone tonight, Rhiannon and Isobel will show you how to *'dance the orbits'* in the morning,' said Douglas.

The sun was setting across distant Mount Alexander when the three walkers arrived at the blue-stone A-frame building Douglas termed *The Clochan*. Many varieties of succulents and cacti thrived in a kind of circular garden surrounding the structure, some were in flower, though specific colours were hard to discern among the evening shadows. They wandered up a gravel path to the main door—little more than a large wooden slab. Though the building was perhaps twenty-five metres long and six metres wide, Rowan knew there wasn't a single window in the structure. Composed of large roughly-hewn blue-stone bricks, it looked chunky and solid, but gloomy—like a northern European bronze age fortress, or a 19th century Victorian prison. And prison it had been for him—he'd endured tedious language sessions there now for months.

Douglas had said little during the walk, and Rhiannon less. She was dressed in a sporty but conservative leotard that colour-matched her black leggings as well as a dark green cardigan. Her long light-brown hair was tied back, and tonight, thankfully as far as Rowan was concerned, she wore no neo-Celtic face paint. The emotional intensity that had accompanied her performance ten days ago was also absent. Instead, she came across as friendly but shy. She also seemed smaller to Rowan—though the sinuousness of her movements made Rowan suspect that she was probably a very good dancer.

'Okay, we're here, but I need to find the right key to open the door,' declared Douglas, putting down several backpacks and fiddling with keys on his key-ring. He eventually found the right key, because the big old door slowly creaked open, allowing the three of them to enter the building.

Rhiannon flicked a switch on the wall just inside. Immediately the interior of the building was lit by a dozen coloured lanterns hanging at regular intervals from beams attached to the building's high, arched roof. Although the exterior walls were made of stone, the two longest interior walls featured thick hardwood boards that someone had taken the time to oil and polish. The two end walls featured the blue-stone of the exterior. In the dimness, Rowan noticed a strange new contraption or art work on the far end-wall. At ground level he noted the metre high hexagonal structure that housed the therapeutic spa-pool Douglas used in rebirthing sessions. Half of the hexagonal pool jutted out into the main room, the other half was hidden beyond the far wall in a kind of beehive stone structure perhaps six feet high at the centre. Rowan knew the spa-pool from his language sessions, but the huge new form that now towered above it looked like an abstract rendition of a gigantic female. It seemed to Rowan as though the figure was about to drop a large infant into the pool.

'Welcome once again to the Hall of Song,' declared Douglas. 'Here in this chamber you'll spend one full night, Rowan.'

Rhiannon wandered down to the large structure and began clambering up a ladder. At intervals, she opened up glass doors in the entity and, using matches, lit up a number of large candles in each chamber.

'We've set up a bed for you close to our Lady of the Seeds— close to the "Womb of Rebirth".'

Rowan took the opportunity to see if anything else in the room had changed since his most recent language lesson. There were the usual deities from all the corners of the globe—dozens of them, perched on furniture, kneeling in obscure corners or hanging down from solid wood rafters. Rowan noticed, however, that only half of the floor area was covered with mattresses. A large number had been piled up near the clochan's outer walls, almost obscuring the large black speakers Douglas made use of in therapy sessions—which were attached to the expensive stereo system that sat on a large wooden table near the front door. The system was familiar to Rowan—Douglas used it every other day to play language tapes.

'You won't be able to convince me to sleep here alone tonight … we're a long way from the house and I've seen the size of some of the rats that hang around this place …' said Rowan.

'I've had the place baited for a week now—most of the rats are no more,' said Douglas cheerfully. He was emptying the contents of his backpacks onto a table standing on the left-hand side of the front door. On it sat a small bar fridge, a gas camping stove and a green kettle. Above the table were shelves containing plates and glasses, and beside the table stood a primitive sink unit.

Mostly Douglas unpacked food, but at one point he handed a torch and a two way radio to Rowan.

'You'll be fine with these—anything goes seriously wrong and you can radio up to the house. There are spare batteries up on the shelf in the usual place.'

Rowan took the two devices reluctantly.

'What exactly will I be doing here, Douglas?'

But Douglas was distracted, 'Doesn't she look glorious?' he said, staring at the large sculpture on the far wall. Rowan followed his gaze and in the better lighting noticed the exaggerated, voluptuous—though not pornographic—curves that marked the work. In the same moment, it struck him that the candles Rhiannon had lit sat in three chambers corresponding roughly to a human female's belly/sex organ, chest/heart and head/brain regions.

'Douglas, you're being rude—your guest asked you a question.'

Douglas looked apologetic, 'I'm sorry—I'm a little hard of hearing these days.'

'Selective hearing, eh?'

'What did she say?' he said, winking at Rowan.

'Oh, never mind! I presume you know that this is where Douglas does his therapeutic work. He offers "Islesian" inspired body work—which combines Reichian and Transpersonal techniques, hence the mattresses. Over there, is the re-birthing set-up—an adapted spa containing salt water. You can actually float in it, though he uses a harness lowered from a beam behind the new sculpture. The large area we've cleared between the spa and the mattresses would usually be kept clear for group-work or therapeutic music sessions, but we'll be using it tomorrow morning to Dance the Orbits.'

Douglas seemed happy with her tour guide routine, but added, 'This is also a good place to birth creative ideas, hence my alternative name for it, i.e. "The Cell of Song". The bed upon which you will lie has birthed many a song, short story, play, novel and work of art—even a screenplay, if I remember rightly.'

'Once again, Douglas, I apologise for my ignorance, but what exactly does this have to do with the biography I'm supposed to be writing?'

'Abraham Isles was a Scotsman fully conversant—at least by 1827—with many of the antiquarian discoveries, as well as the nonsense, of the 18th and early 19th century Celtic revivalists. He'd read somewhere, perhaps in Edward Davies's book of 1809 entitled *The Mythology and Rites of the British Druids*, perhaps elsewhere, that in the old bardic schools of the Celtic lands, initiates were taught various skills, including the composition of original verse, by being left alone for long periods of time on makeshift (often uncomfortable) beds in a *clochan* or windowless building (sometimes known as a 'House of Darkness') with large stones on their chests. Some have theorised that the rock helped focus an initiate's imaginative faculties. Others have argued that the real purpose of the rock was to develop an initiate's capacity to project his or her voice.'

'So I'm to sleep on the bed Rhiannon is setting up for me?'

'That's correct, but it's up to you whether you use your particular stone to meditate, compose a song, or prophesise with,' said Douglas, smiling broadly.

'Are you serious—I'm expected to pass the night with a large stone on my chest?'

'Absolutely! Isles used precisely this technique to compose hundreds of songs between 1834 or so and the early 1850s— during his time in the Australian bush. It's clear that the technique helped bards memorise songs, poems and the like. The master bard might recite a line to an initiate bard and—due to the total darkness in the clochan—the initiate's visual and auditory memory would become remarkably sensitive. There is some suggestion that the initiate's diet was also, let us say, "conducive" to vision-making—though in my experience sleep deprivation works just as well.' Douglas led Rowan past the foam mattresses in the direction of the bed.

'So I'm to experience something like what Isles experienced?'

'Yes, but in your case you'll have a torch close at hand, electric lights if you need them, food up the back—though I suspect that ritual fasting was used by the ancient bards to aid creativity—a comfortable bed, and the luxury of a notebook to record anything that comes to mind. It would be great, by the way, if my humble clochan helped birth a song or two like some of those you wrote for your band! Instead of an "adder stone", or "*gloine nathair*" as it was called in Isles's Scottish Gaelic, I've procured for you this large lump of central Victorian milk-quartz. It contains three ounces of pure gold.'

Douglas paused, apparently struggling with a headache since he was rubbing his forehead.

'Are you alright, Douglas?' asked Rhiannon, almost finished preparing the bed.

'Never better,' he lied, but it was a moment or two before he could continue with his lesson. 'There is evidence that at some point in the mid-1820s, Isles linked his studies in alchemy to the mysterious *Fferyllt*—or astronomer-seers who feature in the *Hanes Taliesin* and were reputed to live in the vicinity of Mount Snowdon. Isles was captivated by the chapter on the Goddess Cerridwen in Edward Davies's 1809 book on ancient druidism. He noted that she consulted the books of the *Fferyllt* in constructing her famous Cauldron of Inspiration. To Davies, Cerridwen was the British Ceres, a corn Goddess—but also a Goddess of Initiation, of Love and other things, for example, she oversaw, with the help of nine damsels—sometimes called *The Gallicenae*—the instruction of bards, *ovates/pencerdds*, and probably, in earlier periods, druids. To Isles, Cerridwen was also a female alchemist—that is to say a healer, one capable of initiating and overseeing transformations of the soul. Finally, it is worth noting that he sometimes imaginatively merged Cerridwen with his own beloved, i.e. Miriam Hobbes, his eventual wife.'

'Now might be a good time to get him to lie on the bed,' suggested Rhiannon, puffing Rowan's pillow one last time before looking at her watch.

'Yes, we need to get some sleep ourselves since we have an early rise tomorrow. Please lie on the bed, Rowan.'

Since Rhiannon was staring directly at him, Rowan felt he had no option but to comply.

'Okay, now what do you see?' asked Douglas.

'I see that monstrous looking female figure.'

'Our Lady of Many Seeds! My favourite name for the Orbits she presides over.'

Rowan felt completely at sea.

'Okay, Rhiannon, the Stone.'

Rhiannon left Rowan's field of vision for a moment—to fumble with something beneath the bed, as it turned out, a large lump of only roughly spherical milk-quartz. She proceeded to place it on Rowan's chest. Given the shape of the stone, his breathing and the fact that he had a broad chest, it was a precarious balancing act to begin with.

'Now what do you see?' asked Douglas.

'A blurry hunk of quartz and a wooden ceiling with beams.'

'Pull your neck back more onto the pillow. Good. How does that feel?'

'Stupid ...'

'Perhaps we should push him closer to the wall?' said Rhiannon. Douglas agreed and they wheeled him closer to the sculpture.

'What do you see now?'

'The breasts and the head of a postmodern Goddess?'

This satisfied Douglas. 'Okay, but I need you to look closer. Can you see the chambers?'

'Yes, I see two chambers in her uh ... body ... lit by candles.'

'Good. Now look closely at the highest chamber—in her forehead. What do you see?'

Rowan struggled to concentrate, 'I see a kind of metal pot.'

'It's a small bronze cauldron—specifically the Cauldron of Knowledge.'

'It's positioned under a lit candle and it is sitting on its side. It won't hold any fluids,' mused Rowan.

'Yes, now look at the second chamber—in her chest/heart region.'

'I see it. What's that called?'

'The Cauldron of Vocation—very important to you right now, eh?'

'It also contains a small bronze cauldron—on its side beneath another lit candle,' added Rhiannon.

There was silence for a moment as Douglas and Rhiannon pushed Rowan even closer to the statute.

'Now what do you see directly above your stone?'

'The belly-button of a postmodern Goddess,' said Rowan laughing.

They shuffled him still closer to the statue. As she loomed above him, she began to look threatening in the dim lighting—a gaudy female giant.

'Now what do you see?'

Rowan had the urge to sit up and discard the ridiculous stone.

'What do I see? What *do* I see?'

'Yes, directly above the stone ...'

'I see the vagina of—is this some kind of joke?'

'No not at all.'

'Are you sure? Well, I see a large green wooden or metal—I can't make out which from here—vagina giving birth to the blurry stone on my chest—like it's a head. Above the artificial vagina is a chamber with an upright bronze cauldron and a lit candle. What is this?' Rowan was completely bamboozled.

'Good, you're in the right position. We've weighted the first cauldron, the Cauldron of Warming, to always be upright, but the other two only turn upright after a certain amount of liquid wax gathers in a spot behind each cauldron.'

Rowan sighed, he was trying to be patient, but Douglas was provoking his arrogant dismissive side again. 'So what?'

'In the Davies book, it was theorised that the Goddess

Cerridwen was an initiatory Goddess who put the novice bard-druid through two mysteries—a Lesser Mystery and a Greater Mystery. The Lesser Mystery involved a death-rebirth experience catalysing intense emotional outbursts, perhaps in a House or Chamber of Darkness not unlike this one, followed by an epiphany composed of feelings of liberation, clarity of perception, and the like. In short, a kind of rebirth and sloughing off of poisonous emotions symbolised by time in the waters of Cerridwen's womb.'

'Symbolised by that spa over there?' asked Rowan, only barely containing his cynicism.

'Yes, in a manner of speaking. Now perhaps the initiate bard would be ready for real learning—might even be trusted with a certain number of sacred songs, stories, charms and the like. The epiphany of the Gwion-Cerridwen story (as interpreted by Davies) struck Isles almost as a personal religious revelation since the Cerridwen story was set near his grandfather's farm in North Wales—i.e. at Bala Lake. The Medieval alchemists had labelled a similar phase of 'the Work' as the 'Nigredo'. This was how Isles was thinking as he underwent his own Dark Night of the Soul in the mid-1820s'. Douglas pressed solidly on the stone sitting on Rowan's chest as he spoke.

Rowan cut in, 'I've never heard of the Gwion-Cerridwen story … what's it about?'

Douglas looked incredulous, 'Well, there's a full version of it in one of the books I've left you up the back. Your homework tomorrow will be to read the book which contains both the story and some of the major 19th and 20th century commentaries.' Douglas stopped talking a moment to rub his fingers against his forehead.

'Are you alright?' asked Rhiannon, 'Still getting sharp head pains, I see—that's two in as many minutes.'

'It's a stabbing pain down the right side of my skull and into my neck. It'll pass in a moment,' said Douglas, frustrated at being side-tracked.

Rhiannon turned to Rowan, concerned. 'How often is he getting these attacks?'

'Say nothing, Rowan,' said Douglas, mimicking a lawyer, before turning to his step-daughter, 'If they get bad enough, I promise to make an appointment with Dr Useless Incompetent, M.D.'

Rhiannon laughed. 'You promise?'

'Scout's honour, your Majesty.'

'Rowan here seems to have helped you re-find your sense of humour. You're certainly looking happier since he's been around.'

'How about you tell Rowan the Cerridwen story while I recover a minute?' said Douglas, still rubbing his right temple.

'Basically it's an old Welsh tale, perhaps a myth, perhaps even a creation myth, about Cerridwen, a witch—or a shape-shifting moon Goddess—who owns a magical cauldron and is mother to an ugly boy and a beautiful girl. She employs a servant boy to watch over the cauldron—which she's using to bless her ugly son with wisdom and creative genius. The servant spoils things, however, by spilling the Cauldron of Inspiration's brew and undergoing the initiation into ancient spiritual mysteries himself—by accidentally tasting three drops of spilt liquid. He immediately gains magical powers and there follows a shape-shifting duel between the boy and an angry Cerridwen. This concludes when she, in the form of a hen, swallows him—in the form of a grain of wheat. After nine months in Cerridwen's stomach/womb—her swallowing him appears to be um ... a veiled sexual metaphor—the boy, Gwion, is reborn as Taliesin, the greatest of the ancient Welsh bards.' Rhiannon's acting talents made even this highly truncated version of the story sound interesting.

'Well summarised,' said Douglas.

'But where did Isles get the stuff about cauldrons within the body?' asked Rowan, momentarily fascinated. 'It sounds like an indigenous British yoga—and certainly there are alchemical elements.'

'In the 1820s Isles gained access, through whom we do not know, to Irish oral teachings perhaps linked to what we today know as "The Cauldron of Poesy" MS i.e. a 15th century text found in, of all things, an Irish legal codex. Isles adapted its obscure teachings about cauldrons within the body and soul, and their effects on poetic inspiration and mental well-being. His eventual theory of the Orbits borrowed heavily from that old text as well as the long tradition of bardic teaching behind it.'

'And how is this relevant to me?' Rowan was almost accusative—he hated being given the role of class dunce.

'Well, you're birthing a new "self in orbit" right now—due to the crisis with your wife, and with your vocation.'

Rowan closed his eyes, 'So, I'm to lie here in the dark with a great rock on my chest. Symbolically, I'm to imagine myself stuck between the legs of Cerridwen. During this experience I'm supposed to be birthing a new self?'

'In 19th century Neo-Druidic terminology you're struggling to right the Cauldron of Spiritual Knowledge. Once upright, the Nine Damsels of the Cauldrons, the *Gallicena*, may once again breathe their inspirational song magic upon you!' said Douglas, with an odd solemnity.

'He's snug—let's go. I promised to phone Ian up at the house at 10pm,' said Rhiannon, impatiently.

Douglas released the pressure on Rowan's chest, 'We'll be back around 11am in the morning, with Isobel, to Dance the Orbits! I've left copies of a number of the key 18th and 19th century books that influenced Isles on the table at the back—the Davies book for example, Rousseau's *Emile*, Blake's prophetic books, some alchemical texts of the period, Goethe's *Faustus*. There's also a modern biography about Mesmer and some biographical details about Isles from an essay on his life. You can start reading them after sunrise if you like.'

'I have to keep this rock on my chest until sunrise?'

'Yes, though you can set it down to go outside to the toilet— or to write in your notebook.' Douglas signalled to Rhiannon, who placed an ornate green notebook and a black pen on a small stool beside Rowan. After extinguishing all lighting but the three candles burning in the three chambers of Cerridwen's body, Douglas and Rhiannon left the building. Rowan was alone with the Goddess.

CHAPTER SEVENTEEN

ABRAHAM ISLES AND THE GIGANTIC POD-WOMAN

Rowan lay in the near-darkness for a long time. The sculpture of Cerridwen that towered above him—probably one of Isobel's creations—seemed menacing from this angle, especially given the dim lighting. Obviously he was in the hands of a group of New Age lunatics. But he hadn't signed up for therapy, especially not therapy based on the outdated teachings of a 19th century druid revivalist. *The job description didn't mention druid studies,* he muttered sarcastically. At least the pile of books at the back of the room looked promising—especially the extract from a biographical summary of Isles's life. The literary and scholastic influences on Isles seemed legitimate enough—though Irish, Welsh and Scottish scholars of the 'druidic revival' were a notoriously eccentric bunch. Rowan's problem was that the more he learnt about Isles, the more certain he became that he was primarily an occultist. Douglas obviously wanted Rowan to write the biography of a colourful druid/alchemist—not a project he could afford to put his name to.

As he stared up at 'Cerridwen' from the discomfort of the camp-bed, he began imagining diabolical shapes swirling around in the darkness. He had to admit, Douglas was comic relief from the soullessness of modern academia. That world, so utilitarian and bureaucratic, so addicted to process and posturing, was anathemic—Rowan saw it clearly now—to genuine creative thinking. Everywhere, lecturers in literature, history, philosophy, cultural studies, and the like were being forced to view their work according to economic paradigms. The grey-suited bean-counters of hyper-capitalism were the puppet-masters behind every arts lecture.

The growing awareness that this unimaginative approach to ideas—and life—had infiltrated his consciousness was beginning to trouble him deeply. He hoped that Douglas was right, that he was birthing a new self, a new Rowan. He looked up at the huge, abstract head of the Goddess of the Three Cauldrons and muttered, 'Okay, if you're a goddess of healing and soul transformation, now would be a good time to manifest.' The Goddess responded with total silence.

After half an hour on his back, he felt irritated by the effort involved in keeping the stone balanced on his chest. He felt tired and his arms were becoming numb in places—he also longed to simply go to sleep. For a while, he considered trying to compose a poem or a song to pass the time—as Douglas had suggested. The impulse, however, sent him close to memories he was desperate to avoid—*No songs or poems this night,* he thought.

After another twenty minutes, he decided enough was enough—the candles of Cerridwen were growing dim and the entire exercise struck him as a total waste of time. He found the torch he'd been given and jumped out of bed before placing the cumbersome stone on the bed. He then walked slowly to the back of the room to find a light and make a coffee. He aimed to peruse the biographical material on Isles. Since Douglas was paying him for an evening of work, he felt obliged to do something useful. Ten minutes later, he was settled on a foam mattress reading the only essay in the folder. It was entitled 'Born in the Century Storm'. It puzzled Rowan that the name of the author had been blacked out.[2]

Despite his tiredness, he scanned the document with interest. Isles had been born in northern Scotland in 1803 to working class parents—a Welsh father and a Scottish mother. The extract covered his formative and young adult years: his upbringing and education; the details of his move to London around 1820; his exposure once there to Rousseau's work, as well as Owenite, Mesmerist, alchemical and Celtic revivalist thinking; his breakdown after being rejected by fellow Owenite, Miriam Hobbes; his experience of Mesmerist/neo-druidic therapy; as well as details of his first attempts to develop a system of thought capable of synthesising elements from the works of various thinkers. The extract closed with both Isles and Hobbes (by this stage married) under arrest for distributing radical 'unstamped' literatures. Although Hobbes was quickly released, Isles was found guilty and eventually shipped to New South Wales as a convict in 1833. Douglas had already discussed some of the material covered in the extract and the absence of historic records concerning Isles's life now seemed perfectly understandable given his lowly birth.

For the first time Rowan felt drawn to the story. The circumstances of Isles's shipment to the colonies interested him—obviously he was pro-reform, something like an early unionist/socialist. Given much of the family on Rowan's mother's side were solid working class people, he quickly

---

[2] Note by the Editor: Interested readers can peruse all of Extract 1 at the back of this book (in the **'Miscellaneous Documents'** section). Ref: Extract 1: Chapter 1 – *'Born in the Century Storm'* from **Abraham Isles and Miriam Hobbes (a biography)**.

warmed to both Isles and Miriam. Likewise, the fact that Isles's personality merged Celtic and alchemical occult tendencies with radical Enlightenment political beliefs interested Rowan. He yawned, then took another sip of coffee—maybe the caffeine would keep him awake.

He was struggling to remember his late 18th and early 19th century history. He remembered broad social trends, certainly, and a handful of significant dates and names, but not much else. He went over in his mind the excesses of the Ancient Regime; the shock of the French revolution and the chaos of the 'revolutionary period' that followed; the course of the Napoleonic wars, including the eventual defeat of Napoleon at Waterloo in June of 1815; the reactionary conservatism of the Concert of Europe; the melancholy, creative achievements of the Romantics; the renewed impetus for reform in the revolutions of 1848; the rise of Britain as a global empire under Queen Victoria; the rise of Marxism, and so on. In terms of Australian history, he recalled the founding of penal colonies in New South Wales and Tasmania; the oppression of Aboriginal peoples just about everywhere; Batman and the founding of Port Phillip; the gold rush period; and so on. He found a lot of Australian history tedious and thus he struggled to remember details.

He yawned again, making a mental note to buy a dozen history books dealing with specific aspects of the period. The urge surprised him; he was beginning to think like a history academic. Uncomfortable with this, he closed the folder and returned it to the back table alongside the other material. After switching off the lights, he returned to his makeshift bed. Stretched out once again with the quartz stone on his chest, he found himself staring up at Cerridwen's weirdly sculpted vagina and upper torso. Something had changed, but for a moment he couldn't work out what it was. Miraculously the second cauldron, the Cauldron of Vocation (the *coire ernma*), was slowly turning itself up-right. He gasped. It had happened so gradually that it seemed, in the dimness, almost like it had been turned by an invisible presence. Though there would be a scientific reason, it felt like an epiphany. For some time afterwards, almost despite himself, he stared at the third cauldron, willing it to tip upright. It didn't happen, however, and eventually he drifted off into sleep.

Whenever Rowan slept in unfamiliar places, he tended to dream a great deal—sometimes he had nightmares. Not long after falling asleep—on his back, still clutching the stone—he dreamt he was looking up at a gigantic, perhaps carnivorous, female monster. It appeared part human and part plant, and it danced and swayed in the gloom among the roof beams of the building. Suddenly, a huge pod head, black and shaped like a massive clam, slipped out of the creature's vaginal cavity coming to rest not a metre above Rowan. As it fattened and grew in length, it began to droop downwards until its massive pod-like head rested on his chest. Terrified, Rowan attempted to push it away. The attempt proved ineffective. Something was desperate to get out of the clam-like shell that now pinned Rowan to the bed—perhaps some kind of large chick or reptile. A physical struggle ensued inside the pod until its clam lips were prised open thirty centimetres or so. And then something gave way and out popped the rubbery, blue head of a middle-aged man—someone Rowan immediately recognised. The man said, 'Help me out of here! Can you pry open this shell a little further so I can get my shoulders out— it's very cramped in here?'

'I'm trying, mate, but the weight of this thing has me pinned to the bed.'

The guy, though up-side down, looked more closely at Rowan. His face, like a new born infant's, had lost its rubbery blue-black texture and was flooding with colour, i.e. blood.

'Don't I know you?'

Rowan suddenly recognised the man; it was Eric.

'Hi, Eric—how the hell did you end up inside that thing?'

'You don't choose your family, your enemies or your friends.' Eric's skin now grew amazingly bright, making his entire face seem smooth and animated. There was no trace of the depression that had dogged him throughout his youth.

'You don't look sad anymore, Eric,' said Rowan, remembering again the circumstances around Eric's suicide.

'Shit! I just realised, you're dead. Talking to each other isn't possible.' An age old fear of the dead gripped him—clouding his thoughts and making his heart beat fast. Instinctively, he pushed away the pod-clam that held Eric's body. Eric looked confused, 'Rowan, I need a hand—to get out of this thing.'

But Rowan had been seized by the god Pan. He jumped off the bed desperate to flee Cerridwen and her strange fruit. Once liberated, he addressed Eric again, 'Why, Eric? Why? ... you know I attended the funeral to say goodbye.'

The clam-like pod began contracting back into itself—into the womb of Cerridwen—reversing Eric's hard earned efforts to emerge. Less and less of Eric's head was visible. Rowan felt himself running in the direction of the clochan's exit. As he ran, he risked a glance over his left shoulder. Eric had disappeared completely, only the swarthy plant-giantess, swaying menacingly among the rafters of the building, remained. Still, Eric's last words echoed about the room, 'I bet you were stoned.'

CHAPTER EIGHTEEN

DANCING THE ORBITS
(Friday, January 17th 1997)

Rowan woke just after sunrise to the sound of a kookaburra. The interior of the building was still dark—there were no windows anywhere. He remembered only vague details from the nightmare. Perhaps the weight of the stone on his chest and the strangeness of the 'bedroom' had triggered it. The theme, however, was a familiar one. He felt about for the torch. Once located, he directed its beam up at the statue of Cerridwen. He noticed that the third cauldron still hadn't tipped. He felt irrationally disappointed. He yawned and then realised that he hadn't been able to stay awake all night with the stone on his chest. Using the torch, he searched the floor for the block of quartz. Weird painted shapes, Isobel's alchemical orbits, greeted his efforts. Luckily, it was undamaged on the floor beside the bed. Rowan felt relieved—though only a stone, he didn't want to return it broken. After picking it up and placing it on the bed, he walked briskly to the back of the building to make tea and grab some breakfast.

Douglas, Rhiannon and Isobel turned up about an hour later. They were in high spirits when they arrived, but business-like. They immediately selected three large foam mattresses and dragged them from the back of the room to positions directly in front of 'Cerridwen'. These they placed at intervals making a kind of broken line, with each mattress placed roughly two metres apart and linked to a particular orbit painted on the floor. Rowan noticed that the 'orbit mural' began with a circle (now containing a mattress) painted about three metres from the wall directly in front of what he'd nicknamed 'the spa' directly beneath 'Cerridwen'. It was labelled 'The Self in Orbit'. Another two metres out, the second circle/orbit line was labelled 'The Lovers'—it also contained a mattress. The next orbit line also had a mattress and was labelled 'The Orbit of Kinship and Close Association'. There were two other orbits beyond these, but Rowan had difficulty reading their labels. From the art-work, he guessed that one was the orbit of society, the other—outer—orbit was probably that of the natural world. Outward pointing red and yellow lines (rather than unbroken orbital circles) were painted two metres beyond the orbit of the natural world. Rowan thought the lines looked like fiery snakes and had no idea what they symbolised.

Isobel and Douglas decided to sit cross-legged, with backs upright (they looked to Rowan almost Buddha-like) on the mattress in the Orbit of Kinship and Close Association, whereas Rhiannon sat on the mattress within the Orbit of the Lovers.

'Feel free to join us, Rowan—yours is the mattress attached to the orbit of the Self in Orbit,' said Douglas, with closed eyes and his hands resting gently on his knees. Rowan, who was leaning against the 'spa' wall, did as he was asked.

'Did you manage to stay awake?' asked Rhiannon, who was dressed in the same dancer's outfit she'd worn the previous night.

'I probably managed two hours all up—balancing the stone

is hard on the arms,' said Rowan, feeling uncomfortable that Rhiannon was sitting in the Orbit of the Lovers. He'd felt the first stirrings of attraction to her yesterday—even though she'd shown no interest to date. Such desires, he reasoned, were understandable given his new status as a single man.

'Any songs or poems?' asked Douglas, his eyes now open and looking directly at Rowan.

'No, but the second Cauldron went upright early in the night—that was kind of weird.' Rowan was trying unsuccessfully to mimic Douglas's posture—minus the pot belly of course.

Rhiannon left her mattress to attend to Rowan's posture and breathing. Her arms were warm as she alternately pressed against his shoulders, chest, lower back and stomach whilst asking him to keep his breathing rhythmic and deep and his spinal cord straight. Now and then she lifted his chin or pressed gently on his forehead, 'You need to keep your head upright for this exercise.' When she was happy with his posture and breathing, she returned to her own mattress.

The other two said nothing throughout this process, preferring to concentrate on their own breathing.

'What exactly is the purpose of this, Douglas?' asked Rowan after fifteen minutes or so.

'In a moment Isobel is going to take you into a very light trance state. It's required if you're to address some of the issues you wrote about on your "Orbits" chart.'

Rowan felt uneasy sharing his personal issues with Isobel and Rhiannon, 'I didn't sign up for therapy, Douglas—I've told you that.'

'Don't worry,' said Douglas, between breaths, 'you can choose whether to address an issue or not. All we're doing is giving you first-hand experience of how Isles's system would address various life challenges.'

'While I'm at it, what exactly was the purpose of last night's exercise? I don't understand what I was supposed to achieve. Nothing actually happened.' Rowan trailed off, suddenly aware of Rhiannon's gaze upon him. She clearly wanted him to stop talking and concentrate on his breathing.

'Your *coire ernma* went upright at an auspicious moment—that's something,' said Douglas, between intakes of breath.

'But nothing else happened.'

'Everything important begins in eventlessness,' said Isobel who broke from the breathing posture to stretch specific muscles gracefully like a yogi or a dancer. She was very supple for an older woman. Ordinarily, Rowan would feel physically inferior to both her and Rhiannon. In recent years his body had come to feel heavy and sluggish—largely due to the long hours he'd been spending at computers. Douglas, however, had changed all that. The relentless cricket training had made Rowan both more muscular and more graceful in his movements.

'The three cauldrons of creative inspiration suggested to Abraham Isles important truths about the workings of the human soul.' Douglas was still looking at Rowan. 'Recall, he was looking to merge the transformative possibilities of alchemy, with insights about the role of "soul cauldrons" in the body and mental life. As a result, he developed a number of general principles concerning the nature of human well-being. In the late 1820s he started to develop exercises that could help undo the damage to children that Rousseau had so brilliantly written about in *Emile*. He highlighted two aspects to Rousseau's thinking that the French philosopher had neglected. Firstly, he noted that the civilising process critiqued in *Emile* most often revolved around impediments to natural movement and/or natural expression. Secondly, he noted that such impediments were always related to a frustrated "need" for specific persons or environments to act in specific ways. The sum total of interactions with needed persons and environments, past and present, he referred to as a person's "unique solar system". He theorised a limited number of "soul planets" or "soul orbits" to the average person's "solar system"—they are beautifully depicted here for us on the floor of our clochan: The Lovers, Kinship and Close Association, Society, and Nature (what he called The Green Orbit). Isles also classified energy exchanges between the self and the "needed planets" of an individual's "solar system" as either "joyous" or "vexatious".'

Rowan interrupted, 'But what about that outer circle—the one with the fiery serpents?'

'Good question—for the moment let us just say that one answer is *Ceugant* or infinity. Rather, to Isles, infinity *plus* that which exists within each human being, but originates outside the structures of suffering, intra and interspecies competition, etc. that rule our existence. Isles adapted beliefs about the various "circles of existence"—being *Annwn*, *Abred*, *Gwynvyd* and *Ceugant*—current among Welsh revivalist druids of the nineteenth century. Such beliefs have since been traced back to the work of the 16th century writer, Llewelyn Siôn. Whether they represent genuine druidic beliefs is rather beside the point since Isles was not interested in reviving the original, untarnished purity of anything. If the Universe had a flaw— represented by the persistence of suffering—then to him there was no *pure* origin story buried by history to revive.'

'There must be a simpler way of describing this material,' said Isobel, yawning theatrically.

Douglas paused before continuing, 'Isles was interested in chunks of theory he could incorporate into his own system.'

This made sense—Rowan was already aware of Buddhist, Hermetic/alchemical and Gnostic elements in Isles's thinking.

'Was the goal of his system to transcend a basically fallen existence?' Rowan asked.

'No, not exactly, and this was at the heart of his breach with Hermeticists and Gnostics—as well as some 19th century druids. The primary goal of his therapy was to convert "vexatious orbits" into "joyous orbits". To this end, he merged cathartic trance techniques taken from Mesmer and elsewhere, with a range of special exercises designed to cleanse and heal "vexatious orbits"—i.e. special breathing exercises taken, so he said, from "the Alchymists".' Douglas paused again, before signalling to Isobel to take over.

'Douglas is a little old for some of the orbital exercises developed by Isles. This morning, he's asked Rhiannon and I to take you through some of them instead.'

'He smoked like a chimney as a youngster and he's paid the price with emphysema,' translated Rhiannon. 'If you see him smoking, Rowan, he's to be reported to me instantly,' she continued, mimicking a dominatrix with a whip.

'According to Douglas, this Isles fellow also incorporated an old Celtic concept—that of the *nwyvre* or sacred soul heat—into his system ... probably in the late 1820s. At times he seems to merge the concept of *nwyvre* with that of the *awen*. Strictly speaking, however, *awen* describes an energy that fuels creative inspiration.'

Douglas couldn't resist interrupting, 'Given Isles was a composer and writer, it is likely that the two energies became indistinct for him at times.'

Isobel glared at Douglas then cut him off, 'What we'll be demonstrating today is quite traditional. We'll be seeking to stimulate the flow of healing *nwyvre* energies throughout your body via the "cauldrons" or "switching points". However, we'll also be looking at some of Isles's innovations to that old way of thinking.' Isobel paused, 'Douglas, you *should* perhaps explain the next bit—I'm not that clear about it.'

He tried to sound humble. 'For Isles, *nwyvre* energy extended beyond the body wall and beyond the present moment in time. To him, *nwyvre* energies circulate between the self and the various "orbits". Likewise, *nwyvre* energy can atrophy in spots beyond the body wall (i.e. in the "*mesmeric*"/memory field of the "*subtle body*"); in particular, it could atrophy in "vexatious (or traumatic) orbits". Traumas, particularly the kinds of socialisation traumas Rousseau had so thoroughly detailed in *Emile*, impede the proper flow of *nwyvre* between various current "orbits" important to the self—a recipe for all kinds of problems, both within individuals and between individuals.'

Rhiannon interrupted, 'He can read all about the theory later. No offence, Rowan, but what you need right now is to get out of your head and into your body.'

'I agree—but he does need some background, Rhiannon' said Isobel, 'Are we through for now, Douglas?'

He nodded in the affirmative.

'Okay,' said Isobel, 'then let us return to the deep breathing exercises.'

The room went quiet as everyone settled to their breathing. This time Isobel occasionally pressed on Rowan's chest, head or shoulders. Sometimes she asked him to breathe faster or more deeply into his diaphragm. Rowan tried to follow her instructions, but after a short time he began to feel light-headed.

After a while, she took both his hands and pulled him gently to his feet, 'Push up on your toes, bend your knees gently and lift each hand, palms facing upwards, until it's ninety degrees at the elbow … That's right, balance yourself—and keep breathing deeply. We're "kindling *nwyvre*" energies by breathing and adopting this posture. The idea is to draw the energy through certain balance points in your body, i.e. through the symbolic cauldrons. Keep your chin up … good! Now, what do you see?' She moved behind him for a moment leaving Rhiannon in his direct field of vision. She was wearing a half mask painted green and black, and was standing in a relaxed but dignified posture. Rowan noticed she stood directly above the orbit painted on the floor as "the Lovers' Orbit".

'I see Rhiannon wearing a half mask painted with green and black symbols.'

'You're having some difficulties in your love relationship with Kerryn, is that right?' whispered Isobel from behind Rowan.

Rowan winced and then closed his eyes, 'I don't want to talk about that here. I thought this was only a demonstration.'

'Keep breathing' whispered Isobel, 'we're not going to force you into anything.' Her voice sounded soothing and hypnotic.

The prolonged deep breathing, Rhiannon's mask and the soothing rhythms of Isobel's voice were sending Rowan into a strange mental space. 'Are you trying to hypnotise me?' he asked, in a groggy voice.

'Isles only ever used a light trance,' answered Douglas, trying to mimic Isobel's soothing tone, but sounding gruff and wheezy instead. 'He disagreed with Mesmer's tendency to completely erase an individual's free will during hypnosis. For Isles, the patient needed to explore blocked *nwyvre* beyond the body wall with the aid of free will. Patients had to *make a choice*.'

'Shsss, Douglas,' said Isobel, 'Rowan, look at the woman in your current "orbit of love" and imagine she's the Kerryn you know—but imagine also that she's *more* than the Kerryn you know.' She trailed off, giving him room to visualise Kerryn.

'Now, can you verbalise the *nwyvre* energy between the two of you?'

Rowan bit his lip, 'I can't say.'

'You can't say or you don't want to say?'

'Okay, okay … dead energy, drained energy—there's a blockage.'

'Where's the block? Point to the block—you can move closer to Kerryn if you wish.'

'She wanted children. I didn't want …Look, this isn't a nineteenth century therapy, this is adapted psychoanalysis.'

'Where's the block?'

'In my chest and in my stomach …'

'In your jaw, too, by the sound of it,' said Isobel as she pushed gently on his lower back whilst pulling his shoulders back, 'Keep those legs bent—don't stiffen up.'

With Isobel alternating pressure and directing his breathing, he soon had the urge to raise and lower his head rhythmically in synch with circular movements seizing his shoulders, lower back and hips. As he did, he felt a strange warmth creep up his legs and into his lower abdomen.

'Where's the block? Show us.'

As the warmth crept further up his trunk, he found he wanted to sob, 'She moved toward me, she wanted children. I pushed her away because I wasn't *me* around her.'

'Let's act it out,' said Isobel as Rhiannon began to approach Rowan slowly with her arms outstretched.

'Pretend to push her away, Rowan. Go on, gesture "NO" with your hands. And pull and twist your torso back and away as you do it.'

Rowan did as he was asked—he felt even more emotional.

'Speak *at* and *through* the "orbital" block.'

Rhiannon slowly, gracefully approached him again, her arms outstretched.

Rowan reared and twisted back and away, 'I'm not ready. Don't force me. Don't try to control me!'

'Louder …'

'There's stuff I have to resolve. I'm not ready. You can't …' Rowan was sobbing as he mimicked pushing the masked dancer away a third time.

'Say it …'

'You can't trust me—I'm a fake. I don't support people. I'm

like my father. I'M *NOT* READY. BACK OFF!!'

The sobs turned to anger as Rowan sank to the mattress. The heat in his belly and legs had spread to his chest, arms and head, but it was a bitter, acidic heat accompanied by anger, self-loathing and sadness. The release of emotions went on for a good ten minutes. Eventually someone switched on the stereo system and well-positioned speakers piped mournful Celtic music into the room. Now and then Rowan felt Isobel's hands on his back or neck, drawing out more emotion or comforting him.

When he eventually calmed down, Rhiannon and Isobel were sitting cross-legged on their mattresses and Douglas was up the back preparing tea for everyone. 'Do you like honey and milk in your tea?' he asked Rowan, almost shouting, 'it's Mallee honey made by bees from our region. Apparently local honey helps if you have allergies caused by local grasses.'

'White with honey,' croaked Rowan, before looking sheepishly at Isobel.

'What happened there?' she asked, 'Most people don't go into "vexatious" orbits quite so quickly.'

'I've had a tough few weeks, perhaps. And my rehab therapist back in the 80s was into cathartic release techniques.'

'How long were you in therapy?'

'Just long enough to get off the drugs—a shit childhood and a career in the music industry made me think it was cool to be smashed for years at a time.'

'Why didn't you keep going with the therapy?' asked Rhiannon, gently.

'I don't know—I met Kerryn and things improved. I had no desire to look back, nothing to look back at. Dad was a rich prick bent on revenge. Mum did the best she could, but life was hard for her after they divorced.'

Rhiannon looked thoughtful, 'Refusal of the call, eh?'

'What do you mean?'

'You settled for stability and security?' she spoke quietly, as though she wasn't judging Rowan, but somehow that made him feel worse.

'Not entirely. To be honest, after the rehab, my sad-assed up-bringing—courtesy my sad-assed parents—seemed only part of the story. Society, with its systems of oppression, seemed to be the other part—and so, I became a social worker. I don't like to individualise every incidence of misanthropy, and counsellors and psychologists are useful, but what we really need right now are *community psychologists*—people capable of healing the sicknesses of whole societies.'

'I do not disagree,' said Rhiannon, aware he was getting defensive.

During the uncomfortable silence that followed, Douglas joined the three of them carrying a tray with four mugs of tea.

Isobel continued as Douglas distributed the mugs, 'Rhiannon and I had a few more exercises planned—we didn't expect you to go so deep so quickly. Usually there's resistance.'

'Lots of resistance,' chuckled Rhiannon.

Rowan didn't know whether he'd impressed them by his access to emotion or worried them with his emotional instability.

'Anyway,' continued Rhiannon, 'there are hundreds of "orbital exercises" or "dances" supposedly developed by Isles and his wife Miriam. All are based on removing specific "*nwyvre* blockages". A significant number relate to girls and women and were developed by Isles's wife who disagreed with Rousseau's attitude to women.' She paused to sip her tea.

'The other important thing to note,' said Douglas, taking up the slack, 'is that each exercise was supposed to be accompanied by a specific song composed by Isles. The surviving diaries feature hundreds of sketches—illustrating orbital exercises—as well as the lyrics to hundreds of songs. Unfortunately, the musical notation accompanying the songs is missing. Either that or he coded the musical notation into the diaries somewhere.'

'I can't see much difference between Isles's system of postures and modern body oriented forms of psychoanalysis,' said Rowan, still feeling groggy and vulnerable.

'There are similarities, but the thing is,' said Douglas, 'in that exchange then between you and Rhiannon—at the moment the blockage beyond the body wall gave way and the *nwyvre* flowed—albeit through bitter feelings ... Well, Isles would say that a god was present—though he wouldn't have used the term 'god'. He preferred other terms: "The Principles", the "Domestic Gods" or the "Guardians of the Orbits". He referred to all the orbital guardians combined as "the Government of Souls". To him, each of us is composed of a divine self— attached to the Government of Souls—and a mortal self struggling to manifest the will of the various Guardians on earth. When the orbits become "unblocked" and *nwyvre* flows freely beyond the body wall—i.e. between the self and the orbits—the divine and the mortal parts are at peace. There is "joyous equilibrium".' Douglas smiled at Rowan, 'Does that sound like psychoanalysis to you?'

Rowan looked down, 'I just can't come at gods, Douglas.'

'Not gods—*Guardians* of particular *Orbits*.'

'Archetypes, Polytheistic Gods, Guardians of the Orbits. What does it matter—gods by any other name. Sorry, but I just can't come at them. Give a god an inch and he'll take a mountain range.'

'I suspect the Guardians, or whatever we call them, don't really care what we think about them,' said Isobel, '"summoned or not", eh? Was it Jung said that, Douglas?'

'I think so, my dear.'

'I'm not, *your* dear!'

Douglas flinched theatrically and then took another gulp of

hot tea. Rhiannon was lying on her back, one leg crossing the other. To Rowan, she looked either bored or whimsical.

'Summoned or not', continued Isobel, '*they* will be present.' She crawled over to sit beside Douglas and immediately slipped her arms around his shoulders.

'I prefer personal responsibility to divine mandate,' said Rowan curtly.

Isobel smiled, 'If we're not occasionally reminded that a part of us transcends what Isles called "the flaw in the fabric of the cosmos", don't we risk allowing the flaw itself to define all that we are?'

'Hell on earth begins with our tendency to ask our "gods" to exempt us from the necessity of exercising free will,' said Rowan mischievously.

Douglas cut in, 'Isles was actually big on free will—but he allied it to the Imagination. Shall we leave it at that for now? You need time to process what you've just been through.'

'Isles was profoundly creative,' interrupted Isabel, 'but it is still possible that Abraham Isles is simply the literary creation of one Douglas Green. After all, the afore mentioned old bugger refuses to reveal to any of us, including his sometimes lover, *moi*, his source documents. When will you show me copies of Isles's diaries?' she asked, whilst planting a huge kiss on Douglas's left cheek. 'Not that I mind. Perhaps *Green* is the mortal side of the Orbital Guardian *Abraham Isles*. Hail Great Moloch Isles! Or is it: Hail Great Moloch Green?'

Everyone laughed, even Douglas.

'Speaking of gods, Rowan,' Rhiannon sat up to speak, 'If I were you I'd be learning a lot more about Apollo, Dionysus and Hermes. Douglas tells me that one of your own "blocked orbits" is to do with composing and performing music.'

CHAPTER NINETEEN

THE INSTABILITY OF NOW
(Thursday, February 6ᵗʰ 1997)

One morning in early February, Douglas barged into Rowan's hut saying, 'Are you up, Rowan? We have important ideas to discuss.' Rowan sighed as he dragged himself out of bed to greet Douglas. After the 'Alchemy', 'Orbits' and 'Cauldrons' lessons Douglas had shared nothing new about Isles for weeks. When asked about guidance in researching the biography, Douglas had invariably changed the topic or stated flatly: 'The time isn't right yet ... have patience, young apprentice!'

Isobel had departed for an exhibition tour of Europe in the last week of January and Rhiannon had returned to Melbourne soon after. Rowan had noticed Douglas's spirits sag thereafter, leading to days where he'd pestered Rowan to come up to the house in the evening to share a meal. During the dinners, however, he'd seemed mentally hyperactive—sometimes he'd grappled aloud with obscure philosophical problems posed by thinkers Rowan knew nothing about. Other times, he'd speculated in depth on scenes out of classic novels or plays. Most worryingly, however, he appeared to be ill—a number of times Rowan had heard him vomiting and coughing after doing basic physical chores. He was also complaining constantly of migraines.

Rowan was no better off. He'd been struggling to get up in the mornings for weeks and lacked the motivation to do anything much besides work. Only the busyness of Douglas's training and study schedule kept him engaged with the world at all. Just as worryingly, for the first time in a decade he craved alcohol and marijuana. His 'social worker self' diagnosed depression. A possibility that had led him to an important decision—one that he now intended to break to Douglas.

This morning, however, Douglas seemed to be struggling to deliver a revelation of his own. He stood in the hut's lounge fumbling with a key-ring that contained a number of ornate looking keys.

'Sit down, Rowan. Do you want a coffee or a pot of tea?'

'All in due course, Douglas. I have to go to the toilet first.'

'That doesn't stop you deciding between coffee and tea,' Douglas joked, but his voice seemed unusually strained.

'Okay, make it a coffee. What's up? I suspect this morning's PD session is going to be a doozy.' Playing the role of dutiful employee made him feel inauthentic given what he had to tell Douglas. He'd received a casual job offer the previous afternoon—a part-time tutoring position in Cultural Studies at his old university. It came through only a week before the first semester classes were due to start and involved one semester's work tutoring for a unit called 'Contemporary Literary Theories'. There was no guarantee of work beyond the first semester. Other more substantial positions he'd applied for had all fallen through. Despite the drastic income reduction, he felt that the tutoring position at least represented a genuine academic position. He'd also be near a number of long-term friends, as well as his mother. He hoped these influences might jolt him out of his downward spiral. He'd decided to phone that very morning to accept the position. The only issue now was how to break the news to Douglas.

'You look like death warmed up. Didn't you sleep last night?' asked Douglas, whilst placing the old black kettle on a gas plate and lighting the burner. Rowan wandered into the bathroom without answering.

'Have you been keeping up with your readings—especially that essay on the new physics I gave you yesterday?'

'I didn't read anything last night. I've been doing some thinking instead—some of it in bloody French, Gaelic or one of the Aboriginal languages!' Rowan shouted, as he flushed the toilet before deciding to brush his teeth.

'You need to have another go at entering into those Mesmeric trance states Isobel and Rhiannon introduced you to.'

'I've told you before, Douglas, I'm not here for therapy.' He spat out some toothpaste, then continued speaking between brush strokes, 'I'm not saying that Mesmerist-Druidic-Alchemical paths aren't useful to some people, it's just that, well, Freud came along between Isles and us.' He spat out more toothpaste and placed the brush back in its unhygienic metal clamp. 'And the stuff about trance states, induced by music that supposedly lets us tap into the "etheric frequency" of particular "orbits"—to be honest, Douglas, it's not my thing. I'm no occultist.' He ran a small bowl of water and selected a shaver.

'The trance stuff is very important—and by the way, most of Freud's theorising was confined to energy exchange systems operating within an individual's psyche. The impact of society—of relationships, *orbits* if you like—on his claustrophobic "inner" world was only very roughly sketched out, in *Civilisation and its Discontents* actually. And the influence of the physical environment didn't feature at all.'

Something was definitely up—Douglas was talking faster than usual. Rowan felt bombarded with information fragments from numerous undelivered lectures.

'It's too bloody early in the morning for this, Douglas. My brain doesn't work before 9am—and like I said, I've had a lot on my mind.' He wandered back into the lounge where Douglas handed him a cup of coffee. The old man wore an odd expression.

Perhaps, thought Rowan, *he's going to talk about some of the unanswered questions forcing me to leave.* He listed them in his mind: What became of Isles after arriving in New South Wales? Why had Douglas taught him French and that weird Koori hybrid language? Also, why exactly did he have to be able to bowl at 130km per hour?

'Where are we going for today's lesson?'

Douglas pointed at the couch and said, 'Here is just fine since it's close to the study.'

Rowan looked across at the now partially open door of the study. 'Oh you've opened it again.' The door had been locked since his return from a trip to Melbourne the previous weekend. Obviously, Douglas had been preparing some kind of stunt. Rowan felt his heart rate increase slightly. Douglas turned—mug in hand—toward the hut's main window. Rowan followed with his eyes. The two men watched the sun rise amidst a veritable archipelago of low-lying thunder-clouds skitting eastward. Douglas seemed to be composing himself for a major announcement.

When he spoke, his words came out slowly and in a whisper, 'The thunder-clouds have been moving fast all night. They were supposed to bring rain, but did you hear any rain? I didn't and I was up most of the night planning this conversation.'

'I heard no rain either and I was also awake most of the night,' said Rowan.

Douglas sighed as though about to set down an immense burden.

'After I leave this morning, you'll be permitted to go into the study and have a look around. In there, I've placed a summary of the life of Abraham Isles post-1833. However, before you read it, we need to engage in a little "hypothetical". Are you up for that?'

'Sure—I'm always up for a hypothetical at sunrise,' said Rowan, before taking a gulp of his coffee.

'Good.'

There was a long pause as Douglas took a deep breath, 'A while back you made a list of "transpersonal events" that you've experienced. The point of the exercise was to expose the limitations of an entirely secular—that is 'Old Science'—world-view. Do you remember the exercise?'

'Vaguely …'

'Well, the hypothetical I'm about to present builds upon aspects of that exercise. Did you notice a pattern behind some of the events you listed?'

Here Rowan could be genuine, 'I guess there was a certain logic to them. Many involved "knowledge at a distance"—of people or events out of my immediate sensorial field. Some concerned knowledge of future events.'

'Good. Well, suppose the universe was composed of an infinite number of alternative presents and, by extension, alternative pasts and futures. Do you think that might be possible?'

Rowan smiled—a bit left field, but modern science fiction writers were obsessed with the idea. 'If one accepts the reality of subatomic instability as presented to us in quantum physics, then yes, I'd say it sounds *theoretically* possible.'

Douglas was pacing the small room like a trapped animal. He seemed to Rowan to be choosing his words with excruciating care, 'Okay, supposing as an extension of that possibility, gateways were to occasionally appear between two or more "alternative worlds" — perhaps due to a crisis in one or other of the alternative ...'

'I don't follow.'

'Let me put it slightly differently. Let's suppose shockwaves generated in one alternative world — due to mass trauma, or impending mass trauma — were able to leak across into parallel realities. We might call such leaks "ontological ruptures".'

Douglas had entered *le terraine fantastique* and Rowan had to concentrate hard to keep up with the fast evolving argument.

'To take our hypothetical a little further, Rowan, we might ask: is it possible for certain people to, as it were, leave their own reality and enter in some way a parallel reality — perhaps for a prescribed period of time, perhaps permanently? We might theorise minor forms of such journeying: dreams, day dreams, imaginative creations, and the like. Or we might theorise more substantial "travel": partial identity transfers (something like the experiences shamans have in trance, for example). Perhaps, near total identity transfer is also possible.'

Douglas stopped pacing. He took a sip of his drink and stared out at the phantasmagoria of red, yellow and purple cloud formations outside.

Rowan felt increasingly pleased with his decision to accept the Cultural Studies tutoring position.

'Now, let's also suppose that Abraham Isles knew intuitively about these other worlds — though obviously not in the way a modern quantum physicist or a cosmologist might theorise their existence. He believed that all life is interconnected — therefore the other worlds must interpenetrate our world in subtle ways. By the 1830s Isles saw himself as a *walker* between coexistent worlds.'

'What, as per the old Celtic notions of the ordinary world and other worlds?' asked Rowan.

'Certainly he began there, but by 1835 he'd moved beyond his Celtic roots—perhaps due to experiences among the tribes of South Eastern Australia, perhaps not. Either way, the diaries affirm his growing belief that leakages between coexistent realities had a purpose—basically to offer us other options for living.' Douglas paused. 'We've talked a lot about Isles's notion of "the flaw in the fabric of the cosmos" and how he developed the postural system to transcend it. Well part of this process involved commitment to the Imagination. To Isles, the Imagination stimulated the empathic faculties of the self at the same time as it opened us up to better ways of living.' Douglas stopped talking abruptly; to Rowan he appeared pale and was struggling for breath.

'Are you okay, Douglas—you don't look well?'

Douglas brushed aside Rowan's concern and ploughed on, 'Isles speculated that the postural system *plus* the Imagination might even be able to alter the rules that govern a universe. He wanted a spiritual system to oppose the generation of new forms of suffering. Death, ultimate evidence for the existence of an ancient ontological flaw. Eat or be eaten! The strong shall devour the weak! Fight! Perish! Kill! Grieve! ... *Grieve.*' Douglas faded off into silence—his features had softened markedly, as though all the effort involved in explaining Isles's philosophy had led to some sort of epiphany.

'Haven't we been through some of this material already?' asked Rowan, softly. But Douglas was back staring at the strange cloud patterns in the sky to the east.

'What if it was possible' Douglas said, 'to merge my current identity with another version of myself in an alternative reality where alternative historic decisions and actions—alternative acts of will—had created less suffering, less death, for some individuals or groups? Wouldn't I—wouldn't you, Rowan—be interested in contacting that other self?'

Rowan tried not to sound incredulous, 'Do you uh … believe you can merge your identity with another version of you or are we talking about travel via visions, dreams and the like?' Even as he spoke, he found himself thinking about Anika and Eric. Yes, he would certainly like to live in a world where he'd made different decisions in his early twenties.

'I've had shamanic trance experiences—I can enter into trance almost at will. I try to avoid unwarranted skepticism about such experiences—besides, one doesn't argue with hundreds of gold nuggets does one?' He laughed cryptically, still staring at the cloud patterns.

The social worker in Rowan had a hunch that Douglas was about to divulge something important. He'd experienced such confessions many times over the years. He'd learnt that some part of almost every delusional client wants to trust the worker or therapist enough to ask for help. He tried to stay as open and non-judgmental as possible in such moments. 'And what do your trance experiences involve?'

Douglas ignored the question—whatever was bugging him, Rowan thought, had built elaborate defences.

'Isles wrote many diaries—essential reading for any biographer. Likewise, a diligent historian would want to view any undeciphered—thus far, anyway—transcripts of his sacred songs. We're talking about the hundreds of songs he composed between the early 1830s and his death.' Douglas turned to look directly at Rowan.

'Will I get to look at some of the diaries? Where exactly are they?' Rowan tried not to look too sceptical about what he was hearing.

'I don't own the manuscripts—his descendants make the decisions about who gets to read them. I do however possess a summary of Isles's life post-1833. It sits on the wooden desk in your study. There's also other material in there I'm sure you'll be very interested in.'

'In there?' Rowan glanced in the direction of the unlocked door. For some reason, he felt a wave of vertigo every time Douglas drew attention to the study.

'After we've finished our hypothetical, I'll be letting you have a look in there,' said Douglas, struggling once again to breathe.

Rowan waited for him to recover before using his best social worker voice, 'Maybe we should return to the hypothetical then?'

'Yes, let's return to the hypothetical.' He began pacing up and down again, absorbed in his thoughts, 'What would it be like to wake up one day in a parallel present?'

Rowan tried to remember how the psychiatrists he'd worked with answered such odd questions. 'Well, I imagine it would feel pretty weird—especially if you were unable to share the experience with others. It might feel like mental illness.'

'Possibly, but that's to pathologise the experience prematurely. Whatever unfolds in coming weeks, don't you think it's a useful exercise to contemplate alternative pasts, presents and futures?'

Rowan had lost his train of thought, 'I suppose so.'

'To return to the poor fellow who wakes up in an alternative present. Perhaps we could hypothesise that he might feel like a writer or poet, an artist or musician. After all such *artisans* are always experimenting with "reality"; with the givens of the "past" and the utopian possibilities of the "future". They cross between realities routinely, don't you think?'

'I suppose so; perhaps it's the reason so many of them have problems adjusting to ordinary life.'

'Exactly, it's almost in their job description to warp and twist the ontological structures that define their world—and they do it in the name of free-will and the Imagination. Some hope to right old wrongs, others seek relief from poisonous remorse, still others hope to birth affirmative futures.'

Rowan was struggling to keep up.

'In the postmodern period we write, we compose, we think, we paint under the sign of Thoth/Hermes and his wife Sesheta—the *imaginative* travelers between worlds. The beautiful hybrids. Whatever else unfolds—that's something to remember.' Douglas stopped his pacing to face Rowan again.

As Rowan met his gaze, he realised that the old man was somehow saying goodbye.

'Look, Douglas, I have to come clean with you. I've been offered a casual tutoring position at my old university and I intend to take it.' He felt like some sort of traitor.

'I completely understand.'

'It's not that the material on Isles doesn't fascinate me—it does, it's just that …'

'No need to explain, Rowan, I get the picture.'

'But I'd really like to read the article and the other material in the study.'

Douglas cut him off abruptly. 'One other thing, before I leave you to fend for yourself, young apprentice,' he said, his mood, suddenly lighter. 'When the average person thinks about the possibility of "alternative worlds" etc., he or she typically envisages worlds ruled by the same structural laws that rule our world. However, what if an alternate present was *structured* differently to our world, what if things impossible here were possible in the other world? Similarly, what if some of the fundamental building blocks of our reality were missing in other realities or were less solid there?' Douglas's face was a mask to Rowan.

'I'd find that very confusing—the imagination would have to do a lot of work,' answered Rowan. 'I mean, all of it is theoretically possible, but I very much doubt we'll ever really experience such things—perhaps when we die.' Rowan was doing his best to appear open to what Douglas was saying—especially now that he'd dropped the resignation bombshell.

'It's probably just as well you've decided to move on—Rhiannon has been worried about me lately, she phones every night, you know. She wants me to undergo some tests in Melbourne. I'm struggling to remember names a lot these days. Do you know, I used to be able to recite the Rhyme of the Ancient Mariner from beginning to end out of memory? I'd occasionally do it for the students when I was lecturing on Romantic literature. Not anymore. Old age is a bastard, Rowan, don't let anyone tell you different.' Douglas trailed off, leaving Rowan with the impression that he was undergoing a long slow inward collapse.

'What are you being tested for?'

'Seems they're browsing the entire *catalogue*: dementia, Alzheimer's, acquired brain injury due to minor stroke (I had a funny turn during a group session in the clochan last November that I kept from you) … what else, oh yes, they want to do scans for a possible brain tumour, etcetera, etcetera. It's been getting worse over the past few months. My energy levels are way down and Rhiannon thinks I'm dwelling obsessively on the past a lot. I'm sorry you haven't seen me at my best these past six months.' He seemed to genuinely believe he'd failed Rowan as a mentor.

'I've learnt a huge amount about my uh self here—things I could never learn at a university.' As he spoke, he realised he meant what he was saying.

Douglas walked over to the sink, 'I'm glad you didn't find our time together a complete waste of time. Besides, you're

now a very good cricketer—in fact you remind me of ....'
For some reason Douglas couldn't end the sentence. Stifling
emotion, he turned to the sink and began washing his coffee
cup compulsively.

'Enough heavy talk for one morning! As I said, feel free
to read the material in the study before you leave. I have to
insist, however, that you do not, under any circumstances, take
anything out of the room.' He was facing Rowan again, this
time with his right hand outstretched.

'Absolutely,' said Rowan, as he shook the older man's hand.

'Also, given the fact that you've resigned you aren't permitted
to switch on the computer in there under any circumstances.
It's the twin of a prototype quantum computer currently being
developed in the US,' said Douglas, turning his back on Rowan
again. 'When engaged in calculations, it may well destabilise
quantum energy fields by accessing multiple parallel realities
at once—the goal, so they tell me, is to accelerate processing
capacity.' Douglas took something out of his pocket.

Rowan thought: *How much nutty pseudo-science do I have to
endure today and what the hell is a quantum computer?* Outwardly,
however, he kept calm and said, 'Okay, Douglas, I promise not
to play with the uh … quantum computer.'

'Good' said Douglas, turning to Rowan with a handful of
what looked like crystals. 'Now, do you like crystals? These are
extremely pure quartz crystals—I found them up the top of the
hill many years ago. I'd like you to have them.'

Rowan took the crystals, which were quite large and
remarkably smooth and transparent. 'Thank you Douglas. I'll
er … put them on my book shelf.'

'I find it fascinating,' said Douglas, 'that silicon dioxide—
which is found in those quartz crystals as silica—is fundamental
to computing. Such compounds allow us to maintain precise
frequencies and atomic states in radios, digital clocks,

computers, cell phones and the like. Our civilisation owes much to these humble compounds. Remarkable, don't you think, that indigenous shamans and healers the world over also used quartz crystals?

'Yes, something of a remarkable coincidence,' said Rowan, in a level voice.

'But everything changes and adapts, even quartz and silica apparently,' continued Douglas, turning his back on Rowan and walking slowly back to the kitchen window. 'The quartz-silica compounds used in my quantum computer have been atomically micro-engineered to reduce quantum decoherence—this is fundamental to increasing processing speeds. New worlds await us!'

'A new era for the computer sciences,' said Rowan, wanting to end the conversation.

Douglas stooped over the sink for a moment and coughed before saying, 'I'll make sure all arrears are paid into your account—and don't feel you have to leave right away. I'll be gone a week, so there's no rush.'

'I'm sure there's nothing major to worry about,' said Rowan, kneading the crystals.

'Thanks for the vote of confidence. I hope the finalisation of your divorce gives you a new start—it seems to have knocked you about a bit.'

'The divorce is only part of it—maybe you've taught me that. I sometimes think that instead of reading about the gods and goddesses of the world and hitting cricket balls this past six months I should have been in therapy with you.' In that instant, Rowan knew with certainty that returning to Melbourne wouldn't fix any of his real problems.

Douglas let the admission stand without comment.

'Who will you get to complete the Isles book?' asked Rowan, aware he'd just thrown away the only stable thing in his life, i.e.

a job that paid good money.

'Maybe it wasn't meant to be written right now,' said Douglas, as he left the hut.

For a long time after Douglas left, Rowan didn't move from the couch. Instead, he drank the remainder of his coffee and stared out the window—a few stray clouds moved swiftly across a gradually lightening sky. As he drank, he kept glancing at the door to the study—just in case Douglas had any other surprises up his sleeve. The door was slightly ajar and despite the early morning dimness, he saw that his wooden desk was stacked with some new folders.

He found it surprisingly difficult to rise from the couch and enter the study.

CHAPTER TWENTY

QUANTUM WAFFLE AND THE CONVICT

When Rowan finally plucked up the courage to enter the study, he did so tentatively, trying to convince himself that the madness he would surely encounter there would be benign, given Douglas's benign personality.

The room was as sparsely furnished as ever—though as promised a brand new computer stood on the work desk. *The legendary quantum computer*, thought Rowan. Hesitating only briefly, he reached over and switched it on. *Quantum occult waffle be damned!* While the computer booted up, he scanned the rest of the room.

The next addition he noticed was a manila folder containing a small wad of A4 papers. It sat on the writing desk beside the computer's keyboard and was entitled: Chapter Two 'Life in the Colony of New South Wales' from *Abraham Isles and Miriam Hobbes (a biography)*. Beside the folder there was an ornate box containing some foreign money. Most of the notes were coloured red, black or yellow, except two notes that featured green and blue spirals. The currency was *yarkuks* not dollars. On the wall above the desk Douglas had pinned a large map of South Eastern Australia. The names on it were strange to Rowan, perhaps Aboriginal names, and the state borders didn't seem to exist as Rowan knew them. In the centre of the map, encompassing Northern Victoria, indeed across the space usually occupied by the names of Victorian towns like Echuca, Shepparton and Wangaratta, the phrase 'Republic of Marin-e-bek' was written in large, bold capitals. In brackets the name was translated into English as 'The Splendid Land'. Despite this, the English place names Rowan was familiar with only started to appear a hundred kilometres or so north of the Murray River, though it was not named the Murray on the map. Instead, it was called the 'Indi River'. He felt relieved to see that Yass, Goulburn, Cowra, Orange, Bathurst, Wollongong, Sydney and Newcastle all appeared on the map. However there was no national capital city—no Canberra. Puzzled, he looked further south only to find that Melbourne was also absent. In its place was the name 'Dinas Bunjilaka'. To its north-east he noticed that Bendigo was named 'Big Gold Mountain'. South-east of there (uncannily close to Douglas's property) the name 'Dinas Yarkuk' appeared. The nearby English translation read: 'City (or *fortress*) of Quartz'. Immediately west of there was a place called 'Bora Tanderrum'.

Next to the map was a framed A3 photocopy of what looked like a genuine cricket article from the Auckland Star. It covered a recent New Zealand v Australia one day match. For some reason, Douglas had circled the name of long-term New Zealand bowler and tail-end batsmen, 'Daniel MacIntyre', on the scorecard.

Rowan then noticed that the computer screen had locked to a display featuring an unsolved, highly complex, mathematical equation followed by a bright red rectangular dialogue box.

CALCULATE (SELECT) A BETTER OPTION NOW!

Rowan stared at the screen a while then picked up the folder containing the A4 pages and returned to the lounge. Once there, he put it down before making himself another coffee.

After preparing the drink, he opened the manila folder and started to read the stapled A4 document within. The extract began with Isles adapting to convict life in the colony of New South Wales:

> In early 1834 Isles was assigned as a 'labourer' and 'mechanic' to a squatter family that had established a sheep run in the northern foothills of the Snowy Mountains, fifteen miles south-east of what became the township of Yass. The property—which was barely within the borders of the 'nineteen counties' of official white settlement—was on the edge of Ngunnawal and Ngarigo country. Isles arrived at a time of intermittent conflict between the colonists and local Aboriginal tribes. Unfortunately for Isles the squatter he'd been assigned to was a brutal Englishman prone to drunken episodes that frequently culminated in the indiscriminate flogging of his convict charges. Isles—one of ten convicts posted to the squatter during the mid-1830s—observed and sometimes endured the man's brutality for about a year before matters came to a head.
>
> During an uneasy truce between the invaders and a local Aboriginal clan some members of the clan began visiting the property to work, trade or

simply converse with the strange white people who had built odd dwellings on their ancestral lands and who had introduced thousands of sheep to the area. Often the lord and his family were away in Sydney on business—the family owned a home there—and Abraham and the other convicts would barter Aboriginal labour or other services for food, tools, blankets and the like.

One day an old woman and a young woman appeared at the hut. Unbeknownst to both Isles and the squatter—the only white men around at the time—a number of young men were hiding in the trees nearby.

The squatter was already drunk on rum and had begun to argue with Isles about the theft of some of his sheep in the southern part of his property, when he greeted the two Aboriginal women.

According to Isles's diaries, the squatter became aggressive when the old women shielded the young women from his drunken advances. He ordered Isles to keep the women busy with small talk whilst he disappeared for a few minutes. When he returned he was struggling to load a gun and carried rope over one shoulder. Isles discerned his intentions and tried to reason with him—after all the women, as well as other members of the clan, had been visiting the hut for some months without conflict.

Though the gun was not yet fully loaded the squatter began pointing it wildly at Isles and the women all the time cursing his convict for 'defending savages' and for being a 'Highland savage' himself. Luckily rage, and his inebriated state, frustrated his efforts to load the weapon. He did however manage to grab the young woman—only to find himself attacked by the old women. To fend her off, he began kicking her with his heavy stockman's boots.

Isles decided to act. He feared what the man was capable of with a loaded gun. In desperation Isles took a nearby farm-spade and hit the squatter hard across the back. The shocked and infuriated man let go of the young woman and fell heavily, blood oozing from a large cut across his upper back and lower neck. The man's grogginess allowed Isles to wrestle the gun from him.

As the frightened women ran off into the bush the squatter cursed Isles, 'You'll hang for this—I'll see to it! I might even rope you up myself. Maybe some of your convict scum will lend a hand—no loyalty among the sons of whores!'

Isles stood a distance from the squatter, blood pumping, face pale, grasping the unloaded gun as though it were a life buoy.

Complicating the situation, two Aboriginal men suddenly appeared from behind the hut armed with spears. They ignored Isles and headed straight for the squatter who quieted his cursing momentarily once aware of their presence. Isles knew the two Aboriginal men due to their previous visits to the hut. He signalled to the men that he had the situation under control, but the warriors refused to leave. The squatter, now terrified, began to crawl in the direction of the hut all the time cursing Isles and the Aboriginal race.

The younger of the two suddenly leapt behind the

squatter to thrust his spear deep into the white man's back—resulting in its blood-gorged tip appearing between several of the white man's ribs. The poor fellow shrieked eerily after the assault. After several more spear thrusts it was over.

Isles stood paralysed as the men—quickly accompanied by their women—looted the squatter's hut. Every now and then they glanced over at Isles to assess his intentions.

A little later, loaded down with tools, food supplies, clothing and guns, the group prepared to leave. Before departing, however, animated discussion broke out between the four of them. After some sort of decision was reached, the older man approached Isles. In the broken English they'd been trading in for months, he said, 'You want ... come us?'

Isles—slumped over the squatter's gun and pale after vomiting—looked up with tears in his eyes. He paused only a moment, before nodding a tentative 'yes'. [3]

Rowan scanned the rest of the document quickly. Sadly its contents grew increasingly bizarre the further on he read—to the point where by 1851 Isles had become a key figure in the government of a new South-East Australian nation (Marin-e-bek). The new country was dominated by an alliance of indigenous Australians assisted by 'Idealist' Europeans and Chinese. The indigenous alliance, with assistance from its Idealist allies, slowed and eventually reversed, British advances into South Australia and southern New South Wales throughout the 1840s. The discovery of gold north of

[3] Note by the Editor: To peruse the full text of this extract go to the back of this book (in the 'Miscellaneous Documents' section) and read Extract 2: *'Life in the Colony of New South Wales'* from *Abraham Isles and Miriam Hobbes (a biography).*

Melbourne around 1843 further assisted the fledgling state by procuring for its government much needed foreign exchange to fund military activities. Isles's writings and songs were supposedly instrumental in attracting Idealist migrants and in mobilising European opposition to British attempts to seize the entire Australian continent. The author of the extract also detailed meetings between Isles and Darwin, and Isles and Marx that altered their systems of thought in various ways. Douglas's alternative history of 19th century Australia would have been entertaining to read, were it not for the fact that he'd been paying Rowan for many months to write a biography about a fictional man, living in a fictional country, practicing a fictional religion.

Rowan slumped back onto the couch after finishing the extract. On the surface, it struck him as the product of a brilliant but disintegrating mind. At a deeper level, he felt acutely uneasy and had an irrational urge to go and switch off the 'quantum computer' before grabbing all his possessions and leaving. The sense of unreality grew so intense that for a while he found it difficult to even stand up.

He closed his eyes, aware that his palms were sweaty and his heart was pounding. 'The old bastard is playing with my mind. Come on, Rowan, this is a classic delusional system. We'll ring to accept the tutoring position this morning, then pack and clean before leaving the old bugger to his madness.'

After a few minutes, he felt a little calmer. He even found the courage to stand up, return the folder to the study and shut the door behind him. Oddly enough, he felt unable to approach the computer to switch it off.

CHAPTER TWENTY-ONE

THE ECSTASY OF A DIFFERENT GOD

By mid-morning he'd resolved to ask Douglas some questions about the obviously fictitious Abraham Isles. Intricate delusional system or not, Rowan felt he needed some answers. Around 9am he wandered up to the house intent on a last breakfast with Douglas.

To his surprise, it was Rhiannon who greeted him at the door to the barn-house. She immediately invited him in to share breakfast, but Douglas was nowhere to be seen. Apparently, he would meet her in Castlemaine around lunch-time—he had business there and had left immediately after his earlier conversation with Rowan.

'Douglas tells me you've resigned,' Rhiannon said, after they'd settled into two old armchairs on Douglas's upper storey balcony. In front of them on a small table was a spread of hot coffee, a plate of cut fruit, some toast and two bowls of muesli.

'It's a pity he's in Castlemaine—I have a few questions for

him. He finally allowed me to read some of the source material he has on Isles this morning ... we're six months into my contract, mind you.'

Rhiannon was curled up in her armchair with a mug of something resting precariously on one knee, 'Oh, you've seen more than he's ever shown me then ...'

'What do *you* make of it all?'

'What, the Abraham Isles obsession or the stuff about the Orbits and Cauldrons?'

'All of it—alternative Australias, orbits, druidic cauldrons, life among the Koori tribes, quantum computers. He's given me two weird "history" extracts to read—one outlines an *alternative* history of this region. Intricate stuff and quite well researched, though the idea that the Aboriginal tribes in alliance with European radicals might have held off the British military seems, well, extremely fanciful, no matter how much Victorian gold they got their hands on.'

'I'm in no position to judge since I know very little about Australian history.'

'There's other stuff too—a bizarre map, money and a flag representing a non-existent nation. Has he shown you that stuff?' Rowan tried not to sound too dismissive.

'Well he told me he'd found a box belonging to Isles's descendants in a cave complex at the back of the property. I didn't pay too much attention at the time, but he said someone had um ... left it there for him to find.' She curled up defensively in her seat as she spoke—obviously cagey talking about her step-father's more outlandish ideas.

'He meant: *someone from another reality*. Look, obviously he created the objects himself—but for what purpose?'

Rhiannon let out a sigh, 'Douglas is a genius—ask anybody, but he's almost seventy and he's seen a lot in his life time: extreme poverty as a kid growing up in the thirties, the Second

World War—he was only thirteen when it started—and a failed marriage. After the split up, he decided to educate himself, and then … has he told you? … He lost a son, Harry, to the Vietnam War. Harry was barely twenty when he died.'

Rowan felt the blood drain from his face, 'No, he never told me about that.' A dozen pieces of the Douglas puzzle immediately fell into place and he felt disappointed that Douglas hadn't trusted him enough to share the information.

'What about the Koori stuff—his language skills are almost uncanny?'

'That also goes back a long way—to before I was born, actually. A year or two before he left for Vietnam Harry fell in love with Lyn, a Koori girl from up Swan Hill way—they'd met at school. She was pregnant with a girl, my niece, when the war took him.' Rhiannon sounded sad. 'Harry's girlfriend had a very hard time of it after he died—no money, no job, no education and a dead "husband". Douglas helped out. His interest in all things Koori started there, and the Koori community accepted him. After a few years, he began to see things very differently.'

'What things?' asked Rowan.

'Australian history, European denial. He loved his grand-daughter, it was that simple. That politicised him.'

'Where are they now?'

'Lyn is a Koori health worker up Mildura way—a community leader. And Kieran, my niece—though she's close to my age—trained as a pharmacist. She lives in Melbourne these days. Haven't you met them yet? They check in on Douglas every now and then. Lyn is always at him about his smoking, just like me. We'll be seeing Kieran tomorrow. She's meeting us at the hospital.'

'He never told me,' said Rowan.

'He's a bit forgetful these days. Or maybe he didn't want you to know. He never got over Harry's death, so is it such a bad thing that he's become obsessed with other realities—other histories—in his old age? I bet there are things in your past you'd like to change,' she looked down at her mug before taking a sip.

Rowan had a hunch it was a leading question. 'Sure, who wouldn't want to change things about their past,' he said, hesitantly.

'For example?' asked Rhiannon.

Rowan felt ambushed, 'I guess I'd like to change a lot of things about my past—some things more than others.' He took an involuntary deep breath before continuing, 'Firstly, I'd like to have been around for a good friend, Eric, in the days before he committed suicide.' He paused thoughtfully. 'Also, I would like to have treated Anika, my girlfriend at the time, better. I should have placed her ahead of my career as a musician—and I suppose that would have required me to have been creative in a less destructive way.' Rowan went quiet.

'Douglas says you're afraid to fulfil your potential as an innovative musician.'

'I'm afraid alright,' spluttered Rowan, 'afraid that I might hurt people important to me if I give myself over to the scene. Afraid, I guess, that I might become like my father.' He knew he seemed defensive.

'Douglas has a different take. He says, and I quote: "Rowan is in a double bind. He needs to create and perform music, but he fears the impulse. In truth, he's afraid of the transformative power of authentic creativity—afraid of the journey. He's unwilling to embrace the ecstasy of a different god."' Rowan thought he caught a hint of Douglas's mischief in her eyes.

'A different god? Different to what? I don't believe in gods and the only journey I'm taking is a 150km drive back to Melbourne!'

'I don't know. That was all he said on the matter. You know

how enigmatic he can be—I wouldn't take the comments too seriously.'

Rowan massaged his forehead slowly, trying to calm down. Rhiannon, however, had more questions.

'And the third thing?'

'The third thing?' He was still smarting over Douglas's comments.

'That you'd want to change about your past.'

'Oh, that's easy—I wish I'd been raised by a more loving father.'

Rhiannon spoke more quietly, 'Douglas says that one way to deal with the sadness of unfulfilled need is to spend some time imagining better pasts, presents and futures.'

'But his imaginings are a little *too* real for my liking. He's developed a very intricate delusional system.'

Rhiannon stared at him a moment. She seemed about to defend her step-father, but checked her tongue. In that moment, Rowan thought he saw a version of the same slow emotional collapse he'd witnessed in Douglas earlier.

'Do you remember the psychoanalyst Wilhelm Reich?' she eventually asked.

'Yes, he broke away from Freud in the late twenties or early thirties to found the body oriented approach known as "orgone therapy". My D & A worker was a Reichian, he was always on about breaking down character armouring and the like.' Rowan tried to lighten the moment by pretending to be a stiff-jawed action hero but Rhiannon wasn't smiling.

'Do you remember how Reich ended up?' She sounded sad.

'Didn't he end up fighting the US government over his *orgone accumulators*? And I recall he tried to observe *orgone* and dead *orgone*—DOR was it—floating about in the atmosphere.'

'You got it. Things got bizarre. Point is, Reich was a fundamentally good human being—and light years ahead of many modern psychologists. His madness, if we even want to call it that, was that he preferred to locate the causes of human destructiveness in forces *outside* of us—in "Dead Orgone". This cosmic principle explained human actions others blamed on innate 'evil' or 'sin' or the 'Id'. Reich was both a genius and, quite possibly, mad—at least by the end. However, he was *pro-human* mad. To him the core of each human being is authentic and loving—essentially *good*. Reich's "frontier thinking" pushed him beyond both Freud's system and mainstream psychology. I think that something similar has happened to Douglas.'

Rhiannon's theory made him feel even more depressed. If Douglas was indeed delusional, why had Rowan bought into it for so many months?

'I mean for me,' Rhiannon continued, staring pensively in the direction of the hillside, 'the Orbits theory is his theory *start to finish*. I don't understand why he refuses to claim it, trademark it even—it's very innovative. And I don't care where he dredged it up from—his own subconscious, a planet in the Andromeda galaxy, alternative reality land or an invisible friend called Abraham Isles—the fact is, it gives people a useful way of looking at their relationships. The other stuff—on alchemy, the cauldrons, Abraham Isles and Marin-e-bek—well, I don't know.'

'I do know. I think it's all pure fantasy,' said Rowan, feeling angry at his own gullibility.

'I'm not so certain. Recall W.B. Yeats attributed *A Vision*, as well as many of his later poems, to spirits who communicated with him via his wife—she would go into a trance and *voila!* Who am I to call Yeats mad? And surely you know about C.G. Jung— *the dead returned from Jerusalem*, and all that, to give him the system of Analytic Psychology.'

She leant over to butter some toast before continuing, 'We'll see what the tests say. Either way, it's probably good that you've decided to resign. I talked to the accountant the other day and do you know that paying your wage, as well as funding all those avant-garde publishing turkeys Douglas is so fond of, has almost sent him bankrupt?'

Rowan contemplated this bombshell.

'I had no idea—he told me he was being paid by a foreign university.'

'Maybe he was,' she stopped a moment to take a bite of her toast, then proceeded after swallowing, 'but nowhere near enough. As he became more and more obsessed with Isles, a lot of his old publishing work—at least the profitable part of it—started to dry up. His only real income came from the therapy sessions and at his age he can only conduct a few in a week. They exhaust him. He's totally dedicated to his clients.'

'What about the gold?'

'What gold?'

'Down there in the mine.'

Rhiannon looked puzzled.

'That day you did the alchemy-druid presentation ... Douglas let me wander down the tunnels. There was gold in the tunnel walls.'

'Oh yes, he said he occasionally finds nuggets down there—calls them "gifts of the Quartz Lizard"—but not enough to put the accounts into the black. He thinks the quartz is more important than the gold and doesn't like to "disturb" it too much.'

Rowan felt foolish and defeated. Out of the blue, he asked Rhiannon, 'Do you think I'm a good person?'

She looked at him gently before answering, 'Yes, I think you're a good person, but you need to look after yourself.'

Her words sounded so genuine that he had to fight back unexpected tears.

'That's true, I'm not in a great place at the moment. I know it's the right thing to quit the job, but I have nothing to return to in Melbourne—no wife, no real job ... just casual stuff ... and no accommodation of my own.' He knew he sounded pathetic.

'You'll come through—Douglas also thinks you're a good person.'

She took some red grapes from the plate before swivelling to get a better look at something that had caught her attention outside.

'What do you see up there?'

'Something large—moving under those gums.' She was focused on a spot further up the hillside. A moment later, on a whim it seemed, she said, 'You know, I sometimes think that Douglas would die happy if he could just once hear the music.'

'Hear what music?'

'Isles's music ... He talks about it all the time—like it's the gateway to the promised land.'

Rowan focused on the cause of the movement up the hill, 'That's a huge kangaroo up there ... the size of a very tall man. Amazing! And it looks like it's waiting for someone or something.'

Together they stared at the beast for a while before Rhiannon settled into her armchair, 'Delusional, fictional or factual, he *really* wants to hear someone sing Isles's songs—even a couple of them.'

'You're right—I think they signify spiritual transcendence and peace to him.'

'That's Douglas for you, always in search of the caduceus of Hermes, the Grail or the Philosopher's Stone—the *something* that allows us to transcend the unfairness of life.' She placed her empty cup on the table between them—it seemed to indicate that the conversation was ending. He had one more question however.

'Why is he so obsessed with bloody cricket?'

Rhiannon hesitated a long time before answering, 'Harry was a very good cricketer. He could have played professionally — instead he signed up for the Vietnam War.'

Rowan made an involuntary whistling sound — did Douglas see him as a kind of substitute for Harry? The possibility didn't bear thinking about.

'You're right,' Rhiannon said after a while, 'that is a huge kangaroo up there. But what exactly is he waiting for?'

CHAPTER TWENTY-TWO

THE LINE BETWEEN HERE AND THERE
(Wednesday, February 12th 1997)

It was six days before Rowan found the energy to pack his things and return to Melbourne. For a while after Douglas's departure, he lounged around the hut reading whilst a fan blew warm air over his body. He'd taken to browsing Jung's three books on alchemy—strangely enough the notion of the alchemical *nigredo*, as transformed by Jung into a kind of spiritual Dark Night of the Soul, comforted him somewhat. A couple of days later, he decided to open the old, blue suitcase to have another look at his old *Interstitium* band paraphernalia. After spending a couple of hours listening to the old recordings—jam sessions, interviews, etc.—he started poring over posters, news clippings, and, in the end, photograph albums. The photographs brought back painful memories as well as regret—especially the photographs of himself with his friend, Eric, and with Anika.

As the days piled up, he knew he was obsessing overly about

the mistakes of his past and he felt sluggish and indecisive. Although he was moving back to Melbourne, he couldn't find the energy to look for a place to live. An irrational part of him imagined that Kerryn would put him up for a week or two—though he hadn't phoned her to ask. Besides, she had a new life now. In the end, he decided it would be better to live with his mother for a few days—a different kind of defeat.

The morning of his planned departure for Melbourne proved to be a scorcher. He was sweating as he loaded up the blue Falcon with books and boxes—the car, at least, was properly serviced due to his months on a good income. He was returning to Melbourne with a good bank balance. *How like my father that is*, he thought, as he threw the last bag of clothes in the back of the car.

His decision to leave had been quickened by the fact that the hut's solar batteries were going flat. The fan stopped working mid-morning, soon after the fridge. To remedy the situation, he knew he'd have to drive into Harcourt to buy some petrol. He'd then have to trudge up the hill to start the generator—the effort required seemed beyond him. He hadn't shaved or combed his hair now for a week and, in his more lucid moments, he was certain he was clinically depressed.

As he cleaned out the fridge for the last time, he realised he'd left the computer on in the other room for almost a week. He willed himself to enter the study to switch it off—it had become a symbol of Douglas's mind-games. Once in the study, however, he felt angry at Douglas and pressed a key to bring the machine out of hibernation. The red dialogue box was still on screen. On a rebellious impulse, he defiantly clicked the box and left the room with the machine still on.

CALCULATE (SELECT) A BETTER OPTION NOW!

The power will run out soon anyway—and so what if Douglas finds out! Rowan thought.

After wandering back into the lounge, he noticed movement out the window of the main room. A group of people in colourful clothes were walking up the hill, possibly heading for the clochan or the state forest behind the block. Rowan wandered outside and paused for a moment under the veranda. Although the sunrise was making it difficult to see who the intruders were, he thought he saw an older, stocky woman and three younger figures, all female and all Aboriginal. One of the figures looked like a young girl, the other two were tall and thin, probably teenagers or perhaps young adults. Rowan felt his pulse race irrationally—they had a weird aura about them, something to do with the way the sunrise gave them large shadows that almost reached back to the hut, or perhaps it was to do with the graceful, almost floating, way they walked. Similarly, he suspected they were already aware of his presence, though none turned around to look at him.

Rowan steadied himself. What were they doing trespassing on the property so early in the morning? He resolved to follow them. If they were trespassers, he had to let Douglas or Rhiannon know. Feeling he needed a story should they prove legitimate, he decided to put on his shorts and pretend he was going for a swim in the back dam. It was so hot and humid that it seemed like a good thing to do anyway—before hitting the road. He changed quickly, grabbed a towel and nonchalantly pursued the women, who by then had wandered over the hill and out of view.

As he walked, he found his mind racing. Despite the

inventiveness of the trumped up article on Isles, everything in it helped explain Douglas's actions over the past six or so months: the mysticism and alchemy, the texts on Celtic revivalism, the language studies, perhaps even the cricket. Unfortunately, it all made sense — at least to an old man slowly losing his grip on reality.

Had Douglas convinced himself that Rowan was about to 'cross-over' in some shape or form to an alternative reality? The thought froze in the thinking — making Rowan shiver. As he walked, he realised that he couldn't throw off a sense that something was about to happen. The landscape seemed surreal, feverishly heightening his senses — it was as though the trees, the soil, the sky, the boulders all around, even the sun as it climbed the heavens, were aware of his every movement and thought. The boundaries between his existence and theirs seemed to be crumbling. He walked a little faster to ward off his unease.

He was sweating profusely as he reached the trees and large boulders at the hill's crest. Shielding his eyes with his hand to reduce the glare, he searched for the four women. They'd halted among large boulders half way down the hill and were sitting in a circle sharing food. One of the two younger Aboriginal women saw Rowan and spoke to her mother at which point all four turned to look directly at him.

The way they stared, however, made him uneasy — they seemed to be looking straight through him, but he also felt they were waiting for him in some way. None spoke a word as he clambered down the hillside intent on asking them why they were on Douglas's block.

As he approached, he noticed that no one in the group was actually following his movements, instead they stared fixedly up hill at the place they'd first spied him. As he drew level with them, he saw that they were seated on rocks beside a small cave entrance formed by two of the largest boulders. The boulder formation was about twenty metres off the path. The sun's glare was less intense from this angle, but something about the scene gave Rowan the creeps. The clothing worn by the group members was ornate, almost African in appearance—graceful wrap-around dresses coloured dark red or dark green, featuring designs he'd never seen before.

'I'm Rowan—a guest of Douglas's. He's the owner of this block of land,' Rowan stood directly opposite the older women who sat cross-legged on a large flat rock. She looked to be in her fifties. She turned slowly to stare at him—as if she wasn't quite sure he was really there.

None of the group spoke, but they all followed her gaze. After a moment, four faces were staring directly at him.

'I was about to take my morning swim,' he pointed to his towel, 'when I noticed you all—do you know this is private property?'

One of the younger women, the one to Rowan's immediate left, giggled nervously—this set the young girl off too.

'He knows us,' said the older woman, as if through an echo machine 'and he doesn't mind, never has—says it's our land anyway. You have your swim, Mister. We'll be off into the forest before you know it.'

Rowan felt a little silly; obviously they were friends of Douglas, perhaps they were even engaged in secret women's business and thus resented his presence. He stammered an apology, 'I'm sorry, he never mentioned you. I'll just have my swim and leave you to it.'

Again the girl on the left giggled nervously as she stared at Rowan. The older woman, however, didn't respond to his apology, instead, she began humming in a low voice—which silenced the youngsters.

Rowan now felt he had to actually go for a swim—he didn't

want them to think he'd followed them and spied on them, especially if they really were friendly with Douglas. Besides, the older woman had an aura about her that he wanted to avoid. He knew that his sense of reality had slipped a cog or two over the past week. The Aboriginal visitors were only heightening the sense of slippage—though his reasoning told him they couldn't possibly be the cause.

Maybe a swim in the cool water of the dam would help him compose himself before leaving the property for good. As he walked, a front of low clouds suddenly obscured the sun. The towel around his neck rubbed aggressively against skin already chapped raw from weeks of sunburn and sweating linked to the endless cricket sessions. Likewise, the dry February grasses that occasionally scraped against his calves and ankles irritated him no end. The landscape, if anything, seemed even more animated and expectant after his conversation with the Aboriginal woman. He thought for a moment about Douglas's belief that everything in nature possesses its own unique mode of communicating with human beings. The idea only made him more anxious, so to calm himself down he began singing the chorus to an old *Interstitium* song: 'Medicine man go fly to the clouds/ Medicine man go speak with the spirits.'

The dam was situated in a small valley close to the state forest. It was sealed off from surrounding paddocks by a rectangular fence with a retractable gate, which Rowan pushed through on the way to the water's edge. The grass here was shorter.

Rowan reached the dam and noted the appearance of a full-blown headache, concentrated in a band emanating from over his right temple. He couldn't shake the feeling that something unusual was unfolding.

He stopped beside a gigantic old redgum tree to the right of the dam and proceeded to take off his t-shirt and thongs. From this angle the dam appeared as a vast murky brown sheet of water all but merging with the northern horizon. He estimated that at its deepest part it might be 15 or more feet deep. The clouds overhead thickened as he took a series of deep breaths. He wondered whether he should risk another glance up the hill to see if the women were watching him—part of him didn't want to risk a swim, the water seemed muddy after the recent rains, perhaps it was full of leeches and other creatures—huge, mythological king-brown, red-belly or tiger snakes. He knew snakes could swim. Then there was the possibility that car wrecks loomed just under the water line—in the old days many farmers dumped old cars and other rubbish in dams for want of a local tip.

Impulsively, he shot a glance back up the hillside and was shocked to see that the group of women had spread out across the hillside and were descending on the dam—or more likely the gate to the state forest—from various angles. The oldest, Rowan noted, was walking down the path straight towards him (the child in front of her as she walked). The other two were positioned fifty or so metres to her left and right. They all moved with a slow graceful, float-walk. All were about to converge on the dam's gate. Rowan felt panicky and decided in that instant to enter the water—he had to get a grip of himself. Perhaps he was dehydrated—the last three days had been very hot, high thirties to low forties, and under such circumstances his body usually began to malfunction. Or perhaps he was experiencing the early stages of some kind of physical illness, the flu perhaps or food poisoning, or something worse.

His headache grew stronger as he paddled tentatively, deeper into the water. Thick mud oozed between his toes and he imagined gigantic yabbies prodding his pinkish flesh as huge leeches sucked his blood.

The thumping sensation in his right forehead intensified and he felt strange sensations—gravel then grass scraping slowly across the right half of his face. His right arm also twitched disturbingly and he felt more and more disoriented and groggy. He heard something move directly behind him and turned to confront a huge grey kangaroo as it hopped into view from behind the dam wall not fifteen metres away. It stopped abruptly, then stood upright on its tail and hind legs, close to the gnarled redgum tree. It seemed aware of Rowan, who suddenly noticed a sign nailed to the bough of the tree. It said simply: UNIVERSITY THIS WAY.

Rowan felt hemmed in on all sides. The water around him was cool and he concentrated on this sensation as a means to calm the paranoia engulfing him. Uncomfortable with the feel of the mud between his toes, he decided to immerse himself in the colder, deeper water and on impulse dived in head first.

Calmed somewhat, he began to swim in the direction of a wooden platform at the centre of the dam — from there he could take a breather until the women passed.

At first the colder water felt good — the head pains retreated as the cool shock of dam water reduced his core body temperature. Perhaps the problem really was heat induced dehydration.

However, about ten metres from the platform, he felt first one calf, then the other, succumb to cramp. Painful sensations shot through his legs and he had to roll over on his back to try and deal with them. The action, however, made the sensations of gravel and grass return in full force and he had flashes of himself turning over and over … in the water … or was it in a field? And an injury to the head, and voices — panicky voices. Topsy-turvy, over and over in the water. In the grass? In a field? The spasms of pain worsened, and his right arm buckling, and the low-hung rain clouds and muggy air … earth, sky, water, sky … over and over … He tried to use his arms to paddle to the platform, but his right arm wasn't working properly, and besides there was no water, just grass, green grass, and sickening vertigo. He felt himself vomit … into the water? Into the long, green grass? Then everything went still, silent, blank as he slipped into unconsciousness.

BOOK TWO

PART ONE: DINAS YARKUK (THE CITY OF QUARTZ)

INTERSTITIUM

A dream realm, perhaps—though usually he is not asleep. Rather, a place—an interstitium—between infinite possible worlds, universes. And each world launched by a given life option chosen at a given moment in time. Each nurtured in the place of Emergence, the place of the World Tree—bright organism that encompasses all possible worlds. In the interstitium, created and uncreated worlds crowd together under one vast space-time continuum—each exhibits a desire for plenitude.

But is Rowan capable of choice, or is someone or something choosing for him? The Government of Souls perhaps? Is the heavy burden of the incomplete—of regret and guilt and thwarted desire, loading, skewing, weighting the outcome? The Hindus would speak of Karma—a force drawing him, like a magnet draws metal, to a particular world, destiny, set of limitations. He moves only gradually over many days and weeks, from the place of Emergence—the Tree Place, the place of eternal branchings—to a solid world, a world different to the world he knew prior to the accident.

He weathers the uncertainty, the periods of moving to and fro, back and forth between worlds. Some days he is pulled backwards, sometimes violently—usually in the evenings, in the hospital, on the edge of sleep—to the place of Emergence, of endings and beginnings, annihilations and creations. A strange place—he half believes it death—a crevice between worlds. In the interstitium everything is clear—he observes all the intricate patterns and possibilities of any number of personal destinies. His life appears as a network of all his possible pasts, all his possible futures. Each destiny glows in a vast abyss containing many other destinies—though sometimes he perceives infinite frequencies and channels instead. Curiosity makes him want to explore these worlds, though when he snatches randomly at a destiny or fate, he always hears the same nurses and doctors speaking, and feels them tending to his injuries and bodily needs.

For weeks after coming out of the coma, he is aware of a certain thinness—a certain insubstantiality—to the world he's been drawn to. Perhaps the gateway between worlds wasn't properly shut—the world of Melbourne and Adelaide, of Sir Donald Bradman and Banjo Patterson, sometimes threatens to overwhelm the world of Marin-e-bek, Bunjilaka City and Dinas Yarkuk, a world in which Abraham Isles is a national hero. A physicist would theorise that Rowan is experiencing periods of 'ontological leaching'—specific simultaneous realities are merging in some way.

Sometimes, in the middle of simple tasks—whilst eating or drinking—he is forced to stop and take a deep breath. The old world appears super-imposed for a moment on the new, solid world he now inhabits. Double exposure! Vertigo! Dizziness! Nausea! Rowan observes Rowan attempting a different task in a different dimension. The other self, familiar but steadily more distant manifests as a ghost-self, a self behind a white sheet or tarpaulin, a self restrained by a thin but effective barrier. Double exposure! Vertigo! Dizziness! Nausea! Though just as quickly, that other self melts to nothingness. Vacuum sucked — into and back — to the receding world, the receding Rowan … Only stray mind-ons, psitrons, neutrinos remain — he clings to them as a sailor clings to shipwreck debris, all abob on a storm-grey ocean.

He emerges, he is emerging, as Rowan Sweeney — academic, former international cricketer and the author of a forthcoming book on Abraham Isles and Miriam Hobbes.

CHAPTER TWENTY-THREE

AWAKE IN A BRIGHT NEW REALITY
(Monday, Feb 24th 1997)

'Are you okay if I speak in English?' said the male Koori doctor, 'My English is a little basic, but it says here that it's your main language.' Rowan noticed a female nurse, also Koori, standing beside the doctor.

Rowan nodded tentatively, but thought: *What an odd question.* He had come to wearing a neck brace—the right side of his head felt swollen and numb. As the doctor talked, he was aware that he was seated upright, though with neck support, in a special chair close to his hospital bed. He was also aware of a dull pain in his right arm, which he noticed was in a sling and a cast. Behind the doctor's left shoulder Rowan noticed a large painting of rock art images—the reds, yellows, ochres and gentle orange pigments of the weathered rock seemed strangely comforting and soothing to him.

For the next ten minutes or so the doctor put him through a series of exercises and tests. For example, he was asked to grab the doctor's fingers and squeeze hard, also to bend each leg in turn up almost to his chest before pushing hard against the doctor's hand. There was also a reflex test and ice was applied to his ankles, knees and hips to test Rowan knew not what bodily functions.

After he'd finished, the doctor stepped back, wiped his hands with a white towel and smiled. He then gestured to the nurse who produced a small data entry device.

'Now that you're conscious, we'll need to run a few more neurological tests: a CAT scan, another MRI scan, some brain-functioning tests, etc. We're just checking to make sure there aren't any hidden issues—infections, cognitive deficits or memory loss—now that you're out of coma. On the whole though, I think you've come through all this remarkably well, given you've been unconscious for two weeks and weren't wearing a helmet at the time of the accident. We've had you on steroids to reduce brain swelling.'

Rowan was having trouble connecting what the doctor was saying to his own understanding of his memories.

'Last thing I remember, I was swimming in a dam.' He spoke slowly, with a slight slur—perhaps due to the accident or perhaps due to medication, 'I felt a cramp, in my calves, and then the sensation of rolling over and over in the water. Or was it a field? That's odd ...'

'It *was* a field—close to rice paddies—in the mountains of northern Vietnam. Not far from Sapa—you had a motorcycle accident. Do you remember? You've been unconscious for two weeks. The university organised to have you flown home a week ago, your insurance company covered the cost.' The doctor spoke slowly, allowing Rowan to take things in at his own pace.

Rowan didn't remember traveling to Vietnam or riding a motorcycle, but he did recall a scraping, lacerating sensation across his face—tarmac then grass and earth, and excruciating pain in his right arm.

'Well, you've certainly had some odd things to say as you've been coming out of the coma,' continued the doctor, 'But audio hallucinations and vivid dreams are not unusual under the circumstances—at times you may feel psychologically disoriented. In fact, given the shock of the accident to your brain and nervous system, we may expect this kind of phenomena to continue for a few days or even weeks yet. You may also experience some memory problems—partial amnesia accompanied by scrambled memories and associations.' He paused, not wanting to overwhelm Rowan. After a moment, he turned to the nurse beside him and said something in a language Rowan didn't understand. The woman immediately set to work changing the dressing on Rowan's head wound.

'The nurse will change this dressing for you, plus we'll need to give you a different neck brace now that you're awake and partially mobile.'

'I don't remember Vietnam at all,' said Rowan, as much to himself as to the doctor. As he spoke, he rubbed the cast on his injured shoulder with his other hand, 'and I never ride motorcycles.'

'It's hard to get an injury like this swimming in a dam. As I said, there may be some memory loss for a while. You're still on anti-inflammatories for the shoulder injury, and this morning, after you woke up, we added pain-killers—the combination may make you drowsy.'

He winced as the nurse changed his head dressing. She'd turned his face toward a small hospital window on the right. Though the curtains obscured much of the view, he did notice that the building opposite looked circular in design. The exterior walls, going up many levels, were painted with colourful Aboriginal designs. It looked like no hospital he'd ever seen in Victoria.

'Am I in Melbourne or Bendigo?'

'The doctor paused for a moment and exchanged puzzled glances with the nurse, 'Neither of those places—you're at a hospital on the outskirts of Big Gold Mountain ... not far from Dinas Yarkuk or, in English, The City of Quartz—you'll be transferred to a rehabilitation centre there in coming days. You're a teacher and a researcher at the university there—do you remember that?'

Rowan felt his heart beat quicken, 'I recently finished my PhD. There was a man who employed me to teach and research, but I don't remember working at a university.' Rowan felt the hairs on the back of his neck stand up. Nothing made sense. He noticed the doctor and the nurse looking a little alarmed.

'We're in Victoria right?'

'Well, from our records you're a citizen of Marin-e-bek and a permanent resident of New Albion. You lived in Marin-e-bek as a child, but your parents migrated to New Albion in 1977. You returned to Marin-e-bek to play international cricket from 1986 to 1990. However, in 1991 you returned, once again, to New Albion—to Sydney actually, to study. That was a year after the end of your international cricket career.'

'I only ever played cricket at school ... except for a few seasons. Marin-e-bek? Where ... *what* exactly is Marin-e-bek? My family live in Australia. I'm an Australian.'

'You have a Get Well card over there from your father and sister who live in Sydney. Sadly your mother died some years ago in a car accident. Sydney is the capital of New Albion.'

'No, not Sydney—mum lives in Geelong and dad, for what he's worth, lives in Queensland these days—on the Sunshine Coast. They've been separated since I was young.'

'As I said, there will be some scrambled thinking for a while. How old do you think you are?'

'I'm 33. I was born in February 1964.'

'That's also what my records say—see, all is not lost!' The man looked relieved.

Suddenly Rowan was aware of vague memories of young adult years spent in Sydney. They were less vivid than his Victoria memories from around the same age, but the fact they existed at all confused him.

'When will I be able to see my, er … father?' Rowan struggled to calm himself and process what he was being told. He didn't want to upset the doctor and nurse, who seemed friendly.

'He's been informed of your accident, but has been unable to cross the Marin-e-bek/New Albion border. It's closed at present, but don't worry, I'm sure they'll open it again soon. The political situation has deteriorated while you've been in Vietnam.'

With each new piece of information, he felt more anxious. Perhaps it was best to relax, even to sleep, and let the healing process take its course.

'Okay, I'll leave you in the capable hands of the nurses— all being well you'll be transferred to the rehabilitation centre at Dinas Yarkuk in a few days. The centre has an excellent medical clinic.'

Rowan startled again at the strange name.

'Also, Lionel, from the university's Board of Elders, wants to see you as soon as you're able. Apparently he lectures with you in the Religious Studies department. He's very concerned about your health—as is a young lady by the name of Imogen Bright.' The doctor winked, but declined to elaborate. 'You're supposed to be teaching classes in a few weeks, but I'll be telling them more like a few months. And you're writing an important book. Obviously you'll need a functional memory for all of that.'

Some part of Rowan, even in his groggy state, realised something was radically wrong. He felt himself floating for a moment up near the ceiling—looking down on the scene with perplexed terror. Another, less dominant part, however, seemed perfectly at ease with the situation. The memories of Sydney were associated with that part.

'Are you okay?' The doctor stooped closer reaching for Rowan's left wrist to check his pulse.

'Yes, I'm okay. I'm just trying to take things in. I think you're right, I'm having a few memory problems.'

'And that can sometimes create a sense of what we call *derealisation*—when we don't know aspects of our self, when we have to take aspects of our identity on trust. It's a common experience after traumatic accidents. Luckily the memories usually return—albeit gradually. The psychologist at Dinas Yarkuk will help you—after all we don't want you to lose all those cricket memories, do we?'

Obviously, Rowan was known as a cricketer here. Perhaps the reason Douglas had been training him for months. It was all too fantastic to take in.

The doctor backed away slowly and said something to the nurse. This time Rowan recognised the language, it was something like the Pan-Koori conglomeration Douglas had tried to teach him. But had he really known a Douglas on a block of land in central Victoria?

'I think you need to get some sleep,' said the doctor,' the memory recall process is making you anxious. There's no pushing this—the memories will reconnect in their own good time. I've decided to up the tranquillizer component of your medicine for a little while to reduce your distress. I'll check in again later this afternoon.'

CHAPTER TWENTY-FOUR

WHO IS IT ENTERS THROUGH THE GATES OF TIME?

The neurological and psychological tests took up most of the afternoon and some of the results weren't due until the following morning. The psychological tests proved most troubling—he was easily confused and his anxiety at the mismatch between his memories and reality had not abated. There was also a delay in the administration of the psychological tests, since a government psychologist, Ms Abella Lapierre, had to be brought in at the last minute. Rowan felt tired before she even started.

Ms Lapierre was a friendly and competent forty-something woman with large eyes and a distinct French accent, though she spoke impeccable English throughout the session. She took down his description of his life as an early career academic with growing solemnity, even asked him to elaborate on what he thought he would be teaching and where he'd studied towards his PhD before he clammed up. His research topic also interested her. 'You're writing a book on Abraham Isles, the Adamantine Wizard, and his wife Miriam Hobbes? They're important figures in early Marin history.'

At least she's familiar with their names, thought Rowan, surprised that Hobbes appeared to be of equal importance.

'Well', she said brightly, upon completing her tests, 'a bit of a fruit-salad in there due to the accident, but the main scaffolding of your life is in place. You are indeed an academic named Rowan Sweeney, you were born in 1964 and you are conducting research into Abraham Isles *and* Miriam Hobbes. A good start, but from there things go a bit awry. Some of your life details don't match up. You didn't study toward your PhD at 'Melbourne', wherever that is, you studied at Sydney, and you didn't almost drown in a dam owned by Douglas Green, you had a motorcycle accident in Vietnam.' She leant back to look more closely at the test results sprawled out in front of her on a table.

In terms of brain and nervous system functioning, she found no significant impairment—his language skills, in English anyway, were normal; reflex and general motor responses were also normal; general intellectual functioning was almost normal. The only significant issues were symptoms related to partial amnesia and mild identity confusion/dissociation— which she believed were triggering anxiety attacks that could turn into full blown panic attacks if untreated. Like the hospital doctor, she thus recommended anti-anxiety medication.

Near the end of their discussion, however, she paused for a moment as if pondering something.

'There's one other thing I'd like to have checked. There's a spiritual counsellor situated in Dinas Yarkuk—he works with me now and then. You might know him: Lionel Wirrarap?'

The name Lionel rang a bell for Rowan, 'I'm supposed to meet with a university representative named Lionel today or tomorrow. Apparently he teaches with me in the, er ... Religious Studies department at Dinas Yarkuk.'

'He might be the same person! Look, he may have an interesting perspective on your identity confusion problem. Let's hear what he has to say—he may recommend some other treatment options.'

As Rowan sat outside in the late afternoon sunshine—the television in the day room only added to his anxiety—he tried to assess his situation. He hadn't told the psychologist the half of it. After answering a few questions about his life he'd clamped up—unwilling to reveal anything else until he knew more. However fantastic and implausible it seemed, it was clear that he possessed the memories of two distinct people. Just as disturbingly, all the evidence seemed to suggest that he'd woken up in an alternative reality.

The Australia he'd known didn't appear to exist. In its place were five nations—two to the north, one to the north-west, one to the west and Marin-e-bek itself, a country encompassing Tasmania, Victoria, and bits of South Australia and southern New South Wales, from Rowan's reality. He felt waves of vertigo every time he contemplated this new situation.

A little later a nurse came to wheel him inside. On a whim, he asked if he could have a go at standing up.

The nurse called for another nurse and together they helped Rowan to his feet. 'You haven't lost too much muscle tone over the past two weeks—nevertheless, let's do it slowly. We don't want you hurting yourself.'

Though he felt weak and dizzy he managed to stand up with assistance.'Good—very good! Now, can you keep standing without us helping you?'

He succeeded for several minutes before nausea kicked in and he felt like vomiting. Once back in the wheelchair, he noticed that his legs and lower abdomen were trembling violently—like he'd just run a marathon.

The various medications helped him sleep that night, though he was haunted by a repetitive dream involving another version of himself. His dream-self sat cross-legged but gracefully upright on a wooden deck at sunset among the boulder formations at the back of Douglas's property. He was naked from the waist up. As Rowan approached the deck, his dream-self began an impressive sequence of yoga-like postures. He seemed to panic, however, when Rowan approached the deck, refusing to look up and desperately increasing the speed of the postural sequence. As Rowan moved closer still, his dream-self made a stop sign with one hand and said in English: 'Don't come any closer!' The hand was covered in blood. 'My burden!' said the dream-self, also staring at the bloody hand. The dream ended with the other self staring at someone or something further up the hillside before turning back to Rowan and saying, 'Don't tell my family that I tried to kill myself on that road—it would break their hearts.'

Rowan woke early the next morning feeling groggy, but hungry for some breakfast—cereal slop designed to get his intestines working. The nurses also wanted him to try showering unassisted.

As he stepped out of the shower and reached for a towel, he was taken aback by the image of himself in the bathroom mirror. On the whole the Rowan staring back at him was identical to the Rowan he'd always known—broad-shouldered, of medium build, slightly above average height and sporting longish brown-black hair. The large scar on his face, however, was new, likewise the plethora of bruises all over his body. He also had numerous Celtic tattoos engraved on his chest, belly and back. The tattoos were mostly coloured green, red, yellow and black and featured circles, spirals, stylised animals and planets. He also noticed a number of enigmatic Koori designs. He approached the mirror to examine a large circular tattoo covering his stomach—the tattoo depicted Isles's entire 'System of the Orbits' in miniature.

He moved back from the mirror fighting a sense of vertigo. It was as though Douglas's crazy neo-druidic ideas had been branded all over his skin. The tattoos confirmed the other self's devotion to Isles's spiritual system. The idea of himself as a religious person made him anxious. He turned away from the mirror abruptly struggling to comprehend what was going on. Imagining himself as the other Rowan turned out to be the best way to calm his jagged nerves.

Later that morning the male doctor of the previous day arrived with good news about the outstanding test results. Though Rowan didn't understand the terminology, he gathered that all being well—after only another day or two of observation—he'd be transferred to a rehabilitation centre close to the hospital.

After checking a few specific things, the doctor asked Rowan whether he felt up to receiving some visitors. 'Lionel Karrapgundidg (also known as 'Whirrarap') and Imogen Bright are here from the university—they're colleagues of yours, I believe. I've told them you may have difficulties with memory and that today they may only visit you for half an hour. Are you up to it?'

The thought of meeting two people who supposedly knew him made him immediately anxious.

'I could ask them to come back tomorrow if you wish?'

Rowan took a deep breath, 'No, I'll be okay—so long as they understand my condition.'

'I'll explain—but I think it's important for you to meet Lionel, in particular, soon, given the university's medical staff will be monitoring you once you're back in Dinas Yarkuk. Also, Lionel works a day a week in their counseling wing.'

The doctor then spoke in Pan-Koori to the nurse before

leaving the room. A few minutes later an older Aboriginal man entered the room. The man was balding, of small build and with heavily tattooed forearms and biceps. He wore a simple collared, burgundy shirt and black slacks and carried a bundle of carefully arranged eucalyptus leaves and a small wooden vessel with two reed straws. He was followed by a dark-haired twenty-something woman dressed casually in a brown skirt and black t-shirt. Rowan suspected that they didn't know each other well since they sat opposite each other at the foot of his bed.

Only after the man had deposited his foliage and cup, and sat down, did he make any effort to look at Rowan. The woman, however, kept glancing at him and almost tripped whilst placing her seat as a consequence.

'Hi, Rowan' she said tentatively, 'my God you've been bashed about a bit! The doctor says you might have a few problems putting names to faces, even familiar faces.'

Lionel, who had his palms pressed together beneath his chin, looked inscrutable.

'Do you know who I am?' the young woman asked gently. Rowan noticed that she had a thinnish face with perceptive green eyes.

'I've been told you're Imogen and you work at the university,' Rowan said, trying to be friendly. 'I vaguely remember you, but my brain is a little scrambled.' There was something about her manner that seemed familiar, even comforting.

'You may only have met Lionel once or twice—he was overseas on study leave for most of last year. Isn't that right, Lionel?' Imogen seemed to want Lionel to take over. Instead, he said something in Pan-Koori that Rowan didn't understand and watched for Rowan's response.

'Lionel says he prefers not to speak in English. He says you met him when you first took up the research post and have been in regular contact since then. He also says that although his real name is Lionel Karrapgundidg—literally 'Man of Quartz'—you can call him Whirrarap like everyone else does.' Rowan detected that the presence of the older scholar was making Imogen choose her words carefully. She seemed to be trying to convey both intimacy and academic professionalism. She looked again at Whirrarap and he nodded, perhaps content with her translation.

'How are you feeling?' she asked.

'The doctor has given me a clean bill of health—well apart from the cast, the dizziness when I stand up, the scar on my head and billions of scrambled brain-cells.'

Rowan noticed the old man grin a little and had to junk his assessment that he was moody and overly serious.

'No permanent damage then—that's great news! I'll tell all the staff in the Religious and Cultural Studies department when I get back this afternoon. They're all asking after you— even Karujin, the groundsman, who asked me to tell you, and I quote: "Hope that bang on the head makes him realise what he's been missing out on as an international cricketer!" He's anxious to hear about the prognosis for your bowling arm.' Imogen laughed musically then paused before surveying the room, and then the view outside. Rowan suspected she was searching for things to talk about. Lionel, on the other hand, sat quietly, observing Rowan.

'I'm glad you're doing so well,' said Imogen, looking back at him, 'and I hope that all your memories become unscrambled very soon.' The last statement suggested she had a personal interest in his memories. 'The doctor says you may even be back teaching in a month or so. That'll make the Dean happy—he's had to employ a tutor to deliver the early lectures for your first semester unit.' She paused and began fumbling nervously with some of the bracelets and bangles around her left wrist. Rowan suspected she was from New Albion rather than Marin-e-bek—

though he didn't know where this information came from.

As she fumbled, Whirrarap stood up without speaking and wandered over to the small white medicine basket beside Rowan's bed. He picked up the packet of anti-anxiety tablets and began reading the label. Imogen watched him, perhaps— Rowan mused—hoping he'd speak more freely instead of making everyone feel uncomfortable with his quietness. Moments later, he obliged.

'These … they take time to work,' he said in English, 'should be used for a short time only. There are better ways to help you adjust.' He shook the box as he spoke. 'Here, have a drink of this.' He offered Rowan the wooden cup and straw.

'I'm fine, thank you—I'm not very thirsty.'

'It's not poison. Look, I'll drink first,' said Whirrarap, before taking a sip.

Not wanting to appear impolite, Rowan accepted. It turned out to be water.

'Marin-a-wyhne-yer-am!' said Whirrarap, placing the box of medication back in its basket and returning to his seat.

Rowan looked blank.

'I hope you enjoyed "the splendid water!"' said Whirrarap in English.

Imogen broke in, 'Well, Rowan, the doctor says you get tired easy at the moment so I'll return another day. Maybe once they've moved you to the rehabilitation centre.' She stood up and walked a step or two closer to the bed before bending over to hug him and whisper: *'You look after yourself, okay? Do what the doctor's ask. We'll talk soon.'* She then left the room.

He'd enjoyed her physical closeness—and she was attractive and self-confident. He suspected, given her manner, that they were either lovers or were close to being lovers—though, inexplicably, a part of him was aware of deeper waters.

Lionel seemed to assess Rowan's response to Imogen's hug. Having made up his mind about something, he leant back in his chair, becoming inscrutable all over again.

'Is there something you need to er … tell me, Lionel?'

'I prefer not to talk in English; my main languages are Koori and French. Apparently these two languages are a problem for you right now. Have you forgotten them?'

Was Lionel conducting some kind of examination—maybe assessing how long it might take for Rowan to recover enough to teach?

'My English has returned the fastest. I'm able to comprehend French and Pan-Koori, but people have to speak slowly,' Rowan said in broken French.

'When I first met you, you were very fluent in Pan-Koori—you sounded like a native speaker.' Lionel was speaking slowly in Pan-Koori now.

Rowan couldn't think of anything to say in response, besides, the thought of using the Pan-Koori language only highlighted his predicament. His anxiety was on the verge of escalating into a panic attack. After sitting there in silence for a minute or so, Lionel's mood changed. He stood up quietly and shifted his seat closer to the top end of Rowan's bed before sitting down and putting both his hands over Rowan's uninjured left hand. The gesture was so simple and sympathetic that tears welled in Rowan's eyes.

Eventually Whirrarap stood up and said in English, 'I'll visit you at the rehabilitation centre. Once you're feeling better we'll talk about how far along you are with the Isles project. I'll be supervising your research now—right through to the publication of the book.'

Rowan flinched, 'I'll do my best, but the accident has really knocked me about.'

The old man smiled sincerely, 'You'll do just fine—after all you've come all this way to hear the music.'

'I'm just saying that I'm not myself right now.'

'We call it soul loss or soul fragmentation, but that's to look at it in an overly negative way, eh?' Lionel winked. 'Given the times we might perhaps ask: Where has *he* gone, little soul? And just as importantly: *Who is it that enters through the gates of time; should we welcome him as friend or banish him as foe?*' He was looking directly at Rowan. 'I very much hope he is a friend.'

Rowan feigned incomprehension.

Rowan was soon transferred to a rehabilitation centre close to the hospital at Big Gold Mountain. He remained there for a further week before the medical staff allowed him to return 'home' to Dinas Yarkuk for outpatient monitoring.

Wirrarap visited every second day. His usual routine was to sit with Rowan drinking tea or playing chess, cards or dominoes for about half an hour. Almost on the half-hour, he'd lose interest in whatever game they were playing and produce a book, magazine or object illustrative of contemporary life in Marin-e-bek. These included Rowan's car licence, debit card and government medical ID as well as money, newspapers, tourist brochures, maps, etc.. Sometimes he'd switch the TV on and they'd watch a show together, sometimes in Pan-Koori, sometimes in French or English with Koori sub-titles. Other times he'd show a video or would switch on the radio. He never asked for Rowan's opinion about anything he was showing him and he didn't discuss the logic behind what he was doing except to say, 'All these things will help you remember'. Whenever he noticed Rowan getting anxious, he'd end whatever activity was causing the problem and chat for a time or brew a tea.

After about five days familiarising Rowan with 'Marin society', he brought in material specific to Rowan's life:

graduation photographs, cricket photographs, family pictures, a love letter from someone called 'Kharaika' (with a New Albion stamp attached dated January 7th 1992), images of his current home and of the university. He also brought in extracts from Rowan's published writings and lecture notes. Still later, he produced two chapters from Rowan's biography on Abraham Isles. He noted that the chapters covered similar terrain to the essays on Isles that Douglas had possessed.

Imogen also appeared once or twice during this period — though Wirrarap was present both times. She maintained a professional distance during the visits — only ever asking about Rowan's medical progress or filling him in on university gossip or her own PhD thesis. Rowan learnt that he'd been her supervisor since last November and that she was researching mystical themes evident in the works of key European Romantic poets.

On the second visit Wirrarap asked her to describe to Rowan in detail aspects of her PhD project. Rowan listened patiently, despite not being overly interested in the era — the materialist in him disliked her fascination with the supernatural. He became more interested, however, when Imogen outlined her plan to analyse some of the material from postmodernist and feminist perspectives — though she listed a number of theorists he'd never heard of. He advised her to read the usual suspects thoroughly, i.e. Derrida, Foucault, Kristeva, Eagleton, Cixous, etc. At which point, she became puzzled and tearful.

'Are you alright, Imogen?' asked Whirrarap.

'Yes-yes, of course … *No* actually.' She looked at Rowan. 'Maybe that knock on the head *has* scrambled your memory or something. You never mentioned those thinkers in our supervision sessions last year.' She paused, struggling to stay calm. 'It's just hard,' she continued, 'I'm teaching at the moment—more than last year—and I'm only a year away from completing. You said in December, that I was "right on track" with my research, but after a list like that I doubt I'll be finishing any time soon.' She played nervously with her bangles as she spoke.

Wirrarap was about to speak, but Imogen had more to say, 'And you haven't mentioned any modern experts on alchemy, Hermeticism or Kabbalah in that list—can I take it that I at least have it right in those areas? Funny, that was all you wanted to talk about last year.' She started scribbling down some of the names he'd mentioned on the back of one of her thesis pages.

Rowan knew he was making the mistake of spouting knowledge alien to the world he was now in.

'Well, there's always an immense amount of reading in a PhD—perhaps I didn't want to over-load you. Don't research those more obscure thinkers just yet …'

'Perhaps it would be better to wait until Rowan is thinking a bit more clearly, Imogen. He doesn't want to send you off on a wild goose chase.'

'I have to be honest,' chimed in Rowan, 'I don't remember much about your thesis, though I must have read it a couple of times last year. Wait until I have another chance to read it before you do any new reading.' His pulse was racing.

Imogen stopped scribbling, 'Are you sure? I'd rather read these thinkers now than two or three months from now.'

'Why not leave the manuscript here for Rowan to read at his leisure—especially that summary at the beginning,' said Whirrarap.

'I'll get back to you as soon as I'm able.'

Imogen nodded doubtfully, but left the manuscript just the same. When she eventually rose to leave, Wirrarap had wandered down to the kitchen—perhaps to make some drinks.

Imogen stared down at Rowan—obviously puzzled.

'Very odd. I think this accident has changed you. Though not completely—you're the same, but you're also different. More, what is it … forthright or something. You're less, well *mystical* and more New Albion in outlook. Very strange.'

'Is that a good thing—being more *New Albion in outlook?*' asked Rowan.

'I'm not sure. I mean it usually is for me … Paul is also from New Albion, for example. But I'm starting to think that's not such a good thing.' She paused. 'Anyway, we'll talk about that when you get out, eh? I've also made some important changes— you'll like them.'

She was gone before Wirrarap returned.

CHAPTER TWENTY-FIVE

REVISING THE CONCEPT OF HOME
(Thursday, March 6th 1997)

Rowan left the rehabilitation centre on a rainy evening in early March. There followed a drive with Whirrarap south-east of Big Gold Mountain—along roads he couldn't recognise in the dark. Rowan was amazed at the regularity of wildlife corridors both under and over the roads. Likewise the land either side of the road featured regular clusters of homes built in woodland clearings.

Eventually the familiar contours of the boulder country north of Harcourt (in his world) signaled they were approaching Mount Alexander. Soon after they took a left turn into the eastern foothills of the mountain and, after a drive of perhaps fifteen minutes, he realised they were close to Douglas's property, though the familiar hillside—now on his right—featured a mass of dimly lit buildings.

'Where are we now?' he asked Whirrarap.

'To our right is the western most suburb of Dinas Yarkuk—

though our science campus is at the top of that hill. They set themselves apart from the rest of us. Behind the lights and beyond the hillside are the town's central parklands. It's a twenty minute walk from there to the town centre and university.'

'If you don't mind could you drop me over there in that laneway—I recognise this place. I'll meet you at the other end of the uh … park in thirty minutes or so.'

'Are you sure—the park is unlit until you're almost at the centre of the town and it's been raining heavily?'

Eventually Whirrarap had agreed, though he'd kept Rowan's luggage and he'd hunted down a torch in the boot before leaving. It was still drizzling when Rowan began his walk up through the houses to the park. Most things looked different and he felt a dull despair at the absence of Douglas's barn-house and out-buildings. In their place, he saw a large building decorated in Koori animal designs. It was fenced off from both the surrounding suburb and bushland to the east—though Whirrarap had called it parkland. A sign written in Pan-Koori, French and English on a tall barbed wire fence in front of a car-park said, "MUCT Science Precinct'.

Given the carpark entrance featured a boomgate manned by soldiers Rowan decided against exploring the campus and instead made his way up a path to the north of the precinct—through the bushland/parkland where the clochan, and further along, the dam and boulder formation had existed.

As he walked, the moon came out and all around him grey-box, yellow box and other gums and native trees stood still and quiet, moistened by the rain. He heard the sound of water flowing and every now and then the murmurings of night birds or the scratching sounds made by possums fossicking around on the ground or cavorting in the foliage of trees. He found comfort in the familiar smells of the bush, the pungent breeziness of the eucalypts after the rain, the subtle perfumes of understory plants. Thankfully too, the moon, stars, clouds and wind continued to behave as they'd always done. For a few magical minutes he was able to convince himself that he was back in the Australia of his original self.

Similarly, though there was no dam in the small valley below the hillside, just a small wet-weather creek, he managed to find the boulder formation he'd known, and further along, the huge gnarled redgum tree close to the park's perimeter. Nailed to the tree was the sign that said: 'University This Way'—though it was in three languages. The tree seemed like a long lost friend.

A few hundred metres into the walk, he met someone walking in the opposite direction. As they passed, the man—obviously in a hurry—slipped and his luggage spilled out onto the muddy ground. Rowan used his torch to help him locate the muddied possessions.

'It's pretty slippery on this path', said Rowan, as they recovered soiled clothing and other objects.

'Thanks. I have to make tracks—the bus leaves in twenty minutes for the big smoke—Bunjilaka City.' The man's accent was the same combination of French, English and Pan-Koori that Rowan had encountered with the medical staff—though the man was speaking in English. 'I had a late class, and given the rain this afternoon this path is hard work. So much for a short-cut—I should have taken the main road. Where are you headed?'

'I'm heading up to the university.'

'You from round here? … You don't sound like you're from round here.'

Rowan answered cautiously, 'I've been away a long time … overseas and up north.' The man pulled a towel out of his back-pack and began cleaning a couple of his possessions before repacking them. Rowan wiped mud off what turned out to be the man's photo-album then passed it back to him. The man received it then looked more closely at Rowan.

'Yep, I thought you were from up north—from New Albion? There's a certain "professional" way of talking up there, but you also have a Marin accent.'

Rowan wanted to withdraw from the conversation, but it seemed impolite to move on when the man still needed the torch.

The man stopped packing for a moment then looked very closely at Rowan. 'I recognise you from somewhere ... even in this light. Don't tell me—I'll work it out. You were on television. I know—you're Rowan Sweeney the cricketer! And you'll be taking me for the unit on Axial Age Religions.'

Rowan felt like a pretender, he was no cricketer despite Douglas's best efforts. The man stood back as though replaying a series of television memories alien to Rowan.

'Unbelievable! You really are back in Marin-e-bek—we didn't believe you'd actually be teaching us. Someone said you'd been injured in Vietnam.'

'That's true, I won't be taking any classes for a month or so—at the very least.'

'Well, I hope you get better real quick. I play cricket myself— you'll have to tell me one day why you gave up. I mean the ... uh ... incident, you couldn't blame yourself for that.'

Rowan tried to pretend he knew what the "incident" was without having to talk about it.

'The guy was a professional. He should have been able to handle a bouncer. You can't be blamed for what happened.' The man spoke tentatively—as though trying not to offend Rowan.

'I'm supposed to be meeting someone up at the university,' said Rowan, changing the topic, 'I presume I'm on the right path?'

'You'll see the main lights of the town and university just over the crest of that hill—keep walking from there, down through the park, past the old diggings until you come to a road in a gully.

It's another half kilometre or so up through the town centre to the university from there.' The man had finished repacking his luggage and was ready to move off. He paused a moment, however, to ask one more question.

'It says in the course book that you've spent the last few years studying in Sydney. What do you think, are they really building up for an invasion?'

Rowan was taken aback—the Sydney of his Australia would never invade central Victoria.

'I have no idea. I'm a Cultural Studies, and er … Religion and Spirituality academic. You'll have to ask the Politics people, though I'm back here after all—obviously something about New Albion didn't agree with me.'

The man looked disappointed, 'I guess the humanities disciplines are irrelevant to most New Albion people these days. It's all sport and conquest up there—oh and *money* of course. No wonder you came home.'

The word "Home" made Rowan flinch, though he held his tongue. The conversation wasn't helping with his anxiety levels.

'There's a university cricket team, staff and students can play. You have to play—we're shit. We've had to rope in Swedes, Hollanders and Angolan's just to field a team—guys who have never bowled a ball or held a bat in their lives. Anyway, have a think about it. Otherwise I'll see you in class.'

'Yes, see you in class,' Rowan said, as the man headed off into the darkness.

Soon after, Rowan reached the crest of the second hill and despite the light rain, he made out the lights of the township and university to the east. As he descended through sparser woodland, the noise of traffic became more insistent.

Instead of heading straight for the university, he decided to take a look at the main street of Dinas Yarkuk. Wirrarap had shown him some videos and photographs of the town. He'd also organised some money ('yarkuks') for Rowan. He noticed that the place, though dominated by shops displaying signs in Pan-Koori, was quite cosmopolitan—on one block alone he made out Thai, Mexican, Indian and Italian restaurants. However, the normal rules of western town planning didn't seem to apply. There were buildings of all shapes and sizes, featuring architecture from almost every culture on Earth in evidence. Most of the shops and businesses—bookshops, alternative health premises, coffee shops, theatres and internet cafes—had closed for the night. Nevertheless there were people everywhere—eating and drinking, chatting, playing games, listening to performers, exercising on patches of lawn, and so on. Obviously the small CBD area catered to a large international student population.

As he reached the township, the rain started up again. He turned right at the main road and headed toward the university in a south-easterly direction. Behind open ground near the university's front gate, he noticed student dwellings and heard party music thumping out across the campus. He took shelter under a verandah for a few minutes and listened. The song playing had a distinct late adolescent feel about it—longing, pain and joy converted into acoustic guitar progressions and Dylanesque singing (in English). For some reason he knew instantly that the party was being held by New Albion students. Marin music usually exhibited traditional Koori dance rhythms, seemed less individualistic and the lyrics were typically written in Pan-Koori.

After about ten minutes the rain let up and Rowan wandered up past the university's main buildings (which were decorated with gigantic native animals) to the academic residences. He eventually came to a gate hung with a sign stating: 'Warden: Academic Residences'. He entered and before long was knocking at the door of a cottage. A smallish, bald-headed man dressed in a long night-gown and slippers greeted Rowan with unforced civility — despite being woken from sleep. He introduced himself as Dr Grella and possessed a flashlight and umbrella. Before long, he was shuffling ahead of Rowan along a narrow, overgrown path behind his own cottage.

'Lionel told me you'd be back.' said Dr Grella in French.' He said you have memory loss, a sore arm and a neck brace, but otherwise you're fine. Very lucky — under the circumstances.'

Thank god, thought Rowan, Douglas had forced him to brush up on his French.

'Your cottage is up here — my wife cleaned it up for you this afternoon — it got a bit dusty while you were away in Vietnam. Wirrarap asked me to give you the key.'

'Excuse me,' said Rowan in French, as they passed buildings apparently built into the hillside 'but Lionel said he'd drop off my luggage.'

'Yes, he dropped it off twenty minutes ago,' said Dr Grella, 'and asked me to reacquaint you with the building. Apparently the accident knocked you about a bit.'

Though it was difficult for Rowan to form a full picture of his surrounds in the dark, the campus grounds appeared to merge in many ways with the surrounding forest. Rowan would learn later that his cottage, was part of a complex of thirty set among five acres of native bush on the hillside behind the university campus. The cottage gardens weren't fenced off from each other — making the bushland and gardens 'common land'.

Finally, they halted beneath a sheer escarpment.

'This is it — I bet you're glad to be home,' said the old scholar, directing his light upwards to reveal a small cliff-face featuring numerous windows. Rowan was staring at a cluster of two storey cliff cottages. The stone path to the front door of his cottage was flanked on both sides by large boulders and slabs of stone only barely visible beneath a veritable jungle of native groundcovers and climbers. Attached to the front of the dwelling was a rickety verandah featuring a table, some chairs and a collection of well-watered ferns.

'Oui', said Rowan clumsily, noticing more flowers and climbers either end of the verandah.

I don't recall living in an underground house, thought Rowan.

'I know I told you this last year, but Wirrarap insists we start all over again. Just tell me to stop if I'm boring you,' said Dr Grellis as they approached the front door.

'These cliff dwellings are quite efficient in terms of energy usage and comfort. Even when it hits 40 degrees Celsius—not unheard of during the summer months—you'll find that the house stays quite cool inside.' Dr Grellis paused for a moment to focus his torch and unlock the front door.

'Your luggage is just inside the door—if you need anything, or if you have any problems please use the pager in the kitchen. Other than that I'll leave you to it.'

Rowan felt like he was entering the very bowels of the earth.

Apart from the rough-hewn interior walls however, the rooms of the house were nothing unusual. Overall the dwelling was simply furnished—*No obvious display of consumer spending power,* thought Rowan. He wandered upstairs first and found himself exploring two bedrooms and a bathroom. The downstairs area comprised a large living area cut in two by a breakfast bench several metres long. On one side stood the kitchen dining area, on the other, the lounge area. Behind the kitchen was a hall-way which led to two other rooms—a laundry and a study.

The study featured a large desk with a computer, and a good sized scholarly library. The computer looked modern enough, and judging by the connecting wires was hooked up to the Marine-bek version of the World Wide Web. Behind the computer was a large library of DVDs, videos and CDs—related, as far as he could tell, to the units 'Rowan' taught. As he surveyed the bookshelves, he noted many cheap paperback editions of global classics in French, English and Pan-Koori. Disconcertingly, he recognised very few modern commentaries on the classics and even fewer modern theoretical texts. History, literature, philosophy, and religious studies books featured strongly, but there were very few books on sociology, psychology and cultural studies.

As Rowan explored each room, he came across photos of his other self as an international cricketer side by side with images of him as a devotee of Abraham Isles's spiritual system. There were also images of his mother and father—they looked identical to his own mother and father except for clothing and the fact that they were pictured together into their forties and fifties. His father's face also looked softer and less pinched than the father he'd been raised by—his mother also seemed happier, less weary and stressed. He felt a surge of emotion—all these images from a life he hadn't actually lived.

In the second bedroom Rowan found a kind of shrine featuring small Islesian posture statues and prayer scrolls. When he looked closer, he was shocked at its purpose. The statues and prayer poems specifically addressed 'unhealthy guilt and remorse'. A small newspaper clipping was pinned to the wall behind the shrine—it was dated December 15th 1990 and captured via a photograph the sickening moment 'Rowan' had killed a young Aotearoan tail-end batsman called Daniel MacIntyre with a bouncer. Cricketer 'Rowan' had retired from international cricket after the incident.

The piece jogged a memory. He recalled the newspaper article Douglas had pinned up in the study beside a map of Marin-e-bek. The Daniel MacIntyre of that world was still playing international cricket in 1996.

As he explored the cottage, he grew fearful that his other self might suddenly appear in the form of a ghost or doppelgänger. To cope, he took two more of the sedatives he'd been prescribed. He then decided to shower, all the time struggling to make sense of the day's revelations.

Despite the medication, he was unable to sleep and eventually took to reading extracts from the incomplete Abraham Isles biography MS he'd found in the study. After the shock of seeing the author's name—"Dr Rowan Sweeney"—he scanned the contents page, the introduction and several early chapters. The introduction contained more pages than Douglas had given him to read. Similarly, on the contents page Rowan noted three chapters on Isles's wife, Miriam Hobbes—a chapter summarising her life, another on her political contribution to the founding of Marin-e-bek (including her championing of constitutional rights for women) and a third on her contribution to the postural system developed by Isles. Rowan skipped the sections in the Introduction describing the first 30 or so years of Isles's life and went straight to the additional pages dealing with his later years—which included a brief summary of how his sacred songs had been composed, distributed and eventually de-emphasised. The pages also outlined the role played by Isles and Hobbes in the new nation of Marin-e-bek from the 1850s until the 1880s and argued for a reassessment of the contemporary importance of the spiritual system they'd developed.[4]

Rowan noted that "Dr Sweeney" seemed as bamboozled as Douglas had been about the music accompanying many of Isles's songs, stating in a note: 'It is believed that the musical notation system under-pinning several hundred of Isles's songs (some published in lyric form, some not) was coded into images strewn throughout his diaries. If a code exists, however, this author— like dozens before him—has been unable to break it.'

---

[4] See Extract 3: *'The Lost Songs of Abraham Isles'*, from *Abraham Isles and Miriam Hobbes (a biography)* by Rowan Sweeney, at the back of this book (following the Miscellaneous Documents section).

As Rowan struggled to fall asleep, he realised that two distinct sub-selves were active in his personality—one was dominant, the other was secondary.

When he thought about how the two selves functioned in consciousness, he decided that the dominant self, the one that he felt most comfortable with, held to thoughts and memories related to the other reality. When that self considered his circumstances, Rowan tended to feel panicky. The secondary—or less dominant self—struck him as foundational (almost instinctual), though it seemed oddly distant most of the time. It served as a kind of memory remnant of the Rowan of this reality. Its memories were less intense than the memories of his primary self, though this self also served to calm Rowan when he felt anxious.

Interestingly, this self also possessed knowledge his dominant self would discard as occult nonsense—notably, knowledge about consciousness migration. Had the other Rowan, in his life as a spirituality academic, grown to accept such ideas? These memories, however, were vague—perhaps because his dominant self resisted their re-emergence.

He also noted that his secondary self possessed skills in various languages—notably French, Pan-Koori and Gaelic. Likewise, knowledge concerned with being a professional cricketer, as well as general knowledge of Marin culture and society. The memories emerging of his father, who lived in Sydney, were particularly confusing. In this world Rowan's parents had never divorced. His mother, however, had died in a car accident in the early 90s. The memories of his father suggested a very different Dylan Sweeney to the one he'd known. He sensed a long-term harmonious relationship between father and son.

CHAPTER TWENTY-SIX

LIFE IN THE ACADEMY
(Monday, March 24th 1997)

The towers of the Cultural and Spirituality Studies department were on his immediate left as he dodged students heading for the carpark after their 9am lectures. The sky was overcast and the air was chilly as he walked. It was late-March, over a fortnight after his release from the rehabilitation centre, and his arm and head wounds had all but healed. Only days ago the doctor had approved both the removal of the plaster cast on his injured arm and the removal of the neck brace. He was supposed to meet Imogen in her office at the base of one of those towers at 10.00am. He felt nervous and had taken two sedatives to lessen the stress of being back at work.

The past fortnight had been very difficult. After the release from the centre he'd holed up for a week in his unit feeling anxious and overwhelmed. Whirrarap eventually turned up to give him a guided tour of the university, nearby town and surrounding district. Rowan had taken the opportunity to buy some clothes of his own—a pair of black jeans and a number of dark coloured t-shirts and collared shirts. 'Very New Albion *avant garde*,' had been Whirrarap's wry comment. They'd then discussed aspects of his health: 'How is your memory—any improvements yet to your French and Koori?' 'A little, but I have a long way to go,' Rowan had lied—though in truth he'd been busy relearning the languages since his New Albion accent and tendency to only speak English puzzled people who knew him. The other Rowan had been fluent in Pan-Koori, French and English. Luckily, people blamed the accident for his language loss.

On a recent visit Whirrarap had gently grilled Rowan on other issues. Apparently the Dean wanted to know when he'd be able to return to teaching. As a consequence, Whirrarap had inquired about his memories of the Axial Age Religions course material. The subject matter comforted Rowan greatly since all of the key historical events and primary texts were identical to what he'd read about with Douglas—though the modern academic interpretation texts were often different. Rowan told Whirrarap that he had a handle on the material, but that the prospect of teaching made him anxious—largely due to his language difficulties. 'We can get around that,' Whirrarap had replied, 'the tutor, you see, doesn't know her Buddhas from her Shivas.'

He'd also asked whether Rowan had made any progress on the Abraham Isles and Miriam Hobbes book—a question delivered on behalf of the Marin Cultural Board of Elders. Luckily Rowan had read the draft chapters of the book as well as extensive notes for one of the remaining chapters whilst holed up in the unit. This news had delighted Whirrarap who had responded, 'We need you to write a brief report over the next week or so concerning where you're at with the book research. There's a Board meeting early next month and they want you to attend—to discuss what help you might need. The draft of the book will need to be available for copyediting by late June at the latest. If you can't meet the deadline they'll need to appoint someone else soon.'

Rowan had agreed to complete and present the report—he'd also agreed to deliver the Axial Age Religions lectures from April 8th onwards. 'But I'll need to deliver them in English if my memory hasn't returned. And if it gets too difficult, I may have to simply stand at the lectern and read from the lecture notes.'

Whirrarap, and later the Dean, had agreed to the conditions, and Rowan had spent the next few days reading up on Buddhism, Hinduism, Islam and the like and trying to assess exactly how far along the Isles project was. His training as an academic helped considerably. He believed that there were only two chapters unwritten. One concerned the unique contribution of Isles and Hobbes to modern notions of 'oppression'—Rowan had some ideas for that chapter already. The other, however, was causing major headaches due to his limited musical expertise. It needed someone to decipher a coded musical notation system supposedly hidden in the pages of eighteen of Isles's diaries. Given there were no copies of the diaries in the cottage, or even in the university library, it was impossible to give that chapter a completion date. He'd discussed the problem with Whirrarap who'd said that the Board wanted to assess his well-being before 'returning' copies of the diaries to him.

Rowan walked across the crowded University courtyard before climbing the flight of stairs leading to the Cultural and

Spirituality Studies department. Though it was mid-morning—prime time for lectures—a make-shift stage had been set up and hundreds of students were busy in the paved square painting placards and banners or adjusting costumes for some sort of protest. Large crowds made him feel claustrophobic—he even thought about returning to the unit until the protest was over. He didn't feel up to dealing with a noisy demonstration on his first day back.

After climbing some steps, he entered the main building. It was much quieter inside. *Perhaps most of the staff and students are in lectures*, he thought, as he looked for Imogen's office. On the phone the previous evening she'd promised to 'take care' of him on his first day back.

She wasn't in her office when he arrived—though her door was open. He stood outside for long moments wondering what to do next. He'd counted on her being there to meet him and show him to his office which was somewhere down the hallway.

'Hey, Rowan—I'm over here!' shouted Imogen.

As he turned, he noticed her emerging from a small room carrying a stack of stapled photocopies as well as some hardcover books. Her dark hair was almost down to her waist and she had a spring in her step. She looked happy to see him.

'Great to see you back,' she said, as she breezed past him on the way to her desk where she quickly offloaded the pile of photocopies and books.

'It's all happening out there in the square,' said Rowan, surprised at the attraction he felt toward her.

Imogen looked up, 'Why don't we head to the staff-room for a coffee? We can view the protest speeches from the balcony there. It's serious stuff—there's a lot of anger at New Albion aggression along Marin-e-bek's northern border, not to mention the human rights abuses in their refugee camps and detention centres.'

Now that her hands were empty, she seemed to want to hug him, but checked the impulse for some reason.

As he followed her to the staff-room, he struggled to retrieve memories to do with her role in his life. Apart from them being co-workers in the same department, he knew that he was also her PhD supervisor. Obviously she was intimate in some way with the other Rowan, but he needed to know the details—how far had their relationship progressed prior to his departure for Vietnam? He hadn't seen her since his release from the rehabilitation centre—she'd been away at a First Year Bachelor of Arts orientation camp for much of that time. Although she'd phoned a number of times whilst away, he hadn't returned her calls. His anxiety had stopped him answering calls from anyone—including a couple from his father and sister in Sydney.

After making coffee they sat down at a large table covered in newspapers (some in French and Pan-Koori), union information and other bits and pieces. Imogen sat opposite Rowan, glancing at him thoughtfully whilst sipping from her mug. Rowan didn't know what to say, but some part of him sensed hidden complexities to their relationship.

'You know you have the student from hell,' she said, breaking the silence.

'I beg your pardon ...'

'You have Philip "Godstar" Wallaby in your class—he's the student from hell.'

'You're joking? And *Godstar* has to be a self-adopted name.'

'No, he was born with it—he brought it with him to Marin-e-bek five years ago. Members of his family were among the first refugees to flee the New Albion purges. He was given a special scholarship to study here at MUCT.'

'Refugees … from New Albion?' Rowan sipped at his coffee, unsure how he should talk to her.

'Yes, Godstar Wallaby is a New Albion refugee. I ought to charge you tuition fees!' she said, flicking her long, dark hair in mock amazement.

'Things are getting crazy up there by the sound of it.'

'You were studying in Sydney, epicentre of the craziness—mass media indoctrination, a corporatised newspaper industry, 24-hour commercial TV and every school child must salute the flag and sing the national anthem daily. The Neo-con alliance has governed now for thirteen years. The opposition is under-funded, persecuted and full of wishy-washy careerists.'

As she spoke, Rowan drifted off into memories of large-scale street protests in an urban area. He remembered sullen men and women chanting aggressively in English. Many wore cowboy hats decorated with red, white and blue flags. They were marching fifteen abreast beneath huge skyscrapers. He also remembered a sea of crosses stabbing the air as a tall clean-cut man in a business suit fulminated about God, New Albion military power and capitalism. 'Our bounty—our gift from God—is but one side of a covenant. And that covenant is a reaffirmation of the *original covenant* made between God and fallen man through the suffering of Jesus Christ'. Rowan remembered the crowd's frenzy—people sang hymns as the man spoke. 'The Lord always has a purpose … Can you tell me his purpose in making New Albion strong?' he'd paused dramatically allowing the audience to shout answers at him whilst stabbing the air with their crosses. '*His* purpose is to have *us* eliminate all stains of idolatry and socialism from the soil of this Great Southern Land.'

'Looks like you know all about our northern neighbours. Painful memories eh?' said Imogen thoughtfully. 'Many New Albion progressives are in exile these days. The rot up there began with the censorship laws of the mid-to-late 80s. And then all publicly owned media was privatised, likewise the higher education sector—arts, humanities and social science programs being the worst hit.'

'The aim being, as always, to silence anyone who understood what they were up to,' said Rowan, comforted that a version of the left-right divide also existed in this reality.

'See you do remember! After 1993, however, it got much worse with the advent of "Patriotic Revisionism". University lecturers, high school teachers etc. could only teach the 'Patriotic tradition' and thus the history of the white invasion of Aboriginal lands was changed into a story about "settlement" and "bringing God and civilisation to the culturally inferior Aborigines",' Imogen sounded angry—making her seem even more attractive to Rowan.

'And Godstar is a refugee from all of that? Sounds like he has good reason to be upset. I don't think there'll be a lot of disagreement between us.'

'But he directs some of his anger at the non-Marin academics on staff.'

'Maybe we just need to acknowledge his anger,' said Rowan, playing devil's advocate.

'He likes to critique everything lecturers say and he knows his stuff—has multiple degrees. The world is a grand conspiracy—rich, white, corporate psychopaths and warmongers are trying to take over the world!'

Rowan smiled, 'He has a point—they are to blame for

many of the world's problems. And postmodernism is hyper-capitalist start to finish.'

Imogen looked astounded, 'Since when have post-modernism and economics interested you? Last year you taught that stuff only grudgingly.'

Rowan thought fast, 'postmodernism started to make sense after the accident—bits of me were shaken to Kingdom Come. I've discovered I have no real self.'

Imogen laughed nervously then took another sip of her drink. Outside, in the square, the crowd was getting louder. A group was chanting something in Pan-Koori that Rowan didn't understand

'Godstar will be your best mate if you spout that stuff in class,' said Imogen.

'He can't possibly know everything.'

'He knows *a lot*. His mother is an academic still living in Sydney. His father is an Aboriginal activist and native doctor. He comes at everything from the perspective of philosophy.'

'We didn't do much philosophy at, er ... Sydney. We had a "minimalist" menu: Western Marxism, the various feminisms, Existentialism (especially Heidegger and Sartre), psychoanalysis and the post-modernist thinkers...' Rowan felt himself merging memories of his studies in Melbourne with the other Rowan's memories of studying in Sydney. He bit his lip in frustration.

'Who is *Heidegger*? I've never heard of him.'

'I'll tell you about him one day, he's a lesser existentialist.' Rowan realised, once again, that many of the key thinkers he was familiar with didn't exist in this reality.

'Which reminds me, when are you going to give me the report on my PhD project? I looked up some of those thinkers you mentioned, but couldn't find any references to most of them.'

'I haven't done the report yet,' said Rowan, feeling flustered 'but probably best to believe the pre-accident Rowan. Just do what I told you in December and forget Derrida, Foucault, etc. Post-accident Rowan is broken.'

'Shit!' said Imogen, cutting him off, 'they're getting really loud out there. I can barely hear you mumbling! Let's take our drinks and go watch the start of the revolution.'

CHAPTER TWENTY-SEVEN

NEW ALBION: MILITARY DICTATORSHIP

'Last night the New Albion air-force attacked hundreds of desperate refugees as they tried to cross into Marin-e-bek,' shouted a tall red-haired man dressed in a collared black shirt and tartan trousers. He paused after each sentence to glance at his notes. A crowd of several hundred students and staff listened intently as he spoke. 'At least thirty refugees were killed and many others, including children, were injured.' He paused again, struggling to contain his fury. 'During the operation,' he continued, 'bombs hit a hospital carpark on our side of the border—killing two visitors.'

The crowd broke into a chorus of boos and hisses. 'New Albion's flagrant disregard for human rights is a grave matter, but we're also witnessing illegal covert military operations against neighbouring states and discriminatory legislation against minorities. Together they illustrate New Albion's flagrant,'—*he likes the word flagrant*, thought Rowan— 'disregard for human rights and international law. It is time for the international community to act decisively and soon!' The crowd, including Imogen and Rowan, clapped and cheered.

'Tonight in Bunjilaka City a number of organisations have organised a mass protest rally outside the New Albion embassy. We expect over one hundred thousand people to attend.' There were more loud cheers, as well as some protest chants before the red-haired man was allowed to continue.

'We've hired dozens of buses to shuttle concerned students and staff to the Bunjilaka protest tonight. Before you board, however, please add your name to the petition over there by the drinks stand.' He paused to point in the direction of three tables of student volunteers. Each table sported pamphlets, pens and sheaves of petition paper. 'Since we know students are poor and sometimes have trouble feeding themselves— especially after they've paid for books and er ... alcohol—' There was isolated though hearty laughter, 'we're thankful that Islesian and Indigenous Community Centres in Bunjilaka City have offered to feed all regional protestors tonight for a nominal fee. So after you sign the petition you can also grab a food and drinks voucher for two yarkuks.'

The man handed the microphone to a tall Koori man wearing only a red, black and yellow scarf and a pair of blue jeans. His chest and stomach had been painted with various traditional designs in red ochre and white clay and he held a guitar. He was followed on-stage by a woman with short, blonde hair, dressed in a simple white dress and black boots. Together they began performing a stirring, melancholy protest song in Pan-Koori. Rowan guessed it was a song of lamentation for those who had died the previous night since many in the crowd began wailing and crying before the completion of the first chorus.

'I need to go back inside,' said Rowan.

'You've gone pale—what's up?' Imogen looked alarmed.

'This is all a bit raw for me on my first day back. I need to sit down a minute.'

He felt panicky and was relieved when they went back into the staffroom away from the crowd.

Imogen went to fetch a glass of water after helping him to sit down. After ten minutes he began to feel better.

'Do you want me to take you home?'

'Not right now—too many people out there. I've been experiencing panic attacks since coming out of the coma—they often hit without warning,' said Rowan.

'I didn't realise they were so severe.' Her hand lingered on his shoulder.

'You're forgiven. By coming in here I've avoided a more severe attack.' Imogen seemed on the verge of saying something important when Rowan cut her off. 'Why on earth is their air force bombing our hospitals?'

Imogen sat down beside him, her hand still on his shoulder her sandalwood perfume strong to his senses, 'The New Albion government accuses the Marin government of leniency toward "undesirables". They say that many of the refugees are subversives, maybe even terrorists. The borders are shut right now because New Albion is demanding the return of two their own Koori activists responsible for handing footage of government tanks rolling into Wiradjuri country near Wagga Wagga to the international media.'

Rowan didn't understand the political situation, 'So there are refugee camps north of Dinas Yarkuk?'

'Jesus, your memory, Rowan!' Rowan flinched and then looked at the floor. 'This past year alone, thirty thousand New Albion citizens have crossed the border into Marin-e-bek—another forty thousand are being held in camps on the New Albion side of the border. The trigger for the exodus came when the government quarantined pension payments and tax system family payments to all Koori families who refused to send their children to New Albion public schools regularly or, get this, were caught *teaching their children* a tribal language.'

Rowan almost choked on his water.

'Then there are the consequences of the 1995 racial purity laws. Aboriginal children are now being separated from their parents if they are deemed to be part white or Asian or whatever.'

'Surely the international community …'

'They're economically and militarily powerful. And there's a suspicion that the US are in on the deal—a whole continent to mine! They sell New Albion a lot of conventional weaponry and are rumoured to be overseeing their nuclear weapons program.'

'The world's largest democratic superpower secretly backing an authoritarian regime—wouldn't be the first time,' said Rowan, not wanting to sound completely ignorant.

'*Democratic* … the US? They abandoned democracy in the early eighties to become a formal Plutocracy—government by corporations and wealthy individuals.' Imogen paused to take a sip of her drink.

'So things started to go wrong in the 1980s?'

'Correct! See you do still possess one or two brain cells! In the mid-1980s the New Albion elite embraced the US strain of Neo-Conservatism. Am, I boring you?' she mock yawned, 'I'm boring me! This stuff is common knowledge—for people who manage to stay on their motorbikes.'

'It's not common knowledge to me anymore. Some days I think there's a vacuum between my ears,' said Rowan gloomily. To him the New Albion government ticked all the boxes as a military dictatorship. 'Sounds like we're on our own against an international bully?'

'The Marins aren't the only ones worried about the New Albion/US alliance. The other continental nations are also fearful. Even the Aotearoans are worried—though they traditionally keep out of continental politics.'

'Will they all back Marin-e-bek in the event of a war?' He knew he sounded dumb.

Imogen tried to veil her amazement, 'Lucky you aren't teaching Marin history! Yes, they are all allies—progressive Aboriginal-Immigrant nations similar to Marin-e-bek—but even combined they'll be no match for New Albion.'

'What's the story with their camps?'

'There are two types: detention centres, which are for political prisoners and suspected terrorists, and refugee camps proper. Most Marin refugees fleeing New Albion are placed in a refugee camp and typically cross within weeks. New Albion citizens wishing to leave have a much tougher time—initially they're also placed in a refugee camp—there are dozens all along the border. Sometimes, however, the government gets suspicious and some people are transferred to the detention centres. Activists are calling them *concentration camps*.' Imogen paused—she seemed distressed just talking about the camps.

'Is that why you came down here?' said Rowan, suddenly aware that her hand was back on his shoulder.

'Yes, I just got out in time,' she said, 'I've had to accept recently that I'm living in exile—it would be dangerous for me to return now to New Albion. Can't understand how Paul still wants to play gigs up there. Each time he travels across the border, I worry he'll never come back.' Her hand left Rowan's shoulder and she stood up to stretch.

'Looks like I also left just in time,' said Rowan thoughtfully, 'lucky I have a Marin passport.'

'And have *cricket* connections—the bastards still love their cricket.'

'It sounds like the indigenous people of New Albion have had it bad for some time,' said Rowan, on the hunt for more historical context.

'During the late 19th century and for much of the twentieth

century they did okay. After Marin-e-bek became independent New South Wales also became a nation—"New Albion'. Wanting peaceful relations with Marin-e-bek the northerners negotiated a treaty with their indigenous tribes. Then came the self-managed reservations, economic compensation, health and education initiatives, common law rights around accessing sacred sites on crown land (with money put aside to gradually buy-back sites on private property) and so on.' She paused to check Rowan's pulse—seeing it had slowed considerably, she continued, 'The new state also enshrined in law a number of political rights: minimum quotas for indigenous people in cabinet; an indigenous person as Governor General; and a certain number of exclusively indigenous seats in the parliament.'

'Sounds like a pretty good deal,' said Rowan, ashamed at the paltry efforts made toward indigenous self-determination in his Australia.

'Not as good as the deal the indigenous people of Marin-e-bek secured for themselves. Hey, look at your pigeon-hole. It's full to the brim,' said Imogen, pointing at a row of boxed shelves on the far side of the staff-room. A label on one of the pigeon-holes said: **Dr. Rowan Sweeney**. He stood up slowly and wandered over to the pigeon-hole to recover a huge pile of envelopes and paper scraps.

'Welcome back, eh?' said Imogen, brushing up against him gently as she recovered her own mail.

'What's this?' said Rowan, struggling to organise the documents. He passed Imogen a piece of green A4 paper that said: "Organisation Day: Meet the new CEO, 9.30 am this Friday (28th March). Lecture theatre 3.05".

She smiled, 'Just what it says I suppose—a general staff meeting, just before the mid-term break. Attendance will be mandatory—it's in our employment contract. It'll help you remember what this place is all about. It's a real zoo, believe me.'

'It can't be too traumatic, can it? I don't know the CEO from a bar of soap.'

'There'll be some kind of major announcement on the day—you just watch! They never spend money like this ...'

'Like what?'

'... the free lunch and a staff dinner in the evening. Not unless they want to sugar the medicine.'

Rowan sighed, 'I'm having enough trouble preparing for teaching. The last thing I need right now is a dose of university politics.'

Imogen handed him back the notice then leant close before whispering, 'I'll hold your hand on the day if you like.'

He returned to the table and sat down—he was feeling dizzy again.

'Don't be scared of the big bad CEO—he's unlikely to bite ... yet. And think of the day as a good way to keep your job.'

'I don't really care about *keeping my job,*' said Rowan, slumping back into his seat.

Imogen knelt down beside him, 'I have my eleven o'clock class in ten minutes—though the turnout will be small on account of the protest. Do you want me to walk you back to your office?'

He felt himself retreat from her touch, but accepted the offer.

Puzzled at his body language, she took a deep breath before selecting her next words, 'You know, I understand if I'm too complicated. All that stuff with—well you know—Paul. While you were away, I sorted things out. I went cold turkey in late January at a clinic in Bunjilaka City and I've split from him permanently. It's the only way to keep off the drugs. Besides, he's been on tour in New Albion for weeks now.'

She was about to say more when a senior lecturer in Norse Mythology—an old man with a long, white beard—entered the staffroom.

Rowan and Imogen looked at each other in silence until she said, 'We have a supervision session tomorrow. Can we discuss the problems I'm having with structure then?'

As they wandered along the corridors to his office Rowan thought about his 'father' and 'sister'. For weeks he'd avoided answering the worried messages they'd left on his answering machine. He'd bought time by sending them a brief letter describing the accident, his recovery to date and his anxiety about talking to people on the phone. After the chat with Imogen, however, he was worried about how safe they were in Sydney. Sooner or later he'd have to meet with them—which would involve pretending to be the person they knew and loved. Surely they'd realise that he was an imposter. Besides, he'd avoided his father in the other world for many years— the thought of him being abrasive and obnoxious in this reality was too much to bear. Most importantly, however, he wasn't ready to deal with the death of his mother—as far as he was concerned, she was alive and well and living in Geelong.

CHAPTER TWENTY-EIGHT

THE CULTURE MACHINE

Rowan's office was on the second floor of the Cultural and Spirituality Studies building. It was sparsely furnished, but homely, containing an old desk, a computer, three tall bookshelves, two chairs, an archaic looking phone and a filing cabinet. The bookshelves were lined with books on religion, mythology, alchemy and all things supernatural. There were also a number of books on Isles and Hobbes, but no copies of any of Isles's diaries. The room had a window view and from his desk he looked out over a rock pool and native fernery.

After a phone call to the IT department Rowan started up his computer and logged on. The web was down, but everything else seemed to be functioning okay—though even here he experienced mild culture shock. The operating system was one he was unfamiliar with—though the basic commands seemed to be generic between realities. It took him some time to find the folders in which the other Rowan had stored his personal files.

Frustrated at having to consult the operating manual constantly, Rowan eventually decided to browse the books on the shelves. His other self was certainly a specialist in all things religious and mystical and Rowan made a mental note to grab a box from somewhere and take thirty or so of the books home for further study.

Just before lunchtime, he visited the library to confirm his library card and lending rights, but was approached endlessly by staff wishing him well with his recovery—most spoke in French or Pan-Koori. Imogen popped in at noon to check how he was going. After solving a couple of computer issues that had bugged him all morning, she suggested they wander over to a campus café for some lunch.

'What's with all the costumes?' asked Rowan, pointing at a woman wearing a flowing white dress embroidered with Koori and Islesian sacred symbols as well as a wreathe of green leaves on her forehead. She danced barefoot among flowering gums, myrtles and native hibiscus trees close to the café.

The woman's dancing was slow and self-absorbed—frequently disturbed by abrupt pauses as if she were trying to remember certain postures. It puzzled Rowan that she seemed unaware of the presence of staff and students as they passed. Also, she appeared oddly insubstantial, casting only a mild shadow. Stranger still was the fact that she had the brown hair and facial features of a woman he'd known in his other life—his ex-girlfriend, Anika Miraj. 'She's an Anomaly—we've seen more of them than usual these past few months.' Imogen paused to look briefly at the woman before acknowledging the delivery of her sandwich and coffee.

'An Anomaly?' asked Rowan.

'Yes, an Anomaly—though this one is a bit stereotypical: the archetypal Muse or Moon Lady of ghost-stories, Alchemy and glossy celebrity magazines! Probably harmless enough—and of only local importance.'

Rowan was baffled, 'Of only local importance?'

'Yes, Anomalies usually either warn us about things hidden to us or they give us a glimpse of a possible future. There's been a spate of trans-local Anomalies across the country of late. A lot of people in the government are on edge about it.' She paused to tuck into her sandwich.

'Some examples?' Rowan had never heard of the phenomenon and the woman's presence was making the hairs stand up on the back of his neck.

'Baffling stuff—a horse, a cow and a sheep limped into Big Gold Mountain just last week. There must have been five or six spears in each animal as they wandered through the park and the main thoroughfare, guts hanging out, bleeding everywhere and making weird noises. They stayed around for two days.' Imogen put her sandwich down for a moment as though unable to eat.

The idea that his new reality didn't obey all the laws of classical physics made Rowan's head spin. 'Do they only manifest as ghosts and phantoms or are there other kinds of Anomalies?'

Imogen looked puzzled that she had to explain such stuff to him, 'Look Anomalies are space-time ruptures, or inter-dimensional ruptures if you like. They're usually associated with periods of emotional or spiritual upheaval—either for individuals or groups.' She looked thoughtful as she took a slow sip of her coffee.

'So they show up during periods of upheaval?'

'Sometimes, but lately there have been stories of *possession*—inter-dimensional entities taking over someone's body for a time.'

Rowan gasped and forgot to say thank-you when his

sandwich and coffee arrived. They ate in silence for a while and he found it difficult to take his eyes off the woman.

'She's dancing postures developed by Abraham Isles and Miriam Hobbes,' said Imogen casually.

Rowan rubbed his eyes before focusing back on Imogen, 'She looks like someone I used to know.' After speaking, his eyes darted back to the dancing woman.

Apparently the Anomaly had sensed Rowan's attention because she was slowly dancing and miming her way across the courtyard toward him. The facial likeness to Anika grew clearer as she approached and he now believed that she was speaking rather than singing or chanting, though he heard no sounds. Was she warning him perhaps, or trying to give him some advice?

Imogen sensed his growing anxiety as the woman drew nearer and said 'If you find her disturbing, you can send her away by averting your gaze. After a minute or two she'll realise you're not evoking her, at which point she'll move on. When you engage with any Anomaly you attract and amplify its presence.'

Rowan struggled to tear his eyes away from the figure. He was trembling and the blood had drained from his face. 'I've never come across this sort of thing before.'

But Imogen was still playing the tourist guide, 'The longer we stare at them the more incarnate they become—up to a point. For example, we may be able to physically touch them and even hold a conversation. Apparently, they can be quite interactive with the right people. Though they're as likely to vanish without warning.'

The woman stood beside Rowan now—leaning over him. Her full lips almost touched his ear. Her scent, like some kind of flower, triggered long forgotten memories of—no doubt about it—Anika.

Imogen tried to divert his attention from the creature, 'I blame the Marin-e-bek authorities for the Anomaly epidemic. They've encouraged the critters with their respect for magic. If you encourage the people to believe in the occult, they begin to dream weird things into existence. We don't get nearly as many Anomalies up in New Albion. Though there is a certain charm to them, I guess,' she began shooing the Anomaly away as if it were a fly or a wasp.

Rowan, meanwhile, had closed his eyes and was breathing in short, jerky spasms as if he had asthma.

'Try to breathe more deeply,' Imogen said, whilst touching Rowan's hand. 'That's it, you're doing well—I'm sure she'll go away in a minute.'

As predicted, the figure slowly began to dance away in the direction of a myrtle tree. The woman became statuesque in its shade, before vanishing slowly over ten minutes or so.

It took Rowan a while to steady himself.

'Obviously the accident has made you forget a few basic things about life in Marin-e-bek,' Imogen said. 'If it helps, there are other Anomalies in the area right now. See that blue-metal monstrosity over there?' she pointed inside the café at a large work of art embedded in the serving area of the café. He stared for a moment or two at what looked like a gigantic machine— some sort of cross between an octopus and a metal dragon. It was also embedded in some way in the floor above since its pipes and pulleys merged with the café ceiling. It looked dilapidated since its paint was flaking and some of the metal work looked buckled.

'It looks like a gaudy modernist art installation. There's nothing anomalous about it—is there?'

'Officially, it's called *The Culture Machine* and it's supposed to be fed from a central furnace area deep in the bowels of the university,' Imogen paused a moment, using her teaspoon to gather up remnant froth in her cappuccino. 'The general principle is that students are fed a "nourishing" concoction of culture during their education. This nourishment is supposed to help create a humane and cultured personality worthy of receiving the trust of ordinary people. To the Islesians the Culture Machine was symbolised by a dragon, but to some Indigenous people it took the form of a large quartz creature dormant in the earth. Both traditions see the creature as a double-edged sword—dragons, for example, can assist us or destroy us with fire. '

Rowan noticed a large sign on the object that said, 'Higher Knowledge Must Address the Flaw in the Fabric of the Universe'—obviously referencing a key Islesian concept. He also noticed that the machine's many pipes—though presently cordoned off—ended near a serving area. Had it once actually distributed food to students? A shiny sign in front of the now cordoned off area said, 'The Culture Machine Will Soon be Replaced by Calci-Comp—a New Economically Efficient Way of Distributing Knowledge to our Youth.'

Rowan turned back to Imogen.

'Where's the Anomaly—that looks like political art to me?'

'In late February, food served using the device gave recipients a twenty-four hour virus.'

'It probably needed a good clean.'

'After an initial fever the students and some staff became politically RADICAL, in upper case, for twenty-four hours—quite funny really. The Medieval Christianity lecturer had to be locked in his room. He was wandering about the campus ranting about New Albion Neo-colonialism—literally foaming at the mouth like one of those Axial Age prophets you're always on about. He'll never be able to live it down.' She drank the last of her coffee and ate the rest of her salad sandwich in silence. Now and then she looked over at him—as if seeking the right moment to say something important.

Rowan, however, no longer felt hungry. He only wanted to return to his unit as quickly as possible.

Imogen walked him home. 'I'll lock up your office later if you like. Are there any books you need?' she asked, obviously concerned about his state of mind.

By the time he reached the unit, however, Rowan looked calmer. 'Thanks for coming back with me. I think I'm trying to do things a little too fast at the moment. The Anomaly spooked me.'

Imogen bit her lip—he'd observed that she did that a lot, 'Rowan, we need to talk about us. Do you think I can come in?'

'Sure—why don't I boil the kettle for a cuppa, or would you prefer a cold drink?' he said, sensing she was building up to some sort of confession.

'A cold drink will do.'

Once inside, she sat on the couch while he poured her a blackberry cordial. Suddenly, she looked small and vulnerable.

'I owe you an apology, Rowan. It's been a while coming, I know.'

'For what?' And he really meant *for what*—he had no idea what wrong she'd perpetrated.

'After New Year's Eve—you must have thought ...' she looked at him pleadingly, her eyes wet with tears.

He had no idea what had happened on New Year's Eve.

'You're such a lovely person—a bit mixed up at the moment, sure, but it must have hurt you deeply to see me back with Paul a couple of days later. I mean, I must have given you the impression ...'

'Look, I understood your need to work things out with, er ... Paul.'

'New Year's Eve was really beautiful—and I don't feel like

doing drugs around you. Maybe it's a cultural thing, you see in New Albion—well, you've lived there, you know what it's like—we're brought up under immense pressure to perform, to acquire lots of *things* and to make a fetish of our individuality. And you're right Paul is a narcissist—a selfish shit. *Look at me! Aren't I talented? Every girl wants me.* But the poison is all through our culture—and it's taking me time to get it out of my system. Relationships are corrupted up there. We move from one lover to the next and we're only supposed to be friends with people who take us places. It's as though long-term relationships don't matter—despite the influence of the barking mad fundamentalists. I'm not asking you to understand, I know you were born here—here relationships are everything, and every relationship is sanctified in some way.' She was still weeping as she moved closer to Rowan on the couch.

For a while they sat side by side. Rowan enjoyed the sensation of her body pressing gently against his own. The closeness made him feel less anxious.

'I knew you were pissed off with me when you left for Vietnam. The drugs got out of control—he does a line of cocaine every other day, plus the pills and the rest. He has the constitution for it—says it makes him creative! "I write my best songs under the influence," he says, but it fucks with my mind after a week or two. And of course he can't help himself—I tell you, the women in that industry! Like damn blow flies. I caught him one night with some blonde chick from Scotland.' Her sadness was threatening to turn into anger.

Rowan kissed her forehead and smoothed back a curl of brown hair.

'I went into rehab—Mum and Dad paid for it. I even took time off my PhD. I've learnt a lot about myself—"codependency" they reckon. Though I told them: *he's not the slightest bit dependent upon me.*'

'Why are you telling me this?' asked Rowan.

'Can you be patient? With him it's always so difficult—so fucked up—whereas it seems so easy with you. I mean, I haven't actually *promised* you anything have I? It's not like I really cheated on you. I'm really fond of you, Rowan—when I first heard about your accident, I felt a stab in my heart. That told me a lot.' She kissed him gently.

'Things are also complicated for me,' he responded, 'but I'm sure we can work things out.'

She was breathing hard as she looked at him, 'You've never mentioned complications before. Is that Anomaly woman about to re-enter your life or something—what was her name?'

'Anika—but that was a long time ago. I'm talking about other kinds of complications.' He was thinking about his ex-wife, the accident and the fact that everything he'd believed about reality had vanished after a short swim in a dam.

'Let's see how we go. For me, recovering from addiction is one day at a time—so long as you understand that.'

Rowan wasn't listening—one hand was already caressing her left breast.

CHAPTER TWENTY-NINE

RESTRUCTURING THE ARTS
(Friday, March 28th 1997)

Maxwell Fife—MUCT's new C.E.O.—sat quietly at the front of the giant auditorium as lecturers and tutors from many discipline areas filtered in. Dressed in an expensive grey suit, a white business shirt and shiny black shoes, he looked completely at ease in his leadership position. Staff were already calling him—somewhat facetiously—'the great communicator', since he possessed the oratory skills and charisma of a skilled politician.

He'd dropped the title of University Chancellor within days of his appointment, and after just a month in the role he'd railroaded the board of the university into sacking most of the senior management team. They'd been replaced by a largely New Albion educated team, drawn from the private sector. Of late he'd been making noises about finding 'the best middle management team on offer'—which made the departmental heads and the unions very nervous. He'd also forced the university's IT centre to instigate a surveillance system by the name of "Electronic Efficiency Monitoring" (EEM for short). Fife was also working hard to casualise large segments of the university's workforce. More importantly, there were rumours abroad that he intended to alter irrevocably the University's traditional educational philosophy.

'I'm always delighted to talk directly to the staff, particularly in this case the academic staff, the very *engine of our success*,' said Fife leaning back in his chair. Rowan was seated beside Imogen, close to the rear of the auditorium.

The staff warmed up only slowly. 'Perhaps we could all introduce ourselves to you, Maxwell. That should give you some idea about the diversity of courses on offer here. It will also educate you about the *philosophy* of the university,' said a tall gray-haired woman Rowan had never seen before.

The next thirty minutes were somewhat tedious as every lecturer in the room described their teaching areas, their administrative duties and, for some unaccountable reason, their time fractions.

Rowan marvelled at the complete uselessness of 90% of the courses on offer. He struggled to comprehend how the place managed to attract a thousand new students—half of them international—every year. Where would its graduates find work in the Marin—never mind the international—economy.

The room was swarming with medievalists (as Rowan labelled academics escaping from the real world). Teachers of all the major spiritual approaches were represented, though for some reason religious scholars from the major traditions of his home reality—Christianity, Hinduism, Islam, Judaism and Buddhism—seemed under-represented. Next came Rowan's own compatriots—contemporary Western culture theorists, psychologists, sociologists, historians, media studies experts, language scholars, literary theorists, experts on politics and international relations and, of course, philosophers. For some reason quantum physicists, cosmologists and biosemioticians had been lumped in with the philosophers.

People were still arriving as the creative arts scholars began outlining their work areas (and time fractions). Quietly spoken writing lecturers spoke first, followed by the more flamboyantly dressed teachers of painting, photography, sculpture, film-making, etc. Next came the performing arts people—comedians, performance poets, dancers and musicians. The alternative and sacred medicines people were next. Finally, the most colourful group of all spoke, teachers of indigenous art forms from all over the world.

The introductions trailed off after an agonising thirty minutes and Rowan, who had not chosen to stand up and introduce himself, sat bemused by the lack of scientific/technological and commercial courses on offer at MUCT. For example, MUCT offered no Engineering, Business Management, Western style Medicine or Pharmacy courses—to name but a few of the absent disciplines—and it offered only a generalist science degree.

'Okay, that gives you a good run down of what's on offer here at MUCT, Maxwell,' said the Vice Chancellor nervously.

'Yes, thank-you—all of you—though I must be honest, there were few surprises. I've been here almost a month and it still amazes me that there is, well ...' Maxwell was struggling for the right words and opted for a digression instead. 'You all understand, of course, that in my world—and make no mistake about it, mine is a *brutal* world, that's why we CEOs get paid so much—there's a lot of risk.' He seemed to be growing in confidence. 'I'm responsible for a great deal of government money—tax payer's money, students' money and international aid money. Now it is true that *this* university is also privately funded, but I honestly believe that it's time to start introducing more courses that will assist us to pay our way in the world.'

Someone from the philosophy department interrupted Fife, 'But innovation should not be defined in terms of economic imperatives alone. Our physics people, for example, have been experimenting with the world's first quantum computer—a world transforming project that may not turn a profit for years.'

'Are the physics people located in the science precinct?' Rowan whispered to Imogen.

'Yes, to the west of Dinas Yarkuk—but that's supposed to be a secret project. Though rumour has it that the first experiment, conducted back in February, failed due to—wait for it—the malfunction of solar panels at the facility! Still, they got enough data out before the shutdown to permit them to write a dozen boring data analysis papers.'

Rowan made a mental note to find out more about the facility—memories of Douglas's 'quantum computer' still haunted him.

Maxwell had moved on after the interruption. 'Experiments that may contribute to the development of profitable future technologies are not at issue here. All I'm saying is that offering courses that make our graduates job ready is in everyone's best interest.'

Margaret Ballanga from the Sociology and Cultural Studies department decided to interrupt. 'We get the picture, Maxwell. Don't we?' she said, pausing and turning briefly to the audience before continuing. 'Part of the reason we've asked you here today, Maxwell, is to let you know that this place is different to any other higher education institution you'll ever *work for*. There are dozens of institutions in Marin-e-bek turning out practical professionals. Similarly, the vocational training system takes care of the country's demand for competent trades-people. We exist to fulfil a different social purpose.'

Rowan was fascinated by the apparent lack of respect for the new CEO.

'So, we have a few questions for you.' Margaret spoke in a low, menacing voice.

Fife, however, would have none of it, 'Margaret, with all due respect, I didn't come here to debate *ideology*. The sole purpose of this session is to introduce myself to you all. The later sessions will be different. We'll be speaking to all university staff members about the government approved restructure we'll be undergoing over the next few months. I think perhaps it would be better to save your fire until after we've unveiled details of the modernisation process.'

Margaret, however, was not so easily silenced, 'With all due respect, Maxwell, the 'process' was formulated without consultation with any of us. Besides, it is never too early to question you about the ideological perspective behind these plans. Are we looking at a Neo-Liberal, Neo-Colonial take-over of this university? Are we witnessing an attempt by the New Albion government and its multinational friends to attack Marin-e-bek's commitment to supporting the arts and critical intellectual cultures?' There were muted mutters of support from the audience.

Fife smiled condescendingly and took a moment or two to answer, 'Margaret, thank you for making us aware of your concerns. However, I'm far less complicated than you appear to want to paint me. I'm a numbers man, that's my job, to be *realistic* about the numbers—so many Yarkuk in, so many Yarkuk out. If we're to survive as an institution someone in this place has to take on the occasionally unpopular role of accountant.' He smiled ironically at the Vice-Chancellor then said, 'your job, Margaret, is to assess *ideology*, mine is simply to do the sums.'

His tone was like a red rag to Margaret the activist bull. She pulled out her flamethrower, 'Money is power and power always applies some sort of *ideology*, Maxwell! Let me put the question in a simpler form: Is this attempted cultural colonisation of our country the curtain-raiser to an outright invasion by the New Albion military?'

Fife pretended to be astounded, 'Margaret, you'll have me dropping nuclear bombs on Bunjilaka City next! Come, come—with all due respect—that isn't an appropriate question for a humble CEO.'

There was silence in the audience—maybe some felt Margaret had gone too far.

Fife took the opportunity to describe the many higher education roles he'd been given in New Albion and across the Pacific. Rowan noticed that he repeatedly told them he'd been raised Anglo-American.

After telling everyone that he was always available for a chat, he left the auditorium and everyone adjourned for morning tea.

Rowan took a seat at the back of the auditorium, for the second session of the morning. The room filled quickly, but many of those arriving looked bored. At the front of the theatre a large group of smartly dressed (in the New Albion style) people were seating themselves—probably the new team of educational managers appointed by the CEO, thought Rowan. The audience was larger—numerous administrative and technical support staff seemed to be in attendance.

The Vice-Chancellor strolled into the theatre on time with a box full of folders, some computer discs and a lap-top computer. He had short black hair streaked with grey, a collapsed chin that made him look like a toad, the beginnings of a middle aged spread and an overconfident manner (though Rowan thought he looked a little nervous).

After he'd hooked up the lap-top to a projector, he introduced himself. 'I'd like to welcome you all here today – especially those who are new to our university.' He nodded politely in the direction of the twenty or so educational managers behind him.

'We've all heard Maxwell's address this morning, so I think we all understand the thinking behind the proposed restructure.

My job this afternoon is to talk a little about the specifics of what the changes will mean for each of you—also, to introduce each department to its new academic manager. I know that there are many concerns about the restructure. From my perspective, however, I see the large funding injection we've received from the New Albion government and its private sector partners as a wonderful opportunity to completely modernise how we do business here at MUCT. Their demand that we *always* link educational content to clear job outcomes is the key condition accompanying their funding injection.'

Rowan felt oddly comforted hearing the Vice Chancellor put so much emphasis on the economics of higher education—he'd been bombarded by such thinking in his home reality. Though bored, he listened patiently as the man droned on about 'business models', 'the competitive international market', 'educational product', 'market penetration', 'client satisfaction', etc.

After a while, however, Rowan turned his attention to the remarkable contrast between the dress code of the new 'educational managers' at the front of the theatre and the people in the audience. A love of colour, particularly yellows, reds, greens and blacks, predominated among the academic staff. Even among the non-Koori academics he noted long flowing shirts with green and black spiral designs, tattoos with the same designs, light baggy trousers, bangles and bracelets and rings and strange necklaces—even among the men.

For some, Koori and Islesian designs merged seamlessly—especially where Celtic 'circles of being' symbolism met Koori circle designs symbolising camp sites/watering holes and other sacred landscape features. Likewise, the Chinese Koories had their own unique ways of presenting themselves and celebrating their ancestry.

To Rowan, all this colour and symbolism contrasted sharply with the blue and grey suit uniforms worn by the male educational managers at the front. Even the female managers had erased all evidence of individuality—most wore black or grey trousers or skirts with black or grey tailored suit tops over silk-white shirts. All the men had short hair, and even the women were keeping their hair under control—none wore it longer than shoulder length. Rowan noticed that some of the managers also sported university logos stitched to their suit tops—always over their left breasts. Others wore token Marin-e-bek flag-badges, always over their right breasts. A much larger version of the flag was on display behind the Vice Chancellor.

Rowan studied it closely as the Vice Chancellor presented a string of unintelligible pie-graphs. The flag was in two horizontal parts. The top four-fifths featured two stars on a black background—representing, Rowan had learnt, Sirius and Canopus, in Marin tradition the protectors of the entire country. The stars were in opposite corners of the upper black rectangle, as per their appearance in the south-eastern night sky. Between them, Rowan noted a design featuring green spirals with radiating orange lightning flashes. Rowan knew from his reading that this design symbolised the Islesian perspective on the old Celtic Circles of Being theory: *Abred* ('the world as is'), *Gwynedd* ('the ideal world') and *Ceugant* ('the world transcending the conflict between reality and ideal'). The bottom quarter of the flag was coloured dark red—symbolising the land.

Rowan became more and more drowsy as the Vice Chancellor retreated further into corporate speak: 'educational managers will assess all courses and individual units for vocational outcomes' ... 'we need to adopt flexible, resource efficient delivery models' ... 'we'll be benchmarking New Albion university standards' ... 'Marin-e-bek's cultural values will be protected throughout the restructure' ... 'we hope the Unions and the Council of Elders will see the sense in all this', etc.

Near the end some audience members tried to ask questions. The Vice-Chancellor, however, parried the attempts. 'We understand there'll be a lot of questions about the restructure — but we'd like you to save them for our half hour Q & A session in the theatre at 4pm on Monday. And please remember: the restructure is a complex phenomenon that takes a fair bit of explaining. Our main task for the rest of today is to gather faculty groups into their assigned rooms. From there you'll meet your new educational managers who will provide you with resource packs outlining the process to be used to phase out uneconomic courses. They'll also discuss how our new efficiency assessment processes will be applied to all other courses over the next couple of months.'

With those words he ended the meeting.

CHAPTER THIRTY

FRONTING THE BOARD OF ELDERS
(Friday, April 4th 1997)

Some days, Rowan woke believing his new world to be the only real world. In those moments, the other world, so vivid after the accident, became a kind of dream world. If he focused on academic or domestic tasks for a while, he found that he rarely thought about the bizarreness of his situation. Immersion in the routines of life seemed as good a remedy as any for the memory clashes that emerged whenever he spent too much time alone. All in all, he reasoned, it was probably not unlike living with a mental illness. In his life as a social worker he'd helped clients manage periods of severe identity confusion. The task now was to live the advice he'd given others.

As the days went by, he realised that the two identities were starting to knit and merge at deep levels of his psyche. The main challenge was to accept the existence of two sets of life memories for each stage of his life. He was aided, however, by the gradual emergence of more and more of the 'other' Rowan's memories and knowledge. It also helped that people don't ordinarily remember things in connected linear ways. He reasoned that what we usually remember are clumps of experience associated with particular locations or people—such clumps often seem disconnected from adjacent memories. Rowan, for example, remembered weekends with his grandparents separate from chronologically adjacent school memories. He found that focusing on memory clumps belonging to a specific 'Rowan' seemed to reduce his anxiety levels.

Nevertheless, some days were easier than others. Some days a minor stress would throw him off balance for hours at a time. He wasn't looking forward to his meeting with the university's Board of Elders, for example—nor his first Axial Age Religions lecture.

On the day of the board meeting, Whirrarap appeared in a small white vehicle powered by electricity—unusual for him since Rowan mostly saw him riding a motorbike. He'd noticed that most Marins rode motorbikes, bikes or petrol-electric hybrid scooters around town. They only used cars for family or group outings. This Marin habit reminded him of transport habits he'd observed in a number of Asian countries. His 'Australia', however, had been known as a nation of gas-guzzlers. As the global stocks of fossil fuels had decreased, Australia's middle classes had taken a special delight in purchasing larger and larger vehicles.

The drive to Mount Leanganook was pleasant and Rowan sat back enjoying the scenery. It was a warm day, though not excessively so—early April in this region could still turn in 40 degree days. As the bush and farmland streaked past, he noticed a stark contrast between agricultural and land usage practices in and around Dinas Yarkuk and Victorian land usage practices. Firstly, he saw no cattle and very few sheep for the entire journey. Instead kangaroos, wallabies and emus grazed over large stretches of a landscape featuring native grassland linked by large clumps of native forest. Although mass cropping techniques were being used, Rowan noticed few of the food staples common to European dominated Australia. Fields sown with native fruit trees/plants, grasses and vegetables dominated instead, as well as some plant crops he didn't even recognise. They made him wonder whether some of the original native foods had been genetically modified since the 19th century.

More fascinating still, great tracts of box-ironbark forest and woodland—complete with mature understory—stood, where in Rowan's memories, there had been pasture for sheep or cattle. Peering into these forests, he noted gigantic trees hundreds of years old. As they drove on, Rowan realised that barring large urban population centres on the coast, the population of Marin-e-bek had to be substantially less than the numbers resident in the Victoria and South Australia he'd known.

'What's the population of Bunjilaka City these days?' he asked Whirrarap. 'My memory still needs a lot of prompting,'

'Getting up there now, two and a half million perhaps.'

'And the population of Marin-e-bek—what's that now?' He hoped Whirrarap wouldn't think him stupid.

'About five million people.'

Rowan thought about this figure for a long time, 'There must be a lot of people living in small towns or on the land.'

'One of the conditions of nationhood was that each tribal region would be funded—from national coffers—to create at least one major town at a location selected by local elders.' He sounded puzzled at Rowan's ignorance.

'Besides, if we spend all our days in the city we lose our connection to country,' said Whirrarap, concentrating on a bend in the road. Rowan noticed they were now climbing the thickly timbered slopes of Mount Leanganook—'Mount Alexander' in his world.

'Here,' said Whirrarap, handing Rowan a piece of paper, 'in case you've forgotten.'

Rowan was holding a paper headed, in Pan-Koori: **Order of Proceedings: Marin Cultural Board of Elders Meeting, April 4ᵗʰ 1997**. He stared at it blankly then put it on his lap.

'Have you memorised your part from last time?'

'My part?' asked Rowan, 'I presume I wait outside the room until I'm asked to enter and deliver my assessment.' Rowan looked more closely at the paper—the page was laid out like a play or screenplay with names attached to specific dialogue.

'People have come a long way for this— the Great River region, Garriwerd and further West, Bunjilaka City, the mountains to the east, etc.. They'll need feeding and our local Land Council is the host.'

Rowan noticed his own name below the words (in Pan-Koori) "Ceremony of Welcome and Approach". Apparently there were certain Pan-Koori phrases that he was supposed to speak—luckily English translations were given at the bottom of the page.

'I speak these words when the president of the council invites me into the circle?'

'Yes, and remember don't enter the circle until all present give their approval. Do you remember from the last time?'

'Only very vaguely—it would have been just prior to the accident?'

'In early December, actually,' said Whirrarap. 'I suppose you've also forgotten the melody?'

'Yes, you'll need to uh ... teach that to me as well,' said Rowan quietly.

They passed through a small township nestled in the northern slopes of Mount Leanganook before taking a left turn up an even steeper incline. As they drove, Rowan enjoyed spectacular views of the forested plains and hills to the west and north. The car came to a halt in a carpark full of small vehicles made by motor companies with unfamiliar names. The meeting house, close to the top of Mount Leanganook, was a large single storey circular structure made of mud-brick and rendered concrete. It had wide verandas featuring ornate wooden chairs, tables and other furniture. Above the building fluttered a large Marin-e-bek flag—its red, yellow, black and green colours strangely dreamlike against the clear blue skies.

Rowan struggled to remember the melody to his section of the ceremony. The essence of his part was simply to confirm to the group that he entered the sacred precinct as a friend of the Cultural Board of Elders. Whirrarap had listed the people likely to be present: tribal, Idealist and Chinese scholars, as well as practitioners of numerous art forms, e.g. artists, writers, musicians, story-tellers, dancers, etc. Some local Land Council representatives might also be present due to the link between culture and country in Marin-e-bek. Whirrarap also said that descendants of Abraham Isles would be attending, 'To decide whether to return copies of the diaries to you—so please be polite.'

Rowan was given a seat outside a large auditorium. It was labelled 'Honoured Guest of the Board'.

'The "Call to Approach the Board as a Friend of the People and Friend of the Land" will be enacted once everyone has arrived', whispered Whirrarap, 'We have a large turn out— there must be a lot going on. We might be here a while! There's fresh water over by the rest couch and a toilet round the corner. Remember: wait for someone to call you in and remember the melody.'

Whirrarap turned before walking through a large double door into the meeting area, which was composed of a central stage area (dug, Rowan, surmised, into the earth). On the stage sat an ornate bench (perhaps ten feet wide), three chairs and a large whiteboard. Circling the stage area were desks and chairs tiered to five levels. The area immediately behind the stage seemed to have been cordoned off. There were also a number of rooms behind and to the right and left of the main meeting area—some, Rowan observed, were offices containing computers, phones and the like. One looked like a food area and another appeared unused. Tinted windows featured on most of the outer walls of the building and indigenous and Islesian sculptures, paintings, ceremonial equipment and photographs were on display throughout. Glancing outside, down the hillside, Rowan noticed emus and kangaroos grazing peacefully near a billabong covered with hundreds of native lilies.

Turning his attention back to the gathering, he noted men and women engaged in lively conversation. Occasionally the discussions appeared heated—he hoped they weren't arguing over the Isles/Hobbes book project. It was over an hour before the glass double doors opened and Rowan heard a booming voice ask him to declare his intentions before joining the assembly of the Cultural Board of Elders.

'Who is it walks the land of the Dja-Dja Wurrung to meet with the cultural guardians of MUCT?'

'Rowan Sweeney, born in the tribal lands of the Woiwurrung. I come as a friend of the assembled Board of Elders,' sang Rowan in a croaky voice.

The declaration made him aware that he knew almost nothing about his Marin-e-bek childhood—despite having worked his way through all the photo albums in the unit.

Many of the representatives present nodded their approval to the president and soon after, his voice boomed out again in perfectly modulated Pan-Koori syllabics, 'We welcome you as a friend of this council and the people of Marin-e-bek.'

A young female usher led Rowan down the stairs passed a dozen board members to a seat on the stage just to the left of the president. Rowan also noted that Whirrarap had moved to a seat near the stage area—close to the president. Rowan's throat felt dry and he was sweating excessively out of nervousness.

After a few aimless minutes the president looked over to Whirrarap, who responded by rising slowly to address the assembly.

'Dr Rowan Sweeney addressed this assembly late last year regarding his progress with the Abraham Isles and Miriam Hobbes research project. At that stage he felt sure that the manuscript would be available for pre-publication editing by June of this year. He had only two chapters and the conclusion to write. One of the chapters, however, dealing with the musical content of Isles's sacred songs (supposedly extant in his early diaries owned now by the Isles estate), was proving difficult to complete. As we all know, Isles is rumoured to have written the song melodies in some kind of archaic cipher language perhaps related to his neo-druidic and alchemical studies. As Rowan's supervisor for the project, I advised the board that we give him another month or so to decide whether he required the assistance of a folk music expert and a data analysis engineer in order to complete the chapter.

Unfortunately, as I reported in late February to this assembly, Rowan suffered a serious motorcycle accident involving head injuries whilst in Vietnam on holiday. The accident resulted in serious memory loss in some areas (notably language areas), which is why I'll be translating from English into Pan-Koori for you this afternoon. He also experienced a degree of identity confusion which occasionally leads to anxiety attacks.'

Various people expressed sympathy to Rowan as Whirrarap signalled him to stand and walk to the centre of the stage area. 'I should also point out that during Dr Sweeney's period of incapacitation, guardians of the Isles estate requested that all loaned facsimile copies of Isles's song diaries be returned to them for safe-keeping. Obviously this means that Dr Sweeney's current assessment has been conducted in the dark to some extent. Despite these problems, Rowan has re-familiarised himself with the research material, such as it is, over the past few weeks and has agreed to deliver to you today the assessment before you.'

Rowan felt credible as a sick person—his arm was still in a sling and his head wound, though more or less healed, was still clearly visible as a large white scar on the right side of his forehead. Whirrarap shook his hand as he entered the stage and whispered, '*I had your Assessment Summary photocopied, the members are reading it now. Some advice: keep it short and sweet, read only the opening two summary paragraphs and read them slowly. I'll translate into Pan-Koori for you.*'

'*Where's the mic?*'

Whirrarap looked puzzled, '*There isn't one—every Marin knows how to project the voice at gatherings like this.*'

'*Of course,*' whispered Rowan.

'Firstly, thank you for inviting me here today. Although I obviously did not choose to have an accident, I nevertheless feel apologetic, since it has delayed the completion of the Isles/Hobbes project you've entrusted me with.'

He paused to clear his throat discretely. People were listening intently. He wondered: Did he sound like the Rowan they'd met previously or was it obvious to some at least that he was an Anomaly?

'You'll see from my summary that there are only two chapters to complete.' He paused so that Whirrarap could do the Pan-Koori translation.

'I do not intend to make substantial changes to any of the biographical sections of the manuscript, nor to the chapters outlining Isles's spiritual system. In this sense the book is eighty-five percent complete. I'm also close to completing the chapter on Isles's contribution to later models of intersectionist oppression. In reviewing my notes, and recalling my earlier readings of Isles's song diaries, I do feel that I urgently need the assistance of an international folk music expert, as well as that of a skilled data analysis engineer if I'm to successfully decode the musical notation system supposedly coded into the diaries. I'm unable, at this stage, to give you a completion date for that chapter, which might also require extra work writing out the music for hundreds of Isles's songs. I also want to say that I'd understand completely if the board decides to employ someone else to complete the book.'

Rowan looked around briefly at Whirrarap and the president before taking a step back towards his chair. Whirrarap, however, looked alarmed and gestured for Rowan to stand his ground.

'Any questions for Dr Sweeney?' boomed the president, an old Koori man with a large, bushy grey beard almost down to his solar plexus.

A tall woman dressed in stylish clothes merging Chinese and Koori sacred designs, stood up to ask a question.

'Firstly, I'm so sorry to hear you had such a life-threatening accident. It is wonderful to see you doing so well and we thank you for putting in such an effort to prepare this report for us. I don't want to ask a question so much as make a comment. Given your obvious mastery of the nuances of Isles's spiritual system, as well as your deep knowledge of his biographical details, I feel it would be counter-productive at this stage for us to take you off the project. Rather, I think we need to provide funds to pay for the experts you've requested. I also hope that the Isles estate quickly return the facsimiles to you so that you can continue with your research.' She nodded in the direction of an older European couple sitting in the back row.

'Hear-hear!' said several members of the audience.

'All of these options will be discussed in closed counsel soon enough,' said the President, 'however I've noted your comments and agree with them. Any more questions?'

A small but trim middle-aged man smartly dressed in a suit—and with tanned skin—rose to speak in French.

'I just wonder, Dr Sweeney, given your injuries whether you'll also need a language expert. I notice you're speaking exclusively in English here today—quite a change from your last appearance before us. Whirrarap mentioned that the language areas of your brain have been damaged, do we know whether that is a permanent condition likely to affect the completion date for the remaining chapters?'

Rowan tried to stay calm—although the man was trying to be friendly, it was obvious he suspected something wasn't quite right.

Rowan decided to attempt to speak in French, 'I have indeed sustained some damage to certain language areas of my brain, only my English seems unaffected at present. My French, as you can see, is reasonably intact. Highland Gaelic is of course a difficult language for any inhabitant of Marin-e-bek to understand, let alone speak. I've lost some ground there, but I'm recovering the knowledge fast. I'm also having trouble speaking and interpreting Pan-Koori fluently—though again I've made a lot of progress over the past month or so. This causes some problems with source documents written after 1860 when Pan-Koori became the main language of Marin-e-bek, however, the chapter on Isles's music focuses on his native Gaelic and English since those are the languages used in the diaries—as well as a little Welsh.'

The man stood again to make a follow-up comment, 'Given what we've heard here today I'd say your English has actually improved since the accident—an interesting phenomenon.'

Rowan felt his heart-beat accelerate. Luckily, Whirrarap rescued him, 'We are not here to interrogate Dr Sweeney on the finer points of the neurological trauma he has suffered. All I can tell you, and I've observed the various stages of his recovery, is that he's made exceptional progress this past month or so—I have no reason to doubt the specialists who say that his cognitive and language usage abilities will return to normal within the next six months.'

Rowan felt drained by the time Whirrarap joined him in the carpark for the trip back to Dinas Yarkuk. After the morning tea adjournment—where he'd chatted briefly with board members and the descendants of Abraham Isles—he'd gone for a stroll in the gardens surrounding the meeting house whilst the board had deliberated on his report in greater detail.

'They've agreed to fund the folk music expert—I have someone good in mind. Also, you'll need these.' Whirrarap handed Rowan a small leather suitcase.

'What's in this?' asked Rowan.

'Full colour facsimiles of Isles's song diaries. The family agreed to give them back to you. As before, they are not to be shown to, or discussed with, any unauthorised person. Please keep them locked up in your safe when you aren't working with them. Finally the board agreed to fund detailed computer analysis of the song diaries—do you know anyone we can trust from the science campus?'

CHAPTER THIRTY-ONE

THE FOURTEEN POSTMODERN VICES
(Saturday, April 5th 1997)

'What do you think so far?' asked Imogen, before taking a sip of her wine. A group of young Koories dressed in black jeans and black t-shirts with images in red of various native animals had just left the stage after a rousing group performance that had built up from a single voice mimicking bird cries to a whirlwind of voices—each occupying a particular frequency. Rowan guessed the group was amplifying and adapting sounds common in the box-iron bark forests.

'Very impressive—I really felt like we were in a forest, but with every creature kind of communicating directly with us. The performance poetry down here is really unique, though I wish I could remember more of my Pan-Koori and French,' he said, marveling at how well Imogen and her flatmates had set up their lounge for the party. A section of the small room had been cleared for the performances.

'With that last piece, the only option is to go with the flow—

to: *give up the alienated thought patterns that separate us from the animate cosmos,*' Imogen said, leaning closer and making him forget the poetry performances completely for a moment. She wore a long black peasant dress over a green under-tunic.

'The stuff I'm used to—the uh Sydney scene—is very individualistic and young person melodramatic: "I'm having sex in a share-house. I had a rough childhood and now I'm saying *fuck you* to consumer society". But this stuff—the chanting, those weird primeval time rhythms and the animal mimicry—I've never heard anything quite like it.'

'I'd probably write Sydney style poetry!' declared Imogen.

All night Rowan had been anxious about how they were behaving in public. They'd spent a lot of time together of late, even though he'd respected her wish to take things slowly. She tended to be keen to hug and kiss when they were alone, but seemed reserved, sometimes cold, when they were out in public. She'd introduced him to her friends as a 'workmate' since she felt students gossiped incessantly about their lecturers and tutors. Given he was supervising her PhD, she felt that public displays of affection would only encourage the scandal-mongers—even though she was a tutor herself. For the most part, Rowan went along with the act, in part because he didn't know if they were actually in a relationship. He felt more like her part-time lover—with the details of what that might mean still to be worked through. 'It's to protect you,' she'd argued, 'senior academics frown upon any kind of staff-student relationship. It would damage our careers if it became public knowledge.'

Imogen tugged on his arm then led him upstairs as a musical duo began performing a slow, moody folk song featuring ornate twelve-string guitar runs and beautiful vocal harmonies. 'They're only playing covers,' Imogen said, 'and besides, you'll be able to hear them upstairs. There are some people I'd like you to meet.'

Rowan followed—his head full of gloomy vocal melodies and guitar riffs.

As they entered Imogen's upstairs bedroom-come-chill-out room, he noticed alarmed expressions on the faces of a couple of the people in the room. Imogen anticipated the reactions however, and calmed people by saying, 'Rowan's cool, okay? He's different to most of the other staff members—former international cricketers are pretty streetwise! Besides, as honours students, staff are starting to see you more as equals. If you want to smoke dope and attend orgies, that's your business.'

Most of the young people relaxed visibly, though Rowan quickly became aware of another layer to how they viewed him—the 'I'm meeting a celebrity' layer.

A young woman in purple and black shuffled forward to offer him a joint

'Sorry, I can't—I may have to teach some of you guys this semester,' said Rowan, concerned that the dope would trigger an anxiety attack.

'When do you start teaching again?' asked a slim, dark-haired girl with a low husky voice that made her sound both cautious and seductive. 'Imogen told us that you had a nasty accident. I *loved* your lectures on Medieval magic and paganism last year.' Rowan saw Imogen flinch at the girl's tone, but he was relieved she'd addressed him in English. It quickly dawned on him that the group members were from New Albion.

'I'll be back in the saddle in a few weeks,' he said, 'as soon as I can remember my own name. The accident knocked me about a bit.'

A young guy, obviously stoned, giggled then blurted, 'Gawd, imagine a class in which the lecturer couldn't remember anything. Cool! *What* witch-hunts? *Which* witch were we discussing? *The* witch? *What* witch? *When*? Oh, that *witch*.' He trailed off into hysterical guffaws that soon spread to the other stoners.

After the group laughter died down, Rowan sat down next to Imogen saying, 'This gash in my head has made me dumb as dog-shit about a lot of things. Maybe some of you guys could do a better job delivering my classes.' The social worker in him was surfacing—*To communicate with young people don't be afraid to talk straight.* The comment led to another round of laughter, one guy shouting out, 'I'm Professor Dumb-As Dogshit and I'm here to deliver a series of lectures on What the Fuck. I'd like to welcome you all to What the Fuck 101!' More laughter—until one of the girls started having an asthma attack. She struggled to breathe between bouts of uncontrollable giggling. Eventually someone led her downstairs—perhaps to locate a puffer from somewhere.

Imogen took the pause as an opportunity to introduce Rowan individually to some people. 'This is Ungaru—he's from Aotearoa. He's studying, of all things, Druidism and is the only MA in the group. He's a Scottish Maori—or a Maori Scot—and he promises not to talk about cricket, eh Ungaru?' Ungaru had to be over six feet tall. He had broad shoulders and a friendly face.

Rowan shook his hand. Ungaru smiled, then said, 'Actually, I hate cricket—I prefer rugby. And look, it wasn't your fault the guy couldn't bat to save himself!'

Imogen flinched as several of the stoners took deep breaths—obviously his role in the death of the Aotearoan tail-ender was known to everyone present. Imogen butted in, 'Look, Ungaru sometimes mucks up his English. He doesn't perhaps connect the term "to save himself" with the fact that the guy actually died.' She'd grabbed Ungaru's wrist as though restraining him from saying anything else. Ungaru looked mortified.

'Forgetfulness can be a blessing,' said Rowan, 'I don't remember the incident since the accident.'

More introductions followed. Most of those present were typical arts students. He knew he'd remember very few of their names by the end of the night.

As the introductions ended three guys wandered into the room. Two of them looked like typical New Albion musos—all swarthy, long-haired and black-jeaned. The other, Rowan thought, had to be Godstar Wallaby. He was tall, colourfully dressed and deliberate in all his actions. Imogen became nervous as they entered the room and her eyes settled on one of them before willing herself to look away.

'What's cooking?' the guy asked, crouching to find a spot to sit in the cramped bedroom. His eyes flitted from Imogen to Rowan as he spoke.

'Hi, Paul—you as well, Fezz,' said the girl in purple and black, 'we've just been introduced to Dr. Rowan. You know—the Medieval Religious Studies lecturer from last year?' Rowan noticed that Godstar had found a spot beside Ungaru. He also realised that Imogen was deliberately ignoring Paul's gaze.

'Oh yeh—Doc Rowan! Can we call you Doc?' asked Paul. 'Loved your classes last year—even though you failed me. Especially that stuff on the Seven Deadly Sins—wrote a song about it actually. Maybe I should give you an album credit.' Paul sat on a pink cushion close to the door. He immediately took a puff from the bong that was being passed around.

'He almost died in northern Vietnam, Paul—a motorcycle accident. He was in a coma for two weeks.' Imogen seemed to be giving Paul a warning.

Paul leant back, 'Shit—*we have* been away a while! Hope you're okay now, Doc.' His face went blank as he spoke.

'How'd the tour go?' asked Ungaru, 'I thought you guys weren't due back 'til second semester?'

'The bloody Fundamentalists, not to mention the Patriotic fucking Alliance forced the cancellation of ten of our regional gigs. Some shit about us "promoting immorality". I tell you what, that fuckin' country is going to the canines. We were lucky to get across the border last week. Fezz here had to dump a quarter pound of dope in a shitter or the border cops would have had us for bacon.' Fezz, bong in hand, stood up and took a bow. 'Things are getting weird up there,' continued Paul, 'the border's closed every second day—we had to wait three days to cross and I've never seen so many armoured vehicles—then there's the 24/7 sonic boom of fighter jets and the ominous hum of high altitude bombers doing dummy runs above the Great Dividing Range.'

Paul looked thoughtful as he fixed his gaze on Imogen, 'We're through with New Albion—though the Sydney gigs went off, hey Fezz? 30,000 at the SCG—unforgettable! As soon as we're finished studying—if Doc here and his buddies would pass me occasionally—' he paused theatrically to throw a cool glance at Rowan, 'we're off to the UK. Our agent reckons she can book us a "sell-out" tour. We have two songs doing well on the Indie charts over there.' Rowan saw instantly that most of those present were awed by Paul. Dressed in avant-garde black and blessed with long black hair, high cheekbones, full lips and a bohemian way of moving, he was likely to be irresistible to women. No wonder Imogen was infatuated—he was the postmodern incarnation of Lord Byron.

'You not talking to me tonight, honey? I haven't heard from you for ages,' said Paul, looking directly at Imogen. 'I wrote her lots of letters, you know,' he continued, appealing to the rest of the group.

'Not here, Paul—besides I've been busy.' She was gripping Rowan's arm tightly as she spoke.

Paul glared at her—making the rest of the room fall silent. He shifted his blank gaze to Rowan, who observed him with the calmness of a social worker who'd seen just about everything.

'Hey, Doc—how'd you become a Doc.? It takes years to become a secular monk does it not?' There was something like hatred in Paul's eyes.

'Yep, I did five years in purgatory, and the last year—due to all the editing—felt like hell. All that to become an academic.' Rowan felt himself switch into teacher mode.

Paul grinned through the bong smoke. 'Hey, I thought about the Deadly Sins lecture a lot. I thought: you know, Paul, there are actually at least fourteen deadly vices—or should I say demons. Seven is way too few for a fucked up world like ours.'

Rowan had no idea where the conversation was going.

'You bloody Westerners—everything bad is a *demon* or a shit gene,' interrupted Godstar, perhaps trying to defuse the tension in the room.

'Come on, Rowan; are there seven or fourteen demons? And if there are fourteen what are they? I mean, you must have thought about this stuff a lot after swapping cricket for druidism.'

Imogen seemed about to leave the room as Rowan tried to humour Paul.

'Well the last hell I visited, as I said, was completing my PhD. And in the modern academic world demons come disguised as supervisors, members of colloquium boards and, worst of all, international PhD markers.'

'They say demons are experts at disguise, and at possession—you may have met one, without knowing it was a devil,' said Paul, mischievously.

'Are you calling our new lecturer a devil worshipper, Paul?' said the girl in black and purple.

'Not at all—just warning him. We're mostly New Albion citizens and foreigners here—apologies, Godstar—and Rowan's virtually a New Albion citizen himself, given he studied in Sydney for five years. Seriously, after those lectures

I did think about the vices—they maul you daily in the music scene. It's fuckin' party time. Don't judge me 'til you've said no a hundred times to beautiful women ready, willing and high on cocaine. For us Western musos, the Demons either get banished or they get comfortable—there's no in-between.' Paul looked thoughtful for a moment. *So there's a reflective side to the guy,* thought Rowan, *probably responsible for writing the songs.*

'Have you banished your demons?' asked Rowan.

Paul looked uncomfortable with the question and decided to change the topic, 'Universities like this are weird places, don't you think? Thousands of young people in close proximity. And we are in Marin-e-bek after all. You know, I have a theory that they used alchemy, astrology and numerology to design the layout of this town. And of course there's the indigenous background. That mountain in the distance, and all the surrounding area, sacred as all hell—concentrated fuckin' manna or what?'

'If there are fourteen postmodern vices, what are they?' asked Ungaru.

'Easy to answer,' said Paul, 'excessive narcissism, joylessness or spiritual numbness, pettiness or lack of imagination, greed, lack of empathy, falseness, flight from self, distorted lust, love of conformity, scapegoating … How am I doing?'

'That's ten vices—you're four short,' said a docile, overweight guy with a gorilla beard who hadn't spoken previously.

'We also have Reification and Envy.'

'That's twelve,' counted the gorilla, before sucking on the bong.

'Ah, Reification—the parasite that breeds in high altitudes,' said Rowan, amazed at the amount of thought Paul had expended on his theory.

'Oh, I thought you'd be interested in that vice, given it's the one most often associated with scientists, academics and economists. Such folk are prone to high altitude living—ivory tower and all.'

'What is it?' asked Ungaru, getting interested

'An ivory tower?'

'No, Reification—what is it?'

Paul stared at Ungaru without providing a definition—whether because he was too stoned or too shallow, Rowan knew not.

'It's the tendency,' said Rowan, eventually, 'to degrade reality by resorting to words and theories. Paul's right, it's certainly a major postmodern vice.'

Paul pretended to invite applause, before accepting the bong again.

'Come on, Paul—don't keep us guessing. You've only mentioned twelve vices. We need two more,' said the gorilla, stretching out two plump legs.

'Okay, well there's Cynicism and, oh hell, puffing this shit mucks with my memory. Look, I'll have to hand it over to our resident pointy-head. Come on Doc, help me out—what's the Fourteenth vice? You of all people ought to know.'

'Is Cynicism your personal vice?' asked Rowan, starting to dislike the guy.

'Not at all, my demon is Lack of Empathy. I'm a charming psychopath, or so Imogen's always telling me.' Imogen stood up, trembling with anger and some other emotion Rowan couldn't decode. Her grip on Rowan's arm suggested she wanted them both to leave the room, but Rowan wasn't retreating just yet.

'We'll need a better clue—after all this is *your* summary of the human condition.'

'For fuck's sake, Paul, tell us what it is,' said Fezz, becoming impatient with the discussion.

Paul looked smug, 'I propose the fourteenth vice as the vice of Desire for Power Over Others. What do you say, Doc Rowan, am I onto something?'

Rowan said nothing, waiting for the punch line.

'You know I've sometimes wondered what it would be like to actually kill someone. That must be very fuckin' hard to live with—even *if* you did it accidentally. There'd still be this little voice inside asking: *Did some part of me secretly wish to commit homicide?* And everybody knows that the fast bowler's job is to dominate, to gain power, over the batsman. I don't know much about cricket, but *Power Over* is surely a big part of the game, eh Doc?'

'Fuck you, Paul!' said Imogen, whilst trying to drag Rowan to his feet, 'I'm going outside for a while—when I get back you'd better be gone. Sorry folks, we have a gate-crasher at our party.'

Paul flinched, 'Hey, we're all tempted by vice. I'm just empathising with Doc here. I know a little about what it feels like to hurt people unintentionally,' he whined, 'we all have to find a way to live with guilt and remorse.'

Ambushed by other memories to do with guilt and remorse, Rowan looked stunned by Paul's renewed assault.

'Shut up, Paul,' said Godstar, 'you're full of shit tonight—she isn't sleeping with you 'cos you're an asshole.'

As Rowan left the room, he heard someone whisper, 'Jeez, that was heavy! I didn't need that after the Philosophy class we had today on Hobbes.'

Imogen ranted about what a bastard Paul was as she walked back through the campus to Rowan's unit. 'He's just jealous—though he doesn't really give a shit about me. Only wants me around when he returns from a tour. A few weeks together, then off he goes to fuck more salivating groupies! He's been studying here four years now, but is still miles off finishing his degree—prefers writing songs to completing units. Lucky his parents send him money to pay for the booze and drugs.

If his band starts making any real money, he'll be out of here for good.'

By the time they were sitting on the couch in Rowan's lounge room her anger had turned into arousal. She stopped talking abruptly and began kissing Rowan aggressively. Her body trembled violently as she undid the zip to his jeans and reached for his already swelling sex. As he ran his hand over her erect nipples he recalled, for some reason, the shakes and sweats suffered by addicts experiencing cold-turkey. Before they even reached the bed, they were both naked.

CHAPTER THIRTY-TWO

THE FIFTY MINUTE LECTURE
(Tuesday, 8th April 1997)

Rowan stood at the front of the circular lecture theatre as the students filed in. Though it was already 11am, the steady stream of arrivals showed no sign of abating. He'd spent much of the previous three weeks researching material to do with his first six classes, but he still felt stressed. Only the small bundle of A4 pages sitting on the lectern in front of him provided any sense of security—if necessary, he could simply read those pages before quietly leaving the lecture theatre at 11.50am.

This lecture was the first in a six part series outlining differences between Ancient Near Eastern, Greco-Roman and Celtic forms of polytheism. Further down the track were lectures on emergent monotheism among the Egyptians, as well as full-blown monotheism among the Jews, Christians and, later, the followers of Islam. In the lecture notes he'd inherited, Celtic reconstructionism figured strongly, perhaps because as much as a quarter of the class held to Islesian and Neo-Islesian beliefs.

Koori and other Aboriginal perspectives on the core material also featured in the inherited notes. Obviously, aboriginal perspectives on the material were second nature to the author of the notes.

Rowan glanced nervously at a scrap of paper in front of him — it detailed how the first class should proceed: introduction; apology; thankyou to Wu Tsan-Kun for filling in; language notice (delivery will be in English with translation facilities activated for French and Pan-Koori); brief summary of unit progression so far and direction for next two weeks; etc.

He set aside the little scrap of paper in order to browse his lecture notes. As he browsed, he worried that he hadn't made the font large enough for easy reading aloud. It also occurred to him that despite having tutored for a number of years, this was his first official lecture. Of course teaching could be nerve-racking at the best of times, but given he was all but illiterate in two of the three key Marin languages, his nervousness could easily develop into a full blown anxiety attack. To make matters worse, the subject matter required him to occasionally use Hebrew, ancient Greek, Roman, Coptic, Gaelic, etc. terms he barely knew how to pronounce. He'd written some of them out phonetically to minimise this problem.

Approximately seventy students were seated in the lecture theatre making it about two thirds full. The two tutors sat at the back, chatting with students and preparing to take notes. Wu was a thirty-two year old Chinese lady completing a PhD on the origins of Buddhism. Thomas was a quiet middle aged post-doctoral research fellow from Sweden. Rowan was already fond of them both.

He noted a higher proportion of mature age students in the audience than he was used to whilst tutoring back in Melbourne. Likewise, the students appeared to be from all over the world — though the largest groups were Marins of Koori,

European and Asian descent. New Albion students were also well represented. The Marin-Koories and Marin-Europeans wore the most colourful clothing—usually embroidered with traditional symbols. Today they were mostly seated in the Pan-Koori and French segments of the theatre—though a sizeable number of Marin-Europeans were seated in the central English speaking section alongside foreign students.

Rowan gripped the lectern with both hands and slowly surveyed the room.

'Welcome,' he said, projecting his voice strongly, as he'd learnt to do as a singer. 'We'll begin this series of classes looking at some of the late Iron-Age polytheistic traditions—in particular Near Eastern, Egyptian and European traditions. Given I'm uh … an expert on the progressivist spiritual system of Abraham Isles, which had its roots in 18th and early 19th century Celtic/ Druidic revivalism, as well as in Romanticism, I'll be discussing modern interpretations of Celtic polytheism to some depth.'

He then went through his list of 'issues to deal with' methodically until he was ready to begin the class proper.

'Okay, does anyone have any questions?'

The class's response to Rowan's offer was interrupted by the entry of a tall Koori man—over 6 feet five in height—carrying a motorcycle helmet, gloves and a faded red back-pack. He had a long flowing—but tangled—black beard and shoulder length hair, indeed the man was a mass of hair. He looked to be in his late twenties. He was wearing black motorcycle boots, faded brown corduroys and a faded green t-shirt decorated on the front with native animals. Rowan recognised him instantly as Philip Godstar Wallaby—the folk-singer he'd met briefly at Imogen's party a couple of weeks back. He sat down in the Pan-Koori section.

'Hi, welcome to the class. I've just been summarising the general direction of the next six classes. I've asked students whether they have any questions about assessments etc. I'll be delivering the classes in English for the most part, but you can access translations into Pan-Koori in your headphones right where you're seated now. There's also the French option.'

'Yeh, I'll work it out,' Godstar said in English, 'Look, sorry I'm late. I only finished the early morning shift half an hour ago—I had to rush.'

A student seated in the French language section stood to ask a question.

'We were told at the beginning of the semester that you'd be swapping back and forth between Pan-Koori, French and English. Is there a reason why you've decided to deliver the classes largely in English? I thank you for making the translations available, but they make things rather clunky— and I'm already struggling in my studies.'

'Look, I've spent much of the last decade in New Albion, so my Pan-Koori is a little rusty. Then of course there are ...'

He intended to say 'there are the effects of the accident', however, Godstar Wallaby, by now settled in and ready for action, interrupted. 'Now, I have nothing against individuals from New Albion—so no offence intended—but I'd like to know whether this drift towards teaching everything in English is related to the neo-colonial takeover of this institution by a New Albion senior management team backed by New Albion monetary "aid"? In New Albion universities right now it's: *you pay, we tick the pass box.* Up there the rich kids buy degrees that maintain their birthright social standing and the poor kids, refugees and, increasingly, the Aboriginal kids get dumped on. Are we headed the same way?'

The class, especially the New Albion students in the room, listened intently for Rowan's answer.

'Well, Mr ...?'

'Not *Mr*—just Godstar ... Godstar Wallaby is my name, though some call me Philip.'

'Well, Godstar, I know there are a lot of issues at the moment between New Albion and Marin-e-bek. It's also no secret that the union and certain sections of the university's cultural Board of Elders are in discussion with MUCT's new management team. It's not my business to comment here on what's unfolding on that front, but I can say that my delivering these lectures in English has nothing to do with any supposed New Albion takeover of the university. It has a lot more to do with … '

Once again, he was too slow to speak. Once again Godstar's voice boomed out, 'Aren't New Albion academics just business people—bottom line and all that. They tell me there are no educators left up there, just people who prostitute their knowledge on the open-market. It's important for us students to know whether you, as a graduate of their university system, approve of what's going on up there. Maybe you want to see the same system established down here.' Godstar returned to dragging books out of his faded red bag as Rowan answered.

'Well, Godstar, I was born in Marin-e-bek and represented this country at cricket … and although we've wandered far off the topic already … it would be unprofessional of me to outline a political position in this theatre. A lecturer is expected to be apolitical.' Rowan paused for a breath. His pulse was racing and he felt light-headed.

Godstar's voice once again filled the lecture theatre. 'Then again you could be one of those *lazy lefties* that rich nations churn out like whipped cream on the sponge cake of exploitation. One of the identity politics mob—addicted to convoluted theories that *politely* critique hyper-capitalism, racism, etc. Genuine revolt, however, is usually beyond the pale to such folk.'

Rowan stood for a moment with his mouth open as Godstar continued.

'New Albion's lazy left made basic errors back in the 80s. They thought that the answer to all cultural conflict lay in re-

representing reality. The magazine cover, the television image, the word—these things were more important than the global neo-conservative economic and military juggernaut—which, it is now obvious to all Marins, veiled a Neo-Colonial endgame. All truth was pronounced 'relative'—there was no absolute truth. Metaphysics became a thought crime. Lazy lefties typically underplayed the malignance at the heart of the alliance between hyper-capitalism and Enlightenment liberalism.'

There were signs of boredom around the auditorium—maybe Godstar had overstepped the mark.

Rowan thought quickly whilst trying to hide any sign of nervousness or frustration. 'Thank-you, Godstar. Given the obvious depth of your knowledge, you should perhaps be delivering lectures in contemporary social theory and politics.' Rowan paused—a few people in the front row were smiling awkwardly.

He decided to switch on the lectern's mic and move the conversation along by using raw volume to assert some sort of authority (a tactic he didn't ordinarily like to use). 'To give Godstar his due, I can well understand people's apprehension regarding New Albion intentions toward Marin-e-bek and the other nations that share this continent. Their military paraphernalia is clustered on our northern border, as well as in the oceans to our immediate south and east. An invasion seems imminent, and important questions need to be asked as to how conditions in that country have led to the kind of militarism and cultural intolerance we are witnessing. I stand against militarism, political intolerance and economic and cultural Neo-colonialism where-ever and whenever they manifest, and I know that the majority of academics at this university hold to similar beliefs. I also want you to know that the main reason I'm delivering these lectures in English, is that I received a nasty head wound earlier this year whilst touring Vietnam. It resulted in serious memory loss, as well as disruptions to the language control centres of my brain. Though my English remained intact, my grasp of Pan-Koori and French was damaged by the accident.'

Rowan took a deep breath—he seemed to have regained control over the class, 'Now, we need to move on to the subject matter of this course. Godstar if you wish to make any further comments please note that there will be a short question and answer session at the end of the class.' Rowan suspected Godstar would interpret the move as an attempt to suppress dissent. Godstar, however, didn't acknowledge the move directly—instead, he sat quietly, perusing the hand-outs on European polytheism a tutor had given him. There was a long silence in which students stared back and forth between Rowan and Godstar—perhaps expecting more fireworks.

'Okay, if everyone has the hand-out, I think perhaps it's time for us to go through some of the key components of Greek and Roman polytheism. Any comments or thoughts?' Rowan almost kicked himself.

Godstar stood up immediately, 'Please don't take offence at what I'm about to say, Dr Sweeney, but I'm picking up on an overly *New Albion* model of learning and class delivery.' Godstar was waving the hand-out at Rowan as he spoke.

'I'm afraid that's off the topic, Godstar. I meant: any comments on the *content* of the hand-out?'

'I think we're right on the topic. By your approach you clearly articulate a Western, one might even say, a *colonialist* pedagogy. You're sure *you* have all the knowledge *we* need, and that *you* can distribute that knowledge—as an expert—to us passive learning vessels. Such knowledge, by definition, can only be *objectified* knowledge—we're to *consume* your knowledge product in order to qualify for our piece of paper. I note, also, that there is virtually no experiential learning embedded in this unit—spirituality, it seems, is to be analysed not lived.'

'Not everyone in this class will want to experience so many spiritual systems in one semester! Besides, reconstructions of the experiential, i.e. ritualistic, aspects to many of these traditions are highly speculative. Just as importantly, when we come to the monotheistic traditions we note an exclusivist either/or tendency. One does not sample such religions, one is converted to them.'

'I know that your employment contract may well ask you to teach in a non-experiential way, but that's because this country's education system is being forced to embrace New Albion pedagogies—pedagogies alien to how Marin citizens traditionally learn.' Godstar sounded pleased to have brought the conversation back to New Albion Neo-colonial aggression.

Rowan, beginning to panic, interrupted Godstar's critique. 'If I am to re-fashion my work contract to conform to traditional Marin pedagogies, Godstar, I would first need to introduce you to the head of department. I'm sure she'll be interested in how *your* model of learning might operate in the modern world.'

There were nervous giggles, Rowan knew he'd crossed a line—it was bad form to publicly humiliate a student, even one that was continually interrupting the class.

'No offence intended, Dr Sweeney—I imagine you're a very competent teacher—within a New Albion context anyway ...' Godstar was now speaking much louder as a means to compete with Rowan's microphone, 'but the Marin way is that we debate things together, as adults with unique experiences—that is how real knowledge is passed on. We also experience knowledge by way of activating all the senses: touch, smell, sound, etc. Worthwhile knowledge is also linked to transpersonal dimensions of being. Finally, I intend to learn almost as much from other people in this class as I do from you. No offence intended.'

Rowan spluttered inarticulately into the microphone.

Godstar had obviously spent time comparing and contrasting New Albion and Marin-e-bek adult learning pedagogies. The class stared at Rowan in silence, frustrated with Godstar's constant interruptions, but liking the idea that they had something valuable to bring to the class. A few others looked nonplussed—perhaps the idea of participating more in the learning experience terrified them. Rowan decided on a strategy of de-escalation.

'I hope, Godstar, that you will soon find that I'm very much interested in the idea of a kind of Socratic dialogue between learners and teachers. I have no doubt that many of you will have informed and interesting things to say about the subject to be discussed. I won't feel at all threatened by this—in fact I'll be excited. However, I will insist upon certain basic behavioural standards as laid down by the university—one is to allow other students to have their say, another is to not interrupt a lecturer or tutor because this can diminish the learning experiences of other learners.'

He paused, noting that Godstar was ignoring him by pretending to read the course outline.

Rowan let the ultimatum hang in the air—it was his last and most desperate card and there was no guarantee that it would work.

Godstar looked up again and returned Rowan's dead-pan stare with a small smile, 'I get what you're saying and I am interested in what you have to offer in this unit. Before we move on, however, I'd like to make one final comment. No offence, Rowan, but for a New Albion educated academic your grammar is shit-house. I'm finding it very hard to make any sense at all out of these notes!' Some in the class laughed uproariously. Even Rowan had to smile—perhaps Godstar was proposing a ceasefire.

'My apologies—I wrote that piece in a hurry late last night, and now that my brain resembles scrambled eggs, I generally need to do a number of edits before allowing material to go to print. I'm happy to translate anything you don't understand after class. Also, I'm happy to consider student requests for the addition of an experiential dimension to this class. There's an Islesian/Celtic exercise held in a *clochan*, and involving a large stone, that some of you would find interesting to experience.'

Rowan delivered three lectures and two tutorials that week. After the last tutorial on the Thursday, he and Imogen wandered down to the student food court for some lunch. It had been a tough week, but Rowan had come through okay. Godstar had eased up on him by the second lecture, apparently interested in the content of the lectures, or perhaps with the political insights Rowan threw in—many of them coming from theorists unknown to the audience.

They heard people singing and playing guitar as soon as they entered the crowded food court. Imogen immediately went quiet. As they drew closer, Rowan realised why—Paul, Imogen's ex, was the singer, Godstar Wallaby was on guitar and Philip Ungaru—the Aotearoan M.A. student—was doing the mixing. There was also a drummer and a bass player. Imogen flinched when she saw Paul and seemed to want to leave the area immediately. Rowan, however, drew closer—listening to the performance. Paul was singing a contemporised folk song in English that Rowan didn't recognise. Most of the girls in the audience seemed captivated and Rowan had to admit the guy had a good vocal range and a powerful stage presence.

The performance didn't last long. Indeed straight after the song, Paul thanked Godstar and headed for the door—throwing Imogen a peculiar look as he passed. Imogen seemed to freeze at the look.

'Paul has to go attend to some real music business with his

band, so we need a singer. Any takers?' No one in the audience responded, 'You don't have to be good,' joked Godstar, tuning his guitar between phrases.

Rowan stepped forward, 'I'll sing, but I'm a bit rusty and I'll need song sheets.'

Imogen's eyes widened with surprise.

After a short break in which Rowan and Godstar searched for some songs they both knew—quite difficult under the circumstances—the performance continued. They settled on an old Robert Burns song-poem called 'A Red, Red Rose' from 1797, as well as the classic English folk song 'Lord Arnold'.

Godstar helped out with the melody to the Burns song by singing the first verse and chorus, but Rowan soon took over the lead putting in a solid, though rusty, performance. The audience seemed to enjoy 'Lord Arnold' in particular and one or two students even stood up to dance a little.

Rowan bowed to Godstar, Ungaru and the audience at the end, before re-joining Imogen for some lunch.

'Where the hell did that come from?' she asked, 'You never told me you knew how to sing. That almost sounded professional.'

'If you call that singing,' said Rowan, ordering a vegetarian sandwich—he didn't fancy the kangaroo and emu-meat sandwiches and pies on offer.

Before they could talk further Godstar and Ungaru joined them at the table. 'Well done, Doc Rowan,' said Godstar in Pan-Koori whilst offering Rowan his right hand.

'Pulled that one out of your arse or what?'

Rowan shook his hand and smiled at both Godstar and Ungaru.

'Maybe we should jam more often,' said Godstar. 'By the way, sorry I gave you a tough time the other day. I've had a bad week—my father is locked up in a New Albion detention centre and the bastards won't let me visit or talk to him by phone.' He looked glum and vulnerable.

'I know what it's like—my dad and sister tried to leave Sydney a week ago. I've heard nothing from them since.'

Godstar looked thoughtful.

Ungaru took the opportunity to congratulate Rowan on his singing, before adding, 'I've been told that as of next week you're the new primary supervisor for my M.A. We need to organise a meeting, perhaps with Professor MacIntyre present—though apparently she's out on stress leave. Workload issues due to all the changes round here.'

Rowan shook his hand and nodded, 'Well, we should make a time.' He brought Godstar back into the conversation, 'You guys are a tight musical unit—I'd be happy to jam sometime.'

Imogen ate her pie quietly before joining the conversation, 'I suppose we'd better introduce him to Henri,' she said. 'It'll happen eventually anyway—especially if he ends up jamming with you guys.'

Godstar and Ungaru looked uneasy.

CHAPTER THIRTY-THREE

BOOKS FOR THE DEADMAN
(Monday, May 5th 1997)

Rowan's life began to fall into a pattern of preparing and delivering lectures, researching the Isles material and occasionally seeing Imogen. He was moving along slowly but surely with the chapter about the social and political implications of Isles's theory—although he constantly had to check his statements against the backdrop of an altered intellectual landscape. He found himself advancing the theory that Isles held to a complex metaphysical (specifically an animistic or pantheistic) notion of oppression. From the writings he now had access to, it was clear that Isles saw most manifestations of oppression as examples of individual or societal psycho-spiritual depletion—both for the oppressed and for oppressors. Isles had argued that imbalances between the mortal world and the transpersonal world always accompanied damaging social hierarchies.

The chapter on Isles's musical system, however, was at a

total standstill. Although he'd diligently read the song diaries given him by the Isles estate he'd made no progress toward deciphering the notation system supposedly contained in either the words themselves or the numerous images that accompanied Isles's Gaelic, Welsh and English song lyrics. A perusal of surviving 19th century Isles song transcripts—with conventional musical notation—had not helped. These songs had been widely distributed among migrants and some had even been performed in Europe and elsewhere. Though Rowan enjoyed the lilting, haunting melodies of these pieces, it became increasingly obvious that Isles had composed two types of music. One type was populist—crudely designed to unify the various communities and sacred only in a very generalist sense. The Celtic and European folk rhythms to these pieces were unmistakable and some songs suggested martial rhythms.

Rowan had no idea what the second type of songs had sounded like—if indeed they had ever been played publicly. However, given the images that appeared on every second page or so of the song diaries, Rowan knew that they were to do with certain sacred mysteries fundamental to the Islesian system. Images of people in various physical postures indicative of a range of cathartic emotional states, figured prominently. Likewise, symbols of the 'Orbits' were everywhere, as were alchemical and Celtic revivalist symbols. He fancied that the music might be darker, more melancholic, more personal and perhaps more supernatural than Isles's more populist music. How all the symbolic and tonal elements embedded in the words and images linked to his system of musical notation, Rowan could not fathom.

He'd shared his frustrations with Wirrarap who suggested they employ the data analyst as soon as possible. He also said that a 'specialist' was on the way from Dinas Kaurna in West Marin-e-bek. She would be in MUCT by the middle of

May. When he spoke her name—Anika Miraj—Rowan's jaw dropped. He then asked so many questions about his future co-worker that Wirrarap eventually asked, 'Do you know Anika? She is a first rate poet, musician and teacher of music. Has she taught you perhaps?'

The Anika of his world was also a musician and lecturer in global folk music traditions, but she'd never been, to his knowledge, an accomplished poet. The coincidence, if coincidence it was, sent Rowan into a spin. Eventually he'd been given an email address and had sent her, with the permission of Wirrarap, copies of some of the diary extracts. He'd signed his name prominently and had waited with baited breath for her response. The response, when it came, was professional in tone. Rowan read the note repeatedly, but it was clear that she hadn't recognised his name. As the date of her arrival in Dinas Yarkuk grew closer, Rowan became more and more nervous.

During these same weeks, Rowan's relationship with Imogen blossomed. When alone—two or three nights a week—they shared a relaxed domestic intimacy that Rowan enjoyed. She was a lively thinker, with a secular perspective on the world that helped lessen his culture shock. They made love often enough, and apart from occasional bouts of self-doubt—in which she would get down about her looks, her ability to complete her studies successfully or her past relationship failures—he enjoyed her company. But in public, Imogen was much more circumspect—she refused to hold hands or hug and asked that he not speak to others about their relationship. Rowan suspected that she was still hooked on Paul. Unconsciously, he found himself competing with the muso to impress her—even though Paul was rarely up at the university (he wasn't due to continue his studies until second semester).

Perhaps out of jealousy, perhaps out of a genuine desire to return to music, Rowan found himself wanting to write and perform music again. He mulled over Godstar's offer to jam, but couldn't bring himself to phone and organise a time.

Around dusk one night in early May, Imogen burst into Rowan's unit saying that she had some books to return to 'The Classicist' who apparently lived on the other side of Dinas Yarkuk—'In the suburbs,' said Imogen. Rowan was feeling tired after a long day of teaching and initially declined to accompany her, but something dark, almost fearful, in her eyes made him change his mind.

'I've been putting off going for months. These books,' she showed Rowan the contents of a large bag, 'have been overdue since January.'

'Why don't you post them to him or get a friend to deliver them?' Rowan put down the biography on Isles he was reading and looked squarely at Imogen as she bit her lower lip. He hoped she wasn't about to indulge in one of her self-loathing episodes, since he had a lot of reading to catch up on concerning Isles's postural system.

'Henri likes people to bring them back in person. It's all very informal. He likes to chat to students and listen to gossip about happenings up at the university.'

'Is he an academic or a former academic?' asked Rowan.

'No one knows quite what he is—except that he's originally from New Albion and is extremely wealtshy. He's also loves the arts.'

Rowan decided to speak plainly, 'Personally, I don't want to run into Paul over there. Why don't you go—people will talk if I accompany you.'

Imogen looked upset at the comment.

'I know you were warned off by MUCT staff last year—before your accident—but I really need you to meet him.'

'Paul?' asked Rowan, softening his voice and drawing closer to give her a cuddle.

'No, Henri—the Classicist! I need you to meet him. I'd like to know what you think about him and about that place.'

Rowan's social worker self was kicking in—there were dark undercurrents in Imogen's voice that he was struggling to decipher.

'And he'll have a tonne of books on Isles and the history of Marin-e-bek—books you can't get in the university library,' said Imogen, aware Rowan was close to changing his mind. 'Plus, James, one of Henri's protégés, knows people in MUCT's Physics department. Apparently, they're testing a super-fast computer. Maybe it can solve that problem you've been working on,'

'Okay, so long as we have dinner on the way.'

As they ate at a Thai restaurant in the middle of Dinas Yarkuk, Imogen talked about why she'd avoided Henri's place since January. Whilst boarding there with Paul, she'd become addicted to dope, then speed and then, finally, heroin.

'Lots of creative types hang out there—mostly New Albion folk and international students from Asia, Europe and America. He helps them with accommodation, buying furniture etc. Quite a few board there with him. Paul and I lived there when we first came to Dinas Yarkuk. There was always stuff going down—it's a kind of hub with Henri at the centre, due to his money. He's a polite, strangely nondescript, *dead* old man of fifty something years. And he encourages complete freedom of choice. There are rooms under the house ... all decked out— "You are free, my dear, to indulge in any pleasure that inflames your imagination". Stuff happens down there—instinctual stuff. Pretty soon ordinary life—ordinary sex—seems boring.' She looked down at her half-finished dish before pushing it away.

'Were you forced to do anything against your will—we could contact the police?'

'No, we were never *forced* to do anything. That's the problem—you do it all of your own free will.' She shivered and hugged herself compulsively, 'Look, you have to meet him. I want to know what you think—you'll understand when you meet him.'

Rowan undid his seatbelt as Imogen parked the car in one of Yarkuk's older north-western suburbs.

'From what you said at the restaurant, he sounds like a fruitcake. Let's just go and watch a band instead?'

'We don't have to stay long. Besides, there's usually live music at his place.' She leant across and kissed Rowan softly on the lips. 'I don't ask you for many things do I?'

Rowan kissed her back—then pulled her into a deeper kiss.

She lingered before pulling away. 'This is serious Mr Lecturer. I need to know what you think of him—I need to see the two of you side by side.'

'Alright, let's pay the old pervert a visit.'

Imogen looked relieved, 'Now remember, he's odd—very odd.'

'I don't care if he's odd, I'm only here to meet James,' said Rowan, opening the car door.

'That's his house over there—the one up on the hill behind the huge trees.'

It was raining lightly as they walked up to the front door of a big old French-designed weatherboard building. Rowan marvelled at the ancient oaks and elms in Henri's huge garden—obviously he'd distanced himself from the communal feel of the rest of the street. Imogen paused a long time in front of the doorbell.

'You're right, he must be rich. This is an expensive suburb. What does he do for a living?'

'We only know him as the Classicist. It's rumoured he taught in Europe for years—but no one knows where. Others say he was an officer in the UK or New Albion armies, though others say it was with a European army.'

'Is he European?'

'Who knows, but he tells people his mother was English and his father was Dutch. Though born in New Albion, he says he travelled around a lot in his early years.'

She took a deep breath then lunged at the doorbell.

CHAPTER THIRTY-FOUR

THE CLASSICIST

Henri's doorbell sounded like a mini-church organ and took an eternity to die down. No one answered immediately, even though Rowan could see a dim blue light down the entrance passageway

'Maybe the Great Scholar is incommunicado.'

'He's often slow to respond to visitors.'

'Being a black hole to the universe and all,' said Rowan

Imogen ignored the comment, 'He hardly ever goes anywhere. He has a chronic illness, so people usually visit him.'

Sure enough Henri did eventually appear, though it took him forever to hobble slowly down the dimly lit corridor.

When he opened the door, Rowan was struck first of all by the man's ordinariness. He dressed casually in a collared white shirt and khaki shorts. The flesh of his legs was lined with deep blue varicose veins and his ankles, which protruded from brown slippers, seemed swollen. His face was immobile under thinning grey hair and its baggy skin had the translucence often associated with bookish people. He talked slowly, with a dry, wheezy tone to his voice. At first glance, it was hard for Rowan to comprehend Imogen's wariness of the guy.

'Ah, Imogen, it is good to see you again. And I see you've brought along a young man.'

Imogen's voice increased slightly in pitch, making her sound strangely hysterical and girlish, 'This is my new boyfriend, Rowan. He's a lecturer up at the university.'

'*Row-an.*' The old man seemed to taste the syllables. 'Well, I am pleased to meet you *Row-an.*'

Rowan greeted Henri in Pan-Koori. Imogen flinched then nudged Rowan as Henri waited patiently.

'Only English is spoken here,' she whispered, 'or French if there is no other option.'

'Hello, Henri,' said Rowan, this time in English.

Henri paused a moment before asking, 'Have you both eaten? You're most welcome to share dinner with us.'

Rowan noticed that his face barely moved as he spoke.

'Thank you, but we ate on the way out here. I have some books to return.' She handed Henri the bag of books then said, 'Rowan here is on the hunt for material on Abraham Isles, Miriam Hobbes and early Marin history.'

'Imogen tells me you have an amazing classical library,' said Rowan, trying to back up Imogen, 'and apparently someone called James works with you—he's supposed to be skilled at using computers for data analysis.'

'Yes, James is our young Pythagoras—a genuine numbers wizard. He's fixing a problem with my computer this very minute. I'll introduce you to him in a moment.'

Henri suddenly recalled something about Imogen. 'It's been a long time since we've had the pleasure of your company, Imogen. How are your studies progressing?'

'Quite well, I'm doing my PhD now. Rowan here is my

supervisor.' She paused, aware of how bad it sounded to outsiders. Rowan also flinched.

'I'm teaching as well. That's how we met,' she added.

A slow smile spread over Henri's face, 'A boyfriend, a supervisor and a boss in the one gentleman, what more could a lady ask for.'

The three of them stood in silence as Henri contemplated Imogen's news.

'I seem to recall you had a little problem—was it around the time you were with your last young man, Paul, was that his name? He still visits us regularly, you know. He may even finish his degree before the end of the millennium.'

'I think the band and girls—lots of girls—are more important to him than his degree ... or me.'

'Such is the burden of Dionysus, my dear,' said Henri, shepherding them inside with his right hand. 'Welcome to my humble castle. Here-in Western *culture* is revived endlessly— the good, the bad, and the ugly of it! Sometimes the terribly ugly.'

Imogen giggled nervously.

As they walked, Rowan glanced at the packed bookshelves lining the hallway. The house smelled musty—perhaps the books were to blame—and the floorboards creaked violently as they walked. The place was in need of a good vacuum and in places wallpaper peeled from the walls.

'You look as though you're over your little problem, my dear? In fact you look positively vibrant. Perhaps you're in love?' said Henri, as he hobbled and wheezed his way along the corridor.

Imogen scratched her arm nervously for a moment, 'I-I'm doing fine now, Henri. I just had a bit of trouble adapting to living away from home.'

'If we have our health we are blessed indeed,' he said, turning to Rowan, 'you are a very lucky fellow, Imogen was quite popular around here.'

Rowan was too busy checking out the library to register the comment. Above the shelves he noted exquisite copies of Renaissance paintings and blown up photographs of ancient Greek vases.

Finally the trio turned a corner into a large dimly lit lounge area containing more bookcases, a number of computers and several printers. The room also featured musical instruments—mics, guitars, effects pedals, synthesisers, an electronic drum-kit and so on. The place was obviously being used for jam sessions and small-scale musical performances. In the far corner of the room, only metres from a fireplace, sat a pale, thin young man in a black t-shirt and jeans. He was furiously typing something into a computer.

'That's James over there, Row-*an*,' said Henri, gesturing toward the young man. 'James, we have visitors. Do you remember Imogen? She lived upstairs for a while.' He coughed a dry little cough as James and Imogen acknowledged each other.

'Do you still have friends in the physics and IT departments up at the science campus?' asked Imogen.

'Sure,' James said, after a burst of activity on his keyboard.

'Apparently they have a new type of computer—a quantum computer—that calculates equations using q-bits instead of bits. And didn't they conduct an experiment in February or something that they had to shut down due to a solar panel malfunction?'

'The experiment was "classified", which in Marin-e-bek means it's on the front page of the *Bunjilaka Express*!' James exchanged smirks with Henri.

'I'll tell you one thing, though—the solar panel excuse was bullshit. The real problem was that the device destabilised energy fields in the vicinity of the test-site. Weird shit happened. My mate referred to it as "a seepage problem."' Again he smirked at Henri, who ignored the gesture on this occasion.

'Rowan here needs a super-fast computer and a super-reliable data analyst for a project he's working on. Maybe he could use your friend's quantum computer?'

James looked at Imogen as if she were an idiot. 'You won't get within a hundred metres of that device—the facility storing it is guarded by the Marin military. I'm afraid you'll need to use conventional computers.' James pulled out his wallet and after a moment handed Rowan a business card.

'My friend Gareth is your man,' he said, returning to his computer before Rowan could even thank him.

Henri emptied the bag of books onto a small table before hobbling over to an old armchair, which he promptly sank into before speaking.

'The students aren't well serviced by the university library—one tries to do one's best to help students in need,' said Henri, before taking a couple of deep breaths. At the same time, he pressed his finger tips to his forehead and temples and began rubbing vigorously but slowly.

Rowan looked to Imogen for an explanation.

'It's okay,' she whispered, 'he gets severe migraines. He needs to concentrate to get them under control. We should sit over there on the couch. He won't mind at all.'

James looked up from his computer to speak, 'Help yourself to tea and coffee ... and mull. All the gear is over there beside the television set. If you want to borrow a book just make sure you scribble your name, address and phone number in the black book beside the phone stand.'

Rowan and Imogen waited quietly for Henri to emerge from his trance-like state.

'It's quite a place, isn't it?' whispered Imogen.

'Yes,' said Rowan, aware—despite their apparent disinterest—that Henri and James could be listening. 'I'd give my hat for a library like this. Look, perhaps we should let him be tonight—he seems to be in a lot of pain. We could come back another day.'

Imogen's right hand gripped his wrist tightly, 'No, there's more for you to see. You watch, once the migraine is under control, he'll suddenly spring to life again.'

'Is he a writer of some sort?' asked Rowan, noticing piles of A4 paper on the desk beside James.

'Yes,' said Imogen, 'he writes non-fiction essays on Classical topics. He also tends a Classics web-site featuring English language translations of ancient texts written in ancient Greek, Latin, etc. '

'Henri is a true teacher,' interrupted James.

'Has he always been so ill?' asked Rowan.

'No. He used to be a soldier, but something happened in Europe. He won't tell anyone the details. After he retired from active duty, he devoted himself to the classics. He had a kind of epiphany.'

The tone in James's voice had shifted gradually to that of fanatical disciple.

Suddenly there was movement from behind one of the big bookcases and a partly dressed young woman stumbled into the lamplight, heading for the rear hallway. A little while later, Rowan heard a toilet flush off in the distance.

When the woman returned, she stared at Rowan and Imogen for a moment before turning to James and saying 'Who?'

'Ask them yourself, Josie, they have tongues! I'm trying to upload hundreds of files to a dysfunctional server. Not a lot of fucking fun, but that's the internet in Marin-e-bek, eh?'

'I really don't know why you don't take your drug-fucked ass back to New Albion. You hate Marin-e-bek—you're always giving us shit, Mr Imperialist!' The woman also looked distinctly drug-fucked.

A loud grumble, coming from behind a smaller bookshelf, interrupted her diatribe.

'Hold your horses there, Frisser, give a girl a break for Christ's sake!' said Josie before turning to Rowan and Imogen and saying, 'Who?'

'I'm Rowan—I lecture up at the university. Imogen and I were just paying Henri here a visit.'

'Oh, then you might know Frisser. Come out here, Frisser— let the good lecturer see you with your pants down and your rock'n'roll dick ready for action. Frisser is a lead guitarist, aren't you Frisser?'

A thin, pimply young man, wearing only underwear crawled into view from behind the bookshelf, 'Yup,' said Frisser, his eyes settling on Imogen, who refused to look at him.

'Well if it isn't Imogen,' slurred Frisser, 'you know Paul's really missing you, speaks about you all the time.'

Frisser's comment didn't go down well with Josie who had turned to stare at Imogen

'Oh, I remember you' said Josie, 'Imogen the swot. You did well to give him the flick—he can barely read, but he's very good at singing ... and fucking!'

Rowan watched as Josie ignored Henri's migraine and plonked herself in his lap. 'C'mon, Henri, let's perform for the guests!'

Henri, however, didn't stir at all, which sent Josie off on an abusive diatribe. 'Impotent old Bastard,' she shrieked, straddling him seductively and tweaking his ears. Rowan made to stand up, but froze as the towel she was draped in gave way exposing the small of her back as well as shiny white buttocks that were grinding down—in exaggerated fashion—on Henri's clothed groin.

'Look,' she said, turning to Rowan with an expression combining arousal and revulsion, 'Our Henri is dead meat, dead fucking meat. I'm *fucking* dead meat,' she giggled. 'James! Frisser! Look, I'm engaging in necrophilia. Quick, save me ...

from a fate …' she paused as though at the height of an orgasm, 'from a fate worse than … DEATH!!' She collapsed drunkenly against Henri's chest. Tucking her head softly under his chin she slowly stroked his left cheek.

Rowan was speechless as Henri's eyes, like some wizard's zombie, flicked open to focus on Josie. Henri seemed mildly frustrated.

'You really must behave when guests are here, Josie. What will they think of me? A degree of decorum, please!'

'I don't care what they think of *you*,' she purred, happy that he was paying her some attention, 'the puzzle here is: Why don't you get a stiffy when I sit on you? Are you gay? Every other guy—*even* some of the gay guys—get a stiffy. I don't understand that, Henri. It makes me think you don't love me,' she pouted.

'And you, my dear, are a little worse for wear due to the cocaine and your sexual antics with Monsieur Frisser over there.'

Frisser snorted obscenely from his position on all fours—obviously pleased to be called Monsieur.

With surprising strength and agility, Henri half lifted then half pushed Josie backwards onto the musty old carpet. The movement was enough to disorient her, given her state of intoxication. As a result she failed to find her feet and instead fell backwards in a sprawling mess. There she sat with her legs apart—pubic hair on display—gazing insolently up at Henri who handed her the towel she'd previously discarded.

'You need to get some sleep, Josie. The cocaine makes you somewhat anti-social.' He looked across at James, 'Could you show Josie and Monsieur Frisser to the guest room?'

'I'm not going to the fucking guest room,' she whimpered.

'Then I shall have to call the police to have you removed from the property, Josie. And that would grieve me no end. Your sonorous voice, after all, is much loved by everyone around here. Nevertheless, I will not put up with coarse behaviour!'

Josie looked distressed—her head rolled back and forth between her shoulders as if she were possessed by a demon.

'I'm sorry, Henri. I-I'll behave, I promise.'

'James here will show you to your room, my dear. Any more untoward behaviour and I shall have to ask you to leave.'

Josie made an effort to find her clothes.

'You'd hardly believe that Josie is the lead singer of a very loud folk-rock band on the edge of becoming famous,' said Henri, as James, Josie (who had found underwear and a t-shirt) and Frisser (still dressed only in his underwear), staggered together up a staircase round the corner from the lounge room.

'Now,' said Henri, turning apologetically to Imogen and Rowan, 'I'm so sorry. Not the kind of scene I like my guests to witness. Is there anything I can do for you?'

'The books Rowan needs on Abraham Isles and Miriam Hobbe—' prompted Imogen, 'also anything you have on early Marin and New Albion history.'

Henri looked at Rowan more closely, 'Abraham Isles, the Marin pseudo druid. Why on earth would you waste time and effort on such a figure? Ponder well the jury's verdict: degenerate Romantic … then move on, move on!'

'He and Hobbes are very important to Marin history,' said Rowan.

'The slave fancies he can better his master,' said Henri, nevertheless wandering over to a tall bookshelf, 'and thus the chorus sings: *What will become of the Republic?*'

'They rather liked the idea of a Republic,' said Rowan.

'Not *that* Republic,' whispered Imogen, 'Henri only ever refers to Plato's Republic.'

'Indeed,' said Henri, pulling three or four books from the bookshelf, 'the rabble—the *herd*—a wonderfully beastly word don't you think? Nietzsche rather overused the German version of the same. The *herd* are running the government. Everywhere Darwin's apes proclaim the death of the eternal, beatific forms. Hail the godless Ape! Ape is the measure of all things. The organic society has lost its head and the feet pretend to be royal ears. Meanwhile the peasant arsehole believes it can talk like a holy man! Enlightenment constructs a churlish Frankenstein.' He chuckled dryly as he handed Rowan some books. Close up Henri's face seemed almost rubbery. His eyes, to Rowan, appeared fathomless and his breath stank from neglected dental hygiene.

'Thankyou,' said Rowan.

Something had caught Henri's attention on the bookshelf behind where Rowan and Imogen were seated. He strained to reach for it—an ordinary looking book. He looked at the book's title for a long time, 'Hmm ... *The Black Resistance* by Fergus Robinson and Barry York.' He opened the cover and continued, 'It purports to have been published in 1977 by Widescope International. So what we have here are authors I've never heard of, writing a book I've never heard of, published by a non-existent publisher!'

Rowan flinched at the title. He'd read the book closely during his social work studies. It outlined a state by state summary of Aboriginal resistance to British colonisation.

'Well, well, well ... an Anomaly. In this very room! And at such an interesting moment,' said Henri. 'I do believe I'd like to hear a little more about your research on Isles, Row-*an*?' he said, his expression hardening slightly.

But Rowan was also interested in the book, 'How did you get hold of that?'

'Well, I don't remember ever buying this book. Besides, though it's in the history section it's probably not about history at all. The blurb suggests it's a book exploring resistance to "the dispossession of the Aboriginal people" across the continent in the nineteenth century. What an odd book! Quite useless to you, I imagine.' Henri perused the index, 'Yes, quite useless to you. There is no mention at all of Isles, whereas those books I've given you all deal with him—as I said, for what he's worth.'

'And what is he worth?'

'In an ideal human state there are always hierarchies based upon closeness to the divine. Civilised—as against *barbarian*—culture implies an aesthetic capable of discerning degrees of closeness or otherwise to the eternal forms. The closeness of a painting, or poem, or musical composition, or idea *to the forms* represents a shot at perfection ... a glimpse of heaven on earth. Isles certainly adapted an ancient sacred tradition, but he bastardised it through his affection for Rousseau, Owen and, later on, Marx. His ideas are a corruption of the true perennial tradition. Isles sold out to Enlightenment reason. You must read Smith—he's a mid-20ᵗʰ century New Albion historian,' he pointed to a book in Rowan's lap. 'He outlines the damage Isles did to the people of this continent—both black and white—by impeding British military advances and fighting for the establishment of a Pan-Koori nation in the South-East of this continent.'

Rowan felt his blood pressure rising, 'Why aren't *you* living in New Albion then, Henri?'

Henri looked thoughtful, 'New Albion today is also a bastard state—materialistic in ways cherished by the lower middle classes. Its close proximity to Marin-e-bek and the other Aboriginal/migrant states has done it no favours, but the real cause is democracy. Democracy invariably declines into crass authoritarianism.'

Henri struck Rowan as an elitist dinosaur—or rather a kind of reanimated fossil—only really worthy of humouring. Rowan noticed that Imogen, for some reason, had clammed up for the moment.

'James said I need to sign something ... to confirm I've borrowed the books from you,' said Rowan.

'No need, I'll inform James once he's put the over-tired children to sleep.'

'Do you mind if I also borrow that book?' asked Rowan, pointing to the Anomaly book.

'There's nothing in it on Isles,' said Henri, staring at it again thoughtfully.

'True, but sometimes we need to read material that reminds us of how History could have been in order to truly understand real history.'

'Real history is irrelevant,' said Henri, 'the history of the spirit is all that really matters.'

Rowan restrained an urge to debate the statement since Henri was reaching over to give him the book. 'Here, have it—though I expect a five hundred word review upon its return. I've yet to read it. Oh, and perhaps you could write something about your own research—it would help me choose more books for you.'

Rowan thanked Henri and a few minutes later, he and Imogen were escorted to the front door. 'Now that you're well, Imogen, feel free to drop in any time you wish. You too, Row-*an*. Here we have most excellent poetry, good music, remarkable art and marvellous discussions! Drop in whenever you like.'

Imogen said very little on the way home. When Rowan asked her whether he'd passed 'the Henri test' she ignored the question and said, 'Josie's a bitch—I bet she's also sleeping with Paul.'

CHAPTER THIRTY-FIVE

BORA TANDERRUM
(Sunday, May 11th 1997)

Rowan, Ungaru and Imogen arrived at the Bora Tanderrum (the 'freedom of the land ceremonial ground') in Dja Dja Wurrung territory a little after 10am. The site was in steep mining country overlooking forested valleys between Mount Leanganook and Mount Tarrangower. Godstar, who was performing, had given them the invitation. The site was abuzz with people and during the walk from the carpark they noticed people taking photos of cattle Anomalies—half a dozen Herefords with their distinctive red and white colouring. They were leaning heavily against the three metre high fence surrounding the grounds.

As they entered the vast circular precinct— donating to the refugee fund on the way through the gate—the three were asked to state either their country of birth (tribal or international) or their tribal residence area within Marin-e-bek. This meant splitting up a while since Ungaru identified as an Aotearoan,

Rowan as an Idealist born on Woiwurrung country and Imogen as a resident of Dja Dja Wurrung country. They were directed by attendants to specific entry points on the outer circle of the bora precinct roughly corresponding to the compass direction of their people. Rowan entered via the Woiwurrung gate and soon encountered traditional Woiwurrung stories, songs and multi-media exhibits, as well as a live Dja Dja Wurrung 'welcome to country'. He noticed a huge clay oven in the centre of the circular Woiwurrung structure where damper and bushtucker was cooking. The inviting smell reminded him he'd missed breakfast.

He noticed two gates out of the structure leading to the central ceremonial area. The first was a simple bushland path ('the path of the Stars'). The other burrowed underground ('the path of Yarkuk [Quartz])'. Rowan suspected that every Marin tribe had been acknowledged on the bora ground via a shelter and two story paths. Each path was subdivided into three smaller streams—in Rowan's case the first stream, to his left, could be walked by Woiwurrung people, the second (in the middle) by non-Aboriginal residents of Woiwurrung country and the third, to his right, by non-Aboriginal Marin citizens born on Woiwurrung country.

Rowan belonged to the third stream. As he descended, he noticed stories unfolding on the tunnel walls around him. Idealist and Islesian stories were on the right and Woiwurrung stories were on the left. The Idealist/Islesian stories combined art images, video, audio and material art objects outlining both migrant activities on Woiwurrung country since the 1840s and Islesian/Idealist (and other) spiritual and philosophic creation beliefs (notably Western and Eastern). The indigenous stories depicted key elements of Woiwurrung identity, but they also gave walkers a sense of moving through Woiwurrung country (to the South-East) into Dja Dja Wurrung country. Clearly every visitor was being granted both a symbolic path of 'sung' entry into the Dja Dja Wurrung tribal lands and a symbolic place of belonging/rest within those lands. All Marin tribes had built similar structures on specially set aside land. The system had helped unite the tribes at the height of the 19th century crisis and remained central to national cohesion.

At the end of the Woiwurrung 'Path of Quartz', Rowan ascended to a second, smaller precinct that encircled the main performance area (or bora ground). This precinct featured numerous food stalls selling mostly traditional Marin foods. After catching up with the others, Rowan and Ungaru set off in different directions searching for Godstar. Meanwhile Imogen went to talk to some Boonwurrung friends. Rowan noticed that she'd been edgy all morning—perhaps because the event was protesting New Albion government policies. Officially, she was still a New Albion citizen, though he noted that she'd walked the middle stream of the Dja Dja Wurrung 'Path of Quartz'—meaning she now identified as a foreign resident on Dja Dja Wurrung country. She'd deliberately ignored non-indigenous New Albion entrances to the north and north east of the monument—perhaps a gesture of protest against her country of birth.

Ungaru spotted Godstar sitting alone drinking coffee and tuning his guitar in a café near the main food court. He looked glum. 'What's up, brother?' said Ungaru, sitting down on his friend's left with a coffee and a plate of vegetables. Both men were rugged up against the mid-winter cold.

'Bad news from up north,' Godstar said, 'the police raided Mum's home again looking for information about me. The fuckers won't let the old bird be, they scared the shit out of my little brother. I tell you if I had a way of getting my entire mob across the border safely I'd do it tomorrow.'

Rowan joined them with a coffee and some irresistible damper smeared with wild honey.

'Looks like they're going after your lot as well,' continued Godstar, looking at Rowan, '*non-compliant* academics, novelists, artists and journalists. They're flooding across the border. I heard that a creative writing professor from your old university is being held by the New Albion federal police without access to legal counsel—some shit about him being a suspected terrorist.' Godstar took a gulp of water.

'Always the same pattern,' said Rowan, 'first they scapegoat the vulnerable minorities and then they go after the intelligentsia. Obviously the people of New Albion ignored the warning signs.'

'True, in the case of New Albion, the alarm bells started ringing for us Koories in the late seventies. Of late, all the advances of the past hundred odd years—the treaty, tribal reserves, respect for significant sacred sites, Aboriginal seats in parliament, an Aboriginal head of state—however symbolic the position— plus all the health, welfare and educational initiatives—well, they're all being reversed by the current government.'

'What changed in the late seventies?' asked Rowan.

Godstar shot Rowan a puzzled look, 'What do you think? Neo-conservatism came along. Instead of being seduced by Christianity and Old-Science, the New Albion masses fell for hyper-capitalism—the best Imperial ideology since open slavery! Look, I'm too depressed to talk. I need to restring my guitar.'

Rowan took a bite of his damper whilst surveying the crowd for Imogen. Although it was largely an Aboriginal event, Rowan saw many representatives from other Marin communities present—notably dozens of Islesian spiritual leaders, with their distinctive tattoos and clothing embroidered with green and black spirals and orbits.

The day's main focus was obviously political rather than cultural. As he sipped his coffee, a large screen in front of them flickered into life with shots of the ceremonial grounds fifty metres behind them. The crowd appeared sombre and tense.

'Time for the welcome to country,' said Godstar, putting down his guitar to watch the screen.

A bearded old man got things underway by acknowledging the spirits of the land, as well as attending representatives from dozens of tribes, both Marin and international.

'This is a special day,' he continued, 'today indigenous leaders from all across this continent, as well as from Aotearoa, meet at this sacred place—a place instrumental in halting a foreign invasion over 150 years ago.'

The crowd cheered loudly, forcing the man to pause as the noise settled.

'Marin-e-bek was founded as an alliance of tribes and visionary foreigners from many countries. When we translate the name from the language of the Bunurong, we find it means, quite literally, the 'splendid land'. We Marins, however, understand that the *splendid land* in question is more than the high rainfall, coastal country between Bunurong and Gunai territories. In the mid-19th century Marin-e-bek became a metaphor for our birth as a modern nation—a concept to help us defeat those who would would oppress and enslave us.'

Again the crowd broke into cheers and loud applause.

'We all know the story of Marin-e-bek as told in our national anthem—it's one of the few truly intertribal stories handed down to us from the place outside time. The story and the song tell us, that though Marin-e-bek is a 'splendid land' to those who are pure of heart, with 'splendid' fish—and mussels and yams and berries and so on—it is also a land of sickness and death to those who mean us harm. Visitors to the original Marin-e-bek, whether Gunai or Bunurong or anyone else, underwent an elaborate purification ritual designed to test their intentions. If they were friendly and pure of heart, they survived the assessment and were granted Tanderrum, 'freedom of the land'. Sickness evaded them and they gathered the splendid foods of that splendid country without harassment. But if they harboured evil intentions, the beings who watched over that country sent them sickness and ruin. The 'splendid land' became the 'badland' for such people—the accursed land, the evil land.'

The old man paused to catch his breath. The audience listened in silence, pondering his words.

'I speak now directly to the leaders of New Albion. Know that you are being tested and that our patience is wearing thin. Of late, your hearts have sickened. You harbor only evil intentions toward the people of Marin-e-bek. Let it be known that the time of assessment, of provisional welcome to this continent, is almost over. The verdict of the Land itself is approaching. So we implore you, before it is too late, to purify your hearts and remedy your intentions. If you do not, we will resist you on all fronts.'

The crowd erupted, hundreds rose for a standing ovation. Some began singing the national anthem—others chanted tribal songs and danced tribal dances

After the ruckus died down, the speaker turned to the south and in Pan-Koori welcomed brightly painted representatives from numerous southern tribes, who were seated to the east of the main stage. As he welcomed them, some stood and gestured to acknowledge his words.

"We welcome to Dja Dja Wurrung country our indigenous and foreign friends from all across Marin-e-bek and beyond. From our immediate East we welcome our friends among the Taungurong, Bareba Bareba, Ngurraillam, Waveroo and Jaitmatang. A special welcome to representatives from the Ngarigo, Wiradjuri, Ngunawal and Yuin peoples and indeed all the tribes currently experiencing New Albion oppression.

We want to say to all of you, in your time of need, that we have not forgotten you! We want to tell you that the tribes of Marin-e-bek—in concert with our international allies—stand with you as you confront the greatest threat to peace on this continent since the British expansion out of Sydney almost 200 years ago.' The crowd responded with loud cheers and chants as the speaker paused before turning to the north to welcome more tribal representatives.[5]

The list seemed endless and Rowan felt a curious mixture of joy and heart-rending sadness watching the constant stream of proud, colourfully dressed and painted representatives.

After almost an hour the speaker ended by welcoming a range of non-Indigenous representatives to the gathering. He then emphasised the task at hand—raising funds for refugees and educating the public about what was happening in the north. After this the Marin-e-bek national anthem was played with its haunting fusion of Koori and Islesian melody lines, followed by a number of other songs and chants of national significance. All were sung or chanted in Pan-Koori.

Soon after, the gathering adjourned and hundreds of people flooded into the food precinct. Rowan noticed Imogen among them and signaled to her as she joined a queue for coffee and western food. He then turned his gaze back to the huge video screen. The Marin news was on and he watched as successive items covered the growing tension between New Albion and

---

[5] In the MS original the 'Catalogue of Tribes' stretches for two full pages (and includes what we would call South Australian, Tasmanian, Victorian and New South Wales tribes. For the want of space and textual flow in a fictional work we list only extracts from this list: "From across the ocean to our south we welcome our friends from the Neunonne, Toogee, Paredarerme, Lairmairrener, Tyerremotepanner, Pyemmairre, Tommeginne and Peerapper... From the direction of our immediate south we welcome our friends from the Bidwell, Gunai, Bunurong, Wurundjeri, Wathaurong, Gulidjan, Gadabanud, Djargurdwurung, Giraiwurung, Gunditjmara and Djabwarung. From the West we welcome representatives of the Jardwadjali, Bindjali, Buandig, Ngarrindjeri, Ngargad, Meru, Kaurna, Peramangk and Wergaia . We also welcome our friends among the immediate northern tribes: the Wadi Wadi, Wemba Wemba and Yorta Yorta.'

its neighbours. The screen flickered back and forth between the news and live shots of anomalous cattle—Short Horns and Herefords—emerging from the surrounding forests to graze areas close to the ceremonial ground.

'Something's gone seriously wrong up there—they're no longer a democracy,' said Rowan, thinking about New Albion, but puzzling over the strange cattle.

'And where does that leave us?' mused Ungaru, also watching the news.

'In the shit, my Maori friend. Deep in the Neo-colonial shit,' said Godstar.

'Perhaps we should all join the Marin army,' said Rowan

'I couldn't shoot anyone,' said Godstar. 'Some use we'd be, a guitarist with delicate fingers, a trainee tohunga and a … what? Well, what are you Rowan—an ex-cricketer turned Islesian spiritual expert still feeling guilty about a freak accident that wasn't his fault?'

Rowan looked down.

'Anyway,' continued Godstar, 'I'd be useless with a gun or a grenade—my weapons are these fingers, this voice and this …' he tapped on his forehead. 'These weapons promote the life force—the ultimate enemy of all the death merchants.'

'But every two-bit Sydney shock jock also uses words as weapons. How are we any different to them, eh?' Ungaru asked, sounding defeated.

'I'm not trying to oppress anyone and I'm no warmonger. The way I look at it, I'm trying to slay that which is in my oppressor—I'm not trying to slay my oppressor. What about you Islesians, Rowan—how do you see culture's role in resisting evil?'

Rowan cleared his throat to speak, 'I suppose Islesians would say that "culture" should address "orbital imbalances". Such imbalances, if aggregated in a *nation*, can become deadly collective pathologies.'

Godstar, who was still restringing his guitar, interrupted, 'Ah! So Culture as a medicine?'

'Yes, real culture,' Rowan began, 'aims to treat social "imbalances" before they get dangerous. Culture converted into product, culture as mere entertainment, culture as patriotic guff — *the culture machine of the oppressors* — is not what Isles meant by "culture". To Isles, true culture immunises us against *social* viruses.'

'Then you and I have quite a lot in common,' said Godstar, 'I have a lot of time for Islesians — probably why I perform at their gatherings so often.'

But Rowan was on a roll. 'A culture that humanises is a culture that also invokes powers beyond our "world of limits". True culture is an attempt to *disrupt and challenge the very structures of time and space.*'

Godstar looked at Rowan oddly, 'Sometimes you sound like a damn prophet. Not that I disagree with you.'

'What exactly does New Albion want from us?' Rowan asked, trying to avoid sounding like a prophet.

'The wealth beneath our soil. Wealth controlled, at present, by progressive Aboriginal nations to the north, west and south of New Albion.'

'So, whereas in the 19th century the United Tribes used gold to fight off invaders, today other minerals may determine the fate of the Marin state?' Rowan paused thoughtfully.

'That's to adopt the New Albion point of view,' said Godstar, quietly, 'Marin cities were never built on *mere* gold, if anything, they were built on quartz. Take this place as an example.'

'Quartz?' asked Rowan, puzzled.

'Yes, to Marins quartz gifted us the gold that saved the nation. Crystalline quartz was always revered by men and women of knowledge — they healed or wounded through it.

It could also take them to the Land Beyond the Sky. Similarly, it amplifies knowledge and wisdom helping to maintain inter-personal harmony. This monument, for example, was deliberately constructed near the geographic centre of the Golden Triangle mapped out by 19th century gold miners. The mines revealed a vast subterranean "quartz/gold Uluru" almost two hundred kilometres long beneath Dja Dja Wurrung country. But we were never really comfortable with mining. It was always a last resort for us. Consequently the cave/mine art beneath Big Gold Mountain expresses a lot of anxiety. Crushing so much quartz to extract gold can wound the earth—even if the international tourist brochures speak of "primordial cathedrals deep beneath the city".'

'So why call Dinas Yarkuk a *city*, when it's little more than a small town with a university?' asked Rowan, still trying to absorb what Godstar was saying.

'At the height of the mid-19th century conflict with Britain the Koories and Islesians of Marin-e-bek spoke of a *City of Quartz*. What they were really talking about was an ideal state built on knowledge (sacred and profane) from all over the planet. More practically, when the old miners started to work the deeper quartz reefs of the region looking for gold, they declared: "we're building a *City of Quartz* down there!" And they were—the soil beneath Big Gold Mountain is honeycombed with thousands of kilometres of tunnels, some to depths exceeding 1500 metres.'

'So, Dinas Yarkuk and Big Gold Mountain aren't the *actual* (or even the metaphorical) Cities of Quartz,' said Ungaru, now drawn into the discussion.

'No they're not—the townships are but gateways to the *real* city, which, in terms of geography, is underground, i.e. the quartz reefs uncovered by mining. Metaphorically, the *real* city is also the community of artists, story-tellers, etc. that work hard to maintain the well-being of the people and the land/country.'

'So the Central Tribal Lands rest upon a vast *field of quartz* symbolising the life-affirming cultural traditions of all Marins,' said Rowan, almost in a whisper.

'I imagine there are very few places on earth built above so much quartz,' said Godstar as he stood up. His mind was shifting gear to the performance ahead.

Rowan chose his moment, 'Tonight, after this gathering, how about you guys come back to my place to jam some original songs? Not many people know it, but I write and perform songs. Ungaru—would you like the job of sound engineer?'

Imogen, who'd returned with a coffee and some soggy chips, frowned when she heard the tail-end of Rowan's offer.

'Sounds like fun,' said Godstar, 'but it will have to be tomorrow night. I'll bring takeaway and some band gear.' He wandered off in the direction of the main stage.

Ungaru also thought about the offer a moment, then said, 'Why not, eh? I need an activity to distract me from the thesis.'

'Something weird's happening outside the perimeter fence,' said Imogen, organising her lunch 'some sort of epidemic of anomalous cattle.'

'The squatters are coming,' said Rowan quietly.

Rowan, Ungaru and Imogen were settling into seats near the back of the gathering area as a female Elder welcomed Edward Saeed to the stage—a prominent New Albion activist. The elder introduced him in Pan-Koori, saying, 'Edward is the exiled New Albion president of Global Amnesty— an international organisation opposing the persecution of writers, journalists, artists, etc.' Godstar was sitting off stage right with a group of Dja Dja Wurrung performers. After briefly talking about the illegal detention of key New Albion regime critics, Saeed called for the Marin parliament to expand and accelerate resettlement programs for all persecuted New Albion minorities seeking political asylum—whether arriving via the perilous border regions, by sea or by air.

As Rowan leant across to briefly hug Imogen, three shots rang out. Everyone froze before pandemonium broke loose. People hit the ground looking for cover or ran in a panic for the closest exit. Rowan's gaze, however, was glued to the main stage as Edward Saeed staggered backwards—blood pouring from chest wounds—before collapsing to the stage floor. His body convulsed grotesquely as people jumped or rolled off the stage in all directions—looking for cover. Ungaru, alert to the danger, quickly pulled Imogen and Rowan—who was trying to locate Godstar—down behind the seating.

And then they heard it—hoof-thunder, lowing and bellowing as hundreds of anomalous cattle stampeded into the central performance ring. They up-turned chairs, soiled blankets and forced people to jump the fence to escape as they entered. Once inside, they turned—statuesque and serene in the early winter sunshine—to observe the final palpitations of the dying activist. After ten minutes they vanished completely.

***

Footage and analysis of the shooting and cattle plague dominated the news for days. Though the perpetrator of the killing was still at large, the Marin media and some politicians were quick to suggest the involvement of New Albion Special Forces personnel. The bullets turned out to be military grade and a camera on the perimeter of the bora grounds recovered footage of a black-clad figure on a nearby hillside at the time of the shooting—around 700 metres from the gathering and with a clear view of the main stage.

Godstar, though traumatised, opted for an artistic response. He phoned Rowan the morning after the shooting to confirm the jam session, 'Can you write political songs?' he asked, as they agreed on a Wednesday night session.

CHAPTER THIRTY-SIX

ROWAN THE FIGURE-HEAD
(Monday, May 12th 1997)

'The union meeting starts in twenty minutes, just enough time to grab some lunch. Are you coming?' asked Imogen.

Rowan pulled himself away from the computer to look at her. He'd been working all morning on an outline detailing the types of data analysis he wanted conducted on Isles's song diaries. Thankfully, Whirrarap had approved Rowan's choice of an expert—the young IT guru called Gareth that James had put him on to. Gareth was working up at the science campus. Apparently he did language preservation work for some of the Dja Dja Wurrung clans and was also brilliant at wildlife data analysis. Nevertheless, he spoke the impenetrable language of IT experts the world over and the complex needs of the project were taking time to convert into IT speak. 'I'd like to know if there is any evidence of image pattern or image-text pattern repetitions in the diaries,' Rowan had written in his email, 'we're searching for a coded musical notational system.'

Accompanying the email he'd listed specific language traits he wanted tested including, 'repetitions to do with end and internal rhymes, cadence, vowels and consonants, syllable counts per line (including patterns to do with long and/or short vowels) and stress patterns'. He'd also listed specific aspects of the images that he wanted analysed: 'repetitions to do with symbols, image positioning within frames, colour gradations, etc.'

'Earth to Rowan!' Imogen said again, 'Union meeting— you … want … to … come?'

'Yeh, I'll come,' said Rowan, saving the outline, 'I really need a break from this stuff—it's doing my head in. I always hated computer science at school—IT speak is definitely not my thing.'

Imogen laughed, 'The meeting is in room G.05.'

Twenty minutes later members of the MUCT sub-branch of the Marin Higher Education Union wandered into room G.05—a lecture theatre on the ground floor of G building.

As they sat down, Imogen whispered that the turnout was huge by MUCT standards and hinted that there might even be industrial action in the air. 'About time too,' she continued 'my contract is constantly being changed and I'm being loaded down with more and more admin work, marking and *quality compliance* procedures. These days, I have no time to think about course content,' she looked stressed just talking about it. Although he'd only been around the university a few months, it was clear to Rowan what was going on—the university was being Neo-liberalised.

After introductory greetings and acknowledgement of the local tribes by the sub-branch president, a union representative from Dinas Bunjilaka addressed the gathering. Mercifully for those assembled, he got straight to the point, 'MUCT is currently bearing the brunt of a government sanctioned educational experiment. Staff at this university are the guinea pigs. The main elements of this experiment are increased casualisation, rampant infrastructure cost cutting, program cuts and, very soon, large fee increases for students. As Marin government funding withdraws—frankly some members of our current government have been purchased by foreign interests —it is being replaced by foreign private sector funding (much of it coming from New Albion based multinationals).'

As he spoke, he seemed to Rowan to get more and more bogged down in issues related to the interpretation of the 1995 Higher Education Award by MUCT senior executives. After ten minutes he'd almost lost the overview completely and with it, his audience.

'The union executive hereby advises staff at MUCT of our intention to conduct a secret ballot to seek member approval for rolling strike action early in Semester Two.' The sub-branch president then stepped forward to read out a motion proposing the members approve the ballot. After being seconded, he opened it up for general debate.

Rowan listened attentively to the various speakers, but was disappointed at the lack of understanding of how Neo-liberal management techniques work. A number of the speakers, mostly social workers, psychologists and religious studies lecturers, spoke of the need to negotiate with the CEO and management team first, to explain staff concerns and work through issues constructively. They talked as though the management team were fellow social workers and as though all management decisions had been made personally and amounted to simple oversight. The arts people who spoke were more cynical and less hopeful of management changing its approach, but also had no real awareness of what they were up against. Many trailed off into vague esoteric speculations—'the vibe at MUCT is quite negative right now—we need more colour, more musical harmony,' said a tall guy with a beard. Then there were the Machiavellians—guarded speakers with one eye on possible gains for their disciplines or themselves if they voted to hold fire on industrial action. Some were even keen to use senior management innovations to settle old scores with rival disciplines.

Rowan decided to stand up and speak himself after the Bunjilaka City union representative struggled once again to summarise the importance of taking industrial action soon. The president motioned for him to come to the front. He looked a little down as Rowan took to the podium—perhaps the other Rowan had been somewhat conservative. He decided to speak in Pan-Koori.

'Look, I've heard everyone's comments so far and with all due respect, I'm concerned that many of those speaking against the motion are unaware of the key issues here. Let me summarise: management wishes to conduct an educational reform experiment here at MUCT. Ideologically speaking the experiment seeks to impose a nefarious Social-Darwinist educational philosophy on Marin-e-bek's intellectual and creative classes. This agenda is being promulgated by former colonial powers and represents an attempt to silence members of those groups as a precursor to more widespread neo-colonial aggression directed against Marin-e-bek.' Rowan noticed that the union executive, as well as the general membership, were listening attentively to what he was saying.

'We need to be aware that Neo-liberal managers are educated to use techniques that deliberately break down *community*—by that I mean any tendency toward group resistance. They use mathematical models based on microeconomic theorising to manipulate your personal desire for increased status, power and income. Such managers initially tend to use the 'reward the compliant' technique to achieve veiled goals further down the track. The ultimate end vision, a social vision in truth, is the subjection of all the organs of the state to 'market' forces—an ideology proven worldwide to benefit, in the long-run, only the few. We're talking about an ideology of de-democratisation that quietly shifts the blame for poverty to the dispossessed.' Rowan paused—his delivery had been dead-pan, very low key, simply stating the obvious.

'Since the days of the founding Tribal and Idealist Elders,' he continued, 'Marin-e-bek has sought to protect the critical and creative disciplines from the worst excesses of free market capitalism. The new management, however, seeks to turn the artistic and intellectual endeavours of our staff and students into simple products. If successful they will erode everything that Marin-e-bek stands for. They must be resisted here at MUCT and elsewhere.'

People were clapping and cheering. The president and a seconder were about to move to close the discussion when a woman from Visual Arts leapt up to request a vote on a change of motion. She wanted to bring the industrial action forward to the end of semester one—'let's show senior management that we intend to bring the university to a complete standstill unless their reforms are withdrawn'.

The ballot vote was taken, and passed unanimously. Other motions followed: a vote of no confidence in the senior management team, and, most surprisingly for Rowan, a vote to give him an honorary position as Sub-branch Patron. 'We know you've had a tough six months', said the sub-branch president, 'but the position wouldn't demand much energy. The gesture of a former international cricketer standing against the erosion of Marin cultural values here at MUCT would represent a huge boost to our campaign. What do you say?'

Pleased with the reception of his speech and honoured by the invitation, Rowan accepted.

By the time he left the lecture theatre an hour later he'd also agreed to write an essay on educational Neo-colonialism, making use of the 'advanced social theory' he'd presented at the meeting.

'That was a low key, keep your head down sort of performance,' chided Imogen, 'Are you sure you're not getting possessed by that Isles fellow? How did Rowan the cricketer and conservative religious studies academic become Rowan the musician and social activist? I hope you know what you're getting yourself into.'

'Next time I have a rush of blood to the head like that, please slap me forcefully across the face,' joked Rowan, who was already starting to feel anxious about what he'd just committed to.

The Wednesday night jam session with Godstar and two other musicians went well. Rowan impressed his new band members by playing them a number of *Interstitium's* old songs. In their first 'group' decision they'd decided to perform the songs in public within a month. When Godstar asked if Rowan had a name for the band he'd immediately said *Interstitium*.

Though Godstar's acoustic guitar skills were advanced, he initially resisted playing electric guitar due to his dislike of 'angry, spiritless New Albion music.' To try and change his mind Rowan had demonstrated some classic alternative rock riffs on acoustic guitar. With Godstar interested, Rowan grabbed an electric guitar, an effects pedal unit and an amp from the music department and played the same riffs in electric form. Godstar was amazed at the sheer originality of the riffs.

The ad hoc band, with Ungaru as mixer/sound engineer and Rowan as main vocalist, soon started practicing three times a week.

On the way home after the first session, Imogen asked Rowan, 'Where did you learn these things? What the hell did they teach you in Vietnam?'

CHAPTER THIRTY-SEVEN

ANIKA MIRAJ
(Thusday, May 15th 1997)

Rowan met Anika at the appointed time in the university café. He'd wandered down there after delivering a lecture on late Medieval conceptions of the Seven Deadly Sins—his mind was awash with demonology. Anika had arrived early carrying facsimiles of the song manuscripts she'd been sent by Whirrarap. She wore a rainbow coloured dress—thematically linked to the rainbow Lorikeet. Rowan knew she'd flown from Dinas Kaurna in western Marin-e-bek to Bunjilaka City. From there she'd probably hired a rental car for the trip up to Dinas Yarkuk.

She had her back to him and was seated in front of huge windows overlooking an undercover rainforest area. Off in distance, Rowan could see the university's main gate. The sun, obscured by dark clouds, hung low in the sky and some of the waitresses were busy lighting candles on nearby tables. The effect of lights flickering inside the café and the sun setting outside gave the moment a surreal aura. He'd seen the promotional photos, and read the short bio doing the rounds in the staff room: *Anika Miraj, folk musician/lyricist, poet and lecturer in European folk music.* She looked exactly like the Anika of his youth—of medium height, with long brown hair and angular, almost aristocratic, features. And yet he knew she was a different Anika, someone to whom Rowan Sweeney was a stranger.

Seeing her made him feel like a love-struck teenager again, his hands felt cold and his heart beat hard and fast. The Rowan of late 20th century Victoria was bubbling into consciousness.

She was being served a cappuccino as he approached. For a moment, he suspected she was an apparition—an Anomaly. For some years now his dreams of Anika had involved an aura of insubstantiality. This contrasted sharply with his youthful memories, always intimate and sun-drenched—her body young and firm, her clothes stylish and colourful. In the beginning, life with her had been so innocent and carefree. His career in the music industry had ended all of that.

He ordered a light beer from a passing waitress, straightened his collar and steeled himself for the introduction.

'Hi, Anika is it? Is it okay if we speak in English? I'm Rowan Sweeney, I've been writing the book on Abraham Isles and Miriam Hobbes. We'll be working together to try and decipher the musical notation behind some of Isles's songs.' His heart beat wildly.

Anika turned to face him.

'Hi, Rowan,' she said, smiling 'yes, of course I'll be fine with English. It's good to meet you in person at last.'

He was immediately struck by the warmth in her voice and the genuineness of her smile. Two of the many reasons he'd never really gotten over her. He also became aware of a sudden pang of guilt.

'How was your flight from Dinas Kaurna? Trouble-free,

I hope. And you didn't get caught in the traffic north of Bunjilaka City?'

Anika laughed, 'No problems on either score. It's great to be back east for a while. It's greener over here and I had a wonderful morning visiting some art exhibitions in Dinas Bunjilaka.'

Rowan had wondered if Anika, like himself, might be the victim of some kind of Anomaly. Perhaps she would recognise him in some way. His hopes were dashed, however, when she treated him with all the friendly formality of a new acquaintance.

'Apparently you're only here for six to eight weeks, and I've been told you'll be doing some lecturing too, besides the research work? We have quite a deadline, however, so I'm very keen to hear your thoughts on the diaries.' He was doing his best to play the role of new academic acquaintance.

'We have work ahead alright! I've never seen anything quite like it—I mean there are song lyrics on most diary pages, but where do we even begin to look for a system of musical notation?' As she spoke, she browsed the pages of one of the diary copies she'd been sent.

Rowan marvelled at the tanned skin of her fingers and wrists—suppressed longing and sadness surfaced, choking his voice. Out of nowhere, he felt weak on his feet—swaying precariously where he stood.

'Are you okay?' she asked, looking at him with concern.

'It's been a busy week—and lots more work ahead.' He leant on a chair to steady himself. 'I've just done a lecture on the Seven Deadly Sins; Dante's Hell can dehydrate the fittest of scholars. I'll just sit down if that's alright.' He was struggling to control his breathing.

Anika helped him get seated.

'You've gone white as a sheet!'

Her physical closeness wasn't helping him calm down.

'It's one of the reasons you've been employed to assist me—I've been getting funny turns for a few months now.' He stared at the tablecloth as his beer arrived. Anika thanked the waitress.

'Yes, I heard, you're recovering from a serious accident.' She'd returned to her seat to pour him some water, which he accepted.

Staring at the facsimiles was helping him calm down.

She patted his arm after he drank. 'Feeling better or do you want me to call someone? Actually, I'm not feeling great myself. I've had a weird virus these past few months,' said Anika out of the blue, 'can't get rid of it. I hope I haven't passed it on to my son, Neill. He's ten and I'm missing him already.' She stared through the undercover rainforest towards the university's main gate as though pondering something odd about the virus. 'The virus gives me weird dreams, sometimes even daytime hallucinations. A Kaurna medicine expert I'm friends with—Western medicine was useless, I have to say—told me: "Someone or something from the subtle dimension is trying to make contact."' She stopped abruptly, aware perhaps that she was speaking to a stranger. 'You look like you've got a bit of colour back.'

Rowan wanted to hear more about both the virus and her life, but felt he didn't know her well enough to pry. Besides, a child meant there was also a man in her life and he didn't want to hear the details of that right away. 'Everyone is feeling a bit anomalous around here—in fact full-blown Anomalies are ten a penny at the moment,' he joked.

'Same in Western Marin-e-bek at present. The spirits don't like the military build-up on our border. New Albion politicians have the scent of blood in their nostrils and it'll take a lot to stop them,' she sighed, before gazing at the facsimiles in front of her.

'What do you make of them?' he said, feeling more relaxed. A strange idea occurred to him—hadn't Douglas mentioned something about partial cross-overs—perhaps Anika was experiencing a partial cross-over. The thought, though lacking evidence, appealed to him.

She stared at the plethora of alchemical, astrological, neo-druidic and orbital symbols that decorated almost every page of the manuscript. They were always separated from the lyrics. 'They look like magical pictures. Are you sure we're looking at a music notation system?'

Rowan peered at the page in-front of Anika. 'Apparently there's a clan saying that translates as: "The pictures lead to the music." Unfortunately, the last original guardian of the diaries died in 1916. Apparently he took the code for Isles's notation system with him to the grave.'

'Great,' said Anika, 'a most helpful last guardian of the tartan.' She laughed a gentle, musical laugh.

'Well, we have about six weeks to sort out the bagpipes from the harps! We've also been asked to neatly incorporate the results of our code breaking, that is, three hundred correctly notated songs, into my book as appendices. Easy as you like!' They laughed together for a moment before Anika went quiet.

'Strangest thing—I just had a moment of déjà vu. It's like I've been here before.' She stared around the room as though trying to connect furnishings and other objects with the memory she'd just experienced.

'Between your virus and my head injury, we have a good chance of conjuring Abe Isles himself. Maybe we can ask him to do a special performance of his sacred songs,' said Rowan, aware Anika was a little shaken.

'A shame you don't have a background music,' sighed Anika, 'cricket and religion are your areas of expertise.'

'Actually,' said Rowan, 'I'm a bit of a *scratch about* guitarist and alternative rock singer.' He felt annoyed that nobody in this world knew about his musical abilities.

After Anika finished her coffee, they agreed on a research time-table. The plan was to work with image repetitions appearing in large numbers of diary pages—the orbital images being the chief suspects. They decided to work together for two or three hours every afternoon (except on weekends) until either they'd made some progress or had exhausted every possibility. Anika was also presenting a series of guest lectures on remnant paganism in 19th century northern European folk traditions. This meant she wouldn't be available until May 21st to work full time deciphering (and hopefully transposing) the musical notation behind the diary songs.

CHAPTER THIRTY-EIGHT:

IMOGEN IN THE DEN
(Saturday, May 24th 1997)

'What are you trying to do here tonight, melt people's brains?' said Imogen, as she helped Rowan lift the large black guitar amp out of the back of her friend's station wagon.

'You've got to play certain kinds of music loudly. The drums have to pound in the listener's rib-cage and the bass needs to penetrate every cell of the body. It's how you shock people out of their stupor when they're anaesthetised by civilisation.'

Imogen looked doubtful.

'Ask Paul,' he said, in an even tone, 'I bet his band also aim to "melt the ear wax" of the civilised.'

Imogen sighed and then looked earnestly at Rowan. 'I'm a bit on edge. I don't like coming here these days—bad memories— but my boyfriend, who never used to take the slightest interest in contemporary music, well he had his head kicked in by a road and now he suddenly enjoys belting out New Albion-style rock songs at ear-splitting decibels. It's all a bit confusing.'

Rowan let the comment pass. He was trying to remember the lyrics to the second verse of one of his songs.

'Earth to Rowan!' said Imogen, as they reached the front door of Henri's house where they were immediately let in by James. He directed them through to the large back room that would host the band night.

Inside the room a stage area with a sound system—provided by Paul's band—had already been set up. Rowan noticed Godstar seated in one corner carefully tuning his electric guitar. His favourite acoustic guitar stood on a stand beside him. Rowan and Imogen placed the amp beside the drum kit and were just about to wander back outside for some other equipment when Paul and James appeared. Paul, who appeared stoned, smiled obliquely at Imogen, who flinched, but he ignored Rowan altogether—even as Rowan thanked him for providing all the gear.

Paul offloaded a vocal effects unit to James—who was acting as sound engineer—and walked out, leaving Frisser and the other band-members to set up their instruments alone. Rowan's band had accepted the support role and would thus perform first. Rowan thought that a posture of humbleness would contrast nicely with Paul's arrogance. The raw and haunting power of *Interstitium*, tested on stages all across the other Australia, would speak for itself.

Rowan's makeshift band eventually did a sound check using one of the songs Rowan had taught them. Imogen sat at the back—deep in thought and wearing protective earplugs. After the sound check, she and Rowan bought some Indian takeaway and sat down to eat it in a nearby park.

'I'm thinking of giving it a miss tonight, Rowan.'

Rowan looked at her in disbelief, 'Are you serious? Why? I've been counting on you being there.'

'You're not listening to me. I don't like Henri's place—it

makes me feel weird. They make me feel weird—Henri, Josie, Paul, all of them. You do the gig and then meet me back at your place afterwards.'

'Come on, Imogen, you've been spending too much time on your PhD. Take a break before it drives you nutty. Socialise! Dance! The semester is almost over. Time to have some fun. No excuses!'

'You have an attractive workmate now—perhaps you should invite her instead.'

'Anika and I? You must be joking,' he said, a little shocked that Imogen had picked up on his attraction to Anika.

Imogen immediately apologised, 'I just feel weird tonight—like something's going to happen. People become automatons in that place. Zombies, with dead-meat Henri pulling all the zombie strings.'

Rowan laughed, but had to confess that he also felt the strangeness in the air. As if he was being possessed by his old self—the musician self of his long vanquished youth. He made a mental note to buy some dope off Henri—nothing wrong with having a smoke before the gig. He had no desire to get wasted like in the old days, but by god he was going to relax and enjoy himself.

And he did need to relax—the Head of School had been making noises about his relationship with Imogen, though Rowan knew that the real issue was his new role as union figurehead. He hadn't realised that his cricketing profile would give the union the upper hand in their campaign to oppose the corporatisation of MUCT. Unable to tackle a national icon front-on, management had taken aim at his personal life instead.

The union had warned him of moves afoot to suspend him before the start of second semester. The organiser from Bunjilaka City had even quizzed him by phone. 'I assume you're following the code of conduct?' Rowan said 'Yes, of course', but in truth, he hadn't even read the code of conduct. And besides, Imogen was his life-raft. She was only a few years younger than himself—a staff member and a willing partner in the relationship. Hadn't they avoided public displays of affection? As far as he was concerned, it was no business of the university who he slept with. Besides, there was always the option of relinquishing his role as her PhD supervisor.

Then there were the issues with the Isles research. He and Anika had made no progress to date in deciphering the notational system behind the Isles songs and their frustration was growing. The deadline for the book's submission to the publisher was fast approaching and Whirrarap was looking ever more anxious, 'This is an important book, Rowan—we need those chapters completed.' What Rowan and Anika needed, however, was a miracle. The completion of the other chapter, with the aid of Henri's New Albion books on Isles, had appeased Whirrarap and the Board, but sooner or later he'd have to admit defeat with regard to the musical notation system.

Imogen eventually agreed to attend the gig. Although problems between them had been brewing for a while, he believed that they were caused by her idealisation of Paul. Perhaps if Imogen saw that he—Rowan—could also create and perform powerful music she'd lose here fixation on the guy.

Deep down, however, he knew that the performance had very little to do with Imogen. His own issues had begun to surface days ago. He'd experienced vivid flashbacks to his band days—flooding him with memories of Anika, Eric and his old band mates. Interestingly, he hadn't invited Anika to the gig, aware perhaps that as a poet and highly trained interpreter of Marin sacred music she'd find the crass New Albion aura to his music ludicrous, boring or worse. There was also another motivation: he didn't want Imogen and Anika meeting just yet, especially not in Henri's house. Rowan had too many misgivings about Henri's milieu. For the moment, however, he'd decided to set them aside—he was determined to be young, oblivious and creative again. Nothing else mattered, not Imogen, not Anika, not even his reputation as an academic. The music would drown out all the craziness of recent months. *If in doubt*, he told himself, *scream it out!*

The room, though not large, had space for perhaps seventy people. It was already dark outside when Rowan, accompanied by Godstar on guitar and three other musicians—a drummer, bass player and keyboard player—took to the makeshift stage. Rowan took the main mic—he carried an electric guitar hooked up to the mixer, and he was dressed all in black except for small green spirals splashed across the front of his t-shirt. He'd decided to play rhythm guitar for most of the songs, largely to release Godstar, who was the better guitarist, for lead duties.

He was nervous as he greeted the small crowd and introduced the band in Pan-Koori and then English – 'Thanks everyone for coming tonight! We're *Interstititum* and our music comes from a hybrid place—a place between worlds.' A hand-full of people clapped and cheered

The song-list on the floor in front of him contained five songs by his old band *Interstitium*; a song each from 80s and 90s alternative rock outfits *The Saints, Died Pretty, The Divinyls, The Chills* and *Nick Cave*; and two pieces by *Goya's Child*—a largely unknown central Victorian band he'd followed since the early 1990s (he'd also met their first lead singer in Bendigo at the university). Godstar confirmed later that the audience hadn't recognised any of the songs or, for that matter, the bands in question. The first song was a fast-paced rocky number Rowan had written in his youth. It usually helped loosen up both the musos and the audience, and gave the mixer time to adjust the sound quality and dynamics before the band attempted more elaborate pieces. Rowan's old band had tried to aim at creating a show that became gradually more intense—darker even—as the night wore on. They'd tried to climax gigs about forty minutes from the end with two or three songs that invited catharsis. In the last half hour or so of gigs they'd usually played more upbeat songs—allowing people to 'dance and trance'.

Though no one got up to dance immediately, the first couple of songs seemed to go down okay with the audience. Rowan noticed Paul and his band watching from the back of the room— Josie stood leaning against Paul's left shoulder. Imogen was talking to some friends over by the bar. Rowan knew his singing was occasionally out of tune. Though he'd practiced endlessly for the performance his vocal chords weren't as flexible as they'd been all those years ago. His timing was also slightly out—especially when the rhythm changed suddenly. Likewise, he felt strange—as a thirty-three year old academic—singing angst-ridden and sexy songs (songs belonging to his youth) to a group of university students, many of whom were his students. Even as he sang, he knew he'd moved on as a song-writer.

As the gig wore on, he became less and less confident about his performance. Did he really want to punch the air during a particular chorus, or pretend to masturbate his guitar whilst Godstar launched into a heavy lead-break? Many of the instinctual alternative rock gestures he'd used as a nineteen year old now seemed childish and egotistical. Others seemed culturally inappropriate. Despite this, by the fifth song the audience were getting into the songs and half a dozen twenty year old girls had wandered to the front of the stage to dance. Two of the girls eyed Rowan off seductively, and one—a blonde girl with a t-shirt that said "Flower the infidels!"— danced lasciviously in front of him. Happy to pretend to play the part of ancient fertility king, he encouraged the girls' antics with occasional smiles. As more people hit the dance floor, some keen to sing into the mic with Rowan, others just happy to dance, Rowan lost sight of Imogen, Josie and Paul—indeed of anyone but the sweaty throng occupying the dance floor.

The band members seemed to be having a good time—though Rowan sensed that Godstar wasn't impressed with Rowan's response to the soft-porn antics of the dancing girls. By the time they were set to play 'Golem', the dark, haunting anthem his band had become semi-famous for in the other Australia, the dance floor was a sea of writhing bodies.

As a young person, Rowan would enter a semi-trance state when singing this song. The verse lyrics featured long emotional notes backed by a guitar riff laden with echo, wha-wha and low level distortion effects. In the background brooding synth sounds reinforced the mood. In the bridge and chorus, Godstar had to cut loose with vicious power chords whilst the keyboardist played a gothic synth progression heavy with sustain. Rowan's job, was simple—to sing above the music.

As he sang the first verse, he understood, perhaps for the first time, what the song was really about—the demonic side of childhood. Strangely enough sections from Isles's meditations on Rousseau's *Emile* came to mind as the bridge beckoned. He saw in a flash, that the song explored the process of emotional shutting down that Isles had seen as central to the civilising process. The crowd too sensed that something strange was happening and an unspoken group tension permeated the room.

Rowan, however, felt like he was going through the motions. He simply wasn't feeling the song the way he'd done in his youth. Even before he'd finished the first verse, part of him was assessing the disturbing effect the song was having on the audience. The big guitar rhythms soon kicked in and Rowan began singing at the top of his lungs about being silenced and censored. His words quickly descended into heart-rending screams until the relative quiet of the second verse kicked in.

Some of the younger students looked terrified at what they were witnessing. Even Godstar and the other band members were staring at Rowan as if he'd just unleashed dark occult energies. As though—he understood later—he was an Anomaly. In the other reality Punk Rock, Heavy Metal and Grunge had all acknowledged Munch and Artaud's creative legacy—the need to occasionally scream out the accumulated poisons of life. Rowan had listened to John Lennon's Primal Scream albums, as well as music by The Doors and other cathartic rockers. But these students had never been exposed to such music—either that or creative catharsis was reserved for the therapeutic situation only e.g. Isles's system of postures.

He tried to tone down the second chorus, but the damage was already done, many in the audience were spooked. Only Henri, standing near the door to the lounge like some kind of perverse sentinel, seemed unmoved. Indeed, as Godstar ignored Rowan's signal to play the riff for the next song, instead taking the mic and calling an end to proceedings, a wispy smile of amusement, even admiration, played across Henri's features. At the back of the room a young student, obviously high on something, screamed and sobbed inconsolably. 'You old bastard! You bastard!' she howled as someone led her from the room.

CHAPTER THIRTY-NINE

AFTERMATH

Rowan took a guilty gulp of his beer aware he'd read the audience badly. Godstar whispered in his ear, 'What the fuck was that all about? You never did that in practice, are you crazy or something? That's not music, that's … I don't know what that is. We're not running an Islesian exorcism session here; you don't let that shit loose on people without having skilled elders around to assist.'

Ungaru, however, bounded up to pat Rowan on the back. 'Unbelievable!' he said in broken Pan-Koori, 'I've never seen anything like it—though I've heard our tohungas sometimes do stuff like that with sick people. Even the New Albion students in the crowd were dumbstruck.'

Rowan had smoked a joint prior to the show and was aware he might be slightly paranoid. However, he noticed people whispering and drawing back furtively as he pushed through the forest of bodies on the way from the stage to the toilet. They looked like they were staring at a ghost or a crazy man.

When he returned to the room, he bought another beer and decided to search for Imogen. As he pondered where she might be, he passed a group of people leaving the house. He almost spilled his drink when he spotted his dead best friend, Eric, among them. The group also included Ian, the Bendigo academic and former musician; Douglas's step-daughter, Rhiannon; another woman; and a tall guy with a Jesus beard. All wore clothes embroidered with Islesian designs on a black or dark purple base colour and tattoos merging Islesian and Maori designs.

'Eric ... is that you?'

A slightly built man wearing glasses and a distinct black and green "three cauldrons" t-shirt halted to look at Rowan.

'Hi, er ... Look, I'm sorry, but I don't know your name. By the way great performance tonight—amazing stuff!' He spoke English with a distinct Kiwi accent.

'I'm Rowan Sweeney—don't you recognise me?'

The others stood to one side looking bored.

'Er, no—should I?' Everything about Eric's demeanor suggested he'd never seen Rowan before in his life.

Rowan turned to Rhiannon instead, 'I know you too—you're Rhiannon Green, Douglas Green's step-daughter.' Rhiannon and the other woman wore knee-high black boots and striking gypsy dresses embroidered with Islesian symbols.

The woman looked apologetic, 'I think you've mistaken me for someone else. I don't have a step-father—my father is an army officer and he isn't called Douglas.'

'What about you—Ian is it? Do you recognise me? Didn't you sing and write songs for an alternative rock band called *Goya's Child* before becoming an academic?'

Ian looked closely at Rowan. 'Sounds like I'd be earning much better money! Look, I'm sorry, I don't know you. We're part of a Neo-Islesian band and arts cooperative from Aotearoa—we only flew in last week.'

Rowan turned back to Eric, aware he was starting to sound unhinged, 'You look healthy and happy, Eric. I guess that's the main thing.'

Eric looked puzzled, 'Why wouldn't I be healthy and happy?'

One of the women glanced at Rowan before grabbing Eric's elbow, 'We have to go. The sound check for the Big Gold Mountain gig is at midnight. We have a forty minute drive from here.'

Rowan felt deflated as the small group wandered off. He was elated and amazed to see Eric alive, but sad that his former friends hadn't recognised him.

He spotted Henri and asked if he'd seen Imogen. The Classicist was ordering a drink between band performances. Apparently Paul's band were up next, accompanied by Josie Royal.

'Perhaps she's outside,' he said, 'she was talking to her former young man and Josie'. Rowan went outside, but apart from a couple holding hands on a brick wall near the front of the house, and two others obviously conducting a drug deal in the street, no one else was around. He headed back inside and found Henri talking to Frisser. As Rowan approached, Henri turned—his face a mask of sympathy. Whether it was genuine or not, Rowan couldn't tell. Frisser was still talking, 'He'll be busy for a while—he's in the den with Josie and Imogen. You know what he's like—enjoying himself before he goes on stage.' Henri tried to silence him by placing a rubbery finger to his lips, but the news was out.

When Frisser spotted Rowan, he turned and bolted in the direction of the garden.

'Where's the den?' asked Rowan.

'Oh, dear ...' said Henri, 'the divine musicians have decamped to the dungeons for sulfur and illicit inspiration.'

'Where's the den?' Rowan asked again—more emphatically

this time. Henri wagged a campish forefinger at a stairway down the hall before hobbling off to the bar.

Josie wasn't in the den. She was sitting at the top of the stairway leading to the den looking stoned and angry. Rowan guessed that the stairs led to an old wine cellar.

Josie looked up at him as he passed and said, 'He can fuck off. I'm not singing any harmonies for that bastard. He puts shit in his veins, then heads off in search of the ultimate blow job! Sad you,' she sounded sympathetic, despite her jealousy, 'your girlfriend's probably sucking him off right this minute. Feel free to beat his brains out as he comes!'

Rowan descended the staircase oblivious to the aesthetics of the meticulously decorated 'dungeon' he was entering. Renaissance, ancient Greek and Roman, and Hindu art decorated the walls on both sides—mostly erotic images of classically beautiful figures having sex with other classically beautiful figures. Occasionally a mythological motif featured: Leda with Zeus (in the form of a swan); Dionysus among naked maenads; a voluptuous Venus and a red-cheeked Mars making love under a net, and so on. At the bottom of the stairway Rowan followed a long, narrow brick corridor. There were dim-lit rooms on both sides of the corridor, most with their doors open. Only a few appeared occupied. As he passed, he noticed that each room had a theme—the Arthurian room had a large, ornate but fake Medieval bed-chamber at centre. Above and around the bed-chamber were saucy images of half naked knights trysting with large-breasted ladies or sylph like female spirits of the woodlands.

The Middle Eastern room featured a clichéd harem theme. Rowan looked for Paul and Imogen in there, but instead encountered two gay guys in half discarded white robes going for it against a white column.

He eventually found Imogen, cuddled up to Paul, in a room exploring 19ᵗʰ century Parisian bohemian culture. They lay together on a large pink bed dotted with a dozen purple cushions. A vase full of tired, dusty looking peacock feathers stood beside the bed and, as he entered, he saw that the wall to his right was lined with whips and handcuffs, as well as elaborate period costumes strung up on hooks. The two lovers weren't immediately aware of Rowan's presence—they'd obviously swallowed or injected substances and after the initial rush had become oblivious to everything but each other. Imogen's head rested on Paul's chest, and she played with the long black ringlets of his hair. She looked sleepy, almost peaceful. Paul, by contrast, stroked Imogen's pubic region gently. Her brown skirt was almost up to her waist.

Imogen looked up with droopy lotus-eater eyes as Rowan entered the room. It took her a few moments to recognise him.

Paul stirred more quickly, perhaps worried he was about to be attacked, 'Hey, Imogen—it's the Pseudo druid. I thought you guys were through,' he said, buttoning up his trouser zip and straightening his gypsy shirt.

'Don't mind me,' said Rowan, in a shaky voice, 'you're right, we are through.' Blood pounded in his temples and his throat was dry. He had the urge to confront Imogen about her actions, but she was obviously in no state to talk rationally.

Paul stood by the side of the bed waiting—wary perhaps of being blocked from an easy exit. He'd grabbed one of the whips—protection if Rowan turned violent. Rowan stared at the absurd scene for a moment—Paul with his whip, Imogen attempting to straighten her brown dress—then willed himself to turn and walk back up the corridor.

As he mounted the staircase, he heard Imogen shouting behind him in a drug-slurred voice, 'I'm sorry, Rowan—I really thought I was over him. I told you I hate this place. I didn't want to come here tonight.'

Rowan kept moving.

'Besides,' shouted Paul, more confident now that he had a reliable exit, 'you were having a great time with those two girls in the audience. What did you expect, you stupid fuck?'

'Shut up, Paul—he's a decent guy,' said Imogen, in a groggy voice.

Josie watched Rowan pass, then shouted down the staircase at Paul, 'Did you slime, you bastard?'

As Rowan reached the top of the staircase, Frisser appeared. 'The crowd awaits us!' he declared, unaware, to begin with, of what had unfolded, '*the ... er ... show must go on.*' Beside him Josie whispered, 'but not tonight with this little pussy-cat ... no, no, no ... *not* with *this* little pussy cat.' She was scratching aggressively at her left wrist.

As he waited for the cross-town taxi, Rowan listened to Paul's band playing their first couple of songs. He had to admit that the guy was a good muso with an excellent voice. His band's music was a little too 'progressive rock' sounding for Rowan—that was the only popular genre he could compare it to from the other 'Australia'. However, he noted a painfully melancholy strain to the vocals that helped compensate for the more or less uninteresting synth riffs that dominated the music. Likewise, Rowan had to revise his notion that Paul would be an egotistical cock rocker. Paul didn't attempt to dominate the stage—indeed, he often played second fiddle to the backup singers, male and female, and there were long mystical instrumental sections in some of the songs that left him either playing an instrument or simply withdrawing into the background. In short, Paul had a less obnoxious personality on stage.

These observations only worsened Rowan's despair and by the time he was trudging up past the campus buildings to his unit, an immense loneliness was taking hold.

CHAPTER FORTY

THE *CRIDHE-FASGADH*
(Thursday May 29th, 1997)

Rowan called in sick for work on the Monday then locked himself away in the unit for the next three days trying to deal with the break up. Most of the time, he sat on the small couch sipping tea and staring blankly out the front window. He didn't answer the door to visitors, and he failed to respond to phone calls and emails. He also phoned Anika and cancelled their meetings for the first half of the week.

It was only a matter of time, he felt, before the last pillars of his existence cracked and collapsed. He'd endured enough change and trauma of late, to trigger several of his old escape behaviours—drug and alcohol binges, meaningless one night stands and, sometimes, thoughts of suicide. The first two of these temptations would be easy enough to procure. As a lecturer on a good wage, he could buy any brain-numbing substance he desired. Likewise, as a minor cricket celebrity, he was occasionally approached by admirers, many of them female. Some days he had to stop repeatedly to sign autographs during short walks through the campus or town. He suffered most at night, due to broken sleep, vivid nightmares and a tendency to endlessly mull over his personal failings. Then there were the physical tremors and pangs of electric longing to deal with. They hit randomly and lingered for hours. Whether he was craving Imogen, Kerryn, Anika, or someone or something else, he couldn't fathom. The storm was upon him and it was taking all his willpower to keep the ship carrying his battered self afloat.

Kerryn had crept back into his thoughts. Perhaps because he needed stability and she, of course, had been stability incarnate—at least up until their last year together.

During this period, he also experienced several vivid flashbacks to the night the other Anika had returned early from a trip to the country to see her parents. She'd walked in on a post-gig orgy and found Rowan lying stoned and naked on the bathroom floor beside a skinny groupie called Izzy. Several discarded condoms lay cold and grotesque between them on the white-tiled floor. Memories of Anika's face that morning still haunted him. It had been the cause of their breakup.

His mind whirled on, one moment dwelling on the hurts he'd inflicted on others, the next on hurts others had inflicted on him.

By Thursday afternoon the worst of it had passed—several bouts of deep sobbing (a technique taught to him by his detox therapist in the early 1990s) had permitted him some sleep on the Wednesday night. It had also helped him work through some of the sadness to do with Imogen. He soon found himself thinking more realistically about the love triangle she'd orchestrated, and knew with certainty that he didn't want a bar of it—regardless of the grief this caused the other Rowan. Over breakfast, he even found himself tentatively listing the good things about his situation—a mental trick he'd learnt from his mother. The list was surprisingly long: he had a job that paid good money; he was working closely with Anika on a project that tested all of his creative and intellectual abilities; he and Anika were already good friends; although single, he almost felt at home with himself (perhaps for the first time in his life); the Eric of this world wasn't dead, and finally; he was creating and performing music again.

He found himself imagining what Isles and Douglas would have to say about his situation. No doubt they'd tell him to chant specific poems and adopt particular postures to heal his 'orbital imbalances'. In that moment, Rowan decided he had nothing to lose by giving the Islesian system a go.

Whilst preparing lunch, he leafed through the Isles diaries looking for songs designed to explore 'vexatious orbits'. He came across a song to do with 'unchastity'. Though originally in Welsh, he managed to locate a competent English translation. The song began: '*I have come, my beloved, through the furthest gateway/ to the Circle of Abred.*'

The sketch accompanying the song showed the standard hermaphrodite at centre. The figure was down on one knee with head and chest forward and hands to the sides.

Rowan pondered the image a long time: who exactly was being addressed? Unlike many of the postural images, no other figures were depicted, though an astrological calendar circle enclosed the hermaphrodite and a beam of light (or energy) emanated from its heart 'cauldron'. The beam ended in a white full moon with crudely drawn eyes and mouth. *A distinctly feminine moon*, thought Rowan. The decorative design beyond the moon featured standard Islesian orbital symbolism—various planets and solar bodies pierced by thin orbital lines.

The verses suggested that the song was to be addressed

to a mature (full) Moon Goddess—probably the Luna of the alchemists.

Rowan adopted the posture in the image and chanted the lyrics repeatedly for ten minutes or so, all the time attempting to genuinely feel the words by breathing deeply; just as Douglas had taught him.

Though the exercise made him feel light-headed, nothing significant happened. He returned to the image to see if he'd missed anything, and noted a 'Therapeutic Instructions' section overleaf. Although his Gaelic was patchy, it was clear what had to be done, 'This song should be sung for an hour or more by the unchaste lover in the presence of the betrayed lover whilst engaged in a slow backwards and forwards swaying motion (all the time maintaining the posture depicted). If the beloved is absent, or does not desire the company of the unchaste one, a 'substitute' wearing a blank moon mask may be addressed. Note: for mutual healing, another song 'I strike my Unchaste Lover' might be used by the injured party with its martial upright posture and mimed strike actions.'

Another interesting aspect to all the instructions given for postures was the repeated statement: 'This song and accompanying postural exercise may lead to an awareness of other hidden imbalances requiring postural work.' In other words, thought Rowan, every song in theory linked to other songs. After quickly surveying the other songs and postures that the 'Betrayal in Love' imbalance could link to, Rowan noted various deeper imbalances belonging to four levels: 1) 'vexations of the womb, birth and early childhood'; 2) 'vexations of late childhood and adolescence'; 3) 'vexations of adulthood'; and 4) 'vexations arising from the ancestors, revenant spirits of discord and wronged creatures in Nature'. All in all, he counted four developmental layers to Isles's first diagnostic axis. However, there was also another major axis to the system: the 'Relational

Axis'. It linked developmental phases to key relationships embedded in each phase—each relationship implicated several 'Domestic Deities' or 'Principles'. The more Rowan looked at the physical postures, the more he realised he was staring at an integrated therapeutic system of great complexity and subtlety.

He let out a frustrated sigh before sinking back into the couch. The question that had dogged him for weeks—*Where-in the music of the song images?*—seemed to lead to other questions of ever deeper complexity. It was time to do something he'd been avoiding for months. It was time to attend a local Neo-Islesian church—though devotees used the Gaelic term *cridhe-fasgadh*, which translated something like 'the heart's shelter'. With time running out, he decided that he needed to experience firsthand how modern Islesian communities functioned. He remembered that Godstar played guitar for one of the Neo-Islesian centres. Perhaps he could introduce Rowan to some of the community's leaders.

He'd contacted Godstar early in the week to cancel band practices for a while. Surprisingly, Godstar had sounded disappointed—obviously the fall-out from the gig at Henri's hadn't been all bad. They'd then discussed several of the Cridhe-Fasgadhs in the area. Rowan decided to join a large Neo-Islesian community close to the campus since it was the only one in the area influenced by New Science thinking.

'The community hall will be open to the public on Thursday night. You can meet some of the elected officials and therapists then if you like. I'll be playing some music later on, but the main session will be a presentation on similarities and differences between Buddhist thinking and Isles's adaptation of the *Barddas*.'

'I'll be there, and I'll contact Anika to see if she's interested in attending.'

There was a long pause on the other end of the phone before Godstar said, 'Geez, you don't muck around do you—one out, one in. Easy as you like!' He sounded nonplussed.

'It's not like that. She's working on the Isles and Hobbes biography with me.'

'Apologies. Hey, one question—I'm just a bit puzzled.'

'Fire away.'

'Why aren't you returning to the more traditionalist Islesian community in Dinas Yarkuk?'

'Returning?'

'Before your accident, you often attended their gatherings. You even did presentations there to do with your research on Isles and Hobbes.'

Rowan had to think fast, 'After the accident, I guess I've become less traditional in my beliefs.'

Godstar seemed to accept this and agreed to drop by at 8pm to walk Rowan and possibly Anika to the gathering.

The complex belonging to the Cridhe-Fasgadh that Godstar took Rowan to—Anika had been unable to attend—featured design motifs specific to modern Islesians. The main building looked like a huge circular beehive—it had three distinct levels. The first featured entrance doors and some large windows, but was mainly constructed out of huge, rendered mud-bricks. The second level, towering twenty metres above ground level, featured twelve leadlight panes depicting images drawn from what Rowan interpreted as a Marin calendar version of the Cerridwen-Taliesin story. The gigantic cosmological images, lit discretely from within, looked colourful and strangely haunting to Rowan. He stared up at the glasswork in wonder.

Inside, Rowan noticed that the building was organised around Isles's concept of the 'Orbits' as well as cosmological notions of the various realms—*abred, annwfn, gwynedd* and *ceugant*. All round the wall of the first level—*abred*—were images related to mortal life. The dominant themes seemed to be: struggle, suffering, occasional joys, etc. The floor to this level—featuring the beautiful tiles upon which Rowan and Godstar walked—depicted the relational orbits at the heart of Isles's understanding of ordinary mortal life. They began at the centre of the room with depictions of the 'primary orbits' (i.e. key human relationships and life transitions, e.g. birth, puberty, marriage, death, etc) and were embedded in a large circular structure that looked like a theatre or auditorium. From the centre out, circles appeared at regular intervals until the last one merged with the outer walls of the building. The outer 'orbits', as far as Rowan could make out, linked individuals to nature, the cosmos, time etc. There were also narrow staircases in the huge hall—some went down, symbolising descent into the realm of *Annwfn* (the underworld); others went up symbolising ascent to the divine realm of *Gwynedd.*

Given he didn't intend to visit the building's symbolic *annwfn* this visit, he cast his gaze upwards to the narrow mezzanine floor that was part of the outer circle of the second level—the circle of *Gwynedd*, i.e. the realm of the Gods and other mythological entities. He noted huge bookshelves housing thousands of books all round that level's outer wall—a community library perhaps. Towering above the bookshelves were the leadlight windows he'd stared at from the outside. The realm of *ceugant*, the creative and infinite ground of all being in all realms, was symbolised by the hall's domed circular ceiling which depicted beams of light emanating from a central point backgrounded by the starry heavens.

Godstar led Rowan to the community auditorium. They entered quietly—since the talk had already begun—and found seats at the back of the gathering. The auditorium seemed about a quarter full—Rowan estimated that there were perhaps eighty or so people present. The featured talk concerned Isles's use of the *Barddas*—a controversial late 16th century Welsh text written by Llewelyn Siôn—in the construction of his own unique cosmology. It was material Rowan was familiar with.

After fifty minutes or so the speaker opened up to audience questions and eventually the gathering was adjourned for drinks and biscuits. During the break Godstar, who was keen to go and set up for his set, introduced Rowan to the president of the community, a tall conservatively dressed older woman with gentle eyes. Rowan spoke to her of his project on Isles and Hobbes, as well as his wish to undergo therapy and attend regular community events. Godstar wandered down to the stage to tune his guitar and test the sound system. He was to deliver an acoustic performance of certain well known Isles songs and Rowan noticed that the auditorium was beginning to fill up with more people—particularly young people.

The woman, named Jean, said that she was a qualified *Islesian ovate*, or healer, and that she'd be happy to organise sessions for Rowan. There was a nominal payment per session, but Rowan thought it sounded quite reasonable. 'We don't look at sessions as *therapy* in the sense that most Westerners use the term ...' said Jean, looking at Rowan as she stirred her coffee, 'The Islesian postures and dances that have come down to modern times represent a way to confront the inevitable challenges life throws at us. After the initial phase of removing blocks, people begin to dance the orbital sequences in more expressive ways. Postures and dances are then integrated into everyday life and their movements become more instinctive and joyous. Of course, we understand that difficult material may surface for processing, but we try to never let the darkness, the *nigredo* if you like, obscure *nwyvre* (the life force) and *awen* (creative inspiration).'

Rowan agreed to meet with Jean later in the week to begin 'blockage removal' sessions. She then found him a seat in the front row, close to the stage. As he was about to sit down, however, he noticed an old man seated in a wheelchair five or six seats further down from his own seat. The man looked for all the world like Douglas Green, so much so that Rowan told Jean that he recognised the man and requested that he be given a seat closer to him.

'Oh, you know Douglas?' said Jean, 'Unfortunately, I doubt very much he'll be able to recognise you at present,' she said sadly.

'What do you mean?' said Rowan, following as she led him to a seat beside the old man. He definitely looked like Douglas—though older looking and clearly incapacitated.

'Douglas had a severe stroke about four years ago. It destroyed his capacity to talk, indeed to communicate with people in any way—we're not sure how much he understands of what's going on around him. He has virtually no physical movements, we have to do everything for him, but the strangest thing, he seems to enjoy being included in the audience for community events.'

Rowan looked at the man more closely.

'He was president here for some twelve years—he did a great deal for the community. He delivered talks and organised the entire volunteer program during the 1980s—even though he worked at a clinic in Big Gold Mountain and lectured up at MUCT.'

Rowan suddenly felt quite sad, 'Is it okay to sit here beside him—it won't alarm him or anything?'

'Of course it's okay, though try to move slowly around him—no quick jerky movements. He seems to enjoy musical performances most, always sleeps well after them. He lives in a residential unit attached to this complex.' She paused a moment. 'You know some people believe he communicates with them via ESP.'

Jean wandered off to do something as Rowan sat down beside Douglas. A little later Godstar began an acoustic rendition of a populist Isles song—it had been written in the early 1850s to lament the many Koories and Islesians killed in the struggle to repel the British army.

Rowan marvelled at Godstar's ability to conjure complex mood sequences in his renditions of classic songs. Disappointingly for Rowan, Douglas the stroke victim did not move at any point during the performance—even his face remained passive throughout. When the performance was over, Rowan stood up and before leaving gently grasped the old man's right hand before leaning into his line of vision. On the spur of the moment, he said, 'You wouldn't believe how comforting it's been seeing you here tonight. I want you to know that everything is on track—I'm not sure where I'm headed exactly, but I do intend to see things through to the end.' He trailed off—there was no sign that Douglas had even registered his presence.

Then, without warning, the old man's eyelids flickered and for a brief moment Rowan was certain that Douglas was looking directly at him. At the same time the old man's jaw twitched slightly as though struggling to say something. Though he managed no words, Rowan was sure he was staring at the faintest of smiles.

The sense that he was somehow being acknowledged faded quickly as Douglas's features quickly returned to their former impassive state.

Moments later a smartly dressed middle aged man appeared on Douglas's left. 'Do you know Dad?' the man asked nonchalantly.

Rowan looked at the man, his face had the same shape as Douglas's, round and open. Even his build was similar.

'I knew him a long time back—through the centre. He helped

me out during a tough part of my life.'

'I'm his son, Harry. Pleased to make your acquaintance', said the man, 'he quite likes these events.'

'Yes, they're a lot of fun,' said Rowan, as the penny dropped, 'You're Harry?'

The man nodded as he undid the brake on his father's wheelchair and moved into position behind him, 'Yes, do I know you?'

'No, but I think I met your step-sister at a party a little while back. How is Rhiannon these days?'

'My step-sister? I don't have a step-sister called Rhiannon.'

Rowan paused, 'Oh, maybe I've confused you with someone else. I haven't seen your dad for many years.'

The man looked a little uncomfortable, 'Anyway, I need to get him back to his unit. Enough excitement for one evening eh, old man?'

With those words, he slowly wheeled Douglas forward into the main isle. Rowan watched the two of them, father and son, trundle out into the cool night air.

CHAPTER FORTY-ONE

PERSONAL LEAVE FOR AVANT-GARDE MUSICIANS
(Monday, June 2nd 1997)

When he returned to work on the Monday, he had to sort through dozens of emails sent to him in the previous week. One of them carried news of a publication credit. His essay critiquing the New Albion assault on Marin higher education had been accepted for publication by *Global Culture/s* a major British Cultural Studies journal. With union assistance, he'd used events at MUCT to illustrate the points he was making. In checking the publishing conditions, however, he was alarmed to see that apart from being slated for publication in the July print edition of the journal, the essay was already up at the journal's website. 'Please feel free to email us with any editing issues before the end of next week' said the email before detailing copyright conditions and promising a cheque for sixty pounds.

At the very bottom of the page, he noted an html web-link and promptly followed it to view the article. His unease grew after reading the editor's introduction to the piece: 'In this article, Dr Rowan Sweeney, a Marin lecturer in Religious and Cultural Studies at MUCT (Dinas Yarkuk, Marin-e-bek), discusses the Imperialist ideology driving New Albion 'educational aid' to his nation. Sweeney, formerly an international cricketer, employs previously unknown theoretical models to expose the neo-colonial agenda behind the gutting of arts, humanities and social sciences courses at numerous Marin universities.'

The journal was an international leader in the field and Rowan knew that many Marin and New Albion academics subscribed to the publication. No doubt they'd already received a link to the online edition. He felt a lump in his throat as he saved the email before opening more recent ones. Sure enough, starting late Friday, he'd been sent congratulatory group emails from dozens of union people. The emails all contained a link to the article and encouraged union members to share it, 'far and wide'.

He decided to make a cup of coffee in the staff-room all the time hoping Imogen wasn't about. The knot in his stomach grew as the morning progressed.

He was eventually called into Wirrarap's office late in the afternoon. The timing was inconvenient as he was due to meet Anika in the university library at five and had hoped to grab some food beforehand.

Whirrarap looked grave as Rowan entered.

'Sit down, Rowan—we have some things to discuss.' Whirrarap spoke in English, which meant he wanted to be absolutely clear about what he was saying.

Rowan was still feeling raw due to the split up with Imogen. He kept replaying in his mind the moment he saw Paul and Imogen together on the mattress.

'If it's about Imogen, there's no problem anymore. We're

finished—the Puritans are victorious,' said Rowan, bitterly.

Whirrarap studied Rowan a moment before continuing.

'That is an issue of some concern to the Head of School—but there are also other issues we need to discuss. Firstly, the publication of your essay on New Albion Neo-liberalism and Neo-colonialism in *Global Culture/s*. Secondly, the nature of your band's musical performance a week ago at Henri Nacrose's residence. Overall, people are worried about your mental health—perhaps the strain of the teaching, the demands of the research project and the lingering effects of the accident are to blame?' Whirrarap, as always, appeared inscrutable.

Rowan tried to avoid his gaze—a sign of respect in Aboriginal culture. 'I haven't performed music live for years, so I probably seemed a bit over-excited that night. Look, I will not apologise for my songs—if people don't like them, I frankly don't give a damn.'

'Your songs?' said Whirrarap, with a spark of interest, 'You played *your* songs that night? How did you manage to conceal your interest in music from everyone for so long? I didn't know you wrote music.'

Rowan chose his words carefully, 'I mess around constantly with lyrics, lyric melodies, rhythm riffs, etc. in my head. The songs just come to me—always have done. It's one of the reasons I've enjoyed the Isles and Hobbes project.' He looked Whirrarap briefly in the eye. 'I started jamming with Godstar Wallaby a little while back.'

'You're in a band with a student?'

'The guy is close to my age and he's a fantastic muso. You ask him about the songs—we practiced them for weeks before we performed them. They're my songs.'

Whirrarap pulled back in his chair, 'People who attended the performance said they'd never heard anything quite like it before and they didn't know what to make of your stage antics.

Some said it was like an Islesian catharsis session—others thought you were possessed by spirits.'

'I wasn't possessed by spirits and I wasn't trying to be a therapist. I could easily repeat the performance for you right now. I'd emerge from the performance quite capable of rational conversation.'

Whirrarap looked amused, 'Thank Bunjil for that!'

Rowan didn't really care anymore what students, or the Dean, or the CEO or even Whirrarap thought.

'What about the publication of the essay?' asked Whirrarap.

'I had no idea they'd put it on the internet so quickly—it's available to every man and his dog with a simple mouse click.'

Whirrarap smiled, 'If you are indeed sane it's worthwhile pointing out to you—though this may be old news—that the contents of the essay and the influential nature of the journal in which it has been published, when combined with your new position as union "celebrity figurehead", is giving the MUCT senior management a serious headache.'

'They've read it already?'

'Of course—and they're furious.' Whirrarap smiled a tight little smile, 'There'll be consequences—your personal life will come under more scrutiny. What is the English saying about glass houses and stones?'

'People in glass houses shouldn't throw stones,' said Rowan.

'Yes, I've always liked that saying. Look, I'll be straight with you—the situation is complex. You have two options— but please take this as unofficial. It's coming from the Head of School. She will look favourably at any request for personal leave due to illness. You wouldn't be required to teach your second semester unit or supervise postgraduate research students. This would give you time to recover fully from your accident. I think this is a good solution, given there's pressure from senior management to make an example of you.'

'Do they want to sack me?'

'I imagine so, and the "smoking gun" is of course your undeclared intimate relationship with a female student "under your direct supervision."' Whirrarap sounded more formal— obviously he wanted Rowan to be aware of the seriousness of the conduct charge.

'She's a grown adult and she teaches adults! Besides, the relationship is over, she decided to be with someone else.'

Whirrarap sighed, 'All being well you'll return to teaching in January next year. Also, I've pushed for you to be able to continue on with your research duties into next semester—that is if you want to.' He paused to see if Rowan had any questions or comments.

'So, I won't teach next semester, but I will continue with the research project?' Rowan had to confess the teaching had been exhausting. Given the deadline for the Isles and Hobbes book, time off teaching to concentrate on completing it sounded like good news. Besides, the second semester unit on contemporary social theory had been stressing him of late. The more he thought about the personal leave option, the more he liked it.

'If you don't agree to personal leave it's my understanding that senior management will send you a letter of dismissal. It will be opposed strenuously by the union of course, but let's face it, you're in trouble if Imogen is in anyway ambivalent about the relationship.' Whirrarap paused to allow Rowan to digest the information.

'Personal leave sounds like the best option—it's been a stressful period for me, I've barely survived the semester. Some days,' Rowan grew emotional, 'I barely know who I am. And though it was never great between us, Imogen helped me a lot after the accident.' Rowan rubbed his eyelids and forehead.

Whirrarap stood up then wandered round the front of his desk to sit opposite Rowan, 'Are you up to finishing the Isles and Hobbes research—maybe you want to take leave from that project as well? Of course that might delay the book considerably.'

'No, I'm enjoying that part of the job. I just wish we had a breakthrough regarding the notational system. It has to be embedded in those images somewhere ... somehow.'

'As it's turned out, both you and Anika are innovative musicians. If anyone can work it out it'll be you two. No harm done, however, if you can't crack the code since many other scholars have tried and failed. Competent translations of all selected song lyrics into English, Pan-Koori and French, as well as your expert commentary on the thematic and language elements of the songs, may well be the best we can hope for.'

'Anika and I are hoping for much more. We really want to hear Isles's music.'

'If you need any more help, please come and talk to me or to the board. They'll back you on this project despite pressure from higher up.' Whirrarap paused before continuing, 'Can I also suggest that you don't give management any unnecessary advantages over the next few months?'

'Some of the political implications of my actions evade me at times.'

'Then you need to take a lesson from your dead mentor, Abraham Isles. He successfully merged the fruits of his imagination with the constraints placed upon him by reality.'

As always Whirrarap was on the money—Rowan felt there was a lot he could learn from Isles.

Whirrarap returned to his own side of the desk. 'We'll do the paperwork for your leave application tomorrow morning. I have a hunch the union will also be happy to give you some time out. In a sense you've already served a purpose for them.'

'You think I should step down as a *figure-head*?'

'It's up to you, but realise you'll be in the firing line anyway once the book is published—if not beforehand. I presume you understand that?' He stared at Rowan over the lenses of his reading glasses as he spoke.

'Of course,' said Rowan, feeling inept and foolish.

On a whim, he decided to ask a question about something that had puzzled him for some time.

'What do you think of modernity? I mean do you see yourself as a Koori traditionalist or do you embrace science, technology, globalisation etc?'

Whirrarap took off his reading glasses and answered in Pan-Koori, 'I'm not sure what you're getting at.'

'Modernity is a largely European phenomenon, many colonised traditional peoples struggle with accepting its political, scientific and cultural dimensions, even after the period of colonisation ends.' Rowan knew he sounded confused.

'Well, from my perspective we were not really "colonised" as you put it. Through our own resources and through the help of people like Isles, Hobbes and other international progressives from many nations, we fought off the colonisers.'

Whirrarap seemed irritated at Rowan's underlying assumptions.

'Similarly, I do not see "Modernity" as an exclusively European phenomenon. I see it as an international phenomenon, and in this respect the Chinese, the Japanese, the Arabs, the Indians etc. have all contributed a great deal, as have many Marin scientists, thinkers, writers, poets, musicians etc. As you well know our small nation is over-represented in terms of our contribution to global scientific and cultural developments over the past 150 years.'

'So you are saying that all of Marin-e-bek's ethnic groups accept ...'

'Ethnic groups?'

'Okay, are you saying that we Marins more or less accept modernity?'

'We are a profoundly flexible people; when circumstances change we change too. How else do you think Aboriginal Marins survived drought, fire and flood over the millennia? Historically that's been the real secret to the survival of our people. Art, literature, creative thinking, science, spirituality — these are the tools that have always kept us innovative and mentally flexible. They also make life meaningful. Culture should be used by the people to promote successful *adaptation*. Degrade "culture", stifle it, censor it, bureaucratise it—as is happening in New Albion right now—and you have a doomed people.' Whirrarap made a little steeple under his chin with his hands. To Rowan, it made the last phrase seem like a kind of curse.

'So, some traditional indigenous perspectives have had to change?'

'In my opinion the Aboriginal peoples of Marin-e-bek don't understand the term "traditional" as you understand the term. Unlike many other indigenous peoples during the age of colonisation we managed to keep our lands, our culture and our social structures. We met modernity (and at times we contributed to global "modernity") on our own terms, and we had friends to assist us. As conditions changed we rejected what no longer seemed relevant, but our *tradition*, in the sense that I understand the word—that is, the cultural heart of our people—has not changed because it springs from self-determination.' Whirrarap paused before asking, 'What would you have us be—eternal Noble Savages? Primitive fodder for the suppressed dream-fantasies of alienated Westerners?' He forced a little laugh. 'No thank you!'

Rowan felt sheepish—he felt he'd been skirting the real question, 'Every nation struggles with the Promethean impetus behind Modernity. New Albion, we both agree, is in cultural melt-down right now. It seems possessed by Frankenstein's monster—the darker side of Modernity. How does Marin-e-bek pacify this monster?'

Whirrarap thought for a while then said, 'We do not embrace the faddish, the pseudo progressive—change for the sake of change. We only embrace new ideas that we believe can help us adapt to new realities. I identify primarily as a Koori and secondarily as an Islesian. I'm proud of that combined heritage since in my opinion both traditions value the role of culture in a society, which is to assess, to weigh, to judge, to act as a symbolic *house of review*. If, however, we look at the situation in New Albion at present, we observe a dangerous state of cultural entropy—the masses have been conditioned to believe that culture amounts to little more than day time television, talk-back radio and endless sport. Culture is trivialised and therefore meaningless.'

Whirrarap's critique of New Albion society made Rowan worry about his father and sister—last he'd heard they'd been imprisoned whilst attempting to cross the border illegally. He'd told Whirrarap some days ago, and the older man had promised to talk to some of his contacts in Bunjilaka City to try and locate them.

'The real problem,' continued Whirrarap, in a level voice, 'is that they no longer dance. Here everyone dances—the Koories, the Islesians the other migrant groups—we still dance the sacred dances. Hopefully the situation in New Albion is temporary. Indeed, in the sixties and seventies it was a profoundly progressive country.'

Rowan was less hopeful. 'New Albion projects immense economic and military power—sadly, many foreigners believe it represents the true spirit of the Australian continent.'

Whirrarap seemed agitated by the statement. 'At present Marin-e-bek and the nations to the far north and west best represent the true spirit of this continent's many peoples.

History will judge it so,' he said, before staring out of his office window at the courtyard of native trees and shrubs.

For a moment neither spoke, then Whirrarap turned back to Rowan. 'To us, spiritual energies permeate all aspects of our world—including what Westerners call "the psyche". In this respect the Islesian view is not so different to that of indigenous Marins. They speak a common language of respect for Country.'

'Yes, there is *nwyvre,* the sacred soul heat—and it circulates between worlds and between the various ...'

'... relational orbits,' finished Whirrarap. 'Regardless of its name, its unimpeded flow promotes empathy, love and social harmony. In the Marin view of things—whichever "tradition" you draw upon—unnecessary suffering arises with disruptions to the flow of life energy between the various realms. In the view of the Central Tribes, *yarkuk,* or crystal quartz, assists people wishing to keep the various parts of the creation communicating in ways that guarantee mutual wellbeing.' Whirrarap sounded meditative.

'It would be great if cultural health guaranteed the survival of a nation,' said Rowan, rising to leave the office 'but history must stomach the whoops and hollers of many successful but heartless brutes. The flaw in the fabric of the universe is never so obvious as when we start to analyse the way nations behave.'

'Spoken like a true disciple of Abraham Isles and Miriam Hobbes!' said Whirrarap.

Rowan opened the door to leave—he'd already taken up too much of Whirrarap's time.

'By the way,' said Whirrarap, 'your essay is excellent. The thinking is innovative and you are accurate in your assessment of the current situation.'

'Thank you,' said Rowan.

'On a more important topic—I'm sorry that I can't bring you better news concerning your father and sister. The situation up north is very tense—it's almost impossible to get information out of the New Albion government about detention camp inmates. As a consequence our government is using other methods and they advise you to be patient.'

CHAPTER FORTY-TWO

THE MUSICAL PLANETS OF ABRAHAM ISLES
(Monday, June 2nd 1997)

Rowan pondered the implications of the meeting with Whirrarap as he walked across campus to meet with Anika. On the way, he decided to check his pigeon-hole for mail—he'd been waiting almost a month for important books on early Marin history. He was greeted, instead, by a letter from the New Albion government, which he opened with some apprehension. It began: 'Dear Dr Sweeney, this office wishes to advise you of the formal revocation of your Class C New Albion Permanent Resident Visa.' The letter went on to say that new conditions had been introduced concerning the 'moral behaviour' of foreign nationals. In particular recent legislation had widened definitions of 'Resident Sedition' to include evidence of 'material or moral assistance' to foreign groups determined to 'undermine the New Albion state'. Further down the letter, Rowan was informed of his appeal rights—basically an appeal had to be made within one month. The letter also ordered him to pay the New Albion government $3,000 dollars for 'visa revocation costs incurred'.

Though it was vague about who exactly Rowan had 'assisted', it was clear that he'd lost the right to reside in New Albion. He had no intention of paying the 'visa revocation costs' since he hadn't been informed of the reasons for the draconian action.

As he perused the letter again after ordering a cappuccino, he understood more fully the differences between the New Albion of this reality and the Australia of his youth. It was no small thing to set oneself up as a critic of the New Albion government—democracy and fundamental human rights had been seriously undermined by the country's governing and corporate elites. As he greeted Anika, he realised Whirrarap was right, he had to become more considered in his gestures of opposition. He was a public figure now and that meant his words carried extra weight—loose words could have severe consequences for himself and others.

'You look thoughtful,' said Anika, already seated at a table in the student lounge sipping green tea and picking at a dish of fruit salad.

'It's been quite a day,' Rowan said, aware he was feeling tense and stressed. He'd never been in trouble with a foreign government before.

Anika had an extract from an Isles diary out on the table in front of her.

'I've had a tough one too. Fully one-third of the student choir and orchestra have resigned over the past three weeks.'

'Do they have problems with your teaching style?'

'No—at least I don't think so. Haven't you noticed?'

'Noticed what?'

'The phenomenon of the disappearing students.'

'I don't handle withdrawals and besides, we're into the

last week of the semester. No one ever turns up to class then. Everyone is swatting for the exams.' Rowan was still thinking about the letter.

'Many Marin students are signing up for military training. The government just made it easy for them to defer their studies. Everyone thinks we'll be invaded by New Albion before the end of the year.'

'Speak of the devil. This letter ...' he pushed the New Albion government letter in Anika's direction, 'announces that my New Albion Permanent Residency Visa has been "revoked". The bastards! Why would anyone want to live there anyway; it's become a plutocratic dictatorship.' Rowan took an angry gulp of his coffee.

Anika read the letter with interest, 'You've been a naughty boy. That essay?'

'Oh, you've heard about it as well. I doubt it's to blame. The letter is dated Wednesday last week, too soon after the essay for any modern bureaucracy to gather all the necessary authorisation signatures!'

'Then it has to be about the Isles and Hobbes book,' said Anika, suddenly aware of the possible implications for herself.

'Most likely, though I've also become a figure-head for the Marin Education Union of late. And of course there's the cricket celebrity thing. Cricket is a religion up there—maybe they think I'll influence their youth!'

Anika pushed the letter back towards him, thoughtfully. 'Perhaps they see your book as providing moral aid to New Albion dissidents and refugees.'

'Apart from my father and sister, the only refugee I know is Godstar Wallaby. I think you're right, it's about New Albion opposition to the Isles and Hobbes book—especially our attempts to decode the melodies behind Isles's songs. There are 700,000 Idealists in New Albion and Isles is one of the continent's most famous anti-Imperialists and democrats.'

'And then if we add in all the cricket tragics—Northerners who listen to you because you're a fast bowler ...' teased Anika.

But Rowan was still puzzled. There were plenty of celebrities critiquing New Albion foreign policy these days—why had they singled him out.

Anika had another theory. 'MUCT is increasingly funded by New Albion investors and most of the management team are from up there, or are American expats. Maybe senior management have been tracking our work.' Anika sounded worried—she often travelled to New Albion for conferences and to perform.

'The university's Cultural Board of Elders, via Whirrarap, told me as much today. Senior management want me sacked. They're using my, er ... supposed "misconduct" as the trigger.'

'Well there you have it—perhaps someone is reporting back to the New Albion government.'

They sat in silence for a moment, pondering what it all meant for the research project.

Rowan took the opportunity to fill her in about his changed employment status as well as the fall-out over his published essay (including Whirrarap's response). He also gave her a short summary of what had happened at Henri's on the night of the gig.

'How long has Imogen been studying here?' Anika interrupted.

'A couple of years. She tutors in the Cultural Studies department—I mean she's virtually a lecturer.'

'*Virtually*, but not *actually*,' said Anika, quietly.

Rowan let the comment pass.

'Regardless of the true intentions of MUCT senior management, I think it's best we get on with our code breaking attempts, don't you think?' said Anika, trying to lighten things up.

But Rowan was sinking into a deep gloom. On top of everything else, he now had to deal with his New Albion visa being revoked and the threat of being sacked for misconduct. As they turned once again to the song diaries, he found it difficult to concentrate.

'If we're being tracked by New Albion spies they shouldn't be too worried. Very little original material will appear in the biography. We have no hope of uncovering the music behind the songs. I'm about ready to confess to Whirrarap that we're out of ideas.'

'Don't be so defeatist,' said Anika, 'I for one don't intend to have my ass kicked by hyper-adrenalised New Albion thugs for studying texts I can't decode anyway. I'd prefer we give them something revolutionary to deal with—God knows the buggers deserve it.'

The fight in Anika's voice cheered him up.

'The Anomalies are also increasing in number,' said Rowan, 'some people even think I'm one.'

'All artists are Anomalies—goes with the territory.'

'Well, that makes *you* an Anomaly anyway,' he said, secretly pleased that she saw him as an artist.

'Living humans can't be real Anomalies can they? Aren't Anomalies supposed to be ghostly—like all those speared sheep hanging around the river north of Big Gold Mountain, or the Anomaly I saw last night in my garden? He appeared for a moment only, and in side profile—a tall, bearded European dressed in 19th century clothes. He was holding a gold miner's pan.'

'According to Imogen,' said Rowan, 'they can manifest in all sorts of ways. I have an anomalous history book, for example. It was given to me by Henri Nacrose—the Classicist across town.'
Anika considered this information a moment.

'I heard about your performance the other week. All the

students have been discussing it in the music theory class. Your band made quite an impression. It also confirmed a hunch I have about you. Only a trained musician could possibly understand the music theory we've been discussing of late.'

Rowan was on the verge of confessing everything to Anika. He had to force himself to dodge her implicit question. 'Here's a question, Anika. In fifty words or less outline your philosophy on music and creativity.'

Anika breathed deeply. 'Jeez, I'll have to think a moment.'

'I thought I had a philosophy of music—of culture and art generally—and for a time it served me well. But after Friday night—after a lot of things, actually—I've had to scrap it and start all over again.'

'Well you're obviously an Islesian of some description,' said Anika.

'In life generally, um ... yes, but I've come to realise that my understanding of creativity is too influenced by modern Western thinking—you know: "individuality", "success equals fame and fortune" and "cultish secularism". Imbibing such stuff has eroded my creativity. I've lost all motivation. Anyway, enough about me—what about your understanding of creativity?'

Anika took a sharp breath, 'Fifty words is not a lot of words to define something so important?'

'Fair comment—I'll allow you one hundred words instead.'

Anika smiled, 'I suppose I approach writing, poetry and music from a Neo-Islesian perspective. Classic Islesian thinking lacks something for me—it tends to treat the 'domestic gods' as entities in themselves. Modern Neo-Islesians, by contrast, tend to see Isles's 'domestic gods' as projections to do with need. They're given the job of processing the difference between our paradisiacal wishes and needs (i.e. for fabulous and nurturing relationships with others) and the actual relationships we get lumbered with in life. The transpersonal experiences Isles talked about so much are explained by Neo-Islesians in terms of New Science developments—particularly the findings of quantum physics. Don't get me wrong, we don't reject entirely the "Gods and Goddesses" of creativity. I rather like Celtic deities such as Cerridwen, Rhiannon and Bridget, for example. Anyway, if I had to pick a deity it would be Bridget— goddess of love, healing, poetry, fire and alchemy!' She paused a moment, thinking, 'Most of the creativity deities of Greece and Rome leave me cold. The women are always described as either passive Muses for the *male* creativity deities or seductive witches like Circe, Hecate and Calypso. But there is one male creativity deity who interests me.'

'So for you, it all begins with aligning real world relationships with our innate needs. The needs projections are the "domestic gods"?'

'I suppose I allow specific imaginal figures to "tune" my way of experiencing the world. At that point I'm not so much a "musician" or a "poet" or anything really. I'm just a woman with certain skills working her way through specific creative projects that *create her* as much as she *creates them*—which is hard work because when each project ends I have to recreate myself anew with the next project. Also, for me, creativity is a way of relating properly to others.'

Rowan returned to the link between classical and modern Islesian thinking on deities, 'You said that one of the Classical male deities interests you, which one?'

'Hermes, of course! Though to classical Islesians, that would be Taliesin—the Celtic Hermes. Taliesin is prepared to learn from women, specifically Cerridwen and the nine maidens of the Cauldron. I rather like Taliesin as a consequence—he could be my lover!' she laughed at the thought.

'So you'd prefer Hermes to Dionysus?' asked Rowan, surprised.

'Yes! Dionysus is too unstable—he has too much repressed rage. Maybe for a one night stand!' she said, grinning.

'What about Apollo?'

'No, never Apollo. Too boring. Conformist Apollo—with his elevator music, high school musicals and national anthems.'

'That's a bit unfair—but you have a point. Tell me more about how you see Hermes-Taliesin?'

'Hmm, he's not aggressive and he's raunchy but intellectual. He's also a magician and a democrat—light as air, inspirational and athletic! I'd need *that*. Yes, he's fun.'

'He's also a thief!'

'You can't have everything.'

Anika waited for Rowan to answer with more light banter, but Rowan was looking at the ceiling as he kneaded one ear slowly.

'Sorry to change the topic so abruptly,' said Rowan, 'but what did that bearded Anomaly look like and how long has he been hanging around your garden?'

'I've only seen him once—late at night. And I didn't see his face. Why do you ask?' Anika looked thoughtful.

'Next time you see him can you ring me immediately—I'd like to have a look at him.'

'Sure—maybe he'll point us in the direction of some buried gold.'

Rowan laughed. 'I need another coffee,' he said, 'Maybe even some dinner. Let's look at that Orbit material in the Isles diaries again. Our goal is to turn planets into music!'

'While you grab a drink you can think about a fifty word summary for me,' she said, mischievously.

'My philosophy of creativity amounts to a philosophy of music', he said, recalling a similar conversation long ago with the other Anika.

'Interesting though that would be, what I really need is a fifty word overview of what we know about Isles's song diaries.'

Rowan paused, 'Okay, I'll see what I can do. Shall I get you another green tea?'

'Why not—this could be a long night.'

By the time Rowan came back with coffee, tea and a selection of sandwiches, he'd summarised the defining characteristics of Isles's songs in his head.

'Right, fire away,' said Anika, taking a sip of her green tea before grabbing a pen and note-pad.

'Okay, point one. There are around 300 songs preserved in 18 diaries. I've been given copies of all 18, but 2 other diaries are missing. I've also been given all of Isles's known public writings including a book containing twenty currently indecipherable ogham experiments (or letters to Hobbes, according to some sources). More codes! Returning to the songs—they are written in Highland Gaelic (around 150), Welsh, (around 50) and English (around 100). Point two: They are best understood as medicinal songs, and thematically they develop symbols found in alchemy, Rousseau's writings and 19th century neo-druidic thinking. Point three: some of the modifications to Rousseau's thoughts on childhood and civilisation were written by Hobbes and classified as Women's Medicinal Songs. She also created many postural exercises of relevance to women and children. Point four ...'

'You're way over fifty words—I can't keep up. Could you talk a little slower?'

'Okay, but you've made me forget where I was.'

'Point four ...'

'Point four. From comments made in theoretical sections of the diaries, Isles seemed to link musical vibratory patterns to human cellular and 'astral body' vibrations. He discerned between healthy and unhealthy vibrations. To Isles, psycho-spiritual health manifests in healthy 'vibrations', likewise healthy relationships/orbits. It follows that unhealthy relationships/orbits produce unhealthy vibratory patterns. The medicinal songs in the diaries address a range of unhealthy psycho-spiritual "vibrations".'

'Point four was long. I have a sore hand. Point five?'

'To fix "orbital imbalances" Isles and Hobbes developed a huge array of "medicinal postures" in the early 1830s. Think *medicinal dance*—Islesians dance and sing to stay healthy.'

'I was actually thinking yoga. Apparently there are similarities between yoga and Isles's postural system.'

'Except many Islesian exercises involve triggering memories of dysfunctional "Orbital" energy exchanges between people—though yes, like yoga, breathing patterns and the promotion of beneficial energy flows are relevant.'

'This is getting very complex. Why couldn't he just write sweet little love ditties?'

'Some of the songs do address "love imbalances": there are songs to cure unrequited love, excesses of erotic jealousy, marital discord, and so on.'

'We'll have plenty of guinea pigs for those,' said Anika, 'I might make use of one or two of them myself!'

Does she want me to ask about her love life? he thought, but before he could say anything, she was bullying him for point six.

'Okay, point six is really an extension of point five. Behind every posture, and every personal medicinal song Isles and Hobbes pictured *Dynamic Principles*. In English: archetypal "Orbital" exchange experiences: father with son, mother with daughter, mother with baby infant, young adult with mid-life father, lover with lover, etc. Also, relationships between humans and society, and humans and nature. There were planetary components to all this—derived, in part, from Astrological and Classical conceptions of the Gods as planets or solar bodies.'

'Jeez, no wonder no one's cracked the blithering code. Isles had an entire universe in his head. We're out of our depth, me thinks—drowning here, flapping about.' Anika made little flapping motions with her hands then started rubbing her forehead melodramatically, 'Could you run me off a copy of your chapter on this stuff—although I call myself a Neo-Islesian I've never read any of his original teachings. I'll be worse than useless if I don't bone up on the teachings of our alchemy obsessed neo-druid.'

They sat quietly for a minute or two watching the sunset and musing on the immensity of the task ahead.

'All the best works of art take us on a journey,' said Anika, thoughtfully, 'they work on multiple levels. The best creations destabilise us for the better.'

'Do you want to hear point seven?' he asked.

'If it's a short one.'

'I'll do my best.'

'The goal of Isles's medicinal songs was to heal particular inter-relational traumas (his term: 'Unbalanced orbits') via immersion in particular dances/postures and breathing patterns, but music also played a part. He seems to have aimed at a music triggered version of Mesmer's well known cathartic response.'

Anika scribbled down the last sentence then said simply, 'Point eight?'

'Clan tradition states that Isles emphasised the lyrical component to the songs. His written records of musical notation were supposedly kept to a bare minimum—key, time signature and lyric melody only. This musical base, plus the poetry built into the lyrics, carried the medicine to each new generation, perhaps?'

'Fascinating', said Anika, 'so he wants people to up-date the songs constantly?'

'Yes, he encourages us to re-imagine them for different musical genres—pop, rock, rap, punk ... Whatever you want.'

'Punk music? What's that?'

'Nothing important.'

Anika smiled tiredly.

'Bored yet?' asked Rowan.

'You're way over fifty words, but I'm not bored—just overwhelmed. It's been a long day. What's next?'

'The sun is almost down so I'll try to summarise the last points quickly. Point nine: Isles seemed to want his medicinal system to supplement rather than replace traditional Koori song-spirit medicine. He felt the two approaches had a lot in common and we must never forget that he was also initiated into the song medicine of a number of Marin tribes as an adult. He felt his system addressed/cured newly evolved "Maladies of Civilised Living"—again the Rousseau connection. We're almost there ...'

'But where is *there* exactly?'

'Point ten at a gallop. The song lyrics are diverse in terms of: syllable count, rhyme schemes (though archaic Welsh and Irish internal rhyme schemes are common) and stress patterns. There are very few repetitive language structures on display to help us out—no repetitive 'Anglican Thump', for example, and he's constantly experimenting with different metres.' Rowan sounded defeated again.

After thirty seconds or so Anika stopped writing to look up at Rowan, 'Is that it?'

'Yes, apart from the drawings that accompany every song—mostly they depict the Orbital imbalances and cathartic 'postures/dances' etc. being sung about. They're always back-grounded by Isles's trademark "planetary orbits" symbolism. We're currently having all the diary pages, especially those images, looked at by a data analyst. He's doing a post-doc up at the science campus. So far he's found no patterns suggesting a musical system.'

'That counts as point eleven—which just leaves,' she scribbled as she talked, 'point twelve.'

'That's the lost key to the entire system. It will permit us to recreate—hear—Isles's music for the first time since the 19th century.'

Anika stretched and looked out the window again, 'I'd better get back to the unit or I'll miss my guest.'

'You have someone visiting?' said Rowan, not wanting to pry into her personal life.

'Maybe, maybe not.'

'Oh.'

'The Anomaly—maybe it will turn up again tonight.'

'If it does, remember to ring me—I'm not big on Anomalies, but I have a weird feeling about this one.'

BOOK TWO

PART TWO: THE SONGS OF ABRAHAM ISLES

CHAPTER FORTY-THREE

PANNING FOR GOLD
(Wednesday, June 4th 1997)

The Anomaly of the 19th century gold miner didn't appear that night or the next. On the Tuesday morning Rowan signed the leave application papers before returning to the cliff unit feeling both liberated and defeated. Whirrarap had organised for tutors to run the exam and mark the remaining assignments for the Axial Age Religions unit. This left Rowan with nothing to do but focus on the diaries.

He soon realised how much teaching had kept him busy—cushioning the shock of everything he'd been through. Imogen had also helped a lot and he often had the urge to forgive her just to regain some of the stability and friendship she offered. Apparently she'd moved to Henri's again to join Paul—visiting her there, however, was out of the question. Though he still possessed an office, he visited it only infrequently. The diary facsimiles could not be shown—even casually—to unauthorised people and they had to be locked up in a safe whenever they weren't in use.

Godstar had phoned to say that the board of therapists for the Cridhe-Fasgadh had selected a therapist for him. He'd also asked, 'Are you handling the split with Imogen alright?'

Rowan had said that he was coping okay and Godstar had replied, 'Rumour has it that they're already hitting the hard stuff big time round at Henri's. She hasn't taught a class since last Tuesday. She's addicted to Paul *and* the drugs, whereas he's addicted to fucking other girls *and* to the drugs. It won't last, you watch—you're much better off without her.'

The following evening, Rowan headed over to Anika's at dusk to discuss the results of Gareth's work on image-text repetitions in the song journals—the test had been authorised by Whirrarap in May and was now complete. Apart from generalist information about the number of images, how often certain symbols were repeated etc., Rowan had also been given analysis of image positioning within frames (particularly the positioning of cauldrons, planets and alchemical symbols in the drawings) as well as analysis of any links between poetic devices used in songs, e.g. syllable count, rhyme schemes etc. and the images. These results had then been tracked against the mathematical structures underpinning various musical notation systems.

Overall, the results were disappointing—hence his arrival with a bottle of red wine to share with Anika, the idea being to drown their sorrows. Only one finding seemed to invite closer analysis.

Rowan pondered it whilst pouring the red wine into glasses. He then placed large sheets of paper full of mathematical symbols on the outdoor table beside a stack of the photocopied diaries.

'As requested, I examined the central motifs in the drawings—' Gareth had said, 'every alchemical lion, dragon, serpent and peacock, every totemic animal, every version of Luna, Sol and Mercury. I've catalogued colour changes, size changes, frame positioning changes etc. No patterns showed up. However, when I looked at the frame itself i.e. the tiny images of planetary Orbits that run down both sides of each image, some interesting correlations surfaced.'

'What correlations exactly?' Rowan had asked.

'It might just be chance, or perhaps there are astrological reasons for the alterations to the orbits, but all the planetary combinations are different. Likewise, each planet is depicted in multiple ways both within images and across the full array of diary images.'

'Meaning?' Rowan had tried not to sound too excited.

'Meaning the positions of the planets in relation to each other—and in relation to the main outer frame—may well be a clue.'

'The orbital diagrams would also have to link to the song-lyrics somehow—we're after lyric melodies after all.'

Gareth had nodded vacantly in response—making Rowan wonder how well he'd analysed language repetitions in the song lyrics.

'I'd like to do more tests on these aspects of the drawings—it's the closest thing we have to a possible code since the orbits appear in all the drawings.'

'How long before we break the code?' Rowan had asked, impatiently.

'Assuming there is a code and depending on its complexity and relationship with other elements on each page, I'd say we're looking at three months, minimum, unless …'

'Unless what?'

'Unless you or Anika have a flash of genius.'

As they sat down to eat, Rowan explained the results as best he could — given he wasn't a statistician. He tried to explain the uniqueness of the planetary shapes as well as their positions in each Orbital image. He then confessed that overall, the results were disappointing.

'Hence the wine?' said Anika, settling into her chair and lighting the lamp that sat on the table.

'Yes, but at least we have a lead. A long shot, true, and the side-frames containing the orbits are all very narrow. If they represent bars they'd have to be very short given the small number of planets per line. But what the hell, let's celebrate/commiserate anyway.'

'Yes, here's to Gareth!' said Anika, fork in one hand, glass of red wine in the other.

'And here's to the new moon rising!' said Rowan, clinking glasses then taking a gulp.

Anika raised her glass, but stopped drinking mid sip when she noticed that a gust of wind had opened one of the diaries. She stared at the song title in the dim lighting, 'Antidote to the Aggressive Impulses of Tribes and Nations.'

'And here's to Abraham Isles and Miriam Hobbes!' said Rowan, struggling to stay optimistic about the project.

'Yes, here's to Isles and Hobbes — let their music reach the ears of their humble telegraph operators Rowan and Anika!' This time she completed a sip of her wine.

Rowan managed a weak smile, but as they clinked glasses again, he noticed a glint of white appear behind a tree directly in front of them. When he looked closer, he noticed that it was moving and was attached to a larger form — a man.

'Shh ...' he whispered to Anika, who was about to make another toast, 'look over there. Is that your Anomaly?'

They both watched in awe as the figure pottered about among shrubs and bushes, beside a large boulder not ten metres distant.

'Any idea what we should do?' whispered Anika.

'My first impulse is to run for my life,' joked Rowan, 'but I guess we ought to take a closer look.' Rowan didn't like Anomalies—their existence meant reality was far stranger than he liked to admit.

'Okay, let's take a closer look. Do you think it's here for a reason?' asked Anika, rising from the table and signaling to Rowan to do the same.

Rowan looked at the Anomaly then at Anika. His heart was racing and the hairs on the back of his neck were standing up. He felt glued to the chair.

Anika, luckily, was more adventurous. She yanked his arm, saying, 'Come on—what are you scared of? You're the Islesian scholar—this stuff should be bread and butter to you.'

He let Anika lead him into the garden.

The Anomaly had its back to them as they approached. Rowan noticed it took the form of a tall, bearded miner dressed in a straw hat, grubby white shirt, primitive pants and not much else. He was down on one knee holding a gold-mining pan, which he shook gently every now and then. It didn't seem to be aware of their presence and they got quite close before it began to fade out. Seeing this Anika, left Rowan where he was in order to move around in-front of the figure. She wanted to catch a glimpse of his features. As she did this, however, the figure turned to Rowan—who felt the blood drain from his face.

Although it was dark, the man's translucence allowed Rowan to catch a good look at his face. What he saw stunned him—the man bore a remarkable resemblance to surviving paintings of Abraham Isles taken in the late 1840s and later. As it faded, Rowan saw the man stop a moment and stare with delight into his pan. He then turned and signaled to someone invisible— located to the right of Anika. The Anomaly watched the figure approach before displaying a small nugget of gold. He then put forefinger to sun-cracked lips and made a 'Stay quiet about this' gesture before vanishing.

'What the hell was that about?' said Anika, shivering as they returned to the table.

Rowan's fragile sense of reality had taken another hit, leaving him unable to speak for a moment.

'Are you okay—you look like you've just seen a ghost?' said Anika, wryly.

'I believe we've just met Abraham Isles,' said Rowan, still in shock.

'He looked like an ordinary 19th century gold miner to me,' said Anika.

Rowan slumped back into his chair, 'In the early 1840s, quite by chance, a Koori up on the Great River showed Isles a number of large yellow rocks in his possession. Abraham immediately realised that they were gold nuggets of amazing purity. He rode south with the man the following morning in an effort to plot the exact location of the find.'

'I presume they found the location?'

'They camped north-west of here—still in Dja Dja Wurung country (the place the Chinese named, Big Gold Mountain). After an hour's work, Isles assembled a large stash of valuable nuggets. He showed these to a local elder, and later to a northern tribal elder. Historical rumour has it that he spent all that night and much of the next day explaining the full implications of the find to the local elder.' Rowan paused.

'Sooner or later, a gold rush.'

'Yes, and the rest is history—one version of history, anyway.'

Anika wrapped her woolen shawl more tightly around her upper body in order to stay warm, she looked perplexed. 'Okay, I know you're in history paradise here—you've just seen your hero in the uh ... sort of flesh, but what does this mean for our project?'

The sun had almost set as Rowan looked up at Anika. Her lively, angular features and long brown hair were lit only by the table lamp. Yet again he was struck by the irony of their situation.

'I think he's trying to tell us something,' he said slowly.

Anika pondered Rowan's words before speaking, 'Wasn't it weird how the diary opened up to a song about social conflict as the Anomaly arrived?'

'I didn't notice the song title.'

'Well, everyone knows', said Anika, pondering something, 'that if you ignore Anomalies they fade away or move off.'

'So they say,' replied Rowan.

'Well, I think the fact that we were talking about his work *attracted* him, but we probably did exactly the wrong thing after that. We stopped talking and we didn't address him directly. I've also heard that Anomalies appear to particular people for particular purposes. The Anomaly turned away from me to address you. If I'm right, he has something to tell *you, Rowan.* If he shows up again you need to *engage* with him.'

'Great work, detective Miraj, but I'm a little too cowardly to *engage* with a ghost.' He didn't care if he was disappointing her.

'What if he intends to show you the code for his music system?' She let the question hang in the air.

'You sound like you have a plan,' said Rowan, still spooked.

'We'll have dinner again here tomorrow evening—with the diaries open on the table. And we'll talk about Isles's songs. *You* will then ask the Isles Anomaly some questions and we'll see what happens next.'

'I don't think so!' said Rowan, firmly, 'I think we grab Whirrarap, or perhaps Ungaru—he's a trainee tohunga, they deal with spirits all the time—and one of them *engages* Isles. If it is Isles.'

'You're an Islesian—what are you afraid of?' she was almost challenging him.

Rowan thought for a moment. 'I'm afraid of religion—spiritual zealots, authoritarian priests, religious fascists, religious warriors, sexual repression in the name of God, Emperors who think themselves divine, but are really insane sadists, terrorists espousing simplistic ideas about Good and Evil. These things frighten me. What are you afraid of?'

Anika spoke gently in reply, 'I'm afraid of disenchantment, desacralisation, loss of soul—a plague of ennui, alienation, depression, acedia, melancholy. I'm afraid of the heaviness of time and I refuse to live in a world robbed of inspiration, magic, wonder, awe, curiosity—love and adventure. I'm afraid of the purveyors of spiritual *oppression* as much as you are, *but* I do not accept the decree that my consciousness must reside in the narrow reality band staked out by classical science, Enlightenment reason and atheism. I'm afraid of these things, Rowan.' She stared at the table-cloth for several minutes after she'd finished speaking.

She eventually agreed to Rowan's suggestion that they invite Whirrarap or Ungaru, and dropped the idea that he engage with the Anomaly.

CHAPTER FORTY-FOUR

A STREAM OF FUTURES
(Thurday, June 5th)

They met again the following night for dinner. Whirrarap was in Bunjilaka City, probably meeting with important people in the government, so Ungaru was asked to attend instead. Rowan arrived with several basic Gaelic and Welsh greeting phrases that he gave to Ungaru to use on the Anomaly if it turned up. He'd written their key question on a piece of paper in Welsh, Highland Gaelic and English: 'Where can we find the music for your songs?'

As they prepared, Anika and Ungaru tried to persuade Rowan to engage the apparition if it appeared. Rowan would have none of it, so Anika tried a different angle.

'I think I was too hard on you last night,' she said gently, 'I made it seem as though there were only two options: God (or the Gods) *or* Science and Reason. Every intelligent Islesian, however, knows that *dualities* are a big problem for us humans.'

Ungaru—seated beside them at the table—was practicing, without much success, the Welsh and Gaelic phrases Rowan had given him.

'Well if it's Zeus—Father of religious conformity, brutal autocrat and egotist—*or* Prometheus—lover of humans, eternal rebel, scientist and atheist—then I'm with the rebel god,' said Rowan, suddenly aware he was shy about discussing his atheism with Anika and Ungaru.

Ungaru gave up on the Gaelic phrases and joined the conversation, 'But you forget one thing, Rowan.'

'What's that?'

'Prometheus was no atheist. Didn't you read your Aeschylus?'

'The modern age is usually thought of as Promethean, Ungaru—' said Anika, 'think Dr Faustus, Frankenstein, Nietzsche, nuclear bombs, computers, space travel, etc.'

Rowan flinched—clearly she knew exactly what a modern day Prometheus might be into.

'I disagree,' replied Ungaru, 'Prometheus was of the old order. He knew that other Gods had existed—*existed still* somewhere—in Tartarus perhaps. By implication such Gods are friendlier to humans,' Ungaru sounded inspired. 'The *fire* of Prometheus is *not* the *fire* of atheism, classical science or technology running amok; nor is it the fire of reason without soul. These are monstrous fires—they are not of his doing. A true Islesian would say that the *fire* of Prometheus is the *fire* of the Principles or Domestic Deities. It's the archaic pre-patriarchal *fire*—the *nwyvre*, molten *karuna*, empathy, eros, quicksilver thought. In short that which comes from outside the universe of dualities, flaws and suffering. His fire is a spiritual fire, but also a fire of the flesh. We're talking about knowledge of the time before dualities—the time of animals, of birds, fishes and insects, and of trees and shrubs,' he trailed off, unaware of the effect he was having on Rowan and Anika.

'So if we remove Prometheus from the duality that is Science versus God, that doesn't remove the duality, the split, itself. What principle can heal the split?' asked Anika.

'The principle in your Western tradition, would be Mercurius or Hermes,' said Ungaru, 'that which maintains the balance between worlds—between the tendency of the Gods to lord it over humans, and the tendency of humans to seek to annihilate their Gods. At least that's how the ancient alchemists would have seen it.'

Rowan looked at Ungaru thoughtfully, then said 'I'll sleep on it! Are you sure Prometheus isn't a scientist? I could do with an ordinary fire right now—it's getting very bloody cold.' They all laughed—and waited.

The Anomaly turned up again just after dusk. They watched it for a minute or two to see if it would do anything different, but it didn't. Eventually, Ungaru took the diaries and Rowan's phrases down to where it was panning for gold and addressed it in all three languages, one after another, all the time looking at its face.

Anika and Rowan stood out of range—lamps, pens and writing pads at the ready. As had happened the previous night, the figure ignored Ungaru and turned towards Rowan, who immediately felt his heart beat faster.

Only Anika's hand gripping his wrist stopped him from running back up the path to the unit.

Ungaru, assessed the situation quickly, and circled to a position directly behind Rowan and Anika. Once in position, he quietly handed Rowan the diaries as well as the piece of paper with the phrases. 'Go on—speak to it,' whispered Ungaru.

Rowan struggled to breathe as the garden, the stars above, Anika, Ungaru—the entire cosmos—felt suddenly permeable. The Anomaly seemed to collapse Rowan's ordinary sense of time and space—leaving him adrift in multiple worlds/realities and possibilities of being. He spoke the phrases quickly as a kind of spell—a means to stay attached to the fragile reality he'd been stranded in for months.

The figure grew brighter after being addressed and soon began to hum a haunting melody that gradually turned into lyrics that Rowan recognised as Gaelic. Isles was singing the song they'd been led to the previous evening. It was about conflict between groups and nations.

Anika let go of Rowan's wrist to find her pen and pad so that she could begin notating the song's melody—she knew instantly it was the key to everything. Behind her Ungaru did his best to write down the lyrics.

Next moment, Isles pointed down at his gold-mining pan—all the time slowly singing in Gaelic. Rowan felt his consciousness stretch and expand almost to breaking point. Hypnotised by the images swirling around in the pan, he drew closer as all his anxieties and fears began to dissolve into a larger awareness of cosmic well-being and peace. He felt connected to everyone and everything he'd ever known—Anika and Ungaru, Whirrarap, Imogen and Paul, Douglas and Rhiannon, Kerryn and Eric, the trees and the bushes, and the stars and the planets in their various orbits.

Rowan watched as words from the song merged with pulsing orbital patterns and strings of ogham letters. As he kept watching, the Isles Anomaly shook the pan gently whilst singing. Each sung note appeared linked to a particular word syllable, ogham letter and orbit. Isles was singing notes downwards through an ogham progression but upwards from the bottom left of the orbital chart—indicating a partial reverse notation system.

Once the song was finished, the Isles Anomaly stared knowingly at Rowan for a moment before bending down with the pan. In that instant Rowan noticed a small stream of some sort running away from Anika's garden towards the university. Isles gestured for Rowan to bend down beside him—perhaps to observe more closely the gold panning operation. Rowan obeyed and soon found himself awash in what turned out to be not water, but a stream of destinies, possibilities, futures—all emanating, he knew it intuitively, from the decisions of the here and now. Isles drew the pan slowly through the phosphorescent waters—through the tangle of possible futures—then, whilst beginning a new song, he gestured for Rowan to hold the pan.

Though apprehensive, Rowan did as asked only to become aware instantly that this meeting, at this locality, at this particular moment in time could launch only a limited number of possible futures. He was being asked to choose carefully from the stream of futures. Phosphorescent water swirled beneath him as he assessed each of the futures on offer. After what seemed like an eternity, he made his decision—though much remained obscure. Isles, who looked grim and noncommittal, received the pan from Rowan before slowly vanishing. As a parting gesture, he signaled to Rowan to keep quiet about the future he'd chosen.

Although it seemed to Rowan as though an eternity had passed, Anika and Ungaru reported later that the entire encounter was over in a few minutes. Anika had not seen Rowan choose from the stream of futures. Ungaru, however, may have seen something, since his mood became instantly more pensive

'I got the melody down—what did he show you?' whispered

Anika, as Rowan stared trancelike at the last weak flickers of the disappearing Anomaly.

'And I got some of the words,' said Ungaru, still scribbling, 'at least in their phonetic form. Remember, he was singing in Gaelic, a language I know nothing about.'

'Doesn't matter, I know the song. The main thing is the melody,' said Anika, rushing to support Rowan, who seemed about to collapse.

'Abraham showed me the notation system—it's connected to that book of nonsense ogham,' whispered Rowan. 'We need to link nonsense ogham letter lists to specific orbital charts. We then read the ogham letters as pitch/notes and the size of each planet as a note's duration. He's only given us simple lyric melodies—but in a way that's all we need. Rhythm, it seems, is suggested by a poem's meter—i.e. iambic, trochaic, etc. as well as syllables per line,'

'Let's find that song in the diaries and link it to a chronologically parallel ogham chapter to test the theory,' said Ungaru, struggling, for some reason, to get excited.

'It sounds like a coded proto-notation system—like the neume systems used in early church music. If this works we've cracked the code!' said Anika, excited at the breakthrough, but puzzled at the way Ungaru was doing his best to avoid her gaze. 'What happened when you bent down and took the pan from Isles?' she asked Rowan.

'Nothing much,' lied Rowan, 'I was standing in a stream of futures. Isles associated physical gold with spiritual gold—and spiritual gold meant trying to create the best possible future from all the futures on offer. We were panning the future for spiritual gold.'

As he spoke, his legs suddenly turned to jelly. Anika had to act fast to break his fall. Luckily, Ungaru stepped in to help out. Together the three of them stumbled up through the garden to Anika's lounge room.

'We need some coffee!' she declared, before clearing some space on her kitchen table so they could work on deciphering the music for the Isles song.

CHAPTER FORTY-FIVE

A SECOND ANOMALY
(Thursday, June 12th 1997)

Whirrarap called an emergency meeting of the Marin Cultural Board of Elders for the following Thursday. Rowan and Anika turned up with a definitive completion date for the final chapters, but they needed the board to release some extra funds to support Anika whilst she assisted Rowan to complete the project.

When the time came for Rowan to speak, he briefly described their progress—this time in Pan-Koori. 'I hope to give a final draft of the book's last chapter to the board next Friday at the latest. Structural and copy-edits of all other chapters are complete and Anika has already transcribed the melodies of dozens of the songs into conventional musical notation. In order to complete the musical appendices on time, however, we need the board to provide a list of the songs to be decoded for inclusion in the book.'

When he'd finished speaking, he was asked a question about

the Isles Anomaly and how it had contributed to the code being broken. His story made quite an impression on the delegates and there was much hushed discussion afterwards. After Rowan returned to his seat, he was surprised to see Anika rise to speak at the podium. A Central Marin female delegate came to the front of the assembly to briefly introduce her.

'Anika Miraj has something important to share with the delegates.'

Anika looked a little nervous which made her stoop as if to avoid being looked at. Rowan was surprised—she hadn't told him she'd be presenting.

'Although I spoke to Rowan, and later Whirrarap, about what turned out to be the Isles Anomaly, I have not spoken to them yet about the other Anomaly that visited my unit around that time.' She looked tentative and vulnerable as she spoke.

'After Rowan identified the miner as Isles, I realised that an Anomaly manifesting in the early hours of the morning in my lounge-room was actually Isles's wife Miriam Hobbes. At first the Anomaly, a tall figure, like Isles, clothed in a long black dress and woolen shawl, stood one night in the centre of my lounge room. Her arms were up-raised—as though conducting singers in a choir.'

Anika drank from a glass of water and then took a deep breath before continuing.

'After Rowan engaged with Isles, I decided to ask Miriam what she wanted to communicate to me. Although I cannot share with you all that was said—some of the discussion was of a private nature—I can say that she pointed at the fireplace, which at the time was ablaze with burning logs and made gestures indicating she was stirring an invisible pot of some description. After ten minutes or so attending to the invisible pot of liquid or food she produced a ladle, dipped it in the still invisible pot before indicating that I needed to drink from the ladle, which I did.'

The woman who had introduced Anika addressed the crowd as Anika returned to her seat beside Rowan.

'Anika has agreed to answer some questions about her encounter with the Miriam Anomaly on the condition that we don't ask her to reveal the nature of the private matters discussed. Any questions?'

A male delegate immediately put his hand up, 'Thank you, Anika, for sharing that. I know you do not want us delving into your private life, but I wonder could you tell us about the significance of drinking from the ladle?' The host glanced over at Anika for a moment to see if she was willing to answer. Anika nodded a 'yes' then stood up.

She seemed to blush as she answered, 'After drinking from the ladle, I immediately felt profoundly inspired—in the creative sense—something I have not felt for some time. I could not sleep that night due to the host of songs clamouring to be born.'

There the meeting ended—at least for Rowan and Anika. The delegates went into closed session for about an hour, during which time Rowan and Anika had some lunch and wandered around in the gardens surrounding the centre.

Anika was apologetic about the Miriam Anomaly. 'I hope you don't mind that I didn't tell you about the Miriam Anomaly. I instinctively knew she was there about my own creativity. By the time I realised the visitor was Isles's wife, we already had everything we needed to decode the songs.'

'What Miriam needed to reveal to you is your business entirely. Though I am glad I heard the story in the end—pretty weird stuff.' They were sitting among she-oaks overlooking the dam with hundreds of water-lilies. The wind was chilly and Anika wrapped her knee-length jacket tightly about her. To Rowan, she almost seemed lonely.

Anika chose her words carefully, 'I had the sense that Miriam was something like Cerridwen, or maybe Bridget, and that by drinking from the ladle, I was becoming Cerridwen-Bridget in some strange way.'

'So you're becoming a merged ancient pagan goddess called Cerridwen-Bridget?' asked Rowan, as gently as he could.

'Not exactly becoming her—in my beliefs it's important to balance the mortal with the divine.'

'Yes, a good idea. So perhaps my real question is: who exactly is Anika Miraj? I've been working side by side with you for a while now and I don't feel I know you at all.'

Anika looked surprised, 'You've never *asked* who I am before.'

'I didn't want to pry—I don't want to pry now really.' He avoided her gaze and focused instead on a wading bird, some kind of native ibis, fishing in the shallows of the dam.

'Okay, you want a short personal bio for Anika Miraj—Anika is a thirty-two year old poet, musician/composer and lecturer in music. She's been separated for one year from Kirby, but is yet to be formally divorced. She has a child, a son called Neill, aged nine—he's with Kirby at present. She talks to Neill most nights by phone just before he goes to sleep. She and her husband have separated because he has bouts of mental illness that occasionally make him discount her role in his life. When he's well, he's loving, and encourages her in everything she does. When he's ill, he makes her feel as if their life together is somehow lacking and insufficient—a cause of his unhappiness. She'll be seeing them both this weekend. They're driving over from West-Marin. She's been missing Neill a lot, and may even bring him here to live. Though Anika needs more joy and inspiration in her life, she feels guilty about the possibility of divorcing Kirby. This is at the heart of her predicament.' She paused, aware she'd probably confessed too much already.

'It must be very difficult not seeing your son every day,' said Rowan.

'I've had equal share of the parenting since Neill was born—and I've been working close to full time for most of that period. I was exhausted when I arrived here. If I've seemed a little distracted at times, it's because I've been pondering my predicament. After that encounter with 'Miriam' I've become aware that overall I'm on the right path. She made me feel happier in myself.'

Rowan felt the urge to share aspects of his own predicament with her, but stopped himself—aware a confession might jeopardise everything they were working towards. Instead, he pondered for a while what 'becoming Cerridwen-Bridget' might mean. He searched back through his memories of Isles's system and it occurred to him that the Alchemy underlying it held to highly personal understandings of divinity. Isles, of course, termed the gods 'Principles'—since he felt the gods of most European mythologies had been corrupted by oppressive aristocratic values and were thus of little use to ordinary people. One could, however, model the Principles, since they were connected to key life-span relationships. To become a 'Principle' was perhaps to manifest a best possible self in a best possible future.

Anika broke the silence between them. 'I should warn you that when I'm inspired I can be a little scary. Things happen quickly. I can sense stuff coming for me—from the future. It's both exciting and terrifying. I've felt it since my arrival here to work with Whirrarap and um… you, but the future sometimes demands more from me than I'm able to give. That's what I mean by becoming Cerridwen-Bridget—the abrupt demand that I devote myself to a creative project that transforms me as I proceed.' She paused in order to observe the wading bird with Rowan.

The sound of footsteps on the stone path jarred them out of their respective water bird meditations. It was Whirrarap and he looked thoughtful.

'We have a proposition,' he said.

CHAPTER FORTY-SIX

ASSISTED COLD TURKEY

Rowan and Anika were surprised at the board's proposition. They wanted *Interstitium*, with Anika, to perform three of Isles's songs at a peace festival set to coincide with the release of the book in late August. A large music venue in Big Gold Mountain had already been booked, and other New Albion, Marin and international bands would also perform—among them Paul's band. They also wanted the newly renovated *Interstitium* to record a mini-CD of six Islesian songs prior to the event. The concert would be preceded by a cricket match between former Marin test players and a World eleven composed of retired English, Indian, New Zealand, Pakistani, South African, Sri Lankan and West Indian players, as well as four players from the other Australian continental nations—including a courageous former New Albion great. The board also wanted Rowan to come out of retirement for the match. The goal of the day, Whirrarap said, was to protest New Albion belligerence internationally. A Marin Rules final eight match to be held in Bunjilaka City on the Friday evening would also be part of the protest.

The board had also decided to continue payments to both Anika and Rowan until the end of the academic year, provided they agreed to the proposal as offered.

'The Isles estate will inform you which songs can be musically transcribed for the biography, and likewise, which songs they want recorded and performed,' said Whirrarap, struggling to pass on all aspects of the board's proposal. 'Remember that Isles emphasised *originality of response* for performers of his work. Isles's descendents wish to give all participating bands a fair bit of interpretive leeway. The key is to make the songs appeal to young people living here and in New Albion.'

Rowan felt anxious all the way back to Dinas Yarkuk. He knew that he and Anika had an enormous amount of work ahead. First they had to resurrect *Interstitium* before working out how to contemporise the songs they'd be given. He and Anika also had to finish the book on Isles and Hobbes.

'Next time you want to tell me about how you feel the future *coming at you*, please try to give me a few more days warning,' said Rowan, playfully. Anika was sitting beside him in the back seat of Whirrarap's car.

'I didn't mean it like that—I had no idea the board had this in mind.'

He marvelled that she sounded more excited than stressed.

'I think you got the best deal by far. I have a lot of singing lessons ahead, not to mention many hours in the cricket nets. I've performed music live only once in ten years and I'll have to bowl at retired international cricketers in front of a large crowd.' He felt a stress headache building just thinking about it.

'You'll handle it,' she said, patting his knee, 'half of them will be sporting huge pot bellies!'.

'Do you think Godstar and his friends will agree to perform?' he said.

'They'll jump at the opportunity.' As she spoke, she pointed out an Anomaly on the side of the road—a young Aboriginal girl holding a small sack of flour. Rowan flinched then looked away.

Over the following fortnight, Rowan and Anika worked eighteen hour days at their respective tasks. Once the songs to be performed were decided upon, they occasionally took time out to meet and plan the performance. The twice weekly jam nights that Rowan's band had held prior to the gig at Henri's were reinstated, with Godstar, Ungaru and the other two musicians delighted to participate. The news that Anika would join the band and that together they'd be performing at a televised Peace Rally in Big Gold Mountain two months or so hence was also taken well—though Rowan detected a hint of nervousness, even with Godstar who was a seasoned performer. Rowan also found the Koori guy he'd met months ago in Dinas Yarkuk's central park and asked if there were any local first grade batsmen he could bowl at as he tried to train for the one day match to be held on the same day as the gig.

The young student immediately contacted half a dozen high quality batsmen, some from the local league and some who were sports scholarship students at MUCT. Rowan's first training session with the Marin team wasn't for a few weeks and he wanted to be prepared in advance for the session. Even though the game at the Peace Festival would only be a friendly, Rowan wanted to make sure that during his one match return to international cricket he at least looked the part. The thought of being clobbered all over the park by retired world-class batsmen scared the hell out of him. If that happened, or if he bowled wides and no balls, his spell of bowling would feel like hell on earth.

One week into his new routine of writing, cricket training, orbital cleansing sessions and band practices, Rowan had a surprise visit from Imogen. Anika had flown to West Marin for the week to be with her son—he was sick with some sort of flu. Rowan wondered whether Imogen had deliberately decided to see him in Anika's absence. She and Rowan hadn't seen each other since the night at Henri's. Though she'd reportedly returned to teaching, they hadn't crossed paths yet since he'd been avoiding his office for weeks. In truth, he'd grown suspicious that his emails were being monitored and his phone was being tapped. Whirrarap had also warned him and Anika not to speak to anyone at the university about their success at decoding the melodies behind Isles's songs. Out of paranoia they'd worked mostly from their respective units.

'Can I come in?' Imogen said her eyes staring at the floor, her right foot tapping impulsively on the stone tiles.

Rowan took a deep breath, 'Actually I'd rather that you didn't.'

'I need to talk. I haven't contacted you because I thought it would make things easier, but I owe you an apology. I'm really sorry that I hurt you.' She had dark rings under her eyes and looked pale. Rowan suspected drug addiction.

'You've got to get off that shit—you know that don't you?' he said, though he wasn't about to open the door to her.

She bit her lower lip and played with her long dark hair a moment before speaking, 'You're the only one I feel I can talk to.'

'I'm not your supervisor anymore and I'm not your counsellor.'

'He just upped and left last week—off to bloody England. They'll be based there for the next year at least. They've landed a major label record deal—apparently a couple of their early songs have had huge sales. Their UK agent—blonde, skinny, looks like a model—dropped in last week to *accompany* the band on the trip. He didn't tell me he was going until she arrived, that was two days before the flight. His *agent* slept on the sofa … at least while I was around. On the last night we were all stoned and he suggested that the three of us … I wouldn't. He can get fucked!'

'The Marin Cultural Board is counting on him being back in August to take part in the gig at Big Gold Mountain.'

'Oh, he'll be back for that—never misses a chance to promote the band or himself. Rumour has it that your band is also taking part. Perhaps I should find a clinic that cures people who are addicted to musicians who fuck off at the first opportunity.' She sounded bitter, angry and despairing all at the same time.

'I didn't fuck off on you, remember,' he said coldly.

She stared at him a moment, genuinely surprised that her actions had led to him making a definitive break.

He had a strong urge to shut the door and send her on her way. Obviously she was only talking to him now because Paul was living it up with his supermodel agent in London. If he came back tomorrow the cycle, with all its dramas, would begin all over again. He had to admit a part of him wanted to let her inside, hug her perhaps—maybe even make love one last time. This part desperately wanted to believe the lies she was feeding him.

'Besides, you owe me one more supervision session. I haven't written a thing since we stopped meeting. And you still haven't given me any feedback on my manuscript!' She sounded desperate, but Rowan wondered if there was also a hint of a threat, perhaps she'd go to the university management to complain about the 'substandard' supervision he'd provided. The possibility left him indifferent—after all he'd moved on from their programmatic morality and besides, he would likely be sacked soon anyway.

'The academic board relieved me of my duties as your supervisor. They think I'm still a bit nuts due to the accident. Just quietly, you need to think about your relationship with Paul—after all he's an undergraduate student.'

'The board can get stuffed! What do they know about people's feelings?'

Rowan said nothing.

'It's about her, isn't it … Anika? Has she made you feel differently about us?'

'No, she hasn't—that night at Henri's made me feel differently about us.'

Imogen scowled at him, 'You and Paul have a lot in common. Both of you are selfish shits.'

Rowan stared hard back at her, 'Wrong, me and Paul *had* a few things in common. And there's something I haven't told you before—' he paused, trying to find the right words, 'the accident in Vietnam wasn't an accident. It was a suicide attempt. Even though it was only partially to do with us—well, everything had to change after that.'

As he said this, he felt time freeze, and for a second Imogen became Anika, long ago—he heard her voice down the end of a phone line whispering 'Eric's in a bad way. I know you and I are over, but I need you here at the moment. He'll tell you things he won't tell me—I'm sure he's about to have another go. The doctors and his parents don't see it, but I think he'll do it.'

Rowan was jolted out of the memory by Imogen's snort of frustration. She was heading for the front gate. Her shoulders had sagged, and she seemed close to sobbing.

'Imogen,' Rowan said gently, 'I've been undergoing weekly therapy sessions at an Islesian clinic in town. It's been very cathartic. You might think about giving it a go.'

She turned again to face him, 'You're right, it isn't Anika—it was the accident. After you came out of the coma you didn't want me in the same way. I kept pretending nothing had really changed, but it had. Look, I'm so sorry you reached a point where you'd try to .... ' She burst into tears before she could end the sentence.

'After the suicide attempt I became a different person—these days I just want a simple life—no complications.'

'I hate being like this—a *monster*. That's what Paul and the drugs turn me into. I almost said yes to him and his shallow model. That scared the shit out of me—handing my body over like that.' She started to cry more deeply.

'Like I said—give the clinic a go. I'll introduce you to the head therapist tomorrow night if you like, she's an amazing woman. And they have drug and alcohol specialists.'

'I'll think about it, but there's other stuff going on too. Not just in my head this time—that's a relief eh?'

'What stuff?'

'Half the New Albion students are deferring their studies and heading home before second semester starts. There are big debates going on around at Henri's—some want to go home to join the military, others just want to avoid the coming war. I need to make a decision. I miss my family—my dad anyway, and my brothers. There are reports in the news of attacks on New Albion students in Bunjilaka City and Henri is paranoid that the Marin government might have him under surveillance. Henri the spy, ha, ha!' She wiped her eyes with her shirt sleeve as she spoke.

'I can't imagine Henri being paranoid about anything. What are you going to do?' As he spoke, he thought about the fact that the New Albion managers at MUCT might also be feeling the heat and felt mildly elated.

'There's nothing for me in Sydney—who is going to employ

a culture critic in shock-jock radio wonderland? I'm too political and my work is all over the web. I've published two essays critiquing their new censorship and sedition laws—they're incarcerating writers there now, it's all happening. But there's nothing for me here either.' She let the last sentence hang in the air.

'You have a job you believe in. You just need to believe in yourself a bit more. And you shouldn't put up with his shit—he doesn't deserve you.'

'Jeez, New Age Rowan, or what! Rowan found his true self in Dinas Yarkuk.' Her mockery seemed edged with hysteria.

'In truth, I found *useful versions of myself* here.'

She stared at him as if puzzled, before responding, 'You have got to get over this tendency to talk like a bloody Guru.' She looked happier, but Rowan didn't want to prolong the conversation.

'Speaking as a friend now, I'll be available to talk, but we won't be lovers—you need to understand that.'

She couldn't hold his gaze, said 'Professor Rowan finally calls his errant student, Imogen, to task over her tendency to see support for her own thesis in every text she reads.'

'I'll see you at the clinic tomorrow night, 7pm sharp, if you feel like doing anything stupid in the meantime, or the shakes and hallucinations get too much, there's an emergency phone number you can call.'

He found a piece of scrap paper and scribbled a phone number as well as a street address on it. He unlocked the fly-screen to hand her the paper. She took it slowly, all the time looking up at him. 'I will think about this. You know it's hardest at night—the deep ache underlying everything. Of course, I'm cold turkey at the moment, but even when I'm clean the ache never really disappears.' She desperately wanted to be hugged. 'But I have good friends and I left Henri's yesterday. My friends give me towels, hydration drinks—there's a lot of sweating. They hold my hand when the seizures and hallucinations get too bad.'

'I'll see you tomorrow night,' said Rowan, closing the fly-screen.

'Okay,' she said hesitantly, then strode a few paces up the path before turning once again, 'By the way, Henri was disappointed you didn't visit him to discuss your research project.'

Rowan pondered the news for a moment, 'Oh, I assumed he had no real interest in Isles and Hobbes.'

'He's making all sorts of inquires about your project with the other students—maybe you should meet with him.'

Rowan looked at her gently before answering, 'I think not—I don't like the way he treats his boarders.'

CHAPTER FORTY-SEVEN

TRUE BLUE MAX
(Friday, June 27th 1997)

The roads north were clogged with military hardware and the skies were swarming with aircraft—transport planes, fighter jets and reconnaissance aircraft from many nations, as well as New Albion bombers, some reportedly armed with nuclear warheads. The small party had crossed the Great River, with its imposing river red-gums, an hour earlier, and despite rainclouds to the west the skies remained mostly blue as the car approached the flatlands of the border region where Rowan was to meet with his father. His sister had not been given permission to meet with him. Rowan estimated they were headed north somewhere between the towns he'd once known as Albury and Wagga Wagga.

'Things are starting to look very bleak up here …' said Whirrarap thoughtfully, as yet another New Albion fighter jet split the heavens well above the speed of sound. The aircraft was tailed by three Marin (or Alliance) jets and Rowan found himself wondering if these manoeuvres had become routine. If so the two nations were surely on the verge of outright war.

'They've already bombed a refugee camp in the mountains on our side of the border—it was supposedly harbouring "terrorists". Twenty-five "exiled" civilians killed,' said Jake in fluent Pan-Koori. He'd been given the job of overseeing the meeting. He was smartly dressed and sat in the vehicle's front seat next to Whirrarap, who was driving. Rowan noticed that both men grew quieter the closer they got to the border.

Their progress slowed as they passed through a series of military roadblocks. Each time Jake flashed his ID and stated his business, 'We're meeting with a Marin citizen currently being illegally held in a New Albion detention camp 10 kilometres from the border.'

Finally they passed a battered road sign that stated simply, 'Marin-New Albion Demilitarised Zone: drivers are advised that unauthorised personnel are not permitted to carry weapons or explosives beyond this point'.

Rowan spied a cluster of huts and towers standing amongst four large gate posts, two either side of the highway. The two sets of gateposts appeared to be about fifty metres apart and had swing-gates attached— the furthest gate displayed the red, white and blue colours of the New Albion flag. The nearest gate was draped with the familiar yellow, red, green and black colours of the Marin flag. However, beside it, flying at half mast, was a flag Rowan had only seen displayed in Dinas Yarkuk on special occasions—it featured a modified five star motif symbolic of the Southern Cross (though the stars were central and coloured yellow against a black background) above a thick horizontal sliver of red. Rowan knew it was the flag of the Australian Continental Alliance—the very same flag Douglas had left in Rowan's study back in February. The five stars were all of equal size and symbolised both the five countries that shared the continent of 'Australia' and the joint military alliance they'd shared since the late 1890s—though New Albion had withdrawn from the alliance in recent years. Marins joked that the Aotearoans now owned the flag's most easterly star. Rowan knew that the thick red section at the bottom symbolised the earth.

There were many soldiers on the Marin side of the border, most were dug into trenches splayed out at ninety degree angles either side of the road. Rowan also saw what he guessed was the entrance to a refugee camp—it was set amongst tall yellow-box gums about 500 metres back from the road. The vehicle eventually pulled into a covered car-park close to the Marin government huts. Once again Jake was asked to confirm his ID to a border official standing guard over the car-park entrance. Rowan, Whirrarap and Jake were then guided to one of the huts.

Their hut concealed a fortified underground complex of rooms and passageways which the three visitors and their guide entered by clambering down a white ladder.

'Please wait here,' said the tall border official to Rowan, whilst pointing to a drab waiting area close to the foot of the ladder. It possessed five or six chairs and a small table cluttered with magazines—the lighting, however, was negligible and Rowan wondered how anyone would ever be able to read in the dimness. To Rowan's surprise, Whirrarap and Jake were taken to another room about ten metres further along the underground tunnel. That room projected blue light into the passageway.

After a while Jake reappeared without Whirrarap, saying, 'Please prepare yourself, your father has lost a great deal of weight and the stresses of detention centre life have made him somewhat apathetic.' Jake, a thirty something Koori with longish black hair, was genuinely concerned. 'We'll both need to keep our hands in the air as we cross the border monitoring zone (BMZ). Your father is in a nearby hut. You've been permitted fifteen minutes with him—sorry, it was the best deal we could negotiate.'

'Put your hands above your heads and proceed slowly to the electronic monitoring station mid-way between the two gates,' said a loud, crackly voice emanating from the gate tower fifty metres away.

Rowan and Jake did as they were told. The monitoring station turned out to be a small black gateway about two metres high, a metre wide and fifty centimetres thick—not unlike the kind of security units installed at airports.

'Please note,' continued the voice, after they'd reached the gateway, 'you are about to be electronically searched for the presence of illegal substances, weapons, explosives, biological hazards, censored cultural materials, banned foodstuffs, etcetera. You may proceed to the alien hazard identification chamber when the light flashes green. If any discrepancies are discovered, you may be required to undergo a search by a border official or a customs robot. New Albion is serious about protecting its borders. You should also note that footage of this crossing may be shown on New Albion commercial television.'

A light above the gateway soon flashed green and Jake walked slowly into the gateway/chamber for assessment. The operation took only a minute or so and he was quickly cleared for temporary entry into New Albion. Moments later, it was Rowan's turn to approach the black gateway with his hands in the air.

He paused in the chamber with a solid plastic barrier between himself and Jake on the other side. Rowan listened to the whir of various monitoring devices and stared, as requested by a synthetic computer voice, into the chamber's 'digital identity assessment' camera then waited. When nothing happened for two or three minutes, he knew something was wrong.

A few minutes later, he heard a dog barking over by the gate-tower they were heading for. A tall figure with an Alsatian dog on a leash soon emerged from the bottom of the three storey gate-tower. The figure was dressed in a black uniform, a biohazard or riot police mask, black gloves, full body armour, a helmet and black boots—the figure also possessed a holstered gun.

'We've noted that your residency visa was recently revoked,' said the synthetic voice, 'Please refrain from any movement as our border protection personnel conduct further tests and data analysis.'

Jake looked mildly alarmed. Rowan felt his heart beat quicken. What if they found something? Given all the student parties he'd been to lately, it was possible the monitoring system would pick up traces of other people's drugs on his clothing.

He'd know soon because the man with the dog was slowly approaching Jake.

The dog took a quick sniff of the Marin official before losing interest.

'Over here, Max!' commanded the man in English, with an accent Rowan immediately recognised as 'Australian'—at least in his world.

'Please step out of the monitoring chamber, Mr Sweeney— and you'll need to keep your hands above your head, mate,' said the man.

Absurdly, the man produced a note pad that he attempted to write notes on without even taking off his thick black gloves.

'Jesus, you're *that* Sweeney, Rowan Sweeney—the cricketer,' said the man, before attempting to peer closer at Rowan. This caused Max, who was now snarling, to edge to within centimetres of Rowan's groin.

'Max here needs to have a good sniff about—unless you have a phobia about dogs, in which case I'll have to call for the robot. If he thinks there's anything suspicious, I may be required to conduct a full body search, perhaps even a cavity search.'

'I'm not afraid of friendly dogs,' said Rowan, looking down nervously at the large, snarling Alsation.

'Max is friendly, aren't you Max? At least he is to people who are friends of New Albion. True blue, is our Max. You should be alright—it says here that you studied in Sydney up until last year.'

The man let the dog off the leash, allowing it to do what sniffer dogs do best—sniff groins, feet, butts etc.—snarling all the time.

He quickly lost interest in Rowan, however, and returned to his master.

'Welcome to New Albion—you've passed the Max test,' said the man.

Rowan and the government official were then led to a hut behind the main gate-tower to meet with Rowan's father.

Rowan now felt nervous in a different way—what would his "father" be like. Would he be the same arrogant, wealthy bastard he'd known all his life, or had life in Marin-e-bek and New Albion given him a different personality. Would he perhaps pick that the body of his son harboured an alien Rowan. He felt himself begin to sweat profusely—he didn't want Jake reporting back to Whirrarap the news that he'd been identified by his father as an Anomaly.

The figure that eventually walked through the waiting room door shocked Rowan. Dylan Sweeney looked pale and emaciated. He was as tall as Rowan remembered—over six feet—but he'd lost more hair, the remainder of which was grey, and he lacked the haughtiness that had irritated Rowan since childhood. There was a calmness and grace to the man's demeanour that made Rowan wonder whether the man was really his father.

Dylan was accompanied by a female New Albion detention centre official named Margaret. The official reminded Rowan of the young female educational managers that had descended like vultures on MUCT in recent months. She had a thin, though not unattractive face, straight blonde hair cut in a bob and she wore the grey corporate uniform of her company with obvious pride. A small, metal New Albion flag was also pinned to her right breast.

When Dylan saw Rowan, his eyes lit up and he attempted to speak—only to be silenced by the woman.

'You'll be able to talk to your son in a minute,' the woman said to Dylan in English. Again, Rowan startled at the broad "Australian" accent, 'We just need to go through the rules first.' She turned to Rowan and said, 'Your father is being held at present under New Albion law for an illegal attempt to cross the Marin-e-bek/New Albion border. He is due to be tried in accordance with New Albion law. Given our nation is witnessing frequent terrorist incursions at present, it is a police requirement that any discussions held between Marin citizens and New Albion residents in custody be monitored.'

'In other words,' interrupted Jake, 'Margaret and I have to listen in on your conversation. Correct, Margaret?'

She looked put out that Jake had curtailed her *officialese*, but recovered quickly this time looking back and forth at Rowan and his father, 'This meeting will be recorded and you should note that if at any point we ask you to cease discussing a topic, it is a condition of this meeting that you obey such a request. Do you accept these conditions?'

Rowan and Dylan both nodded in the affirmative and all four of them entered a small nearby room before being seated around a table.

Father and son stared at each other for a while until the woman signalled that it was okay to speak. Jake looked uncomfortable with listening in on the conversation and soon wandered over to the room's small kitchen facility to make himself a coffee—obviously he'd been through this process before since he knew exactly where the cups, sugar and teaspoons were.

The woman glared at him, pen poised over a wad of documentation.

'I'm sorry,' said Jake, 'I need a drink. I get dehydrated easily—I need to sit over here a few minutes, you guys go ahead without me.'

'Aren't you required to take notes? Perhaps we should wait until you're ready—remember the subjects are only permitted fifteen minutes.' She sounded irritated.

'I'm not required to take any notes—from a Marin perspective this is a humanitarian visit.'

He returned to preparing his coffee.

'Hi, er ... Dad,' said Rowan, shyly in English.

, 'Hi, Rowan,' said Dylan in Pan-Koori, 'looks like I cocked things up a bit.'

'If you're going to use *that* language,' said the woman, 'you'll need to speak very slowly—my Pan-Koori is not great.'

'Are you well?' asked Rowan in English, feeling an urge to hug his father—a feeling that surprised him.

Dylan paused a moment, perhaps disliking the fact that Rowan was speaking in English, 'As well as can be expected,' he said in English, and Rowan immediately recalled his real father—the man's accent was very "Australian".

'The subjects are advised that they are not permitted to discuss any aspects of the alleged offender's life whilst in a detention centre nor the circumstances under which he was apprehended etc.,' said the young woman, in a flat voice.

Dylan looked down at the table, struggling to find something permissible to say.

'How are you, Rowan? Your sister and I were very worried about you after the accident.'

'I'm recovering—there were head injuries and I'm still struggling with memory, but I've been teaching and writing.'

'That's very good—that book is very important.'

The woman's ears pricked up and she began to scrawl away frantically on her piece of paper. Jake also returned to the table, glancing quickly at Rowan then at the woman. Rowan took it as a friendly warning that he shouldn't mention the book again.

Dylan, however, hadn't seen the exchange between Rowan and Jake, 'They are moving against any Islesians who expose "Orbital Body tattoos" in public at the moment. It's been classified as a *seditious crime*—and community centres have been attacked. No wonder people want to leave the country.' He stared dispassionately at the woman and then said, 'Did you get that, or should I slow down a bit?'

The woman returned Dylan's gaze with a coldness that set Rowan's teeth on edge, 'You are not permitted to speculate on the pros and cons of New Albion parliamentary legislation during this meeting, Mr Sweeney.'

He seemed to collapse physically at the threat behind her words.

'I've been an Islesian all my life—it was never a crime here before. I think practicing the postures as a means to *kindle empathy* and *free will,* helped me become a reasonably good person. Ask my son. Look at him, a scholar, a genuinely caring and loving person—and a wonderful sportsman. I raised him as an Islesian—he didn't turn out too bad did he?' He looked at the woman as though demanding a genuine response.

'It's not my job to assess the worth of your son or of your spiritual beliefs,' said the woman, softening slightly.

Rowan suddenly knew that Dylan had passed on his love of Isles's system to his son. More importantly, it seemed likely this

Dylan's life-long commitment to the Islesian faith, reinforced, perhaps, by a childhood in Marin-e-bek, had affected his personality for the better. Though they'd only been together a few minutes, Rowan knew that this Dylan was the father he'd always wanted.

Rowan decided to challenge the woman—he was beginning to feel angry, 'You are looking after my father aren't you?'

'He gets the same treatment as any other inmate. Food is scarce as New Albion prepares to defend itself against a multi-nation military alliance.'

'I have many friends in New Albion.'

'I am aware that you are a former international cricketer, Mr Sweeney, but you should think twice before threatening a New Albion border official.' Rowan and the woman glared at each other briefly before she returned to her scribbling.

'It is not a threat to insist that United Nations conventions be adhered to,' replied Rowan, trying to control his emotions.

'I am not permitted to discuss government policy with any alien subject.'

She looked up from her documentation defiant.

'I'm detecting symptoms of either severe depression or PTSD in my father and, as his son, I would like to know what your Detention Centre personnel intend to do about that? It is, after all, a condition under international human rights laws that ...'

The woman cut him off, 'New Albion makes its own laws and your father will be subject to them without fear or favour.'

'Are there any diagnostic records—or any casework notes—I can look at. He is after all a Marin citizen.'

Jake chimed in, 'Dr Sweeney is making a not unreasonable request, Margaret.'

The woman paused, 'I will note your request, *Dr* Sweeney, but it is not within my power to authorise that such information be released at present.' Her tone suggested that was the end of the matter on pain of the interview ending.

'Your mother appeared to me last night in a dream,' said Dylan, ignoring the tension in the air.

'You know what she said? She said "You bloody Dill Dylan!" Here that: Dill Dylan. Just like her to joke at such a time. It made me feel much better—Dill 'un … Dylan … Dill Dylan. I miss that woman. Lucky for her she didn't live to see days like these—her beloved New Albion reduced to this.'

The conversation drifted thereafter. Dylan repeated himself often and slurred his worlds as though drugged. After the prescribed time, Rowan stood up hoping to say goodbye to his father with a hug. The woman made to intervene, until Jake distracted her as he stood up by accidentally spilling the last dregs of his coffee over her documents.

'I'm so sorry, Margaret,' he said, as Rowan and Dylan took the opportunity to embrace.

'You finish that book—you hear me,' whispered Dylan, in the confusion. 'You always did me and your mother proud. I'll be okay; they aren't beating me yet—not like some of the activists and artsy folk. They don't like your mob at all.'

For the first time since early childhood, Rowan didn't want to let go of his father. As Margaret recovered her poise and moved to part them, she was confronted by two grown men blubbering like babies.

CHAPTER FORTY-EIGHT

THE PATTERN TO ANOMALIES

Rowan picked at his lunch—the meeting with his father had left him feeling fragile. Having to reconcile the two versions of his father had triggered an attack of vertigo that he was struggling to control. Whirrarap and Jake seemed to understand something was up. 'It must be very hard watching him return to those bastards,' said Jake, between bites of a kangaroo sandwich.

After they'd eaten, he told Rowan and Whirrarap that he needed to stay on until the morning and would make his own way back to Big Gold Mountain. Rowan and Whirrarap left in the four wheel drive soon after, but the old scholar took a surprising left turn westward about half an hour into the homeward drive.

'Where are we going? We needed to turn right back there to get on the south-west highway back to the central tribal lands.'

'We have to pay a brief visit to a National Park in Ngunnawal territory—we're in Wiradjuri country at the moment. Have you been here before?' Whirrarap asked the question in a level voice, but Rowan detected a degree of curiosity.

'Not that I remember, but not all of my memories have returned yet. I remember it rains more up this way than it does in Dja Dja Wurrung country. What are we looking for this close to the border?'

'There's an Anomaly developing around an important national monument that I want you to have a look at.' Whirrarap was concentrating on the road, but something in his voice made Rowan feel that he was being subtly tested. He thought hard, what happened this far north-east of Bunjilaka city that he should know about.

'It must be close to the location Abraham Isles first made his break with European civilisation — isn't there a monument commemorating the event?'

Whirrarap glanced at his companion, 'There is indeed — we're heading for Mount Narrangullen. It's only twenty kilometres from the border — beautiful views of warplanes at sunset!'

'But Isles didn't fight with the squatter on Mount Narrangullen … historians don't know the exact location of the hut where the killing occurred — after all, it was only mentioned once in his diaries — and decades after the event.' Rowan was choosing his words carefully.

'Correct, but we know that he and his Ngarigo friends headed south-west along the river-flats of the Murrimbidgee into the foothills of the mountains. They camped in a cave the night of the incident and Isles climbed Mount Narrangullen the following morning. In his diaries, he says he was overwhelmed by a sense of liberation near the summit. The view is good and for the first time since his incarceration he was beyond British authority — in geographical terms he was just outside the 'nineteen counties' that marked the limits of British dominion in New South Wales.'

Low clouds had turned into mist as the road climbed steadily through densely wooded country. Rowan's felt disoriented since many of the towns and roads sported unfamiliar names. Nevertheless, he knew parts of the country from his days with *Interstitium*. They'd travelled the Hume Highway many times to play gigs in Canberra and Sydney in the mid-80s.

By the time they'd reached their destination—the National Park visitor's hut close to the foot of Mount Narrangullen—Rowan assumed they were somewhere north-east of what he'd known as Mount Kosciusko National Park. That meant they were also south-east of the New Albion township of Yass and therefore west of the city of Canberra—the capital of his "Australia". His pulse quickened as he contemplated the disappearance of an entire city.

'Are you okay?' asked Whirrarap, switching off the car engine, 'You've gone very pale.'

'Yes, I'm okay. I'm just finding it hard to concentrate this afternoon. Dad's in a bad way.' He felt his throat tighten with emotion.

'You stay here a moment while I talk to the ranger—he has something for us I believe.'

Whirrarap took a hefty back-pack from the boot before wandering over to a tall Koori in park uniform. The man seemed pleased to see the old scholar and Rowan watched as they shook hands warmly and started talking. The ranger eventually produced something from his coat pocket and handed it to Whirrarap.

Rowan took this as a cue to leave the vehicle.

'Where's the monument?' Whirrarap asked in Pan-Koori as Rowan approached. The two men looked eerie in the thickening mist.

'Eight hundred metres up that track. A nice walk for the New Albion tourists who used to visit here in their thousands before the Borders were closed last month.' The ranger spoke a strange dialect of Pan-Koori—influenced no doubt, thought Rowan, by his own native language, maybe Ngunnawal or Ngarigo, maybe even Wiradjuri, though other tribes were also native to the region.

Aware of Rowan's approach Whirrarap slipped the object into his pocket before introducing the man to Rowan—again in Pan-Koori, 'Kane this is Rowan, Rowan this is Kane. Kane's the Park Ranger here—he looks after the Isles Freedom Monument amongst other things.'

They shook hands.

Whirrarap spoke again, 'Rowan here is writing a biography on Abraham Isles and Miriam Hobbes. Important work—he may have some idea about what the Anomalies mean.'

Kane nodded, 'Feel free to make them disappear. Do you want me to accompany you to the site?'

'If it's okay with you, Rowan and I would like to visit the monument alone.'

'No problem—I'm happy to go back to the fire. The bloody things give me the creeps.'

'Me too,' said Rowan, 'I'm here on sufferance.'

'How active are the Anomalies?' asked Whirrarap, ignoring Rowan's apprehension.

'They appear around this time every afternoon and always from the same directions.'

Rowan and Whirrarap walked briskly up the steep and rocky path to the monument. The mist was thick and getting thicker and Rowan doubted they'd see anything—including the monument—given the weather.

When they arrived at the huge bronze statues of Abraham

Isles and four Koories—the two women and the two men of the legend—Rowan had to catch his breath. The metal work was wonderfully detailed, but it was the expression of pure joy on Isles's bearded face that most struck Rowan.

'He certainly looks liberated,' Rowan mused, as Whirrarap wandered around the monument's base—occasionally peering out into the mist-heavy woodland.

'Yes, liberated, but this moment also birthed another fundamental principle of the Islesian system.'

Rowan knew the answer instantly—all the research was paying off. 'Yes it does—*the rewards of choice.*' Rowan stared at Isles's face again, fascinated.

'This is the sacred moment *after we decide* to act,' he continued. 'It's the moment after we choose the path of balance—the path that kindles the *Nwyvre* or life force. When we *choose*, we do so accepting all possible outcomes, both good and bad. If we're lucky, we may come to embody empathic energies originating outside our rule bound universe. Isles is experiencing the empathy—the *karuna*—that can rupture, if only for a time, the flaw in the fabric of the cosmos.' Only now was Rowan beginning to understand the concept's full implications.

'Yes, many Marins see this phenomenon as the ultimate form of soul medicine—an antidote to the kind of *disenchantment* suffered by people up in New Albion. Isles, like Blake, saw industrialism, secularism, scientism and rationalism as "the four riders of the soul apocalypse". All his non-political writings emphasise the need to keep the psyche enchanted and open to the mysteries of the Imagination.' As he spoke, Whirrarap was still looking for something out in the forest.

'Of course that's uh … fundamental—though in Isles's system it had occult foundations,' said Rowan, thinking of Anika and struck by a sudden realisation. He'd been a victim of *disenchantme*nt—of the 'soul apocalypse'—all his adult life. He'd stuck with Douglas instinctively—because he'd represented an antidote to disenchantment. The Dionysian rebelliousness of his youth had failed, likewise the Apollonian conformity of his twenties. In a sense, he'd been waiting for a third way to be creative in the world, a way poised somewhere between Apollo and Dionysus.

'New Albion leaders like to call Isles's system *occultist*—a very Christian way of dismissing it,' said Whirrarap, standing up. Something in the bush had caught his attention.

'What are you looking at?' asked Rowan.

'Come and look at this …'

Rowan peered into the mist to the south-west of the monument—what he saw made a shiver run down his spine. A young white bushman apparently talking—or perhaps singing—to himself, was walking towards them. Rowan noted that he was wearing late 19th century clothing. He was obviously an Anomaly since he looked insubstantial—ghostlike. Rowan felt an urge to flee back to the carpark.

Even before he could react, however, he felt Whirrarap tap him on the shoulder. Another older figure from earlier in the 19th century—judging by his clothing—was approaching from the north-east, i.e. the direction of the border, or, in the other Australia, from the direction of Yass township. Rowan felt goose bumps on his arms and legs. Moments later a third figure approached from the north-west—the cricket bat he carried gave him away instantly. Rowan gasped, 'Donald Bradman … you've got to be joking!'

'Shss …' whispered Whirrarap, 'we don't want to scare them off. Do you know that figure?'

'Of course I know that figure. It's the great Sir Donald Bradman—the best batsman the world has ever seen.'

Whirrarap took a closer look, 'Oh yes, you're right—I didn't recognise him at first. A great Marin cricketer!'

Rowan stared at Whirrarap, then at Bradman who was

practising his trademark off drive not ten metres away under a large bull-oak. 'Yes, *the* greatest er … Marin batsman the world has ever seen.'

'They're not from our world are they,' whispered Whirrarap, and there was dead silence between them for a moment as Rowan tried to decide what to say.

'No,' said Rowan quietly, 'look at Bradman's hat—he's not batting for Marin-e-bek is he?'

The three Anomalies moved lazily about the monument. Rowan tried to avoid Whirrarap's gaze as they sat at the monument's base.

'Some of the elders noticed a month or two back that a lot of the Anomalies suggested a kind of narrative. A *particular world* seems to be speaking to us—warning us perhaps.'

Rowan fought an urge to tell Whirrarap everything.

'In my office a while back, I remember you talked about "Australia"—almost as though it was a *country* instead of a continent.' As Whirrarap spoke, he pulled out the object Kane had given him, 'Have a look at this.'

Rowan stared at the object, 'It's an unaddressed envelope with stamps.'

'Look at the stamps carefully …'

Rowan squinted at the stamps, there were five attached. Then it hit him—the stamps were all Australian stamps—the envelope was also an Anomaly. Rowan struggled to breathe, 'Jesus Christ, what the hell is going on here?'

Whirrarap sighed, 'I was hoping you might be able to tell me—the ranger found it in that suggestion box over there two days ago. He wondered whether it was a practical joke.' Whirrarap pointed to a battered green box not three metres away.

Rowan looked more closely at the stamps and soon recognised the 18c Hume and Hovell stamp of the mid 1970s.

It celebrated an expedition from southern New South Wales to the Victorian coast—concluding near what became the city of Geelong. Three of the other stamps depicted people: the 5c Banjo Patterson of the late 1960s; the more recent, to Rowan, 45c Donald Bradman and the 22c Ned Kelly, which Rowan guessed was from the early 1980s. The Bradman stamp showed him in full flight hitting a ball to the boundary, whereas the Kelly stamp depicted the bushranger wearing trademark metal armour and waving a Colt revolver at the climax of the Glenrowan siege. The last stamp was the founding of Canberra stamp issued in the 1920s.

While he worked out what to share with Whirrarap, he recalled a vague detail about Bradman's life—hadn't he spent much of his childhood in Cootamundra, which was to the north-west of their current spot? Likewise—and the connections came in a rush—Banjo Paterson had spent time on a farm at Wee Jasper, only kilometres away to the south-west. The other Anomaly had to be Hamilton Hume the explorer. Rowan struggled to remember details of Hume's life. After his discoveries, hadn't he lived for decades around Yass—which was twenty or thirty kilometres to the north-east? Kelly of course had roamed all through this region before the showdown with police at Glenrowan.

'I have something else to show you,' said Whirrarap, pulling an object, which turned out to be a small battery operated video player and screen in one unit, out of his backpack. 'Back in February staff up at the science campus in Dinas Yarkuk started to witness a recurring Anomaly in the vicinity of a classified experiment being conducted by the physics department. There was some concern that the experiment might have caused the Anomaly.' Whirrarap powered up the unit then loaded a miniature video cassette. 'Take a look at this—it was recorded by security cameras in and around the classified area. The scene looped at regular intervals until May.'

Rowan steadied the clunky looking device on his knee then pressed play.

Although the setting—the interior of an electronics lab on the science campus—was dimly lit there was no mistaking the identities of the five incandescent figures seated around a table—Douglas, Rhiannon, George, Ian (former lead singer of *Goya's Child*) and, puzzlingly, Anika. Another figure, the focus of the discussion, faced away from the camera, but Rowan knew intuitively it was his other self—minus Islesian arm tattoos. On the table stood an ornate box and various objects—among them a small Australian Continental Alliance flag, Marin money and the Auckland Star cricket article Rowan had read back in February. The other Rowan looked agitated, even fearful, as he appeared to answer questions. Now and then Rhiannon rubbed his back or patted an arm, as if to calm him. George and Anika, who looked nervous and spooked, were writing down notes. A few minutes in, Douglas coughed uncontrollably, forcing Rhiannon to hand him a bucket. Unfortunately, there was no sound track to the recording and the date at bottom screen left showed "21.06 - February 21 -1997".

Rowan stared at the blank screen trying to avoid Whirrarap's gaze.

'The coughing man appears to be Douglas Green—a prominent Dinas Yarkuk Islesian incapacitated by dementia for a number of years; the woman is of course Anika Miraj. You are also in the footage, but without your Islesian tattoos. We haven't been able to identify the other people yet.' Whirrarap's voice was level and quiet. 'Do you think this Anomaly is part of the pattern?"

'It's possible—they're from the same world.' He was still processing the implications of the video footage.

'The board decided to send for Anika after viewing this material—but we soon realised she knew nothing about you or Green.'

'She was telling the truth,' said Rowan, realising from the footage that Rowan the Islesian cricketer had swapped places with himself and was now resident in 1997 Australia.

Whirrarap watched him closely. 'Tell me one thing ...' his words sounded immensely heavy to Rowan, 'is it a humane world?'

Rowan felt himself collapse inwards, 'It's good—and it was good—for some. Maybe it was/is good for the majority of "Australians". Certainly for these people—Bradman, Hume and Paterson. All of them great men. And there are worse places on earth, believe me, but ...' said Rowan, struggling for words.

'But?' Whirrarap's eyes implored Rowan to continue.

'Not so good for others. A very tough world for Aboriginal people—though things improved in the 1960s. And this moment ...' he waved up at the gigantic statues of Isles and his Koori friends, obscured for the most part now by the clinging mist, 'this moment never happened.' The statement sounded like a death sentence.

Whirrarap watched Paterson reciting something under a huge gum-tree.

'Can you hear that—what is he saying ... or singing?' Whirrarap stood up, straining his body in Paterson's direction.

Though the melody battled hard to reach them through the mist, to Rowan it was unmistakeable. It was also being sung much slower than he'd ever heard it sung.

'*Waltzing Matilda ... waltzing Matilda ... you'll come a waltzing Matilda with me.*' The words echoed off the statues as Paterson repeated them endlessly.

'What does it mean? I've never heard that song before,' said Whirrarap.

'Paterson wrote it. It's *Australia*'s most famous folk song. It's about a swagman who commits suicide. It means, I think, that in my world,' he paused, following his intuition, 'Isles may have committed suicide. He was being flogged mercilessly, remember—and they were trying to make him *complicit* in atrocities that his conscience perhaps couldn't endure.'

Whirrarap looked thoughtful as the singing slowly faded out.

'These Anomalies, and the others popping up all over the place, lately—they're a warning then?'

'Absolutely, New Albion society has been dangerously dehumanised. They will invade and they will try to take everything,' said Rowan in a flat voice. 'That's all you really need to know. Look, I have an anomalous book I picked up at Henri Nacrose's. Most Marin's would read it as a sick fantasy novel, but it's more than that. I'll give it to you when we return to Dinas Yarkuk. Can we leave it at that for today—it's been a big day for me and these things give me the creeps?'

'Thank you, that *is* all I need to know. We have to get back to Big Gold Mountain tonight. I need to talk to the elders. Do you mind if I say that I pieced this together myself? It might make it easier for you. I don't think it serves any purpose for others to know that you are ... well, you know what I mean.'

Rowan felt relieved, 'Sure, and you are the only one who knows at present.'

Whirrarap smiled at him, and then said gently, 'At least we now know the reason for your presence among us. It must have been very difficult for you these few past months.'

'I have friends—and the Rowan in the video remains as a fairly solid personality base. Bizarre as it sounds; I'm fine most of the time.'

'The question is: what does your world need from ours? Such exchanges, in my experience, are usually mutually beneficial,' said Whirrarap, thoughtfully.

'I suspect it would be a very large list! By the way, I wonder, do you know what lies to the south-east of here? Is there perhaps a city?'

'That's New Albion territory, but yes, there is a rural town—not exactly a city. It's a place of trauma and suffering these days.'

'How so?' asked Rowan.

'There are two types of camp there: one is for refugees, the other is for political detainees. Either way, tens of thousands of people live in a kind of limbo. Of the detainees some have attempted to illegally cross the border into Marin-e-bek, others are serving time for sedition, "moral crimes" and so on. Of the refugee populations, some are Marins denied the means to sustain themselves in New Albion due to economic discrimination, others are New Albion citizens seeking Marin visas or Marin citizens seeking to return home. There are allegations of torture and other abuses in some of the detention centres—we have reliable evidence that even children are being held there.'

They stood up to leave, but were surprised by a tall figure dressed in makeshift armour standing threateningly in the bush to the south-west of the monument. He carried a hand-gun, a Colt, and was waving it about slowly in the air.

'Who is that?' said Whirrarap, after he'd realised it was another Anomaly.

'It's the guy on the stamp—Ned Kelly. He was a famous outlaw.'

They watched Ned for a while, before Rowan said, 'You've never heard of him?'

'No, I've never heard of him. And New Albion people don't talk about him either.' Whirrarap squinted through the gloom at the figure. 'Look at that—he's wearing a big tin-can on his head!'

The figure retreated into the bush then began to fade. 'Perhaps he wasn't needed in your world,' said Rowan thoughtfully.

CHAPTER FORTY-NINE

THE SPIRITUAL OBESITY OF THE WEST
(Thursday August 28th 1997)

Paul Bauccher's band did return to Marin-e-bek to play at the Peace Rally. Upon arrival they were riding high on their European success. Rowan respected them for appearing at such a political event. From the perspective of their government, it was on enemy territory. Their new found status as rising stars on the international music scene along with the fact that they were young New Albions meant they secured a lot of publicity for the peace movement. They refused to speak about their government's actions, which was just as well, thought Rowan, since when Paul had paid him a visit only days before the Big Gold Mountain gig he'd sounded slurred in his speech, pale to look at and somewhat fragmented in his thinking.

At the time of the visit, Rowan had been getting ready to go out for dinner, all the while pondering his book on Isles and Hobbes. It had arrived the previous day from the printers and to Rowan it seemed like a magical object. Anika, Godstar, Ungaru,

Whirrarap, Gareth the IT expert and a few other friends were joining him at 7pm for a dinner celebration.

'Hey, man, how are you doing?' said Paul, slurring his words as he stood at Rowan's fly-screen door.

'Paul ... What are you doing here?' said Rowan, wondering what the guy could possibly want from him. Although nothing specific had ever been said, he was sure Paul saw him as some kind of stuffy oedipal rival—maybe even a symbol of the establishment he hated. Imogen had said that Paul's father was a retired New Albion army officer with a strong disciplinarian streak.

'You know we really fuckin' struggled with the two songs they gave us to rework. How did you guys go?'

'Well, Anika and I had the inside running—we've been transcribing them for months—but I've only performed once in the past decade. You were fucking my girlfriend at the time as I remember ...' said Rowan, trailing off.

'Shit! I'm genuinely sorry about that, man. Nothing personal, hey? I thought you guys were finished—I mean, she didn't say it outright, but she implied it.' He was looking down at the ground, 'besides, I was with her first.' He began shifting his weight from foot to foot.

'Have you come for information about the gig—you know that the cultural board are doing all the organising?'

But Paul hadn't heard him.

'Congrats on your new book. Also, I heard we'll all be on a CD together—advance sales are huge. My agent says "it'll be monster big". Silly bitch—she makes me laugh. It's always: *absolutely fabulous* this, and *absolutely wonderful* that. Listen, are you going to let me in for a moment, I need to ask you something and I'm crap at being vulnerable in public?'

Rowan decided to open the door, 'Alright, come in. To be honest, you don't look too good. Do you want a coffee?' He had to smile. Despite the chaos Paul brought to people's lives, he was a difficult guy to hate.

'Naw, coffee just winds me up when I'm on the shit. Look, I thought you might know where she is.'

'Who?'

'Imogen. Her friends are saying nothing and she's on leave from the university.'

Rowan knew that she'd taken leave from her PhD studies two weeks ago and had left for the South Island of Aotearoa to holiday with her family—there were some long-standing issues she needed to talk through with her mother. She'd been in therapy at the Islesian clinic for over a month and was making real progress with the combination treatments on offer. He wasn't about to tell Paul where she was or what she'd been up to.

'Imogen doesn't report to me.'

'Hey, I have friends in this town, you know—even if half of them are dressed up in dumb-fuck military khaki. Those left reckon you're on with that Anika chick, but still meeting with Imogen on the side.' As he spoke, his eyes darted around the room—probably on the lookout for any evidence of Imogen's presence.

'Then they can tell you where Imogen is. Perhaps she doesn't want to see you.' Rowan spoke the last phrase with more emphasis.

Paul smiled, 'She always wants to see me, mate. She knows I love her.'

'Then why do you treat her like crap?'

Paul's eyes settled on Rowan again. 'You don't understand, mate. You were born here, in Marin-e-bek. People treat each other well here—it's the Koori thing and the Islesian thing. You know: "the quality of your relationships is the measure of your personality". Up there—you have no idea!—even kids are consumers to snare. No one gives a fuck about anyone else. It's enshrined in our capitalist ethos—justifiable selfishness! That's why the idiotic fucks are turning *en masse* to the big simplistic Daddy God. Jesus gives a fuck, he has to—it's in his position description. Just growing up in that damn place fucks with your head—especially if your parents are also patriotic little capital accumulation machines like mine were.' He paused as if tasting his bitterness.Rowan felt a flicker of sympathy. He also realised he'd underestimated the psychological complexity of Paul's relationship with Imogen—two survivors from a culture that had damaged them, almost beyond repair.

'Are you okay, mate?'

Paul seemed amazed at the question. He paused a long time before answering.

'You know we have a lot in common: we both love music and we're both leaders. Only difference is I'm afraid of what I become when I lead. I took this gig—the "rebellious muso gig"—cos I thought: here's a way to oppose everything my Dad stands for. But leadership is temptation is power, and I suppose I've failed—especially Imogen. I just became Dad in a different way.'

'You'll work it out.'

'How do you do it—lead without being stained?'

After a moment or two, Rowan said, 'Oh, to begin with I was stained alright. In leading I was tempted—and like you, I succumbed. I started to accumulate remorse and guilt. Follow your remorse/guilt, don't anaesthetise it. Confronting it may make it manageable. And another thing: many people see you as a leader, so lead with your best possible self.'

Paul stared at the carpet again.

'Obviously you taught me for a reason. I mean, I gave you a bit of shit, but that stuff on the deadly vices, all the classes really, they really got me thinking. And I remember one day you used the term "The spiritual obesity of the West." A great line—I may even use it in a song.'

Rowan had to contain laughter, apparently his other self was an inspirational lecturer.

'Hope she likes my best possible self.'

'She'll contact you when she's ready.'

'So you have talked to her?'

'I know she'll contact you when she's ready. When she's strong enough. She kind of goes to pieces around you—haven't you noticed that?'

'Look, I know I can't say no to a pretty girl, but that's not the same as loving someone.'

Rowan said nothing.

'Anyway, she's obviously not here. I gotta go—we need to practice a rap segment in that Isles song about conflict between tribes they lumbered us with. Should be a big deal concert, eh? So big deal it might launch a New Albion nuclear attack. We'll all be singing as the bombs drop—in my case, kissing my traitor ass goodbye!'

'Did they ask you to sing one of your hits on the night as well?'

'Yeh.'

'Which one are you doing—I like *Night of the Ravens*. Seems appropriate—great guitar work too.'

'That's Frisser's doing—he can really play a guitar when he's off his face.' Paul was standing at the door now, 'But we're gonna do the UK hit *Express Train to Kathmandu*. Everybody loves a "poor me, he/she left me" song—besides, ravens are sacred to many of the Kulin tribes remember.'

Paul opened the fly-wire door and sauntered out into the garden. Rowan watched as he wandered downhill across the grass in the direction of the main campus buildings.

CHAPTER FIFTY

THE MASK OF RHIANNON

The meeting with Paul set Rowan thinking. A lot of people obviously thought he and Anika were together. They were wrong of course, but given the workload of the past few months and the need to meet regularly to discuss the transcription process and the upcoming performance, they'd certainly spent a lot of time together. This had allowed him to avoid the issue of turning the friendship/work relationship into something more. With her departure for West Marin approaching after the rally, he felt pressure to confront something he'd been avoiding for a long time. He realised, it was now or never—he needed to be courageous.

Fortifying himself with Islesian exercises for stress and nervousness that he'd learnt at the community centre, he prepared for his meeting with Anika at four. He'd decided to use an obscure Isles song to try and resolve a long-standing issue. Ungaru had agreed to attend the performance to mix a recording of the song's music with Rowan's live singing. He'd also act as a kind of witness—Rowan trusted him and they'd become good friends over the past few months.

As Rowan ran through the exercises, he glanced across at the only prop he'd use in the performance. It was a green and black plastic mask decorated in Celtic spiral patterns bought from the gift shop at the Islesian centre. It symbolised a key deity associated with the Lovers Orbit in the Islesian system—in other words, the muse or female spirit of creativity.

Rowan and Ungaru were the first to enter the Artspace practice hall at 3.30. The Hall was attached to the Islesian community centre complex and the band had been using it for some weeks. Rowan gave Ungaru the CD recording of the song he'd chosen and asked him to play it a few times whilst he attempted to sing it. After the first attempt, Rowan asked for more reverb and echo on his voice and as a consequence the last run through before Anika arrived sounded quite eerie. Rowan then placed the Mask of Rhiannon on a chair at the centre of the performance space.

When Anika arrived Ungaru quietly left the room for a few minutes.

Anika looked around the hall and asked, 'Where is everybody ...'

Rowan gathered his courage before saying, 'Anika, I need to ask you a big favour.'

Rowan's serious tone made her look momentarily apprehensive, 'Fire away—I can only say no.'

'As you know I've been undergoing "orbital work" for some months now—sounds really corny, I know—but the person I've been working with believes that I need to get certain issues off my chest.'

Anika looked defensive for a moment, 'Are you saying you have some issues with me?'

'No, not really. Look, there's an Islesian song I need to perform for you. I'll explain everything else at the end of the performance—Ungaru has agreed to mix for me as I sing it.'

'Do I have to do anything?'

'You need to wear that mask over there,' he pointed to the mask, 'and stand in an upright position directly facing me as I … well, perform the uh … confession piece.'

Anika picked up the mask, 'What does the mask symbolise?'

'It's the Mask of Rhiannon—she's the Welsh goddess of love, supernatural song and horses. Isles wrote the piece I'm about to perform. It's an Apology song—I'm hoping that you'll wear the mask and play the part of Rhiannon for five minutes or so.' Rowan knew he sounded evasive. Anika, however, was up for a little play acting.

'Okay, bring in Ungaru! I'm more than happy to play the part of Rhiannon—Goddess of love and sex and spells and curses and horses and did you forgot the birds, those marvellous birds? Kneel down before me, apologetic suitor!' she said, hamming it up until she realised that Rowan was deadly serious about the performance.

Ungaru returned and before long haunting guitar music flooded the hall. As Rowan concentrated, Ungaru handed Anika two unrhymed free-verse translations of the lyrics—one in English, one in Pan-Koori. She scanned them with puzzled interest. The first verse, however, was soon upon them. Rowan stared gently at Anika and began singing Isles's song-poem in perfect Welsh. The emotional energy in the song slowly overwhelmed him, pushing him to his knees with chest out, head dipped, and palms visible in-front of Anika who, in-turn, stood upright and silent directly in-front of him. The eeriness of her mask sent Rowan deeper into the experience. In English translation the lyrics read as follows:

I have come, my beloved, through the furthest gateway
to the Circle of Abred.
I have come through many incarnations,
sometimes making progress in the passage of a life
sometimes slipping backwards, at the mercy of Cythrawl.

But always, I am seeking the Splendid Land,
the land of Apples!
And the knowledge of the feryllt
in the mountains of the wise.

And always, I am striving toward Gwynedd,
Circle of the Heavenly Beings.
Wishing, it is true, with all my heart
for the grace distributed by Ceugant.

I have come, my love, by paths circuitous
to the region of the summer stars
from the chaos of Annwn
to the Castle that revolves —
your castle, made of glass.

My name today is Rowan Sweeney
and I have done you wrong
Though my heart stayed true, my body,
in its sloth, enjoyed another.

And now the crows consume my heart
and the wolves gorge upon my flesh,
for I have done you wrong
and shame forbids your mercy.

The music grew in power and speed at the end of the third movement and it was at this moment that Rowan slumped completely to the floor and began sobbing his heart out. Ungaru signalled to Anika to maintain her posture and not stoop to comfort him. The sobs merged bitterness with melancholy and it was ten minutes before Rowan emerged from the experience.

After the sobbing abated, Ungaru, who had witnessed and even participated in many such sessions over the past month, left his mixing desk to offer Rowan a drink of water and a towel.

A few moments later Anika took off the mask and sat down in front of Rowan, whose features looked swollen but youthful.

'Okay, I get the idea of therapeutic release of feelings since I know Isles's system as well as anyone,' she said, her hands in her lap, 'but I don't get the personal context.'

Rowan looked at Ungaru who took a deep breath, 'There's a concept common among shamans, magicians and soul doctors all around the world. The notion that human identity is fragile — easily disturbed.' He sighed, struggling to find the right words, 'Trauma can fragment a soul — allowing in other entities maybe even other versions of a lived self. This happened to me five or six months ago — maybe as a kind of Anomaly, maybe not. Some days I'm the Rowan who grew up in Marin-e-bek and Sydney, other days I'm, well ... another Rowan altogether, from another reality.' He looked down, aware he sounded insane.

'And my part in all this?' she said quietly.

Again, Rowan chose his words carefully, 'When I was younger I knew someone a lot like you. I guess I wronged her — infidelity. I never *really* apologised.' He realised then, that healthy remorse demands ruthless honesty. He knew that healthy remorse is cured not by a single cathartic event, but by a willingness to merge realities — the wounded reality in which the hurt occurred and the unwounded reality, the desired reality, in which Eric lived, Anika was not betrayed, Douglas's son survived Vietnam, indigenous Australians entered modernity on their own terms and the continent's flora and fauna did not experience an apocalypse of extinctions. In this 'splendid world' Rowan was slowly finding the courage to commit to his better self — with all its myriad unfoldings. In such a world, he realised, remorse is never permanently resolved, only lessened by daily commitment to one's best possible self.

Anika seemed to take his words at face value, but Rowan sensed that Ungaru—who had now heard the story twice— knew a great deal had been left out. The Maori scholar had a sixth sense for the transpersonal that sometimes astounded Rowan. It was hard to keep anything from him.

Anika broke the silence, 'Before, then—I was really acting out the part of whom? An ex-girlfriend?'

Rowan nodded a 'yes'.

Something still didn't add up, 'But why Rhiannon?'

He mumbled a partial explanation, 'Well Rhiannon, as I said earlier, was one of the ancient Celtic goddesses presiding over poetic inspiration, love and healing—so say the legends. As a young person I er … felt very inspired by this person. My creativity, particularly my musical creativity, went downhill after I cheated on her.' He tried to end the confession there, but his tongue had an agenda of its own, 'Working with you on this project has reignited some old feelings … I mean, I've been feeling very inspired and alive again.' One slip of the tongue and it was out in the aether—a second confession. He felt himself blushing—a thirty-three year old teenager.

Anika, however, didn't miss a beat, 'How old were you when all this happened?' she asked.

'Nineteen.'

'That's not very old. Teenage boys don't always realise the consequences of their actions. They're prone to impulsive behaviour, and they often come across as selfish and narcissistic. That's not an excuse for what you did, but to me it's what we learn from such experiences that really matters. Are we capable of changing for the better? Only you can answer that question.' She went quiet, perhaps pondering the full implications of what Rowan had said.

Ungaru patted Rowan on the back and said, 'I was setting fire to parks for fun at that age, and smashing my body up playing Rugby Union, eh. I didn't find my brain 'til I was twenty five. Luckily the Ancestor spirits kept me safe and stopped me from hurting anyone else, but it was a close call.'

Anika cleared her throat to speak, 'While we're into confessions. There's something I need to tell you. When I spoke about the visit by Miriam Hobbes to the culture board a while back I didn't share everything that Miriam showed me. She made it plain that I had to give in to the feelings the project was evoking in me. I was feeling overwhelmed at the time—frustrated and weighed down by responsibility, but also excited and inspired. The Anomaly called Miriam told me that I needed to trust the experience and um ... trust my feelings, "Only then", she said, "will the music flow".' Anika seemed about to say something, but checked herself.

CHAPTER FIFTY-ONE

INTELLECTUAL PROPERTY RIGHTS
(Friday August 29th 1997)

Rowan, Anika and Ungaru watched as the rest of the band filtered into the Artspace practice venue in the centre of Big Gold Mountain around 5pm. Rowan's revelations seemed to have uneased Anika and Ungaru in different ways. Rowan could see that although Anika was trying to pretend that nothing had changed, it was clear that his words had affected her deeply. He suspected that Ungaru, however, was contemplating other aspects of the conversation. In some indigenous worldviews Anomalies were interpreted in terms of black magic or even communications from the dead—ghosts, phantoms and the like. Any competent shaman, cunningman (or woman), *tohunga* or native doctor would want to examine closely the entity— *identity*—appearing after soul trauma.

Anika and Ungaru, however, said nothing to the other band members as they arrived and by the time they heard Godstar's motorbike in the car-park everyone had focused their attention on the job at hand.

The last minute practice had to be delayed, however, when Godstar came stomping into the hall shouting, 'Put on the television quickly or we'll miss it—the news channel, Channel 98.'

They had to drag a television out of the Artspace office and reset the aerial by which time it was almost 5.30. As they dragged two old sofas in front of the television, Whirrarap and a woman from the Marin cultural board also turned up and quietly joined the group.

The lead item concerned the Marin Senate's decision to affirm a slate of previously stalled legislation passed a month ago by the House of Representatives. 'The mining and resources legislation will see the establishment of joint Marin and Chinese and Marin and Indian mining ventures in resource rich areas. As part of the same deal, some of the profits from successful joint ventures will be funnelled into extra infrastructure spending, including universities, technical colleges, hospitals, transport and the military across Marin-e-bek. Permission to negotiate similar ventures with American and New Albion companies remains stalled, but there has been some movement this afternoon on German, British and French requests. As a sign of good faith with the international community, the Marin government also announced an increase of 50,000 people to annual immigration targets.'

Following the Senate vote item came a piece on the military build-up along the Marin/New Albion border, 'The New Albion government was today warned by the Marin government that a continuation of practice runs by its high altitude bombers, carrying live munitions including nuclear warheads, close to the Marin border would be interpreted as acts of aggression. However, New Albion Prime Minister, Ricardo Smith, at a lunch-time press conference in Sydney, said that his nation was sending a strong message to cross-border terrorists and their supporters in the Marin government that his people were ready and willing to take whatever action was necessary to secure New Albion's borders.'

A couple of the band members were losing interest, 'I don't get politics,' said the band's bass player, Elizabeth, a skinny young classical musician that Anika had roped into the band after Rowan's original bass player had signed up for the Marin military in late June. Elizabeth picked up bass melodies like lightening and had proved a real find.

'Believe me, it gets better,' said Godstar, enjoying himself as the third item was introduced.

'In conjunction with the announcement today of Senate approval for joint mining and resource extraction projects across Marin-e-bek with the Indian and Chinese governments, Bunjilaka city today played host to a surprise visit by dozens of British, Democratic Republic of China and French warships previously scheduled to take part in joint military operations with the Marin military next month. One hundred Bunjilaka residents were ferried aboard a French aircraft carrier, the *Jean-Baptiste*, this morning to pose for photos and check out the military hardware. Fighter jets and short range bombers from the vessel were heard above the city later this afternoon. The planes will take part in war-games with the Marin air-force over the mountainous terrain to Marin's north-west as well as in the Great River region. Late this afternoon, the Marin President refused to confirm or deny whether any of the planes or ships are carrying nuclear warheads.'

'Given current circumstances these were the only sane decisions the senate could take,' said Whirrarap, in Pan-Koori, 'but once again there is a cost to our liberty—a dangerous game indeed.'

Even as he spoke, however, the television switched to images of young New Albion peace protesters clearing customs at Bunjilaka airport. The narrator said 'Thousands of young people from New Albion have braved threats of government reprisals in accepting a Marin government offer of free boarding and free admission to the Peace and Human Rights Festival taking place at Big Gold Mountain this weekend. They join thousands of their compatriots entering the country through land and sea border checkpoints. An estimated 70,000 plus Marins are also set to protest the aggressive posturing of the New Albion military.'

After interviewing a couple of well-spoken young activists the story switched to the festival timetable. 'Twenty bands from fifteen nations including Marin-e-bek, Aotearoa, France, the UK, China, Norway, Japan and, remarkably, New Albion itself will play at the concert. Besides their own hits, bands will perform contemporary versions of twenty previously unknown songs by one of Marin-e-bek's founding figures, Abraham Isles, a nineteenth century highland Scot who, with his wife Miriam Hobbes, assisted Koori tribes in their war of resistance against British colonial aggression. The concert will coincide with the release of a biography on Isles and Hobbes by MUCT academic and former international cricketer, Rowan Sweeney. The biography features, for the first time, music scores associated with many of the poem/songs and argues that new evidence suggests that Isles was more interested in spiritual matters than has previously been acknowledged.'

Rowan appeared on screen being interviewed. 'The "medicine songs" that music expert Anika Miraj and I have been decoding and transcribing are a treasure trove to Islesian devotees across Marin-e-bek and elsewhere. These will be the first performances of these hauntingly beautiful songs since the 1840s. Anika and I believe that they have universal significance for people experiencing a range of life challenges.'

The clip of Rowan concluded and the newsreader appeared, chatting to her co-presenter, 'To get into the spirit of the day,

Rowan has also agreed to come out of cricketing retirement to spearhead the Marin attack in a "Former-Greats" one day game against a World Peace Eleven. The game takes place prior to the concert.'

'Yes,' said the male reader, 'Sweeney, of course, quit cricket to study Isles's spiritual system in the early 1990s after downing Aotearoan tail-ender, Daniel MacIntyre during a match. Unfortunately MacIntyre died on the spot of a brain haemorrhage. The incident led to the introduction of protective crash helmets for batsmen and close-in fielders at all levels of the game.'

'Let's see how our retired stars go against an impressive World Peace Eleven,' said the female presenter.

Godstar switched off the television.

'There you have it—a day of diplomatic cat and mouse and we're right in the middle of it all!' said Godstar.

The discussion trailed off as some band members wandered off to practice. Whirrarap, however, wanted to introduce Rowan and Anika to his friend, and the four retreated to the centre's main office. Once there Whirrarap said, 'This is Nicole Wirrinun. She's the board member responsible for organising tomorrow's rally. She wants to discuss a couple of things with you.'

Nicole was a slightly overweight woman of about forty. She had a warm, round face that immediately made Rowan trust her. She spoke in Pan-Koori.

'I just need to let you know that we've struck a bit of resistance from the university board regarding both the launch of the book and the plan for bands to perform versions of Isles's songs. As a consequence, I've had to let all the bands know what's brewing. MUCT have gone to the Marin federal court seeking to halt the sale of the book as well as any performances of the songs. Their argument is that the intellectual copyright to the material is, in part, owned by the university.'

'But didn't they sign a contract with the cultural board early on in the piece?' asked Anika, in shock.

Whirrarap piped in, 'It's only a spoiling tactic. They know they'd lose any court case over copyright, which is owned by the family. Likewise, the cultural board paid you two as researchers and has paid the printing costs! It's a political manoeuvre, pure and simple. They don't want Islesian inspired songs performed at the Peace Rally.'

Nicole took over, 'Each band needs to decide whether or not they will perform their songs on the day. A decision to grant a temporary court order in MUCT's favour may be handed down tomorrow morning. The full bench has been sitting today. Rowan, we need to know tonight whether you want the book released at the rally tomorrow or not, i.e. regardless of the court action. Dozens of volunteers are willing to sell it illegally tomorrow, though we've had to temporarily halt its sales through booksellers. As for performing the songs—we'll leave that up to you guys. Given the legal situation, we'd understand completely if you decided to perform only your own songs. You should know however, that bootleg copies of the CD are already available across Marin-e-bek—despite record shops being unable to sell copies,' Nicole trailed off then leant back in her chair.

Whirrarap watched the band set up as Rowan and Anika exchanged coded glances. 'Look the music is not really the issue here,' said Anika, eventually, 'I'm sure our band will decide to perform the songs regardless of consequence. So Rowan, that just leaves it up to you to make a decision on the book. I mean condoning the official release tomorrow may mean defying the Marin federal court—an act that could destroy your academic reputation at minimum.'

Rowan stared at the floor for a while in silence.

'The board will back you all the way,' said Whirrarap, looking concerned. 'This attempt to shut down the protest is unpopular among most Marin politicians and legal people. You won't be on your own if you defy the court, but it may be stressful for a while—and I know you've been through a lot already.'

Rowan addressed Nicole, 'I have no problem with activists selling the book illegally and I for one intend to perform those songs.'

Nicole brightened, 'Good,' she said, 'is there anything else you want to ask me?'

'Actually, I need permission from the board. We have an IT friend—a real whiz. He helped us decode the pictures in the Isles diaries, but the university sacked him yesterday for his efforts—even though he has two children. He's great at building websites quickly. I would like to give him an electronic copy of my book tonight. It would be made available world-wide for free download by dawn. I could then email you the web address, which you could publicise nationally and internationally. Would that be okay with the board?'

Nicole smiled, 'I don't think we'll have any problem with that.'

'Then there's the other matter,' said Whirrarap.

'Oh yes—the more worrying development. The Marin federal police have uncovered intelligence suggesting an attack tomorrow at the Peace Festival. Currently, they're more concerned about the safety of New Albion dissidents and performers and have thus decided to increase security at the rally. However, due to your current high profile they've also authorised increased security in and around the University campus at Dinas Yarkuk. Please be aware that New Albion Special Forces personnel are now active across Marin-e-bek.'

Rowan caught Anika looking at him curiously as they wandered back to the large practice hall. He whispered, 'It's been quite a night, hey?'

'Yes, it's all happening.'

'The security concerns really up the ante, ' said Rowan. 'You should think about returning to West-Marin. You have a son—he needs you to be safe.'

She paused, and then said, 'Nowhere is completely safe—that's obvious enough. In fact, this is the best place to be right now—the Marin army are in town.' She laughed a little hysterically, 'Look, you know how you said this project makes you feel inspired and alive?'

'Yes ...'

'Well, me too—but for me the feeling has a bitter-sweet element.'

'What do you mean?'

'I dreamt last night that I was standing in a circle holding hands with friends—musicians, writers, poets, artists etc. You were there beside me and we were all staring into a dark abyss that was threatening to grow—taking over everything. We were singing an Islesian song quietly, ever so quietly—a song to stop the growth of the abyss—the suffering. Miriam has made it plain that with this project I'm doing exactly what I should be doing right now, and that's inspirational, but it's also bitter-sweet, because it makes me feel sad—something like the melancholy Isles said accompanies awareness of the "flaw in the fabric of the world".' She paused.

Something clicked over for Rowan, 'Maybe that's what I was running from when I was young. A confrontation with the full terror of the flaw. You, on the other hand, seem to have been braver—more able to stare it down. Maybe if we really love someone we're forced to face the flaw *in its essence*—and there's nothing more frightening, or potentially transformative, because we realise that there's only love. It's the only means to transcend the cosmic design fault—and even then, only for a time.' He stared at the ground, afraid to look at her.

Anika turned to face him, 'Love *and* creativity. I'm ready for tomorrow if you are—I have my Cerridwen-Bridget Anomaly you have your … what is it? Your *fragmented personality Anomaly*? With Godstar and the others we'll raise Isles and Miriam from the dead. In a way we already have—the CD recordings sound fantastic.'

Despite the forced optimism, Rowan knew that she was feeling the strain. He had a strong urge to protect her, which surfaced in a desire to give her a hug. She seemed to invite the gesture.

Godstar was calling to them, however, 'Come on you two! Rowan has to join the cricketer *creatures* later tonight. Let's get this practice rolling or we'll sound like shit tomorrow.'

They smiled nervously at each other before joining the others. As they walked Anika whispered, 'If you need to talk— or need anything really …'

Rowan felt a warm glow spread slowly up his spine. 'There is one thing I need badly: a ghostly cricket mentor. I'm so nervous about bowling tomorrow that it'll be a miracle if a single ball lands on the pitch!'

'They won't expect much from you—everyone knows you've been retired for years.'

'Not true,' he whispered back, 'given the identity confusion stuff, there's a possibility I've been retired from first class cricket all my life.'

Anika laughed.

Over the next few hours, Rowan tried to put aside the stress of the day. He'd been talking all day to journalists, band agents, publishers, legal experts, security people, etc. in various languages—Pan-Koori, French and English. He was also increasingly worried about his father and sister. Media interest in the Isles and Hobbes biography and CD, as well as the publicity about his return to cricket had put him in the spotlight as a celebrity activist. He worried that the New Albion authorities might connect his name to that of his father and sister and he found himself debating whether to withdraw from the event as a means to keep them safe. Then again, he reasoned, the damage was already done and international media interest probably represented a form of protection against New Albion detention centre abuses.

CHAPTER FIFTY-TWO

ROWAN SWEENEY, INTERNATIONAL CRICKETER
(Saturday, August 30th)

The indoor training session of the previous night had been gruelling, both psychologically and physically. Though he felt his bowling had been functional enough, he was hardly going to pose a threat to former international batsmen. Likewise, he'd had to leave the team early to help Gareth, his IT friend, set-up and then test the web-site he'd designed so that electronic copies of his book could be downloaded worldwide free of charge. That had involved a drive back to Dinas Yarkuk to the science campus—Douglas's house site in the other reality. When Rowan arrived, however, Gareth started raving about the quantum computer experiments being conducted on the campus—they'd been shut down since February over suspicions they were causing Anomalies to develop in the area. Gareth was excited because the Physics staff had been given the go ahead for new experiments scheduled for December.

It was forty minutes before he and Rowan set to work to

perfect the website so it was capable of distributing electronic copies of the Isles and Hobbes book. The big worry was that the site would crash if too many people tried to access it at once. Although a solution was found by 2am, it was 3am before Rowan got to bed. Once there, however, he woke repeatedly to frightening dreams—no doubt triggered by security concerns, the threat of invasion and the sheer stress of having to front so many people the following day in performances he felt under-prepared for.

The morning brought rumours that Democratic China, Indonesia, France, Britain and India were spearheading moves at the UN to try and halt the imminent invasion of Marin-e-bek and other Australian continental nations by New Albion. News out of the UN suggested that the next 24hours would be crucial in terms of diplomatic initiatives. As Rowan attended a pre-match net practice and warm up session with the Marin "Former Greats" team, he noticed busy skies above Big Gold Mountain—reconnaissance planes, fighter jets and transport aircraft from various nations flew over at regular intervals. Many of the transport planes appeared to be heading north and it was clear that the New Albion military build up of the past few months was now being countered south of the border. Rowan also noticed numerous police helicopters above Big Gold Mountain—no doubt there to monitor the Peace and Human Rights rally.

Moorup Stadium sat on the outskirts of Big Gold Mountain, one of the country's major inland cities and noted for its 19th century mining boom. More recently, it had become a Mecca for artists, writers, thinkers, etc. The stadium was to host the cricket match—though the town centre, with its big old 19th century European and indigenous buildings, standing alongside more modern constructions, would also see lots of activity. Community group stalls, street performers, fairground attractions, etc. were everywhere on the streets of the city centre. The town was known for its massive gothic cathedral, an equally imposing Buddhist stupa, as well as mosques, churches and temples from myriad spiritual traditions—including of course many Islesian community centres. People flocked to the city to explore the huge underground network of gold mining tunnels (up to 1,600 metres deep and decorated, in many cases, with Koori cave art) as well as the many Chinese attractions, including the annual Dragon festival.

As the two teams took to the field for the truncated one day game, Rowan noticed that the stadium was already full. The crowd today, however, sported hundreds of signs and banners alluding to the imminent invasion: 'Stop New Albion Aggression', 'Marins Love Peace/Oppose Neo-colonialism', 'Close down New Albion Concentration Camps', 'Justice for Indigenous Refugees', 'UN Sanctions for New Albion', 'Don't Invade our Nation', and so on.

The media—both national and international—were interviewing crowd members, politicians, activists, performers, etc. as well as victims of New Albion human rights abuses. Rowan began to feel nervous—to the point of wanting to vomit—as the master of ceremonies, using the PA system, detailed the purpose of the charity match and evening concert. He'd spent an hour at a press conference fielding questions about the book—though he'd also had to field a number of uncomfortable questions about his life as a cricketer; notably a question about the day he'd accidentally killed the Aotearoan tail-ender ('I don't discuss that incident publicly—it was a profoundly tragic day') and a question about whether this appearance signified his return to international cricket ('Definitely not—these days I'm a writer/academic and musician').

If ever there is a time for the 'other' Rowan to step forward, this is it, he thought, as he measured out his run-up—all the time trying to control his nerves. He'd been asked by the captain to bowl the second over of the day—if things went okay he'd eventually bowl seven overs in all, four in the initial spell and three at the death. After a few test run-ups to the crease, each greeted by crowd cheers, Rowan wandered down to fine leg to field. As he stood there, he struggled to remember everything he'd learnt about fast-bowling in his sessions with Ramsay Philips and Douglas all those months ago.

By the time his turn to bowl came, he noticed a strange tension in the crowd—which only made him more nervous.

The first delivery, both a wide and a no-ball, drew a collective gasp of frustration from the crowd. He felt like an idiot, but as he wandered back to the bowling mark a strange thing happened. His mind grew crystal clear, like certain quartz stones (*yarkuk*) he'd handled—and quartz in these parts often contained gold, making it a kind of philosopher's stone. He dwelled for a moment on what he'd done well in delivering the first ball—the pace was good, probably over 130km per hour, not express, but good enough to make him seem professional. Now it was all about straightening up his action.

The second ball was on target, slightly faster than the first, but slightly short. The Indian batsman pushed it through the gully region for three runs. Again, Rowan focused on what he'd done well and what needed to be fixed. The next two deliveries were both on target and at the right length. When they were blocked by the South African batsmen, Rowan heard cheers from the largely Marin crowd. He felt immense relief after each ball—the situation was tenuous, but for the moment he was holding his own.

He sent the next ball into the same zone, but was smashed over long off for four. The crowd cheered, but Rowan knew that he needed to introduce some variety to his bowling quickly or the spell would turn into a humiliating ordeal. He fired the next ball in slightly wide of off-stump, hoping to get a bit of out-swing going. The ball didn't swing, but the batsman left it alone. For the last ball of the over—he had to bowl seven due to the no-ball/wide of the first delivery—Rowan decided to take a risk and drop the ball in short. The pitch was slightly green and Rowan noticed the ball cut and skid at the same time taking the batsman by surprise. It whistled past his nose and Rowan was immediately informed by the umpire that he'd bowled his one legitimate short ball of the over.

Eight runs off the over, not great, but—apart from the four—he was doing okay.

As he wandered down to the fine leg boundary to field for the other opening bowler, he took several deep breaths. He felt anxious but excited. The day was beautiful, despite it being late winter—not a cloud in the sky. Whilst fielding, he noted the cut and swing the other opening bowler was getting and recalled the fast-bowling clinic he'd been to late the previous year. 'If your action is high and you're side on and landing well, but you're still not swinging the ball, think about your wrist action. The wrist has to be flexible like a whip—it needs to add something to the overall pace of the ball.'

Sure enough the first ball of his next over, delivered from a high position, at pace with good wrist flexibility and with the in-swinger posture, moved in the air. The Indian batsman, who seemed to want to get onto the front foot to drive, found he had to check his stroke due to the late swing. It struck his front pad and Rowan, his team-mates and the entire crowd appealed for Leg Before Wicket. The umpire considered for long moments, but turned down the appeal.

Though disappointed, Rowan immediately felt more confident. The rest of the over saw the ball swing obscenely causing the batsman to withdraw into defensive mode to counteract the movement. By the last ball, Rowan felt something odd happen in his body. On the approach to the wicket, he felt for a moment as though he were flying. The crowd were behind him and he felt as though he had perfect control over every muscle in his body. As he sprinted in to bowl the last ball of the over, he momentarily imagined himself becoming Hermes-Taliesin—just as Douglas had recommended all those months ago. The result was a quick in swinger that forced the batsman into a hurried defensive shot.

With his confidence growing, he decided to do something interesting with the first ball of the third over. He tried to do two things at once—both swing the ball in at the batsman and cut the ball away from the batsman. The strategy worked and though the batsman didn't get an edge and wasn't bowled the ball beat him completely and crashed through to the wicket-keeper's gloves to loud 'Ooohs' followed by louder cheers from the crowd.

Rowan managed to keep the pressure on, during the last two overs of his spell. Two wickets also fell at the other end, which kept the new batsmen quiet, but Rowan himself didn't manage to take any wickets. Nevertheless, by the end of the spell, he felt he'd done his job and retired to the field feeling that he hadn't made a complete fool of himself.

The second spell, close to the end of the match, was different. The field was well spread and it was easy for the opposition to score singles. The ball was also older and didn't move around as much. However, the World Peace Eleven were down to their last batting pair, leaving Rowan to bowl at a defensive tail-ender and a cautious number six batsman. The Marin captain wanted Rowan to test the pair with short deliveries. Rowan was happy to do this with the established batsman, but he baulked at bowling one to the tail-ender—even though he was wearing a helmet.

Mid-way through the second spell and the tail-ender, who had played for New Albion, hit Rowan for successive fours off front-foot drives. The captain—aware that the run total was getting out of hand—signalled for Rowan to test him immediately with a short ball and moved a man into silly short leg for a possible catch off a fended jab. Some in the Marin crowd, fuelled perhaps by fear of invasion by their northern neighbour, began a bloodthirsty chant of 'Bumper ... Bumper ... Bumper ...' Most of the audience, however, sensed the symbolism of the moment—a bouncer had ended the other Rowan's cricket career—and went deathly quiet.

As Rowan turned at the end of his run-up the chants of 'Bumper ... Bumper ...' died away and the entire audience became hushed. Rowan, desperate to take a wicket and prove that he could compete at this level, began his run-in.

After observing the batsman stare a long-time at the new close in fielder, Rowan decided to bowl an in-swinging yorker at full pace.

He put everything he had into the delivery and watched, as if in slow motion, as it travelled in a line outside off stump before swinging back late. Though slightly over-pitched, it was quick enough and surprising enough to beat the batsman and hit the stumps. Rowan had his first wicket.

The rest of the match passed in a blur. Miraculously the pitch looked less lively by the afternoon and though it came down to the last over of the game, the Marin side were triumphant with three balls and as many wickets to spare. Rowan wasn't called upon to bat in the Marin innings.

CHAPTER FIFTY-THREE

THE RALLY AT BIG GOLD MOUNTAIN

The festive atmosphere accompanying the Marin victory subsided for Rowan as he caught up with Anika and Whirrarap at the Dome of Music half an hour after the match. They were in an emergency meeting with security and military personnel. As Rowan arrived Whirrarap gave him some good news, 'We think we've located your father and sister. A group of five-thousand New Albion activists on the way to this concert rioted after New Albion border police refused to let them cross into Marin-e-bek. Apparently they pulled down the fences around the detention centre where your father and sister were being held before over-running the small garrison controlling the border check-point. Thankfully no one was hurt and the activists escorted hundreds of detention centre inmates safely into Marin-e-bek. Your father is currently having a medical check-up at a military hospital, and your sister is safe for the night at a border refugee camp.'

The news from the security people was not so good since a

potentially explosive situation was developing. The estimated crowd for the concert was huge and large crowds were also gathering in other Marin cities as part of the nationwide protest. The police were concerned about possible violence against performers at the concert, but the main issue seemed to be that MUCT had hired a hundred security personnel to police any attempts by musicians to perform Isles's songs. The move had confused many of the international acts and a meeting had been called for 6pm to discuss the implications.

MUCT's management were threatening to close down—with the help of their security contingent—any band defying the morning's interim court order, which had come down, for the moment, in their favour. The threat was being broadcast extensively in the Marin news and protestors and politicians were already labelling the court action 'neo-colonial censorship' initiated by New Albion agents. Placards had appeared soon after on the streets of Dinas Yarkuk stating 'MUCT Dupes: Hands off Marin Culture.' By seven o'clock there was talk that a violent confrontation would take place at the music festival with Marin anger at its northern neighbour running high. The police immediately asked the MUCT CEO to withdraw his private security contingent from the festival area. The request was rejected and the CEO produced lawyers to argue that it was now the duty of the police to shut down the entire concert.

Representatives from the bands met for an emergency meeting around the same time. With tensions high, a number of international acts decided to withdraw from the main concert, agreeing instead to play sets in the city centre that featured only their own music. The remaining bands decided on a joint media statement agreeing to conform to the demands of the federal court order. After this news reached the media at 7.30pm, only an hour before the first band was due to go on stage, a huge crowd gathered outside the stadium to protest

MUCT's actions. Bootleg versions of the CD were already on sale at the Dome. At another media briefing, Rowan backed the protest movement by stating that New Albion neo-colonial aggression was now being directed at Marin cultural values. At the end of the statement he gave out a web address so that people anywhere could download free e-copies of the Isles and Hobbes biography online. Glancing around the room, he noted that despite the embargo on the sale of the book, almost every commentator had a copy.

When Rowan joined his own band for the 8pm start to the concert, he noticed Anika talking to Nicole from the cultural board about who should open the concert. She wanted Rowan and Anika to perform first, 'Just in case the concert is shut down by MUCT or by the police. Even then, given the volatility of the situation, you might only last a few minutes.'

Anika thought for a moment then suggested a different strategy.

Darkness had fallen by the time Paul and his band went on stage to perform their UK hit, *Express Train to Kathmandu*. 'No need to perform that Isles song you were complaining about … your job is to buy us a bit of time and maybe settle the audience,' Rowan had said to Paul half an hour earlier. As Paul stepped up to the mic, fighter jets, military helicopters and high altitude bombers from a dozen nations provided an ominous, all-be-it distant, sound-track. Surveying the huge crowd, he steadied himself for some comments on the theme of the concert. As he did so, however, a Marin senior police officer back stage right waved him away from the mic and cleared a path for Maxwell Fife, the MUCT CEO. Fife strode on stage confidently and, ignoring Paul, grabbed the same mic intent on addressing the crowd.

'Hello, Big Gold Mountain!' he shouted, imitating a rock-star even though he was dressed in his usual expensive grey suit. 'There has been a lot of misunderstanding of our intentions here today. I would like to take a moment to clear up some of those misunderstandings.' Loud boos greeted his words—Paul, looking stoned and bored behind him, started wandering about the stage with a slight Dionysian stagger.

'Firstly, I am not a New Albion national,' when no one cheered he began to look nervous, 'We have not censored this concert and we are not saying that we alone own the intellectual property rights to Isles's newly discovered songs. Our only intention here is to highlight the fact that the Isles songs that were to be performed at this concert, as well as Rowan Sweeney's biography on Abraham Isles and Miriam Hobbes, were written and created with significant MUCT financial input. Indeed today's events were planned, we believe, without due recognition of that input. The Marin Cultural Board of Elders has brought today's impasse upon itself—and, by extension, this wonderful ensemble of performers—by ignoring MUCT requests concerning revenue and product usage constraints.'

A chant of 'Boring … Boring …Boring' began among the crowd and the senior police officer, growing alarmed, signalled to the CEO to leave the stage. Paul, however, took this moment to begin conducting the crowd, motioning them to chant louder. The CEO glared at the singer, making him grab a live secondary mic to shout, 'We aren't playing any of the disputed fuckin' songs, buddy—so get off the stage and let us do our job.'

The CEO once again ignored Paul and continued with his long-winded legal statement, 'The … uh … Board of Elders have left us with no option tonight but to enforce our IP rights as confirmed this morning by the Federal Court.'

'Git off our stage, asshole,' said Paul, launching the statement as a new chant for the audience. In response the MUCT security men in the front row seemed about to storm the stage. Meanwhile Fife rattled on, 'The court today confirmed our right to halt the sale of specific CDs, books, etc. to the public and to unplug any band acting tonight to defy the court by attempting to play recently recovered Isles songs—songs, I emphasise, over which MUCT asserts ...'

'Alright, we get the picture,' Paul whispered in a low menacing voice, 'we gotta listen 'cos you have a battalion of thug-boy shit-for-brains standing here in the front row to piss in your pocket. Hey boys why don't you tell your Evil Emperor he's really starting to piss us off?'

A few of the security people gestured wildly at Paul, but he turned his arse to one of them and screamed, 'Awww, beefcake ... you're really giving it to me.' Roars of laughter erupted all around the stadium, mingling with the 'Boring ... Boring ...' chant. Soon troublemakers were throwing aluminium cans at Fife who soldiered on regardless.

'To conclude, *we strongly assert* ... limited intellectual property rights ...' In that instant a flattened can hit the CEO squarely on the nose. He looked stunned for a moment then scurried off the stage.

Even before he'd left ominous guitar feedback screeched and thundered in the huge black speaker stacks as Paul's band launched into a version of their UK hit.

Rowan stared at Godstar, then at Anika—barely visible given her crouching position on a platform half way up a second lighting tower. All the band members were twenty metres above the stadium floor huddled on maintenance platforms attached to two lighting towers standing either side of the main stage. Each tower sat on the tray of a large truck and each musician was electronically connected to the main concert's sound system. However, Anika had ensured that they were also connected to the Dome's main PA system—now under the control of Ungaru, who had locked himself into the small glass viewing box containing the controls. He was one hundred metres or so back from the concert stage. Crouching unseen high above the ground, Rowan's band did their best to prepare for acoustic versions of several of the Isles songs.

They watched anxiously as the situation deteriorated on the main stage.

Paul's band finished their own song to loud applause before Paul, who was obviously in an ugly mood began lecturing New Albion viewers about their nation's many failings, 'I mean, I was born in the fuckin' country, best nation on earth they always told me—sun and surf and blue sky and lots of money circulating in the economy. Makes for a lot of spiritually obese people, huh? People who have permitted their psychopathic elites to destroy democracy. People who don't give a shit about their neighbours or the rest of the planet. Anyway, my dad, well he served in the N.A. military for thirty plus fuckin' years—very good at bringing his work home to the children—did lots of dirty work for the dark Empire of Oppression. You know he killed people legally as a vocation of choice. I never understood that. Now Mr CEO from the Dark Empire of Oppression wants to shut us all up here tonight—like they've silenced their artists and journalists and poets up north. But we won't let you do that, asshole. So here is an Abraham Isles song about Oppression—the Rapper tonight is Josie Royal, voice of the heavenly spheres. I'm hoping that the N.A. military boys and girls will come join us down here in a love fest, instead of a death fest. Come on!' he whispered seductively at the TV cameras, 'put down those metal death pricks and rip off those dumb-ass corpse making uniforms and tell your American plutocratic superiors where they can stuff their nuclear bombs ... Do it! ... Do it! ... Do it!—I say, from one New Albion patriot to another.'

Rowan heard the first strains of the Isles song he'd given Paul and knew instantly what would unfold. He watched as far below a line of black uniforms assembled directly in-front of the stage. After a minute of the song the swarm of MUCT security personnel scrambled onto the main stage, some moving suspiciously like New Albion Special Forces soldiers. Despite being heckled all the way, it was clear that they meant business. In the wings dozens of Marin police seemed momentarily torn between confronting the foreign security people and attending to the growing disorderliness of members of the crowd.

Paul, oblivious to the violence brewing, gave the finger to a black-clad hulk lumbering aggressively towards him. The man lunged at him, but only managed to send both of them into the drum-kit at the rear of the stage which led to musical mayhem in the speakers.

Before they'd even reached the first chorus the band's access to the sound system was cut. The Marin police—jolted into action by a directive from a secret authority—now confronted the MUCT security people, ordering them to leave the stage. The crowd, sensitive to the international symbolism, surged toward the main stage—for a moment it looked as if the security people might open fire on the police. And then Rowan spotted Henri. He was talking with the muscular leader of the MUCT security contingent. The man carried state of the art communication technologies, a bullet-proof vest and a semi-automatic rifle. To Rowan, he looked like a professional soldier. *Why on earth is he allowing Henri to give him orders?* thought Rowan. A few minutes later, the entire MUCT security contingent left the stage area after forming a defensive huddle. When Rowan looked for Henri again, he'd disappeared into the crowd.

High above the chaos Godstar seized the moment and the first strains of a slow and infinitely haunting Isles song concerning the Flaw in the Fabric of the Cosmos filled the huge black speaker stacks positioned like a wall beneath the main stage. Anika took the cue and began singing the song's slow and haunting chorus precursor. The crowd immediately quieted. Even the MUCT security personnel looked stunned, until one of them had the gumption to unplug the entire concert sound system.

But the silence was only momentary, as Ungaru transferred the band to the Dome's main PA system. Though the sound was not as clear, it remained loud and distinct, and, at least for the moment out of the control of both the police and the MUCT security people.

The audience watched in awe as red and green floodlights fixed on Anika. She was high above the ground, propped precariously at the front of her platform behind waist high metal bars. Her voice filled the stadium. Then more lights searched the heavens, this time green and yellow and focused on Rowan and Godstar's platform. Rowan stepped forward to sing the low—infinitely melancholy—first verse, before he and Anika's voices merged in the soaring chorus. All the time Godstar and the bass player maintained the rhythm and steered the song's overall dynamics.

As he sang, Rowan imagined all the negativity below being transformed by the music. The process seemed alchemical—as if the band were gently heating and transforming the spiritual poisons of everyone in the stadium and everyone watching on TV. He glanced across at Anika as her voice trailed off into an aching silence at the end the first song. In that moment he could well imagine her as Bridget or perhaps Cerridwen, Lady of the Cauldron: she who coordinates (with her wisdom and haunting voice) nine maidens of poetry and song to heat the Cauldron of Inspiration. *And her Cauldron is but one among many*, thought Rowan. *Cauldrons and Orbits and Quartz Crystals—Orbits and crystals of love, joy, freedom and connection—upright cauldrons! Or*

Orbits and crystals of hatred, despair, oppression and evil magic—inverted cauldrons! Despite himself, he imagined for a moment that he, Anika, Ungaru, Godstar, Douglas, Paul, Rhiannon and all the others were traversing the Circle of Struggle *(Abred)* as one. Striving as one, through the magic fog to bring grace, healing, music and poetry *(the gifts of Gwynedd* and *Ceugant)* to the world of limits. *Such fragile professions,* thought Rowan, *practised by imperfect souls—souls striving against the Cosmic Flaw. Souls aware that each small victory is only ever temporary.*

The band managed to play for their full twenty minutes. They finished with a song Rowan had written after the trip north to see his father, 'Another War'. Below them the Marin police and military worked hard to calm the crowd and escort the MUCT security people out of the Dome.

Part way into the song the main sound system fired up and several singers from the Koori band scheduled to perform next ran on stage to lead the huge crowd through two versions of the chorus. Close to the end, Rowan and Anika (who had been singing harmonies) fell silent and watched as the Koori singers and audience chanted over and over again, at every available camera and radio mic: *'Don't lie-lie-de-lie/ don't lie as the children die/ don't lie-lie-de-lie/ you know mankind is putting out the lights.'*

A hundred Indigenous Marins wearing yellow, black or red t-shirts slowly took over the stage. Arranged in a carefully choreographed dance formation they looked, from Rowan's position high above the stage, like some sort of gigantic lizard or dragon with two lines of red t-shirts facing outwards containing a mass of black t-shirts inside, except for a dozen or so yellow back-bone spikes (people wearing yellow t-shirts). As the song died out they began to move slowly back and forth across the stage in an undulating, snake like motion. The head of the beast appeared to whip around aggressively in front of the MUCT security people.

As the chorus repetitions came to a natural end some kind of group threshold was crossed, and the chanting turned into waves of sobbing and wailing. For a moment, Rowan imagined he heard the collective grief of an entire continent.

APPENDIX ONE

Philip Ungaru's Introduction to *Dinas Yakuk: The City of Quartz*

The text that follows originally appeared at the beginning of the manuscript found on Douglas Green's former estate. It was purportedly written by one Philip Ungaru and originally acted as an introduction to the entire story. Given we've decided to publish the manuscript as fiction, rather than as historical fact, we decided to withhold this material from readers until now — our intention being to maintain a certain tautness in the story's plot that would otherwise have been absent with premature revelations concerning Rowan Sweeney's eventual fate.

Olwen Ghent
Commissioning Editor
Ghwilian Books

> MUCT academic, Rowan Sweeney, was shot by unknown assailants whilst bush-walking in parkland west of Dinas Yarkuk on December 20th 1997. He'd experienced that day a guided tour by local Koori elders of some of the region's important sacred

sites. The attack took place an hour after the tour had ended whilst the party members were enjoying Koori bush-tucker at a local picnic site. Rowan decided to approach an Anomaly frequenting the area—which was close to the MUCT science campus. The so-called "Coughing Man Anomaly" was described by witnesses as a pot-bellied old man wearing cut-off pants, a short sleeved shirt and a straw hat. The figure could be heard from some distance due to its distinctive hacking cough. Those who approached it, said that the 'coughing man' appeared to be coughing up blood. Rowan was shot in the vicinity of the figure and police experts told me that he was probably conversing with the figure as the attack happened. The main party, hearing three gunshots, tentatively went to investigate, but Rowan died on the way to hospital. Some of the elders in the bushwalking party swear they heard Rowan singing Islesian songs just prior to the shooting, and they told me that a photograph of an adult male—identified later as Harry Green— the son of local identity Douglas Green—was found in the mud beside the body. Witnesses also mention the presence beside the body of an unnaturally large wedge-tailed eagle and a 'somewhat talkative' raven. Police found fresh military style boot-prints less than fifty metres from Rowan's body.

Rowan's last public statement, a longish letter published in edited form by the *Marin-e-bek Times* in late 1997, was written some four months after the publication of his biography on Abraham Isles and Miriam Hobbes. Rowan had been researching the book since 1996. As I write, it is November 1998 and I am due to return to Aotearoa after completing my MA studies. My exegesis looked at similarities between Maori and ancient Celtic religious beliefs and my primary supervisor was Professor Eileen MacIntyre, a world expert on early Irish and Welsh religions. Rowan, however, took Eileen's place as my primary supervisor in early 1997. As I prepare for my return to Aotearoa, it concerns me that the story of Rowan's life after returning unconscious from Vietnam up to the point of his assassination in late 1997 has yet to be properly narrated.

I do not want to dismiss all aspects of Rowan's letter of late 1997, however, I think it is fair to say that his letter is not at all comprehensive in its description of many of the events that took place in and around Dinas Yarkuk in 1997. This is not due—as some have suggested—to Rowan displaying symptoms of some kind of personality disorder during this period. Rather, by mid-1997, he and Anika had acquired powerful enemies. We recall that there was much hysteria about the Isles and Hobbes biography leading up to its publication in late August—due largely to suspicion in some quarters about the motivations behind the decision of the Isles estate to release, through Rowan's book, and eventually through the song book and song recordings, controversial new information about the complexity and extent of Isles's spiritual beliefs.

At the time, New Albion and Marin-e-bek were on the brink of military conflict. As a consequence, the new material seemed explosive to some since a number of the songs specifically addressed the destructiveness of war. Unfortunately, Rowan Sweeney's murder was but one of many that summer, and it is important that we also remember the cross-border raids that killed so many in the refugee camps prior to the rally at Big Gold Mountain, including Marin civilians assisting the refugees. It was, and to some extent it remains, a time of great apprehension in Marin-e-bek—even with the recently elected New Albion government appearing to be less aggressive toward surrounding nations and more humane toward its own previously oppressed minorities. Of course, moves for sanctions against New Albion spearheaded by four of the world's largest nuclear democracies, France, India, Britain and Democratic China at the United Nations, helped the Marin cause considerably—but I'd like to think that the internationally televised Peace Rally at Big Gold Mountain also helped turn the tide of international opinion. Thus did the old Marin social strategy of 'adaptive traditionalism' pay rich dividends of liberty during the latest national crisis.

Rowan's decision in his letter to not tell it 'straight' was, in my opinion, directly related to what we Maoris call 'tapus', i.e. restrictions placed upon a person or persons by tribal elders. In Rowan's case, I believe that the Marin Cultural Board of Elders and the Isles estate asked him not to speak about certain matters. However, with his assassin/s still at large, I feel duty bound to present to the public a summary of his life prior to the shooting—as best I can reconstruct it.

I've pieced this narrative together from remembered conversations, meetings, gossip around the university, and interviews with people who knew him or Anika during that period. The reader should also note that Rowan and I had several heart to heart talks in October and early November of 1997. Much of the first third or so of this narrative has been pieced together from those talks—to my knowledge this information has never been made public before. Even Anika Miraj, who worked closely with Rowan between June and his death in December, was not party to all of the revelations he and I shared. I should also say that Imogen Bright, a fellow academic and Rowan's lover from late 1996 to May of 1997, has helped me in my quest to piece together aspects of this story.

My apologies, for failing to adopt 'realist' modes of storytelling. As a trainee tohunga-druid genetically inclined to view the world as a spiritual whole, I have long been aware of the existence of other 'realities', modes of being, etc. that run counter to the views of reality favoured by many Westerners. My own perceptions of the spiritual dimension to the events of 1997 inevitably colour this version of events—probably unfairly since I suspect that Rowan was very uncomfortable with transpersonal phenomena. This divergence in our world-views needs to be emphasised.

However, to my mind, he was a talented seer/magician, especially when it came to composing and performing haunting music with transpersonal themes. I enjoyed listening as he, Anika, Godstar and others performed music and I was party to many of their discussions about music and culture generally. However, I learnt most from Rowan's dislike of injustice and his commitment to human rights. His understanding of 'systematic' forms of oppression, in particular, was a revelation to me, though I knew well enough the affects of 19th century European colonisation on the Maori people of Aotearoa.

This is a fantastic story, even by Marin standards, and I admit that certain strands in the narrative will seem quite bizarre to some readers. I make no apologies for this—history is terrifying and strange, and I refuse to sugar the pill, so to speak, to protect the delicate. I have written this manuscript out of grief and frustration that Rowan's assassin/s are yet to be apprehended and out of affection for Anika and Imogen who have been devastated by his death. My sole intention here is to motivate any individuals with useful information about Rowan's assailants to come forward.

As I write I note that many of the songs Rowan and Anika helped resurrect have been formally integrated into the Islesian therapeutic system, others are routinely studied and performed in schools, on radio and television, and at private and public gatherings across Marin-e-bek and beyond. Such a comprehensive distribution of this Islesian material is to me evidence enough that Rowan Sweeney did not die in vain. This book is dedicated to his memory.

Yours Faithfully

Philip Ungaru
(with the permission of Anika Miraj)
November 1998

MISCELLANEOUS DOCUMENTS

EXTRACT 1

'Chapter 1—Born in the Century Storm' from Abraham Isles and Miriam Hobbes (a biography).

Abraham Isles was born near Golspie, Sutherland Shire in the far north of Scotland in1803. His father was a Welshman who had been transferred in 1795 from Lord and Lady Stafford's estates in Shropshire to work as a gamesman on their Scottish estates (his father, Abraham's grandfather, was a farmer from Snowdonia in North Wales, though he'd also been a soldier). Abraham's mother came from Dingwall, just north of Inverness, also part of the great northern shire of Sutherland. She was of peasant upbringing and thus spoke Gaelic. As a consequence, he grew up well versed in the peculiar, almost pagan, folk traditions of the highland Scots. Many of his mother's kinsfolk, however, were destined to join the great mass of oppressed peasant highlanders to be evicted ('Cleared') from their ancestral lands in the name of Improvement (meaning 'sheep farming'). Between 1807 and 1850 many were forced into coastal hovels and told to fish, others drifted southwards to the factories of Glasgow and Edinburgh. For tens of thousands, however, emigration was the only option: to Canada, America or Australia.

By 1814 whole parishes of Sutherland were being 'Cleared' of people. Upset at the effect of the clearances on his wife's kinsfolk, Abraham's father booked passage that year, with his wife and four sons, for North Wales (where his father still worked as a farm laborer). Here young Abraham was exposed to another Celtic tradition, that of the Welsh and the farm's closeness to Wales's largest stretch of inland water, Llyn Tegid (also known as Bala Lake), though incidental to Abraham as a youth, came to have a major impact on his later intellectual endeavors. His memories of life on the farm in north Wales were idyllic. Abraham's grandparents were progressive in religious matters – they were Baptists, i.e. Old Dissent, a form of Protestantism in the 19th century more usually associated with the middle ranks of British society. This early grounding in progressive Christianity also gave young Abraham early exposure to progressive politics. It is said, however, that Abraham's mother refused to enter a church after 1814. From her perspective, Laird and Reverend had worked in tandem to strip her kinsfolk of land and livelihood in the name of the profits to be made out of sheep. Her sense that Christ himself had betrayed her kin was never forgotten by young Abraham. As she aged, she cut an increasingly tragic figure—often ranting in Gaelic at public occasions (even at her death in 1836, she knew little Welsh and virtually no English). By the time of her death, she had lost two sons; one, a soldier, to the wars of Empire, the other, a felon, to the colony of New South Wales.

It was the church, however, that encouraged young Abraham to pursue his growing love of knowledge. In recollecting his early life, he said that it was the local church minister, Reginald Hobdon, who first taught him to read and write English. One particular saying of Reginald's seems to have helped shape young Abraham's future attitude to life: 'Knowledge is the only antidote to injustice.' Though interested in the classics Abraham nevertheless acquired such practical skills as his father and grandfather could teach him, chiefly farming and mechanics—such skills would serve him well in the colonies.

He professes, as a young man, to have had no clear direction in life. He enjoyed farm work as much as he enjoyed reading and it was only the offer of a scholarship at 17 (to become a Baptist minister and schoolmaster) that, in retrospect, set him on his true life's path. In the summer of 1820, with the encouragement of his family and Mr. Hobdon, he set off for London town. After six months of study, however, he professes to have undergone something of a spiritual crisis— in private he began to see himself as a kindred spirit to the likes of Priestly, Price and Robinson, that is to the 'Rational Dissenters' of the 1780s and 90s. This was the outcome of Isles's first attempt to reconcile the loyalty he felt toward his father's religion with answers to questions increasingly posed to him in London due to his encountering alternative interpretations of the political and social situation in England at that time.

England's disenfranchised middle and lower classes were close to revolution—demonstrations against the new Corn Law had taken place in 1815, the Spa Fields riots had taken place in the same year. Likewise, the actions of the Luddite machine breakers remained fresh in people's memories. There were also the cases of the Pentrich rebels and their foiled plan to seize Nottingham Castle (June 1817); the East Anglian agrarian riots; the iron worker strikes in South Wales; the Cato Street Conspiracy led by Arthur Thistlewood and the Spenceans (1820) and the disaster of the Peterloo Massacre of 1819. All were examples of the smothered revolutionary aspirations of the lower and middling classes. Isles, being at a young and impressionable age, soon became more interested in the ideas purveyed by London's many radical bookshops (and 'Unstamped' [illegal] penny journals and broadsheets) than he was in his schoolwork. He eventually fell in with a group of self-educated Owenites ('the first socialists'). At the same time, he began to seriously question the basis of his faith.

It was, by all accounts, a difficult period for Isles. By January 1821, he had decided to discontinue his religious studies. After a short (and by all accounts tense) trip home to North Wales, he returned to

London and took a job labouring to support himself. At the same time, he continued his education by attending informal early gatherings at institutions not unlike what were later called The Halls of Science – working class institutions that held lectures on scientific ideas/advances, and on New Age topics like mesmerism, astrology, spiritual alchemy, phrenology and modern philosophy. He also seems to have visited South Place Chapel on numerous occasions between 1821 and 1828.

By his own accounts, between 1821 and 1825 he experimented with rationalist and atheistic ideas—especially as they might lead to the development and application of Robert Owen's socialist programme for industrial humanity. It is well to remember that Isles was living an extremely marginal existence at the time. He had first-hand knowledge of the evils of poverty—it was all around him in London. Decades later, in reflecting upon his youth, he stated that he chose to leave the religious question in abeyance whilst exploring Enlightenment ideas about man's place in the cosmos, and the right and proper conduct of citizens toward each other in an ideal state:

'I was interested in whether it was possible to move towards the creation of a just society without resort to the religion of my up-bringing—indeed without resort to any religion at all. I wanted to see how we could make use of the principles of science and reason in order to reach such a goal. This is not to say that I abandoned completely the

world of the spirit, I did not. Rather, I engaged in part-time studies of our interior traditions — experimenting as required, without fear of sulphur or eternal damnation. I hoped at the time that certainty would one day reappear in such matters; perhaps in the gap between what could be achieved by right-minded, rational human beings [intent on overcoming injustice], and what could only be achieved by relations with powers beyond the confines of this material world. I imagined that such a process would one day unveil for me a true and uncontaminated version of religion. Whether it would restore that religious perspective that had given such succour to me as a boy, I did not know at the time. I should confess, however, that even then I preferred the lectures on alchemy, druidry and the myths and legends of the ancient Greeks to lectures on mathematics and all things mechanical … though many a time here in the colonies I have thanked the spirits for every minute of practical learning that had seemed so tedious at the time.'

By the mid-1820s, he had become critical of Enlightenment ideas about the human soul. He'd begun to see spiritual alchemy — via the Hermetic tradition — as a corrective to some of the excesses of both Christian and Enlightenment views of the soul. For a time, between 1825 and 1827, he became obsessed with Thoth, Hermes and Hermes Trismegistus — apparently even conversing with these figures in daydreams, journals and dreams. Scholars have argued that they gave him both models for independent learning and a subconscious means to manage the identity conflicts—ethnic and religious—arising out of his upbringing. Four important ideas entered his thinking due to this obsession: 1) that the cosmos, having been created by lesser deities, automatically generates suffering and dualistic conflicts; 2) that the Hermesian principle—aligned with the Imagination—is beyond the control of those lesser deities and thus offers humans a means to transcend suffering and conflict; 3) that conflict, both within humans and between humans, is lessened when we embrace the ideal of 'hybridity'—for Isles the figure of the hermaphrodite depicted in so many old alchemical texts best symbolised this ideal state; and 4) moving from a state of unawareness ('intemperate duality') to one of transcendent awareness ('crystallised hybridity') was a rigorous process involving clear stages of spiritual development.

In 1825, at the age of 22, he fell in love with fellow Owenite, Miriam Hobbes. Miriam, whose father was a London doctor, was two years younger than Abraham. In his diaries, she is described as 'purposeful, easily underestimated, of even temper (though passionate when it comes to any form of injustice) and unconventionally beautiful'. She also held to proto-feminist beliefs concerning matters of gender equality. To begin with the relationship did not go well and his later diaries attest to the fact that Miriam at first deflected his interest. Her initial rejection of Isles seems to have provoked a crisis in him that, between 1826 and 1828, forced him back upon the musical inspiration of his Celtic childhood. Sometime in late 1826, lovesick for Miriam, he came across an old copy of Joseph Walker's *Historical Memoirs of the Irish Bards* (published 1786) and soon after began hearing 'melancholy music' in dreams and day-dreams.

Before long he had identified himself, at least in part, as an *Ollamhain-re-dan* or *Filidhi*, as described in Walker's book. As such, he set about learning the music of his Celtic forefathers from Irish, Welsh and Scottish musicians and composers who were resident in southern England. Around this time, he also acquired a copy of Edward Davies's monumental work *The Mythology and Rites of the British Druids* (published 1809) and it seems as though he took Section III of that book, outlining the relationship between the Welsh Goddess, Cerridwen, and the bard-druid, Taliesin, to heart. He did his best to view his failure with Miriam as a kind of 'bardic initiation'—though he never referred to himself explicitly as either a bard or a druid. Indeed in a later diary of 1839, he writes somewhat mischievously, 'I am perhaps a *gruagach*'. The word is from Gaelic and has a number of meanings including: 'long-haired enchanter', 'wildwose' (wild-man) and 'seer' (though usually in a folk context). As a 'humble *gruagach*' Isles acknowledged, perhaps, experiences he'd had from a young age commonly ascribed to people possessing the so called 'second sight'. He attests in his diaries to occasionally seeing the spirit doubles of other people (though rather than the word 'double', he uses the Gaelic term *tamhasg*).

Whether he saw himself as a bard/filidhi or a *gruagach*, by 1827 he was performing some of his own music at Owenite dinners, fund-raisers and demonstrations. Skills in musical composition and performance now augmented his already considerable skills as an orator.

Popular myth has it that it was his improved social standing that attracted Miriam's belated attention. This, however, is to ignore the evidence contained in his diaries. There is credible evidence concerning a series of visits by Isles to a London mesmerist in 1827—there is also evidence that the fellow was secretly active in a London druid revival group. It seems that the mesmerist, at Isles's suggestion, used the harp, and occasionally other traditional bardic instruments, to hypnotise Isles into a light trance state with the goal of eliciting 'apparitions most terrifying, though ultimately cathartic'.

The same mesmerist apparently introduced Isles to obscure Celtic teachings known as 'cauldron lore'. The teachings concerned various breathing (and other) exercises designed to 'move' three 'soul cauldrons' stationed in important parts of the body: the belly/groin (*coire goiriath*), heart (*coire ernma*) and forehead (*coire soís*). The breathing exercises were supposed to 'fan the flames' of personal transformation (in the alchemical sense) and were aimed at turning the two higher 'cauldrons' (translated, these days, as the Cauldron of Vocation and the Cauldron of Knowledge) to an upright (rather than prone or inverted) position.

These teachings are known to modern scholars through translations of a 15th century Irish legal codex dubbed by an early translator *The Cauldron of Poesy*. It is possible that the mesmerist showed Isles a copy of this text.

By late 1827 Isles was trying to merge the insights of Rousseau (concerning the dangers of a 'civilised' childhood) with cathartic-hypnotic techniques drawn from both Mesmer and Celtic 'cauldron/bardic lore'. Isles's diaries of the period refer explicitly to personal experiments that merged these traditions. He was interested in the healing possibilities of various species of ancient bardic music. At first, in his melancholy over Miriam, he was attracted to the dolorous *geanttraidheacht* mode. In describing a visit to the mesmerist in mid-1827 Isles wrote: 'I cried tears in abundance today, enough to fill Lake Bala, the very dwelling place of Cerridwen. I hope it pleases her.' Later in the year, he and the mesmerist moved on to other experiments involving trance states and what Isles called 'Benshi Sounds' (i.e. 'Banshee sounds'), by which he means, and here he quotes Walker directly, musical attempts to replicate the sounds of 'Spirits conjured by fuperftition, in the darknefs of paganifm' (Walker 1786 p.99).

The initial goals of these experiments were personal—to undo the damage he'd experienced in early childhood via religious and schooling practices aimed at civilising him (this insight he drew from Rousseau). The traumatic circumstances of his family's migration from Scotland to North

Wales were also addressed during these sessions. The more he understood of the social forces behind his disrupted childhood, the angrier he became at the behaviour of the clan chieftains, absentee lairds and ladies and 'Improver' ideologues that were, even in 1828, dismantling the traditional way of life of the highland peasants.

Apparently the therapy sessions were successful. Isles's diaries attest to a fundamental transformation of his personality during this period. *'The ancients, who loved the Olympians, wrote of the therapeutic effects of their Mysteries on the constitution of soul and mind,'* Isles wrote, *'the heart fair overflows with the ruddy humour, though the initiate has trudged through hell to experience it. I was yet to attain my full happiness at that time, but I was by degrees more content.* Isles also records this transformation as the main reason for Miriam's change of heart toward him (note: the two were engaged in 1829 and married in 1830): *'She noticed in me a transformation of the humours—the darker liquids having ceded ground to the lighter ones. I did not tell her at the time that Cerridwen and the Celtic Mercury had overseen the changes.'*

Although important, it would be a mistake to over-emphasise the role of these spiritual traditions in Isles's later philosophical system. Ideas drawn from these systems were always moderated by a hefty dose of social realism and pragmatism. We note, for example, a gradual tendency (from 1829 on) to distance his thinking from the more outlandish ideas circulating among

Hermetic occultists and Celtic revivalists at that time. He'd always seen himself as a social reformer and, as such, he remained inspired, paradoxically, by a number of Enlightenment philosophers, in particular Rousseau. He was also aware that his particular initiatory 'Cerridwen of the Cauldron', that is Miriam, was primarily a social reformer.

It is worth pausing a moment to state that the foundations of Isles's philosophy (in concepts drawn from 'spiritual alchemy', Celtic revivalism, Mesmerism and early socialism) were firmly in place by the late 1820s. However, it was not until the mid-1830s, with his 'Theory of the Orbits', that he managed to turn the chaotic intellectual musings of his youth into a unique philosophy. The break-through, when it came, appears to have occurred as a result of a number of later experiences: his period as a traumatised convict in the colony of New South Wales; his separation from Miriam at that time; and his encounters with the Aboriginal peoples of South-Eastern Australia.

On the political front, by 1828 both Isles and Hobbes were involved in activities that were bound, sooner or later, to attract the attention of the authorities. By daylight Isles was using his considerable skills as an orator to introduce fellow workers to Owen's ideas—in effect he'd become a union organiser in the days before unions—and by night he was helping to distribute 'unstamped' radical publications to the working and middle classes of London town. Given the class differences between Isles and Hobbes, it is not surprising that, to begin with, Miriam's parents were opposed to their relationship. One can only imagine, however, their shame and distress, when both Abraham and Miriam (by then married) were arrested in June of 1832 for illegally distributing a seditious publication. Although Miriam was quickly released, Abraham was later convicted and sentenced to seven years transportation to the colony of New South Wales. His ship set sail on February 12th 1833.

Upon arrival in Sydney, Isles was sent to Longbottom Stockade, about halfway between Sydney and Paramatta. The stockade consisted of a number of primitive sheds, a kitchen, a storeroom and other smaller buildings. There was also a military barracks. The buildings formed a kind of square looking inwards toward a courtyard and outwards toward Parramatta Road to the south and Parramatta River to the north. The settlement housed members of road gangs, convicts, soldiers, some mounted police and various craftsmen. In his diaries Isles describes somewhat mechanically aspects of his time at the prison farm:

'There were about 16 convicts to a hut – the hut was perhaps 17 feet by 10. We were locked in at sunset and were not let out until sunrise. A hut had no windows, only two iron grills set into all four walls. There was much suffering in the colder weather on account of the cold air and dew these grills allowed in. During the hotter periods of the year we suffered terribly from mosquitoes. We worked for the government of New South Wales in many different capacities—in the nearby forests cutting trees, on carts, in the government gardens, or at the nearby wharf."

It is worth noting that the population of Sydney at that time was around twenty-seven thousand of which only six thousand were native born or emigrants. The other twenty-one thousand were convicts or ex-convicts.

EXTRACT 2

'Life in the Colony of New South Wales' from *Abraham Isles and Miriam Hobbes (a biography)*.

The details about what exactly happened to Isles in the decade following his escape from the squatter's sheep run are sketchy. Indeed, even the details of his escape from the squatter were only written down by Isles a year before his death in 1880. To make matters more difficult for the historian, the diaries he wrote between the 1830s and 1860 or so (which contain hundreds of his songs) have never been published in their entirety by his descendants. We have only the following to go on: 1) severely truncated versions of the diaries; 2) Isles's later life autobiography, and; 3) published and recorded recollections by some of the Indigenous and Idealist people he'd encountered during that period.

The broad outline of his life between 1835 or so and 1845 thus remains provisional even now, some 150 years on. What is certain is that in 1845 he emerged as chief advisor to a large, well-armed inter-tribal, indeed international, military confederation determined to halt any further advances by British colonists into Aboriginal lands south and west of the Great River (known by local tribes as the Indi River). It is not until the late 1840s, however, that the British became aware of Isles as anything but a lost, presumed dead, convict. For all intents and purposes Isles became a different person—The Adamantine Wizard—on the day he left the hut and allied himself with the Aboriginal cause.

Interestingly, just prior to his death in 1880, Isles confirmed for the first time the popular rumour that he'd met with the famous British naturalist, Charles Darwin, in contested country west of Bathurst in late January 1836.

Darwin's guide on the trip over the Blue Mountains apparently knew the general whereabouts of a white man familiar with many of the tribes of the region. Darwin, as he had done in the country around Buenos Ayres in late 1832, all but ignored the military conflicts shadowing the frontier region and decided to head into the disputed territories to try and meet with the Adamantine Wizard.

Since Darwin was aware the man was probably an escaped convict, perhaps a bushranger, special negotiations took place to secure the meeting— not discussed at all in the Darwin's version of events, and only hazily discussed in Isles's later description. What is known is that the two men eventually met on the banks of the Lachlan River near modern day Cowra. Darwin, of course, was in the early stages of developing his theory of evolution and apparently discussed his ideas freely with the older man who was much interested in Darwin's summary of the social, scientific and religious implications of Lyell's *Principles of Geology* which had apparently affected Darwin like a 'slow magnificent revelation' (Isles's words) since his having received the book in Monte Video in late 1832. Isles records being thunderstruck by Darwin's support for Lyell's idea that the earth was much older than Old Testament teachings proposed.

This led to a late night discussion of Darwin's growing belief, based upon data from South America and the Galapagos Island, that living species might be descended from extinct common ancestors. Before long Darwin was quizzing Isles about the Koori people he now lived among. With the stifling heat of the day still hanging over the river-side camp Isles astounded Darwin with a detailed exposition of the wide-ranging abilities of his new friends. To Isles no skill of civilisation— intellectual, mechanical, political or creative— could not be learnt by the Australian Aboriginal and in not a few they were superior to many Europeans he had known. 'These people,' said Isles (as quoted in Darwin's diaries of the time), 'are no throw back to an earlier stage of human transmutation, rather each of them enters the world equipped with the same range of potentials for human activity and reflection available to any European. The parson's myth that they are degenerate humans is but a justification for our own barbarism. We covet their land, their water holes, their women and their every means of material support.'

Darwin objected initially to these comments saying, 'But surely you are not saying that the savages of New South Wales are innately capable of attaining to the level of European civilisation?'

At this Isles snorted before responding. For long moments Darwin was reminded of the silent fury he had occasionally observed in the Captain of the Beagle, 'My dear friend,' began Isles, 'a man of science should not be seduced by ornate toys and trinkets—mastery over such trinkets will never substitute for genuine evidence of a people's capacity for civilisation. Having observed and endured the antics of many a high-bred "civilised" European in this far-flung colony, I must beg to differ on the benchmarks we might establish for testing any thesis describing "Civilisation". When you have repeatedly endured the lash or seen a native women violated by a rum-sodden squatter ape, I beg you return and theorise with me about how we might assess progress in "civilisation".'

Darwin was much taken by Isles's comments and seems thereafter to have revised earlier observations about the 'primitive peoples' he'd met in South America.

Another discussion the following day, 'over delicious green China tea' (Darwin's diary), concerned the complexity and subtlety of Koori spiritual beliefs (a revelation to Darwin). Isles outlined the interconnections between these beliefs (and the supernatural beings they spoke of) and the functioning of 'natural systems' suggesting that they worked to maintain a kind of multi-species 'balance' benefiting the entire system. This idea affected Darwin greatly and helped modify certain Eurocentric tendencies in his thinking— making him focus less on individual adaptations (or failed adaptations) and more on whole system adaptations. Likewise, after Isles spoke against the colonial assault on 'indigenous nature', Darwin gradually became interested in examples of inter-species dependencies and how they functioned to preserve the well-being of entire natural systems.

Isles's discussion of the role spiritual beliefs played in regulating and balancing relations between Aboriginal tribes and the natural environment also made an impression on Darwin. 'I have been given new eyes,' he said in his diary summarising their meeting.

Isles did not reveal his true identity to Darwin during their two-day encounter. It was not until the mid1840s that the penny dropped for Darwin, after the censorship in England of a book containing the teachings of the Adamantine Wizard and after newspaper reports concerning Aboriginal resistance to the British invasion. After viewing a portrait of the by now older Adamantine Wizard dressed in a possum-skin cloak, Darwin noted in his journals: 'I recognise him! The very same fellow I had encountered on my travels west of Bathurst.'

Isles's true identity was also deliberately

concealed from the British bureaucrats he conversed with on the eve of the break-out of the 100 days war in 1845. By this stage, however, his songs and unique philosophical teachings had travelled ahead of him to the major cities of the Old World. To European radicals hungry for political and social reform the Great Southern Land seemed like a New Jerusalem. Isles promised them a better life in the antipodes as citizens of a state based upon genuine democracy, freedom of speech, freedom of religion, and, increasingly, an early form of socialism. He believed that Aboriginal people were superior to Europeans in their love of liberty and distrust of authority: 'Among the Aboriginal peoples of this continent no man or woman lords it over another on account of wealth or family pedigree ... all are equal.' By the early 1840s the Adamantine Wizard had become a semi-legendary figure—someone who aided the black armies of liberation gathering on the fringes of the illegitimate Australian colonies.

It seems that as early as 1835 Isles began composing, and later distributing, the songs and spiritual teachings that would become the spiritual backbone of a plan aimed at stitching together an international army of radical volunteer—soldiers, teachers, healers, artists, engineers, etc., i.e. people of any nationality—willing to support Aboriginal efforts to remain independent of the British and enter the modern world at their own pace. Isles worked tirelessly to further this project and saw such an alliance as the only possible way to stall what he called 'a continental apocalypse'.

He seems to have spent most of that first decade of exile talking to Aboriginal elders all across South-Eastern Australia about British intentions for their territories. It was during this period that he also came to understand how introduced European diseases were impacting on the indigenous population. Although some of the illnesses were beyond anybody's power to treat at that time, Isles had heard of the centuries old Chinese practice of 'variolation'—which had been used to contain outbreaks of smallpox. With the assistance of two emancipated Sydney town Scottish convicts, he eventually secured a medical treatise describing the safe preparation of the smallpox matter to be variolated as well as effective methods of inoculation. The same ex-convicts eventually joined Isles's entourage and agreed to work for a number of years carrying out inoculations of indigenous people up and down the east coast and, eventually, into the southern and central tribal lands—and with great, though belated, success.

During their discussions with Isles, some Aboriginal elders decided drastic measures were needed to hold back the British invasion. They understood that the disparate tribes needed to form an effective military alliance. To them this meant a modification to a common Aboriginal ritual permitting visitors 'freedom of the land', i.e. the right to wander the land and gather some sustenance without harassment. Among the Kulin this process was formalised in the Tanderrum

Ceremony, which involved the presentation of eucalyptus foliage to visitors, as well as a ritual that saw host and visitor drink from a *tarnuk* through a reed straw. By 1840 most tribes in the South-East had set aside land and resources to welcome and feed inter-tribal and, eventually, international migrants (whether warriors/soldiers or workers/craftspeople for new industries). These 'Tanderrum' areas firstly became stockyards for seized 'squatter' stock, and then towns. They also became centres of resistance to the British invasion.

It seems that in 1837 an unprecedented gathering of elders from dozens of South-Eastern tribes was convened to agree upon ways to assist tribes directly affected by the invasion. Somehow or other Isles managed to describe to these elders the full implications of the European incursions. Just how such concepts as the British Empire, the roundness of the earth, the existence of technologically advanced nations many thousands of miles away, Imperialist legal strategies, etc. were conveyed to the elders is not known—but during the late 1830s and early 1840s we see clear evidence of coordinated military resistance across the South-Eastern part of the continent. This resistance drastically slowed the colonisation process.

That such fundamental political changes took place in Aboriginal society over such a short period of time seems, of course, almost miraculous. However, we know that by 1843 Isles was supervising secret gold mining operations in Dja-Dja Wurrung, Wathaurong and Taungurong country south of the Great River. These regions were, at that time, untouched by Europeans—the first wave of squatters having been driven off by the Aboriginal resistance. Once mined and extracted the gold was melted down and sold to international traders unaware of its origins. The proceeds funded the purchase of vast stores of weapons—as well as several warships with Non-British Idealist crews. The gold proceeds also provided remuneration to European Idealists and dissidents flocking to the Aboriginal cause from the early 1840s on and funded vital infrastructure projects. The fact that the Aboriginal leadership permitted such a large-scale mining project is evidence of how clearly they understood the British assault by the early 1840s. Under ordinary circumstances the ecological damage resulting from gold mining—especially the process of crushing quartz—would have been unacceptable to Aboriginal elders. Indeed, gold mining in the Central Tribal Lands was scaled back dramatically once the mid-century conflict with Britain ended.

During the early-to-mid 1840s the Aboriginal struggle came to symbolise an international struggle against any form of oppression—including forms flourishing on European soil. Isles's epic journey to France in 1842 saw him meet with, and procure funds and other resources from, leaders of reform movements in France, Belgium, Germany, and elsewhere. Republican and socialist activist families from many countries bolstered the Idealist population throughout the 1840s. On this trip Isles also met with the ageing English gentleman radical, Robert Owen, who had made a special trip to Paris (incognito) from his home in England. Owen is said to have emphasised the importance of 'mechanical and humanistic education' to Isles and the two men discussed Aboriginal attempts to develop a rapid industrial base capable of resisting the British invasion. Increasingly, after Isles's return from France, gold money was funnelled into infrastructure projects sanctioned by the Great Council of Tribes. A desperate, scramble was underway to build an effective tribal alliance. However, unlike the ill-fated social experiment in cooperative living that Owen had backed in Indiana in 1825, this one in the antipodes, backed by the desperation of South-East Australia's Aboriginal peoples, succeeded.

Though Isles assisted Aboriginal leaders behind the scenes during the undeclared war that broke out between white colonists and the Council of Tribes (aided by dissident European groups) from the late 1830s to the mid-1840s, Isles rarely took part in the actual fighting. We possess documentary evidence that the New South Wales government sent several unsuccessful expeditions to capture or kill him. These doomed attempts only furthered the Isles legend. After the failure of one particularly well-armed and well-provisioned attempt, it was rumoured that the Adamantine Wizard possessed the 'second sight'. This ability, it was said, warned him of approaching bounty hunters through dreams and day-time visions.

From early on Isles advised tribal elders not to attack colonist families or their convict charges—instead, he suggested that they first 'issue formal warnings of trespass, in plain Biblical English outlining the sovereign rights of your tribe to the region and its natural bounty. Demand that the trespassers comply with all requests made by the local tribal authority itself a sub-authority of the United Tribes of Australia.' Many tribal elders distributed threats of fines and imprisonment to colonial trespassers—even though no prisons existed at the time. Likewise, no bureaucracy capable of collecting of even imposing fines. The real punishment turned out to be economic—from 1836 on, there is evidence of the systematic seizure of entire herds of cattle and flocks of sheep from 'squatter' runs beyond the borders of the Nineteen Counties. Likewise, horses, mechanical capital and arms were stolen or otherwise acquired from fragile border settlements and even the corrupt New South Wales government. Many government 'assigned' convicts, and not a few bushrangers, appear to have assisted Isles in these projects. During these years Isles used his radical political views, as well as writings outlining his spiritual system to enlist select convicts, ex-convicts and even some freemen to his cause.

In 1845 an inter-tribal currency was instigated across South-East Australia—the Yarkuk. Initially, it was linked to the French and US currencies—though in truth British currency was also relevant. Aboriginal elders, with assistance from Isles and others, made it known that no agreement for temporary freedom of the land or resources access (bestowed by a traditional custom known among the Kulin as Tanderrum) ever ceded ancestral ownership rights. We have many copies of makeshift legal documents, sometimes in Isles's own handwriting, sometimes in the hands of Aboriginal people who had learnt to write English. Later they became more sophisticated, aided by dissident European legal experts, and represented quite a headache for British governance since copies were regularly sent to other European powers and even appeared as declarations in European newspapers and British radical publications.

Around 1841, as the unpublished diaries attest, Isles saw only three sources of hope for the tribal alliance:

1. an alliance with France or America,
2. the mobilisation of the Irish in the colonies (and any other disaffected groups not so morally destroyed as to be untrustworthy), and
3. selective immigration (i.e. of European radicals and others—e.g. Chinese—capable of building a new internationalist Republic able to resist British designs). Isles hints that this strategy was hotly debated among the tribal elders—and indeed initially rejected for almost a year.

By 1843, he'd factored in the 'godsend' of vast quantities of south-eastern gold. Many hundreds of tonnes of the precious metal were secretly mined, melted down and released on the international market between 1843 and 1849. During this period only a small number of Aboriginal elders understood the link between gold and European conceptions of wealth. This proved useful since captured warriors could not describe the economic source of burgeoning Aboriginal wealth.

This 'secret gold' helped fund the Aboriginal resistance throughout the 1840s and it was not until 1849 that the British came to understand the scale of the operation and its role in disrupting the progress of the invasion. Initially they seem to have believed that rival European powers were funding and organising the resistance.

Isles translated the now famous 'DECLARATION of the TRIBES of New Holland' into English in October 1845—though, in fact, it was only signed by representatives of tribes from South-Eastern Australia. The document— in part modelled on the American Declaration of Independence and also on documents drawn from the French revolutionaries of the 1790s— also bears the stamp of age-old Aboriginal beliefs. Although holding to their own cultural beliefs, it is a remarkable fact that by this time numerous Aboriginal 'scribes' and intellectuals conversant in multiple European and Asian languages as well as a variety of international literatures, histories, philosophies and the like had emerged and seem to have contributed to the text of the declaration as well as to the polemical writings doing the rounds of the European capitals. The Aboriginal scribes were trained, it seems, by a bevy of radical European teachers including Isles and Miriam Hobbes (Isles's wife, who had joined him on the return trip from France). In the margins of the declaration and other Aboriginal publications of the era, we often come across scribbling by Isles and Hobbes—apparently taking care to explain to interested Europeans, obscure terms used by some Aboriginal scholars. The declaration is commonly seen as the beginning of the nation of Marin-e-bek—though the military stalemate that occurred in early 1846, after the 100 days war, when the British were for the first time severely checked north of the Great River (the Indi River), is perhaps as significant.

Around 1843 Isles, after much heated discussion with Aboriginal elders, wrote and, with the help of Joseph Irwin, one of the first European radicals to join the resistance, had published in America his 'little book of invitation', the famous 'Come Ye to the Shores of Our Native Jerusalem'. The book eventually circulated in radical circles in France, Germany, America and elsewhere. Eight ships we know of left French, German and American harbours between 1843 and 1845 containing some 1300 Islesians, Chartists, Owenites, new-Jacobites and socialists from any number of countries. At least as many arrived in the southern tribal lands by other means. After the failed European revolutions of 1848 the numbers increased greatly.

British spies failed to discover the true purpose of the French and German ships upon berthing in Cape Town and Batavia. However, spies loyal to the United Tribes and France gave directions to ship captains regarding safe entry into the Aboriginal lands. It seems that ports secured by Idealist warships were frequented south-east of the township of Adelaide and east of Melbourne in Kurnai territory. Once landed, maps of the eastern tribal lands, including guarantees of safe passage, were distributed to the migrants. These European freedom-fighters then attended a 'tanderrum' welcoming ceremony carried out by local Aboriginal elders where they swore an Oath of Loyalty to the principles of the United Tribes of Australia. The principles were a mixture of utopian mid-century European radical ideals and intertribal Aboriginal ideals and laws—respect for country, the interdependence of all creation and the equality of all. Some Islesian principles were also incorporated into the oath. In exchange for their assistance in particular roles the migrants were paid in French or American currencies and were given access to such food as could be procured from lands specially set aside by tribal leaders. Many thousands of free European idealists found their way to the new nation in these years; still others aided the Aboriginal cause from within the British camp.

By the late 1840s the Melbourne and Adelaide authorities were struggling to defend their territorial gains from increasingly well-trained, well-provisioned and well-armed Aboriginal and Idealist military groups. Isles's diaries record several occasions, however, when all seemed lost. For example, only the arrival of several shiploads of revolutionaries and several more of military and industrial purchases in the southern winter of 1848 allowed the alliance to ward off a concerted thrust by British marines (specially sent to quell the uprising) into the tribal lands north of Melbourne—apparently to link up with military units pushing south from New South Wales.

The force was diverted away from the secret gold gathering regions by Aboriginal units—firstly in an easterly direction, later in a northerly direction. French, German and American Idealists backed by a combined Kulin regiment eventually engaged the marines 100 miles east of the burgeoning township of Dinas Yarkuk. After sustaining heavy casualties a remnant British force returned to Melbourne in September of 1848. New South Wales also abandoned its southern push after meeting stiff resistance south of the Indi River. British nervousness about the European uprisings of the same year starved New South Wales, Tasmania, South Australia and the Port Philip region, of military aid for the next two years. The economic situation in the colonies also deteriorated markedly. During this time Melbourne and Adelaide were in a state of permanent siege.

In the middle of this standoff Karl Marx visited the tribal lands to meet with Isles, Hobbes and the Aboriginal leadership. From Isles's diaries the date is fixed at November 1849. The two agreed on many things—particularly the value of education and the destructive nature of uncontrolled capitalism. However, there was heated discussion about the place of non-monotheistic forms of spirituality in an ideal state as well as the necessity of creating and safeguarding democratic political structures. Isles enunciated his reworked alchemical/hermetic belief that the cosmos conspired against anything but temporary forms of utopia. To him the 'flaw' in the structure of the universe also existed within every human being and it was thus essential that political power never be vested for long in one person or in one social class or group. Marx, ever the atheist, apparently listened patiently as Aboriginal leaders described the way in which the Law (as set down by creator beings at specific geographic sites) helped maintain the economic well-being of groups and the land itself.

The discussions influenced Marx's thinking greatly—not least because the Aboriginal groups, with assistance from Isles's motley crew of migrants and dissidents, were putting many of his principles into practice as they resisted the century's greatest imperial power. His later works emphasise the need for democratic socialist political structures 'post-revolution'. Similarly, we note increased scepticism toward fashionable theories of scientific and social progress. Finally, a grudging respect appears in his writings for non-oppressive forms of animistic and pantheistic spirituality.

In 1849 the world finally learnt of the gold being uncovered in the tribal lands—this news heralded the second great crisis for the United Tribes. They'd managed to conceal the discovery since the early 1840s, but now that the news was out Isles and others knew that decisive action was required. The news was initially welcomed by the increasingly isolated Port Philip and South Australian colonists—dependent for stores and military support by this stage on the good will of the Tasmanian and New South Wales governments. The United Tribes however moved quickly—aware they needed an international ally willing to defy the British. The presence of thousands of French, American and, increasingly, German nationals amongst the armies of the United Tribes as well as the legal assertions circulating internationally concerning Aboriginal ownership of the entire Australian continent gave Britain many legal difficulties. They did not, at that point, 'own the lands upon which the gold was discovered'. The gold was 'Aboriginal gold'. This proved useful to a range of parties since it represented the possibility of limiting British economic and military expansion globally.

The United Tribes wrong-footed Britain by inviting a limited number of French and American mining corporations to: 'partake in the diggings for the mutual benefit of all parties'. Those invited were forced to swear allegiance to the state of Marin-e-bek as a condition of entry into the Aboriginal lands.

Britain of course was furious and immediately diverted a large army to Melbourne to tackle not only the Aboriginal resistance, but also 'unwelcome foreigners determined to challenge the expansion of British civilisation'. Any military advantages were lost, however, well before the army's arrival since the United Tribes issued a crucial ultimatum to all colonists in and around Melbourne and Adelaide. Any who were prepared to swear allegiance to the Aboriginal nation could remain—to mine, farm, etc. as directed by relevant tribal authorities, though with due respect for local tribal customs and authority as well as the principles set out in the Oath of Loyalty. Any refusing these conditions were declared trespassers in the same declaration and liable to punishment if they remained. However, if unwilling to abide by the terms of the declaration they were given the opportunity to return by ship to whence they had come. A full-scale invasion of both cities seemed imminent.

In December of 1851 the southern part of New South Wales and the town of Melbourne were abandoned to the United Tribes of Australia. Thousands of British settlers voluntarily took passage back to the motherland. Incredibly, however, almost thirty-five percent of the British population of the two cities (mostly Irish migrants, ex-convicts and poorer free settlers), as well as thousands of Chinese residents remained. All signed agreements and took the Oath of Loyalty and were issued with a 'Free Citizen Passport' entitling them to 'freedom of the land' (though with clearly specified limitations). Historians have dubbed this event 'the Tanderrum Accord' and it is routinely seen as the origins of democracy in the new nation. Melbourne became Dinas Bunjilaka (Bunjilaka City). Similar ceremonies of renaming occurred in Adelaide and elsewhere. The country of Marin-e-bek was born and the goal of the British 'to thieve an entire continent' (as Isles put it) was severely checked. The new state was formerly voted into existence at a full meeting of South-Eastern tribal leaders on January 26th 1852 (the date was deliberately chosen). Thereafter, the United Tribes mutated into a continent-wide tribal military alliance—i.e. a separate political entity to the nation of Marin-e-bek.

Importantly the new nation now had access to a range of industrial assets essential to the development and military defence of a modern state. Tradespeople, teachers, medical experts and other professionals among the Idealist immigrants undertook to educate the many thousands of Aboriginal men and women wishing to learn about the strange technologies on display in the colonial towns. Likewise, the migrants learnt much from their Aboriginal hosts and enjoyed freedoms they had never known in their home countries. Most importantly, tribes across the South-East eventually set aside tightly regulated agricultural land bundles and residence areas for international and inter-tribal migrants.

Marins of all descriptions—Koori, Idealist and Asian—have never been large meat eaters (many Islesians, for example, are vegetarians), and the herds of cattle and flocks of sheep that decimated tribal lands north of the border never got a foothold in the south. Likewise, the large scale deforestation that took place north of the Indi River did not occur in the south. Nevertheless, Aboriginal land councils did permit experimentation with a number of European crops, and cropping techniques and technologies—they were well aware they needed to efficiently feed a much larger population. Sometimes these techniques and technologies were used to experiment with the mass production of Koori bush-tucker staples. Agricultural experiments, like industrial innovations, usually took place in tribal areas set aside under the 'Tanderrum Accord', leaving the great majority of traditional food sources, waterways etc, untouched.

EXTRACT 3

'The Lost Songs of Abraham Isles', from *Abraham Isles and Miriam Hobbes (a biography)*.

According to the historians Abraham Isles's contribution to Marin-e-bek's emergence as a dynamic multicultural, though Koori dominated, nation has three strands: 1) he was a 'political revolutionary' working to unite the various disparate elements present at the nation's formation; 2) he and his wife were proponents of a mass education system for Marin-e-bek that emphasised the cultivation of free will, relational integrity and nation building; and 3) he was a significant 'spiritual leader' to European migrants, though the nature of that leadership changed from a 'Traditional' (i.e. 1830s-1845) Islesian position to a more secular 'Idealist' position in the latter part of the century. This de-emphasis of the role of his original spiritual system in founding Marin-e-bek became instinctive among Islesian scholars for a variety of reasons worthy of our consideration.

Firstly, Isles's spiritual journals and sacred songs were largely written during his time in the wilderness with the Aboriginal people of south-eastern Australia, i.e. during the period he was assisting them to gather an effective military and economic alliance capable of resisting the British invasion. Once the treaty with Britain was signed and Marin-e-bek was confirmed internationally (however tenuously) as a nation state, Isles and Miriam seem to have taken on administrative and ceremonial roles in the nation's mid-century development.

The times demanded skills that could contribute to economic, social and political development. As a consequence, the spiritual aspect to Isles's contribution necessarily received less emphasis. He and Miriam became figure-heads—along with other civil and military leaders—for the migrant segment of the population in particular (in this sense, he and Hobbes had to tone down their life-long disavowal of Catholicism). More broadly, the two also became key symbols of migrant-indigenous unity—so much so that to this day they appear on the 20 Yarkuk note alongside the Aboriginal elder Nooralie (of the Great River region)—an excellent military leader, and the first president of Marin-e-bek (1853 to 1860). The main task facing the Koori and radical leaderships in the aftermath of the Treaty was to unite, educate, provide for and, occasionally, pacify the diverse population of Koories, European exiles and activists, and Chinese migrants. To Isles, Hobbes and the bulk of the Aboriginal leadership, it was imperative that the European and Chinese migrants be prepared to assist the nation as it transformed into a modern economy under the control of a Koori dominated national parliament.

This was a formidable and delicate task and inevitably involved an emphasis on economics, political negotiation (the so–called 'Two Tiers' parliament being the post-1860 outcome), and the development of modern social institutions and material infrastructure that would be acceptable to both Koories and Idealists. The transformation, then elevation, of the 'Tanderrum' concept to a national level in the early 1840s (with accompanying land-management innovations) gave the new nation a means to unify around a much needed collective identity. By the mid-to-late 1840s, it was also the key to the development of an army and navy capable of resisting marauding colonial powers. This was the period in which the emergent Pan-Koori language was formalised as the national language. The first dictionary, for example, came out in 1853 shortly after elders from the various South-Eastern tribes met to determine the form it would take—an epic process! A formal vote (among representative Aboriginal elders only) to select a flag and national anthem followed soon after. In short, there was much to do and Isles's diaries of 1880 make it clear that both he and the Aboriginal leadership—inexperienced at working together on 'peace-time' nation building projects—were well aware of the tenuousness of the alliances that existed between:

a) the idealistic European migrants (by this stage mostly French, German, Dutch and Irish), the Chinese and the various Aboriginal tribes, and b) between the various Aboriginal tribes themselves, who had known millennia of independence on their tribal lands and were still dubious about any call to unite around the foreign notion of the 'nation state'.

At several points in 1858, for example, the 'Traditionalist' party in the United Tribes almost seized parliamentary power after a national vote based upon the old 'Tribal Quota' voting system. With the parliament hung the Traditionalists attempted to junk important trans-Marin plans related to a range of national infrastructure projects—specifically a rail system, a national road system, a national educational system, a national health system and the further integration of disparate tribal military bands into one national army. The deadlock was only lifted in the parliament when events made the likely consequences of their agenda clear. Thousands of skilled European and Chinese migrants booked tickets home in the week after the election. At the same time, sensing the political deadlock in the Marin parliament the NSW governor ordered British military operations along the New South Wales/Marin-e-bek northern border. After local tribes asked for national assistance to ward off the threat (and the Marin government, in turn, was forced to ask for American and French assistance—gestures of 'goodwill' that cost the country dearly in gold)—it became obvious to all that only a national military backed by a modern bureaucracy could ward off the British. The crisis led to the replacement of the 'Tribal Quota System' with the 'Two-Tiered System' in 1861. Universal male suffrage had arrived in Marin-e-bek. In the new system lower house representatives were democratically elected according to principles of universal suffrage, i.e. one adult male, one vote. The upper house, however, as a house of review and veto was composed of elected regional tribal land representatives only.

This was also the year Miriam Hobbes achieved her greatest political victory. Three months after the new parliament convened for the first time, she worked with her husband and other leaders to force a vote extending universal suffrage to the nation's women. In a brilliant address to a combined sitting of the parliament, she argued that the new nation would be unable to attract the large numbers of Idealist women it needed, if it continued to discriminate against them with regard to property rights, the vote, marriage annulment rights, and protection from 'unwanted physical and sexual depravity'. Significant numbers of Aborginal leaders, aware of the negative effects of existing gender imbalances on tribal social structures, created an international sensation when they backed Hobbes's amendment proposing universal women's suffrage. Marin-e-bek became the first nation in the world to grant women the vote (all-be-it to elect representatives under the 'Tanderrum Accord' for only the first tier of the parliament).

The new nation became a beacon of hope for politically aware women around the world.

The political situation in Marin-e-bek after 1853 alone doesn't explain the current biographical emphasis on Isles as being primarily a social engineer and political statesman. Although the main tenets of Isles's spiritual system were well known in the 1840s and early 1850s, and were used to attract large numbers of radical European migrants to the tribal lands to defend the Aboriginal cause (particularly refugees from the Europe-wide uprisings of 1848 and the Irish) as well as to unite all-comers along pro-democratic, multi-faith lines, Isles, like the Aboriginal people he'd lived among, initially held to hierarchical (initiation based) notions of sacred knowledge. To Isles (and to Hobbes) certain forms of knowledge were dangerous and had to be handled with care—thus only certain people (those who had demonstrated their moral as well as intellectual worth) should be given certain types of sacred knowledge. As a consequence large numbers of his songs, as well as the postures he and Hobbes developed to accompany them, weren't published until after his death. When heavily edited extracts from the 'song diaries' were eventually published, the melodies accompanying the songs were not included.

By 1880, shortly after Isles's death, only Hobbes (who died two years later), two or three family members and a handful of figures within the religious structures they'd set up, had seen the original song diaries. The melodies to the songs, though preserved, had been concealed by way of a musical notation system understood by only a small number of people. As modern ideologies of liberation and scientific advancement, e.g. socialism, communism, Darwinism, existentialism, psychoanalysis, feminism, etc. took to the global stage Isles's spiritual system survived by absorbing some elements of the new movements and rejecting others. Neo-Islesians and Idealists, proved less interested than Islesian traditionalists in the more esoteric principles explored in the song diaries. Similarly, his later life call for the nation's institutions to embody the principle of 'natural adaptation' as a means to ensure the nation's survival in a changing world, encouraged scholars to set aside his earlier spiritual writings, including the song diaries.

By the turn of the twentieth century Isles and Hobbes stood for constant cultural adaptation based upon free education (backed by large-scale, but efficient, government spending) and a model of culture that emphasised genuine freedom of speech. Behind this freedom, however, lay a commitment to ongoing debate on historic and emerging philosophical and spiritual principles from all over the world. As a consequence, Marin-e-bek proved attractive to musicians, poets, thinkers, artists, scientists, etc. from all over the world. Its intelligentsia—whether Koori, Islesian/Idealist, New Science secular, Buddhist etc.—helped birth some of the twentieth century's most important ecological and liberation ideologies. The nation has also produced five Nobel laureates as well as international leaders in many fields.

For scholars interested in Isles and Hobbes the tendency to emphasise selective aspects of their thinking, ends up fragmenting and atomising the profound insights embedded in the song diaries and elsewhere. It is my belief that the time is ripe for a thorough re-examination of all aspects of their original spiritual beliefs, the goal of this study—which is undertaken with the aid of the family guardians of Isles's estate, the Marin-e-bek Cultural Fund and the Marin Cultural Board of Elders.

####

THE CITY OF QUARTZ IS PART OF A TRANSMEDIA PROJECT ENTITLED *SONGS OF THE INTERSTITIUM.*

TO ACCESS MORE ABOUT THIS
PROJECT, AS WELL AS INFORMATION
ABOUT THE AUTHOR, PLEASE SCAN
THE QR IMAGES THAT FOLLOW.

www.ingramcontent.com/pod-product-compliance
Lightning Source LLC
Chambersburg PA
CBHW050608110726
47899CB00001B/23

9780646956329